"Keep your eyes shut until I tell you to open them," she told him softly. He nodded.

"Breathe deeply."

He did so, drawing the warm smoke deep into his lungs. At first the membranes of his nose and throat burned and stung, but quickly the pain was replaced by numbness. The vapors seemed to fill his head—he could feel them billowing through his mind, inter-weaving themselves with his thoughts.

"Breathe deeply," Mary repeated, her voice sounding a million miles away. "Breathe steadily."

There was a sound in his ears. A quiet, musical hum-ming. *It's Mary,* he realized. He felt a tingling in his fingertips and in his lips. Mary's humming took a faint ringing tone. He took another deep breath. . . .

The universe opened around him. He heard himself gasp.

It was as if he could sense the universe—the infinity of creation—all around him, with himself at the very center. A tiny, infinitesimally small point. Alone, vul-nerable, inconsequential.

But then the universe turned inside out—he turned in-side out. The infinity was still there, but now it was inside him. The universe was an infinitesimal point, within the infinity that was Dennis Falk. He gasped again.

In alarm, he opened his eyes.

But it wasn't the grimy black room that he saw. . . .

SHADOWRUN

SHADOWPLAY

NIGEL FINDLEY

A ROC BOOK

ROC
Published by the Penguin Group
Penguin Books USA Inc., 375 Hudson Street,
New York, New York 10014, U.S.A.
Penguin Books Ltd, 27 Wrights Lane,
London W8 5TZ, England
Penguin Books Australia Ltd, Ringwood,
Victoria, Australia
Penguin Books Canada Ltd, 10 Alcorn Avenue,
Toronto, Ontario, Canada M4V 3B2
Penguin Books (N.Z.) Ltd, 182—190 Wairau Road,
Auckland 10, New Zealand

Penguin Books Ltd, Registered Offices:
Harmondsworth, Middlesex, England

First published by Roc, an imprint of New American Library, a division
of Penguin Books USA Inc.

First Printing, February, 1993
10 9 8 7 6 5 4 3 2 1

Series Editor: Donna Ippolito
Cover: Keith Birdsong
Interior Illustrations: Earl Geier

REGISTERED TRADEMARK—MARCA REGISTRADA

To Fraser—This sure beats working, doesn't it?

Prologue

A decker entombed in ice. One of those sights you hope never to see.

All deckers are comrades, y'see. At some level, there's a bond between us, even though we can end up on opposite sides of some particular issue, or shadowrun, or what have you. But put all that aside and there's more kinship between us than between us and anyone else—wives, husbands, lovers, anyone. I mean, there's us, who've seen the electron horizons of cyberspace, who've run the datalines of the Matrix, who've jacked a virtual reality directly into our brains. And then there's everyone else . . .

Anyway, I felt like drek when I saw him. The intrusion countermeasures—the ice—were all over him. I could just see his icon through the dark, translucent tentacles wrapping around him. A silver child, that's what his icon looked like. A silver child being devoured by monsters.

He was dying, I knew that. In the real world, it would have been over in an instant. In the Matrix the ice picks up the decker's icon, then dumps its signal into his cyberdeck. The deck's filters overload, pouring the signal through the datajack, straight into the decker's brain. And then . . . Who knows? Convulsions, the kind strong enough to break his bones. Or his blood pressure spikes so high one of the vessels in his brain blows out. Or maybe his heart stops, just like that. Biofeedback, it kills you as quick and as sure as a bullet in the head.

But in the Matrix time's different, it runs much faster.

In the Matrix I can *see* it happening. I can see him dying. And there's not a fragging thing I can do about it.

I'd decked into the Yamatetsu Corporation's Seattle data core. An easy hack, really. Just pop in through the customer-service line. Yamatetsu markets telecommunications software, and one of their biggest selling points is that all you gotta do anytime you have trouble with a product is hook your computer system into theirs through the Matrix. They'll fix the glitches for you on-line, even while you keep using the stuff. Frag, Yamatetsu actually *advertises* that capability as a sales hot-button.

So that tells me there's got to be some connection between Yamatetsu's development system and the local telecommunications grid. Not like those barbaric companies that are disconnecting themselves from the Matrix. So I cruise in on their support LTG number, smooth as silk. Of course, there's some IC in the first node I come to. A barrier program and some light-duty trace and burn. Makes me laugh how easy I went through that.

And then I'm into Yamatetsu's development system. One more node, and I'm in their main corporate data core. The defense is about the same, mainly barrier and trace and burn programs, with a little blaster thrown in for good measure. I go past that so sweet and smooth the corp deckers will never spot me even if they review the whole network log. I'm a ghost.

That's as far as I needed to go. All I really wanted were the personnel records. My contract was to pull up any dirt I could find on the executive vice-president, a slitch named Maria Morgenstern. I had to deal with some minor-league ice on the personnel files, of course, and if it took me a millisecond to slip by it, I wasn't up to my usual game.

I downloaded the file, dumped it into the memory chips in my head, and that was it. Contractual obligation discharged. I could have jacked out then and there with everything I came after.

But, you know, what the frag? My contract was to scope out Morgenstern top to bottom. But here I was in the main data core of a corp with a really solid rep in the telecom field. Who knows, maybe I could scoop something to sell on the shadow market. As long as I didn't totally hose up and alert the system that I'd been having my way with it, any collateral loot I scammed was all mine, that's what my contract says. So, I figure, I'll just sashay over to the research and development files, and see if there's anything worth grabbing that's not bolted down. I backed on out of the personnel files, wiping my tracks as I went. . . .

And that's when I saw the decker entombed in the ice. I knew he hadn't been in the node the last time I came through, so it had to be that he'd tried to cut and run from another node. The black ice that was killing him must have followed and caught him here.

Like I said, there was nothing I could do but watch. The black tentacles of the ice were wrapped around his perfect silver body, and were starting to squeeze. Nasty stuff, this ice. The decker should have jacked out as soon as he saw it coming. I know I would have. I recognized it right away as something from Glacier Tech—one of the "Beltway Bandits," out of Provo in the Ute Nation, the premiere ice programmers on the continent.

But he hadn't jacked out, probably thinking he'd hang tough and scrap it out with the ice. Bad choice. Even Seattle's decker varsity would have a tough go against Glacier Tech black ice, and the silver child sure wasn't on the hot list. If he'd been a burner, I'd have recognized his icon.

That's when I should have turned away, gone on about my business or just jacked out. But I couldn't do it. I admit it, it was sick fascination that kept me there, the kind of grim curiosity that keeps you watching even when something turns your stomach. I kept my distance, staying to the further reaches of the node, but I watched.

And the silver child saw me there. He turned his shining eyes on me, and I know he recognized me for what I was—not part of the system that was killing him, but somebody like him, a free decker. A spectator. He must also have known I couldn't help him. But how would it make you feel, someone watching you die?

That was when I turned to go, wanting to bug out of that node and make best possible speed for the R and D files, then get the hell out of Dodge. As I did, though, I saw the silver boy move. Something had appeared in his hand, a program construct that looked like a golden apple. Even with the ice tentacles squeezing him, he managed to move his arm and throw the apple toward me.

For an instant, I thought the ice might shoot out another tentacle and pick off the construct. But no, the apple kept sailing over to me, and I reached to snatch it out of the air.

As soon as my icon touched it I knew it was a data file. Lots of data, too, a hundred megapulses or more, despite the size of the construct. It also was locked and encrypted. I could feel that instantly. Was the file what the decker had been after—what had got him killed?

I glanced back toward the dying decker, but he was gone. His icon had vanished, which meant that in the real world—the world where his meat body was jacked into a cyberdeck—he was dead as a side of beef. As I watched, the tentacles unwrapped themselves and started questing my way.

I considered trying for the R and D files anyway—if I was fast, I could stay far enough ahead of the ice to make it—then decided against it. The ice had caught the silver child, crushed the life out of him. I wasn't ready to let it do the same to me.

Sometimes discretion's the better part, and all that drek. I jacked out.

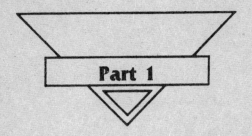

Part 1

Prelude to War

1

2025 hours, November 9, 2053

Sly settled back in her chair. The diminutive decker
whose face filled the vidscreen of her telecom—Louis,
his name was—had just finished his story. His voice was
as impersonal as ever and his face equally expressionless.
But Sly could tell from his body talk, if not from his
voice, that seeing the decker dying in the ice had really
slotted him up emotionally.

And who wouldn't be slotted up? she thought. Running into black ice—getting killed by it—was an ugly
reality of the decker's world. Every time a decker put his
brain on the line and jacked into the worldwide computer
Matrix, he risked running into some intrusion countermeasures program that was just too tough. Risked having
his brain burned out—"slagged down," to use the argot
currently in vogue among deckers—or getting flatlined
by some kind of lethal biofeedback. That was just business as usual, no more remarkable than the risks a mage
took when evoking a powerful elemental, or a street samurai playing bodyguard for a hot target. Among deckers,

it was bad form to talk about ice, except in technical terms or when telling war stories, or bragging about a major score. It didn't matter that Sly wasn't a decker anymore. The protocol would never change. The fact that Louis had described the death of the silver child in such detail revealed just how much it had disturbed him.

She could understand why, of course. For most deckers, death by ice was something that happened "off-stage." If you were the one that got geeked, you'd obviously not be around to tell about it. And if someone else got the chop—decking being a very solitary profession—you'd only hear about it long after the fact, when Joe Schmoe didn't show up at his usual haunts anymore. To see it actually happening and to know you couldn't do anything about it . . . Sly suppressed a shudder. She'd hardened herself to most of the ugly details of life and death in the Awakened world, but seeing the icon of another decker constricted in the tentacles of black ice would have shaken her up, too.

Sharon Louise Young—street handle "Sly"—was careful to keep her own facial expression just as stony. Showing weakness wasn't part of the protocol either, particularly when talking to someone she'd hired to do a job, and would probably hire again. Part of the game of being a "Mr. Johnson"—one who hires shadowrunners to operate in the dark wainscoting of society—was maintaining an ice-cold facade. (Not always possible, of course, but definitely something to aim for.) She shifted in her chair, trying for a more comfortable position, then stretched a mild kink out of her spine.

That brought a frown of displeasure, quickly wiped from her face. Sly knew she wasn't so young anymore, but why did her body have to keep reminding her of the ugly fact? She kept her tall, lean form in good shape, her muscles in tone, with daily exercise. She was still as strong, as fast, as she'd ever been—or at least so she told

herself. But there was no denying that she was thirty-three, no, thirty-*four,* her birthday had been two weeks before. A hard workout—or a particularly strenuous shadowrun—more and more often left her with a backache. And her left knee, which she'd blown out some years back when taking the quick way to the street from a third-story window, had a tendency to throb when it was raining. Which it did in Seattle nearly all the fragging time, of course. Physically speaking, she could still do anything that she did fifteen years ago—plus all her experience making her much *more* competent than she'd been at nineteen—but there was no denying it took her longer to recover afterward.

Sly knew she was still attractive. Her hair and skin were dark, and she had high, well-defined cheekbones— a legacy of her grandfather's Nootka heritage. In contrast, her eyes were bright green, thanks to the Irish blood of her "male biological donor"—she refused to label the fragging bastard "father" even to herself. The overall look was, she knew, unusual, and enough men to represent a statistically valid sample had told her it was alluring. Sure, she had her share of scars. What shadowrunner didn't? But most were in places that only particularly close friends would ever see. She had one facial blemish—a short white scar that bisected her right eyebrow, courtesy of a grenade fragment—but it was far from disfiguring. . . .

She ruthlessly cut off that line of thought. Waste of time, she scolded herself. Work first, vanity later.

The face of Louis the decker was still on the screen. "So you got the paydata on Morgenstern?" she asked.

"I said I did, didn't I?"

Sly didn't like Louis. It wasn't just his manner but his appearance that bothered her on some really deep level. He was a trisomy 11. Thanks to some freak accident of cell division, either his father's sperm or his mother's egg had carried *two* copies of chromosome 11, not the usual one, which meant that the zygote—the fertilized egg—that would eventually become Louis the decker had *three* copies of chromosome 11, not the normal two. Trisomy 11 was a rare but well-studied genetic abnormality that carried with it a certain suite of physical impairments: retarded growth, a weak cardiovascular system, limited motor coordination, and a phenotype or appearance that reminded Sly uncomfortably of an anthropomorphic slug. It also led to mental impairment. The brain of a trisomy 11 was generally unable to attend to the important features of the environment, unable to extract the "signal"—what the person wanted to concentrate on—from the background "noise"—everything else impinging on the senses. Usually this led to the arresting of the victim's mental development at a level not much higher than a newborn baby's.

That hadn't happened with Louis, of course. His parents, who were frighteningly rich, had known about the genetic abnormality even before his birth, and had approached the problem in the only way they knew how: by throwing money at it. Almost as soon as Louis was born, and long before his infant skull had hardened to a normal bony consistency, they'd had a tiny datajack implanted in his infant brain. Specialists had hooked this datajack to a suite of sophisticated computers that fed a virtual reality—similar to but distinct from the consensual hallucination that was "life" in the Matrix—into his mind. The computers had "perceived" the world through microphones and trideo cameras, and had electronically handled the problems of attention and distinguishing between "signal" and "noise" that Louis' own brain would not have been capable of doing. With this electronic assistance, Louis had managed to avoid the mental impairment typical of other trisomy 11s. In fact, his mental capabilities had probably advanced even faster than a normal child's.

At the time, some eighteen years before, Louis had become a kind of media darling. The trideo had featured him in several programs, and researchers had published dozens of papers on his progress and the philosophical questions it raised. Most people who saw these shows or skimmed the literature hadn't really understood what was going on. Frequent re-tellings of Louis' story on "tabloid-style" news shows had embellished matters until the facts became distorted into a kind of urban myth: "Child Grows Up in Matrix." (Actually, Sly had heard rumors that there actually *were* children who'd been raised entirely in the Matrix. But, strictly speaking, Louis wasn't one of them.)

Eventually, Louis had graduated to the real Matrix, developing his skills as a decker. Even so, he was still a trisomy 11. Without extreme medical intervention—again paid for by his parents—his heart would have worn out and his whole cardiovascular system collapsed before he was fifteen. He still needed the assistance of significant computing power (now implanted directly into his small skull) to focus his attention properly. And his sole interface with the real world was through a bulky pair of goggles consisting of miniaturized video cameras and stereo microphones that he wore on his flat face and that plugged into his datajack. Physically, he was almost totally incapacitated. He lived his entire life in a special life-support wheelchair that he controlled mentally through a modified vehicle control rig.

On top of that, he'd come away with a deep-seated addiction to the Matrix. Only when he was jacked in and running the electron environment of cyberspace was he truly alive. He'd once told Sly that anytime he wasn't decking was just waiting.

Sly regarded Louis' small, ugly face on her telecom

screen, struggling to keep from showing her distaste. It didn't matter that she found his appearance revolting, and his personality—predictably warped by his upbringing and nature—even worse. He was a drek-hot decker, no one could deny that.

Most of the time he worked as a Matrix "hired gun" for many Seattle corporations. But he still had time left over to do shadow work for people he liked. And—for whatever reason—he liked Sly. Ever since giving up decking herself, she'd hired him on more than a dozen occasions in the last several years. Never for anything really sensitive, of course: she didn't trust him that much. For really critical projects she chose other deckers. Perhaps not as skillful as Louis, but good enough.

She sighed. "Sorry, Louis," she said, "You're right. You *did* get the paydata. Are you ready to transfer?"

He gave her a slack-lipped smile. "You got it. Ready to receive?"

She hit the appropriate keys on her telecom, opening a capture file. The moment she gave him the go-ahead, he spewed the contents of Maria Morgenstern's personnel file down the dataline. Sly opened a second window on the screen, watched with satisfaction as it filled with text. Good, he got it all. That was one thing about Louis, he was always thorough. No incomplete files, no garbled data. No doubt he'd already gone through the information and corrected any errors that may have crept into the file.

When the telecom beeped to announce conclusion, she closed the capture file and blanked out the data window. "Got it," she told him. "Chipped and locked. Ready to receive payment?"

He didn't answer, but her screen showed his system was already set up to accept the transfer of credit. It took less than a second—*One thousand nuyen, just like that. Oh, well, easy come easy go.* "Pleasure doing business with you," he said with a chuckle. "Now, how about the business of doing pleasure with you?"

She stared at him, knowing he could read the shock in her face. He couldn't mean that, could he? she thought with a start. From anyone else it would have been a blatant pick-up line. But not from Louis, whose warped and childlike body wasn't capable of anything even remotely resembling sex. *Was it?*

He laughed, a grotesque bubbling sound, and a gobbet of saliva dribbled down his chin. "Gotcha," he crowed. "Five points on that one. Ah, poor Sly, still no sense of humor."

Humor? She looked at the slug-like decker with distaste. "Yeah, Louis," she said flatly, "you got me." She reached out to break the connection.

"Hey, wait."

She drew back her finger.

"What about the other file?" he asked.

"What file?"

He shook his head. "The file I got from the dying decker," he said, speaking slowly as if talking to a congenital idiot. "The file he passed me before he died. Do you want it?"

"Don't *you* want it?"

He shook his head again, more vehemently. "*No*," he snapped. "No, I *don't* want it. It's bad luck. Bad karma."

For the hundredth—or was it the thousandth?—time, Sly wondered about the strange superstitions that so many deckers seemed to carry around with them. How could people who dealt exclusively with hard, cold technology be so worried about mumbo-jumbo like "bad karma"?

And it wasn't just Louis. Just about every decker she knew practiced some special ritual or wore one talisman or other to bring good luck on Matrix runs. (Sly's right hand strayed to the pouch on her belt where she kept her rabbit's foot—a *real* rabbit's foot, not something patched together from synthetic fur—that she'd always carried on shadowruns for luck. She felt a momentary twinge of guilt for being judgmental. But this is different, she thought. Isn't it?)

"You can have the file," Louis was saying. "Free of charge, a bonus. Drek, maybe it'll be worth something to you."

She hesitated. "You said it was locked. Did you crack the encryption?"

Yet again he shook his head, looking quite uncomfortable now. "No," he barked. Then with an effort Louis brought himself back under control. "No," he said more quietly. "I didn't touch it. Get ready to receive. Here it comes."

Hurriedly, Sly opened another capture file—just in time to catch the data suddenly pouring into her computer. Again she opened an on-screen window to see what she was getting. But this time, instead of orderly lines of text, the window filled with garbled characters—letters and numbers mixed with arcane-looking graphics characters.

The transfer took a couple of seconds, which meant it was a big file. She checked the status line at the bottom of the screen. More than a hundred megapulses of data.

Transfer complete, she closed the file. "Thanks, Louis," she said dryly.

He shrugged. "If it's not worth anything, just blow it away," he said. "It's yours, do what you like with it. I didn't even keep a copy."

Which meant, of course, that he *had* kept a copy of the file on Morgenstern. But that was okay; most deckers kept copies of the files they "liberated." It was a kind of rudimentary insurance against Mr. Johnsons who believed the old saw about dead men and tales. Sly expected it. "Okay, Louis." Again she reached out to break the connection.

"Catch ya, Sly," the decker said. And he grinned again. "And if you give any thought to my other suggestion—" But she cut him off before he could finish.

She stretched her back again, felt the vertebrae in her lower spine click back into place. Frag this getting old drek, she thought savagely. Seattle, and, more specifically, the shadows she'd been frequenting for the past thirteen years, just wasn't the place for someone feeling her age. She glanced at the holograph taped to the gray wall over the telecom. A white-sand beach, green ocean, azure sky. Somewhere in the Caribbean League, but she didn't know just where. Now *that* was where she should be, someplace where the cold and damp never slotted up her knee. Yep, it was getting nigh on time to retire.

But retiring takes nuyen, she reminded herself, a lot of nuyen. She considered bringing up her credit balance on the telecom screen, then decided against it. Too depressing. Most runners burned up their nuyen on high living and parties, but she'd made a habit of always squirreling away as much as possible. She figured she had maybe seventy thousand nuyen by now. A good balance, but way short of what she thought of as "frag you" money—the amount she'd need to kiss Seattle goodbye, pull a quick fade, and slide on down to the islands. She needed a few more good scores or maybe one serious windfall. I need to make a killing, she thought glumly.

She glanced at the telecom screen. The window was still open, filled with encrypted text. Maybe it's worth something, she mused, then shook her head with a smile. Wishful thinking. Wishful thinking doesn't get you money, it gets you dead. Probably the file contained data valuable to Yamatetsu Corporation, which had encrypted it, but worthless to anyone else.

Her watch beeped. Time to meet with the Johnson

who'd hired her, and pass over the dirt on Morgenstern. The run, which she'd simply subcontracted to Louis, would net her about ten thousand nuyen, of which she'd be able to save maybe half. Better than nothing, but still not "frag you" money.

She closed the data window and powered down the telecom. The encrypted file, whatever it was, was saved to an optical storage chip; it wouldn't be going anywhere. Maybe when she had some free time she'd figure out what it was. If she ever got around to it.

2

2005 hours, November 12, 2053

The alley was dark, noisome as only an alley near the Seattle docks could be. Empty, for the moment, but Falcon knew that wouldn't last. The Disassemblers were after him. He'd opened the gap a little, but they were still close on his heels and not likely to be giving up. Any moment a group of them wearing the gray and white colors of their gang would come pounding into the alley behind him.

The cold, damp air seared his throat, and his right side felt like somebody had slipped a stiletto into his ribs and was now playfully twisting it. His legs were lead-heavy and he could hardly feel his feet pounding against the pavement as he ran. No useful sensations—like whether he was on dry ground or sloshing through an oily slick that would land him on his face—but the burning in his thighs and calves wouldn't go away. "I thought numb-

ness meant no pain,'' he grumbled to himself through
clenched teeth.

Falcon was halfway down the alley, pushing himself
on in what he knew must look like a drunken stagger.
He was a good runner, a fact in which he took great
pride, and had taken off like a fleet-footed spirit the moment he'd run into the Disassemblers.

Of course, that was many blocks ago, many alleys
back. If somebody like him, young, and in good shape,
was feeling so scragged, then a bunch of fat and lum-
bering trolls—all *old,* at least twenty—should be lying on
the ground in crumpled masses, whooping their dinners
into the gutter.

But no, from the hoarse yells he heard behind him
Falcon knew that the original posse of Diassemblers must
have called for help. Maybe the initial six were busy
emptying their guts, but they had friends who had joined
the chase later—when they were fresh and his body was
starting to hate it in a big way.

God, I hurt, he thought. Would it hurt any less if he
just stopped, collapsed behind a dumpster, and let the
Disassemblers catch him? They'd beat the drek out of
him, kick his hoop until he was bleeding from all ori-
fices. But they probably wouldn't kill him. His gang, the
First Nation, wasn't officially at war with the Disassemblers, not at the moment. And he hadn't been wearing
his colors or even been carrying a weapon when they'd
spotted him. He hadn't been on gang business, merely
cruising out to boost some stuffers to fill his empty belly.
Just fragging bad luck that one of the trolls had recognized him.

So, no war, and he hadn't made the potentially lethal
move of wearing gang colors in a rival gang's patch. That
meant that if they caught him they'd *probably* be satisfied
giving him a beating. And if his lousy luck turned,

hopefully he wouldn't be conscious for the whole of the festivities anyway. . . .

But that would be quitting, and if Dennis Falk—"Falcon" to his chummers on the street—was anything at all, it wasn't a quitter. He forced another burst of speed from his legs, ignoring the screams of his muscles.

The alley ended, disgorging him into a narrow road running parallel with the waterfront. He was under the big Alaska Way viaduct. The sound of traffic whined by above him even at this late hour, sometime after three in the morning. He took a hard right, considered flattening himself against a wall behind yet another dumpster and waiting for the Disassemblers to pound on by, then discarded the idea. He could think about accepting the beating, about stopping and hoping the trolls would miss him, but he was just too fragging scared. And by all the spirits and totems, he had a right to be scared. What fifteen-year-old *wouldn't* be with maybe a ton of trolls on his butt?

He risked a glance over his shoulder. Soaked with sweat, his long, black hair fell into his eyes, blinding him. Then his right foot came down on something, something that rolled, throwing him off balance. He screamed in terror, struggled to keep upright. Pain—sharp, burning—lanced through his left ankle. Somehow he managed to recover, took another running step. . . .

Falcon cried out in agony as his left ankle took the weight of his body, and it was like one of the Dissemblers already trying to tear off his foot. He pitched forward and landed hard on the rough pavement. Skidding, he tore the skin from his palms and shredded the knees of his jeans.

Sobbing with fear and pain, he forced himself back to his feet, tested his ankle again. The agony, like molten lead in the joint, was enough to blur his vision for an instant. Broken? He didn't think so, but it didn't really matter. There was no way he could run any further.

Falcon looked around wildly for cover, for somewhere to hide. There were doors in the buildings around him, but he knew they'd be locked. (Who *wouldn't* lock their doors near the docks at night?) And of course there was the dumpster, just off to his right.

Hiding behind it didn't seem like such a good idea anymore. But hiding *in* it . . .

The top of the dumpster was above Falcon's eye-level so he couldn't see what was inside, but it certainly *smelled* full. The big metal lid was open, leaning back against the wall of the building. Once he was inside, it shouldn't be too hard to pull it shut. Then it would be just a matter of hoping the Disassemblers weren't all that thorough.

He had to hurry, though. He could hear hoarse cries of anger and the thunder of running feet. He had only seconds—if that—before the troll gangers rounded the corner and saw him.

It wasn't easy to climb into the dumpster with a sprained ankle, but fear spurred him on. As he dropped inside, the stench hit him like a physical blow: sour milk, urine, decaying vegetables, and a strong overtone of rotting meat. He was glad it was too dark to see what he was lying on; imagining it was making him sick enough. He stood up, keeping his balance with difficulty on the shifting garbage, then grabbed the metal lid and pulled. The rusty hinges creaked—*oh, spirits and totems, what if the trolls should hear*?—but the lid moved. Muscles straining against the surprisingly heavy weight, Falcon lowered the lid carefully to keep it from slamming shut. The hinges seized up before it was all the way down, leaving a gap between lid and dumpster about as wide as his palm. That was okay, though. It meant he'd be able to watch what was going on outside, while the Disassem-

blers wouldn't spot him unless they shined a light in
through the gap or else physically opened the dumpster.
(And what would he do if that happened? Hit them with
a dead cat?)

He'd acted not a moment too soon. The first of his
pursuers burst from the alley almost the instant the
dumpster lid closed. The troll's pasty face almost matched
his gray and white gang colors; if the guy hadn't been
gasping like an asthmatic behemoth, Falcon would have
said he looked dead. His bloodshot eyes were rolling
wildly and a froth of saliva spewed from his lips.

His heart was pounding like a high-speed trip hammer,
but Falcon had to enjoy the sight. If this guy was their
best runner, the trolls would have died of fragging exhaustion by now if only Falcon had been able to make it
another two blocks. Then his grin faded. If they caught
him now, they'd take their physical misery out on his
hide. He squatted lower in the dark dumpster.

Three more trolls lurched from the mouth of the alley,
wheezing like they were about to croak. One bent over,
put massive hands on his knees, and noisily emptied his
guts onto the road. "*Skin* 'im," he growled between
retches. "Skin 'im slow wif a dull fraggin' knife."

"Gotta *catch* the fragger first," the leader rumbled.

" 'e's fraggin' *gone*," the smallest of the group—a
comparative midget at just over two meters and maybe a
hundred and ten kilos—grunted. "Just let the fragger go,
and good fraggin' riddance."

The leader casually slapped the smaller troll, a back-
handed blow that struck with a meaty thud. The slap
would have lifted Falcon off his feet and flung him into
the alley wall, but it barely rocked the troll. He glared at
the leader and spat on the ground, but held his tongue.

"He ain't too far ahead," the leader pronounced. "I
woulda had 'im if the alley was longer."

Don't make me laugh, Falcon thought. If the alley was any longer, you'd be lying in it puking.

"He ain't far ahead," the leader repeated. "Runnin' like a scared fraggin' rabbit, drekkin' down his legs. Scragger, you and Putz go that way." He hooked a thumb that was almost as thick as Falcon's wrist the other way down the narrow road. "Ralph here, he comes with me." He slapped a heavy hand on the back of the troll still hunched over a pool of vomit. "Well? Get the frag go'n'."

The smaller troll and another stumbled off down the road, away from Falcon's dumpster, at the closest they could get to a run. With a groan, the troll that the leader had called Ralph straightened up. The leader had already started to jog, passing so close that Falcon could smell the troll's rancid sweat even over the reek of the dumpster. Ralph cursed, but had no choice but to follow. Passing the dumpster, he unloaded a punch into it, a blow hard enough to rock the massive box and dent the metal. Falcon ducked down low in a resurgence of terror, imagining that massive fist slamming into his own face.

I could summon a city spirit, he thought, a great form city spirit, and send it after them. In his mind's eye he saw the noisome garbage strewn around the street shifting as though a wind had suddenly whipped through the city, drawing together, coalescing into a huge, amorphous shape. A shape that shambled off after the retreating trolls. He could hear their screams, their pleas for mercy. And then silence. I could do it, he thought again.

But of course that was only in his dreams. Often, when he slept, his dreams filled with a sense of power, his nerves hummed with the song of the totems. When he dreamed, Falcon *knew* he'd taken his first step on the path of the shaman—not through any conscious choice; it was as if it were written in his genes, as surely as his high Amerind cheekbones, dark eyes, and straight black hair.

In his dreams, Falcon walked that path, followed the summons of the totem, the spirit that awaited him at the end. He didn't know which totem was calling him—noble Eagle, faithful Dog, sly Coyote, stalwart Bear, or any of the many others. But he could hear the call, feel it thrilling through him, and realized that only when he reached the path's end would he recognize who summoned him. And then he'd probably realize that a part of him had always known.

That was in his dreams. When he was awake? Nothing.

No, not quite nothing. The dreams remained as memories. But that was worse than nothing. He knew, deep down inside he knew, that he would walk the path, that the totems would call him, *were* calling him when he slept. But a shaman must *consciously* choose to walk the path, that's what someone had told him long ago. He must hear the song of the totems and consciously decide to follow wherever they led. Only then could someone become a shaman. He had to seek out the song in his waking life.

"Vision quest," that's what many Amerindian tribes named it, seeking out the song of the totems. Different tribes and different traditions had different ideas of how vision quests worked, but most that Falcon had heard or read about described the would-be shaman going out alone into some hostile environment—a desert, the mountains, or the forest—and staying there until he heard the call. Sometimes the seeker would find mortal friends and allies along the way, sometimes he would not. But if he was really destined to be a shaman, a guide would eventually come and reveal to him the song of the totems. This guide might be a spirit or it might be in the form of a mouse or other creature, but according to all the stories it never appeared in the form that the shaman expected.

That was the traditional form of the vision quest, yet Falcon had heard that certain tribes had rung some very modern changes on the ritual. In the Pueblo Council, for example, he'd heard that some would-be shamans went on their vision quest into the Matrix. (What shape would a guide take there? Falcon wondered.) And then there were a number of groups—not just the new "suburban tribes" that had sprung up around the continent—that considered the city a reasonable place for a vision quest. Would-be shamans would leave their homelands to travel to the sprawls—admittedly, as hostile an environment as anywhere else in North America—and there they'd wait for their guide to come and lead them to the totems.

When Falcon had first heard about it, the idea really captured his imagination. He'd been living in Purity, a particularly unpleasant part of the Redmond Barrens, dreaming of someday leaving the plex and slipping over the border into the Salish-Shidhe nation. Only then, he'd thought at the time, would he have any chance to follow the path.

Then the concept of an urban vision quest had changed his mind. He knew the city; he was raised on its streets. Why should he risk a totally alien environment—the rural countryside of the S-S nation—when he could get what he wanted on familiar ground?

It was a year now since he'd left home, moved the twenty kilometers or so from Purity to deepest, darkest downtown Seattle. A busy year, not all of it spent listening for the totems singing to him. He'd found a place to squat, he'd joined the First Nation gang of half-Amerinds . . . basically, he'd survived, no mean accomplishment.

He hadn't forgotten the vision quest, of course; he could never forget it. When he had free time he put it into research. He was no decker, but he knew enough about computers to access the major public datanets. (That put him a few steps ahead of most of his First Nation chummers, as did the fact that he could read the results the datanets gave him. Most of the First Nationers were illiterate.)

He'd learned that, historically, many tribes had used drugs to sensitize them to the voices of the spirits. So he'd given that a shot. Energizers, speeders, ataractics, hypnotics . . . over the past year he'd tried most of the major types of drugs. They'd bent his brain the way they were supposed to—sometimes leaving him drenched with sweat, cramped and gasping on the floor of his doss—but they hadn't opened his soul to the totems. After a particularly bad trip in which the rest of the gang had to physically restrain him from jumping into Elliot Bay, Falcon had decided that drugs were not the path for him.

Fortunately, it was just about then that he'd found the book. A real book, with paper pages and a synthleather cover. *Spiritual Traditions of the Northwestern and California Intermountain Tribes,* by someone called H. T. Langland. (He'd never found out who Langland was or even if H. T. was a man or a woman.) The book had been for sale in a little talismonger's store on Pike Street near the market. They wanted thirty-five nuyen for it, much more than Falcon could afford. But something about the title and the way the book felt in his hands convinced him it was important. So he boosted it, shoved it up under his jacket and just strolled out of the shop. (The talismonger didn't need it or consider it important, he'd rationalized later, otherwise she wouldn't have been selling it.)

The book was heavy reading, full of long words and complex ideas. But Falcon worked at it and had finally come to understand. Langland—whoever he/she/it was— was a sociologist, and had studied how the tribes of the West Coast viewed the world, and their relationship with the spirits and the totems. There'd been a whole chapter on vision quests, which Falcon had read several times through.

He'd been glad to learn that the city was a valid place for a vision quest, at least according to Langland. But knowing that didn't help much in any practical way. The dreams still continued, the dreams where he sang and danced to the music of the totems, but he had yet to find his guide or hear the call when in a waking state.

Slowly, carefully, he raised his head and looked out from under the dumpster lid. The street was empty except for a rat about the size of a malnourished beagle nosing through a pile of garbage near the mouth of the alley. No sign of the Disassemblers. The trolls were probably dragging themselves back to their normal turf, trying to forget about the Amerindian punk who'd made fools of them. With a grin, he reached up and pushed against the lid.

It didn't move. Sudden fear drove like an icicle through his heart. Had the hinges jammed? Or was there some kind of locking device he hadn't noticed? Images of being trapped inside the dumpster until the truck came along to collect the garbage filled his mind. Collection was every two or three weeks in this part of the sprawl, and judging by the contents of this dumpster, Falcon figured it had been last emptied within the last few days.

No, he ordered himself sharply, calm down. He shifted position, finding some more stable garbage to stand on. Again, he pushed against the underside of the lid. The garbage moved under him, throwing him off balance. He transferred his weight, threw everything he had into it. His back complained, and a lance of liquid pain shot through his ankle. He groaned, tears blurring his vision.

But the dumpster lid moved. With a creaking of rusty hinges, it opened, slammed back against the building. Falcon vaulted over the side into the relatively fresh air of the narrow street, remembering at the last instant to take the landing on his uninjured ankle.

He looked around him quickly. No sign of the Disassemblers. Hopefully, the trolls had given up on him and gone back to whatever it was they'd been doing. He breathed deeply, cleared the reek of garbage—and the funk of fear—from his lungs. He looked up at the sky. Framed by buildings, there was a patch of blackness studded with a handful of stars bright enough to shine through the filth in the air.

And the moon was up, almost full. A perfect night for some of the magical rituals Falcon had read about in Langland's book. He needed somewhere open, preferably a place close to untouched nature, but where would he find something like that in the midst of the sprawl? Luckily, he knew somewhere that might serve. Favoring his damaged ankle, he limped off.

The small park was one of several that surrounded the massive Renraku Arcology. Dominating the region that had once been Pioneer Square, the great truncated pyramid, with its thousands of silvery-green glass windows, loomed over Falcon, its weight oppressing him.

During the day, the parks that surrounded the monolith—each a tiny copse of trees ringed by perfectly manicured grass—were "safe zones." Watched over by Renraku's gray-and-scarlet-clad security guards, they were places for the *shaikujin* who lived and worked in the arcology to stroll surrounded by something that resembled nature. By night, however, the security forces pulled back inside the walls and left the parks to the nocturnal denizens of Seattle.

The park that Falcon chose was at the southernmost corner of the massive arcology, near Fourth Avenue. It was maybe a quarter of a city block in size. Not much, but among the trees at its center he could almost forget for a moment that he was in the midst of the sprawl. He squatted on the damp ground, looked up at the moon riding like a ghostly ship through the scattered clouds.

Holding his hands out in front of him, palms down as though warming them over a nonexistent fire, he began to sing quietly. The words of his song came from Langland's book, words in the tongue of the coastal Salish. Although he couldn't speak the language, the book had thoughtfully provided an English translation, and it was this that ran through his mind. He was only guessing at the pronunciation, and the melody was one of his own creation. But *maybe the totems won't care,* he thought. *Only what's in my heart, in my soul, should matter.*

Quietly he sang.

> *Come to me, spirits of my ancestors,*
> *Dwellers in my dreams and in my soul.*
> *Come to me, guardians, defenders,*
> *Hear your children calling to you.*
> *Come to me, spirits of the land,*
> *Of the forest, and the mountains, and the waters,*
> *Come fill me with your never-ending song.*

He closed his eyes, let the words of his song resonate through the chambers of his mind. Let the melody carry away his pain, and the memories of the pursuit. Let his mind become placid, like the surface of a mountain lake untroubled by the wind.

He didn't know how long he sang. When he stopped, his mouth was dry, his voice hoarse. His knees were stiff and sore, and his injured ankle was throbbing agony. He opened his eyes.

Nothing had changed. He was still in the small park, not in the land of the totems. He hadn't heard the call of the spirits. He wasn't a shaman, just a punk kid hustling to survive in the heart of the sprawl.

He looked up. The clouds had covered the moon, and a chill rain had begun to fall. He sighed.

Stretching his legs, shaking his hands to return the circulation to his fingers, Falcon limped out of the park and vanished into the night.

3

2055 hours, November 12, 2053

This place never changes, Sly thought. The Armadillo was a small, dark bar in the middle of Puyallup, usually filled with a young crowd. She looked around her. As usual, she and owner Theresa Smeland—tonight working behind the bar—were the oldest people there by a decade—or more, in Smeland's case.

Smeland caught her eye as Sly walked in the door. The Armadillo's owner was an attractive, dark-haired woman of about forty, dressed tonight in a plain khaki jumpsuit. The lights over the bar reflected from the three chrome-lipped datajacks set into the woman's temple.

Sly smiled, nodded a greeting. She and Smeland used to be friends. Maybe not close, but better than acquaintances. At one time they'd also been comrades, fellow runners, but that was before . . . Just leave it as "before," Sly told herself sternly, squelching the thought. As she and Theresa had one thing in common before, they had another thing in common now.

Sly raised her hand, flipped it to indicate a small booth at the back of the bar. When Smeland had a moment, she'd stop by the booth with Sly's regular drink to spend a few moments in conversation.

Moving toward the rear of the room, Sly looked around. The Armadillo had little to distinguish it from any other watering hole in Puyallup, or anywhere else in the plex, for that matter. Low ceiling, well-worn composite-tile floor. Small tables and banquettes covered in frayed red terry cloth to sop up spilled drinks. Classic angst-rock issuing from cheesy speakers as background music—something by Jetblack, Sly noted. And a couple of old-tech trideo screens, which the patrons were more or less uniformly ignoring.

The patrons were perhaps younger than the denizens of other, similar bars in the sprawl. And perhaps drinking a little less hard, as though conversation were more the focus than getting wasted on alcohol. Indicative, maybe, but not enough to really set The Armadillo apart from other drinking establishments.

But then Sly let herself hear the hum of youthful conversation. *That* was what made The Armadillo what it was, and what made it one of her favorite places to hang. In other bars, the patrons would have been boasting of their conquests—sexual and otherwise—of the night before, yapping on about sports, arguing over politics, trying to score whatever was most on their minds at the moment. The Armadillo had some of that too, of course. But most of the conversation was about biz. A very special kind of biz.

The Armadillo was one of the premier decker bars in the Seattle metroplex. Everybody there, including Sly herself, had at least one datajack installed in his or her cranium, and some had as many as four or five. (Just for show? Sly wondered. Or can they actually keep track of that many data channels at once?) Reinforced Anvil travel cases containing cyberdecks were everywhere—on tables, leaning against chair legs, or clutched protectively in laps. Most of the first-string and the up-and-comers hung at The Armadillo, called it their base of operations: the console jocks, the Matrix cowboys, the bit-bashers.

For a moment, Sly let herself slip into reverie. It didn't seem so long ago that she'd hung out at another bar like

this. Not The Armadillo but its equivalent, the Novo
Tengu in the Akihabara district of Tokyo. She remembered the earnest conversations and arguments—sometimes
fueled by *sake,* but more often just by passion for the
subject—about the arcana of the Matrix and the philosophy of cyberspace.

Even now, even after having been "off-line" for more
than five years, she still enjoyed listening to decker talk.
Most of it was at the down-and-dirty, bits-under-the-
fingernails level: techniques for dealing with the latest
generations of ice, novel new hacks on old utilities, new
ways to "juice" a cyberdeck to squeeze more performance out of it. The biz—in terms of both hardware and
software, and with regard to the underlying theory—had
advanced almost unbelievably. So much that a lot of the
talk around her might as well have been in Elvish for all
Sly could decipher of it.

But deckers still wrestled with the same philosophical
questions that had so intrigued her in Akihabara. Ghosts
in the Matrix, those rare and strange constructs that
seemed to have no relation to deckers or to normal computer system functions. What were they? Artificial intel-
ligences—AIs—even though the corps claimed nobody
had successfully created one? Or mutating viral codes
that had "gotten smart" in some kind of electronic analog of biological evolution? Or maybe they were the
personalities—the "souls"—of deckers who'd died in the
Matrix?

That's what four elves were discussing at a table near
the booth Sly had chosen. Keeping her eyes carefully
averted, she eavesdropped hungrily.

". . . and what is it that's 'you' in the Matrix?" one
was saying. Sly pegged him as the oldest, an "elder
statesman" of perhaps twenty-three. "It's your persona
programs, right? And they're running on your cyberdeck, right? So what happens when the ice crashes your

deck? The persona programs stop running. And that's it: there's no more 'you' in there to *be* a ghost.''

"Unless the persona programs are still running somewhere else," another suggested. "Like on another CPU in the system." The first shook his head, about to argue, but the speaker kept on. "Or maybe it's the ice that does it. You asked 'who are you in the Matrix?' The answer's the same, in or out of the Matrix. It's your sensorium, the sum total of your experiences. Why couldn't some black ice read your sensorium, kinda like reverse simsense? And then copy it somewhere in the system, while it's killing your meat body? Your body's gone, but your sensorium still exists. A ghost in the Matrix."

For the first time the third piped up. "No," she said sharply, "your sensorium *doesn't* still exist. It's just a program *emulating* your sensorium. It's not *you*, it's software *pretending* to be you."

The fourth elf, silent, merely watched the conversation fly back and forth like a tennis ball.

"Meaningless distinction," the second pronounced.

"Not to me," the third shot back. "Anyway, *I* think the 'ghosts' are just parallel-processing Boolean networks with medium bias."

"Or sparsely connected, or maybe highly canalized," the first decker countered.

And then they were off into the depths of arcana, talking about "the transition between chaos and order" and "attractors" and "state cycles," concepts beyond Sly's understanding. Mentally she detached herself from the conversation, smiling to herself. The words and details were more sophisticated, but the ideas were no different from the ones she and the other Tokyo deckers had been tossing around half a decade ago.

Sly liked The Armadillo, but not just for the conversation. It was a comfortable atmosphere. There wasn't the barely concealed undercurrent of violence she felt in most other bars, particularly those where gangers and samurai hung. Sure, sometimes people got too drunk at The Armadillo, started throwing their weight around. But the patrons were people who used their brains as weapons, not big fragging guns and cyber-enhanced muscles. If there was a fight—a rare occurrence—nobody got killed, or even badly hurt.

More to the point, nobody hassled her. She knew that most of the patrons simply discounted her as a "null-head," a non-decker . . . and something of a fossil. Those few, like Theresa Smeland, who knew Sly and her background also knew enough not to discuss it, not to raise disturbing ghosts. If she wanted to hang with deckers even though she didn't punch deck herself anymore, that was wiz with them.

Apart from the ambiance, Sly found The Armadillo a good place to do business. Over the last couple of years she'd arranged almost a dozen meets with various Johnsons at the bar. Just like tonight. She patted her pocket to reassure herself that the chip carriers and her pocket computer were still there. Checking her watch, she saw it was just shy of twenty-one hundred hours. Her current Mr. Johnson would be showing up any minute, hoping to collect the data she'd dredged up from the Yamatetsu data files on Maria Morgenstern.

She frowned. Louis had finished his run three days before, but Johnson had said it just "wasn't convenient" to meet sooner. That puzzled Sly, even worried her at a deeper level. Johnson had been really eager when he'd given her the contract. He wanted whatever dirt she could find on Morgenstern—not now, but *right* now. She'd gone to Louis immediately, even paid him a ten percent "rush" charge to do the run at once. The conclusion was obvious: Mr. Johnson had needed the dirt either to make a major move on Morgenstern or else to prevent the lady from doing the same to him.

And now he was backing off on the importance of the whole thing. Did that mean things had changed, that getting a handle on Morgenstern just wasn't significant any more? And if so, did it mean he was trying to get out of paying Sly for what he no longer needed?

Sly looked up from the table, on which she'd been tracing complex geometrical shapes. Smeland was making her way through the crowd, carrying two pony glasses full of amber liquid. Sliding into the booth across from Sly, she set the glasses down in front of them.

"Hoi, T. S." Sly knew that for some reason Theresa hated her given name. "How's it happening?"

"Biz?" Smeland gestured vaguely around at the patrons, the bar. "Oh, it's happening. Nothing much changes, y'know." She smiled. "And you? How're the shadows?"

Sly shrugged, echoed Smeland's words back to her with a grin. "Nothing much changes. Still looking for a way to get out of them, into the sunlight."

"Oh, I know, honey." Smeland put her forearms on the table, leaned forward. "How's the vacation fund coming? Almost there?"

Sly sighed. "It's coming. Slowly. Still a long way to go."

"Ain't that always the truth?" Smeland pronounced. "So I guess this isn't quite in order yet, huh?" From her jumpsuit pocket she pulled out a small object—a tiny, multicolored paper parasol—and dropped it into Sly's drink.

Sly touched the parasol with a fingertip, flicked it so it spun. "Not quite."

"Ah, well." Smeland picked up her glass; Sly followed suit. "Some things take time."

They clinked glasses, and Sly drank. The scotch—real scotch, not the ersatz synthahol that Smeland usually served—had a smoky taste as she rolled it on her tongue.

She swallowed, feeling the warmth in her throat. "Yeah, time. What everyone's got so much of, right?"

Smeland leaned closer, conspiratorially, and lowered her voice. Sly leaned forward, too, so she could hear better. "Just heard some buzz from a couple of Dead Deckers," T.S. said, naming one of Seattle's better-known decker groups. "Louis just did some work for you, didn't he?"

There was something in Smeland's voice, something that disturbed Sly. "Yeah," she said slowly.

"Anything . . . like, real sensitive? Did you have him stepping on anyone's toes?"

Sly shook her head. "Just a routine datasteal," she told her friend. "A snatch on some personnel files."

"Nothing else?"

Sly shook her head again. Almost involuntarily, her hand patted at the pocket containing the computer and two chip carriers. One of the chips contained Morgenstern's personnel data. The other held the encrypted file Louis had given her. "No, nothing else."

"That's good."

"Why?" Sly asked. "What's going on?" She hesitated. "Something happen to Louis?"

Smeland's eyes flicked to right and left. But there was no one close enough to overhear. As she craned forward even closer, their foreheads were almost touching over the narrow table. "Louis is gone," she whispered.

"Faded?"

"Dead," Smeland corrected. "From what the Dead Deckers say, he died bad." She grunted. "I never liked the little drek, he gave me the creeps big time. But nobody deserved to go the way he went."

"What happened, T.S.?"

"Some people busted into his doss last night," Smeland said slowly. "The Dead Deckers said they did bad stuff to him, they asked him hard questions, you know what I'm saying?'' Smeland shook her head sadly. ''They wired his wheelchair up to the main voltage, they cross-wired his datajacks . . . Pros, sadistic pros. He took a long time to die.''

Sly closed her eyes. Torture. Somebody had tortured little Louis to death to find out . . . *what*? What was it they were after? The encrypted file? Maybe. But the odds were just as good—better, in fact—that he'd been pulling a run for somebody else as well, and it was that second run that had attracted the unwanted attention.

''You had him on nothing but a simple personnel data-steal? A smear job?'' Smeland was watching her, dark eyes steady on her face. ''Nothing more than that?''

''That's what I told you, T.S.''

Smeland chuckled mirthlessly. ''Good answer. Exactly zero data content.'' She took another swallow of her scotch. ''Well, it's your game. I don't play this drek any-more.'' She was silent for a moment, then went on, ''You meeting your Johnson here?''

Sly nodded. With a sudden flash of apprehension, she tried to remember what she'd told Louis, how much she'd said about her contract. Not much, but Louis was a cun-ning little bugger who could well have figured things out for himself. Did that mean he'd told his murderers? Could that be why her Johnson had postponed the meet?

Paranoid thinking, Sly, she told herself. There's no connection. Louis was probably hiring out to other run-ners at the same time he was working for me.

Smeland was watching her carefully. ''You know,'' she said lightly, conversationally, ''I've got this little hidey-hole in the back, a little room behind the bar. Lots of security systems—cameras, microphones, thermos, the works. Somebody can jack right into all those circuits, keep a close eye on everyone and everything in the main barroom. Did I ever show it to you?''

A broad smile spread across Sly's face. This is why

we have friends, she thought. "No," she said aloud. "But it sounds worth seeing. Why don't you show it to me now?"

Smeland's office was a tiny room, not much larger than some of the broom closets Sly had hidden in over the years. A small desk, covered in paper, a swivel chair that squeaked and had a back support like a torture device. The stereotypical retreat for the owner of a semi-successful watering hole.

Except for the electronics suite. That was top-notch, absolutely state-of-the-art. One whole wall was covered with closed-circuit video monitors, and the control panel was a system designer's dream. Even better, there was a fiber-optic lead attached to a jack. Sly pulled the swivel chair closer, sat down, and slipped the jack into the socket in her head. Data streamed into her brain.

The interface was slightly different from a standard simsense or Matrix connection, and it took her a couple of seconds to make sense of what she was receiving. Then everything fell into place.

With the lead socketed into her datajack, Sly *was* the security system. The dozen or so cameras were her eyes, the microphones her ears; the other sensors became senses that had no direct human analog. Visually, it was like being suspended above the barroom, looking down through a glass ceiling. But she could see into every cranny of the room, a perfect three hundred-sixty-degree view, as though she were looking through an optically perfect fish-eye lens, but without the distortion such a lens always creates. Through a simple act of will, she could focus her attention anywhere, zooming in for a close-up or backing away for an overall view. The microphones picked up the general hubbub of muted conversation, but she quickly learned that she could mentally filter out extraneous noise in order to concentrate on just

about any single speaker in the entire room. So this is what it's like to be omnipresent, she thought with a chuckle.

She'd been a little nervous when she'd first seen the datajack. "Is this system connected to the Matrix?" she'd asked.

Smeland smiled her understanding. "It's isolated. No system access node. No ice here." And with a reassuring pat on the shoulder, Smeland had returned to the bar. Sly still had a few misgivings, but those vanished once she'd explored the architecture of the system. This isn't the Matrix, she'd told herself. It's safe.

The clock on the wall behind the bar read twenty-one-oh-eight. Her Mr. Johnson was late. She focused her attention on the front door.

As if on cue, the door swung open and a familiar figure came through. Not her Johnson. Somebody else, somebody she hadn't seen in a long time.

The elf was tall and thin, his skin the color of mahogany, his kinky black hair clipped so close it looked almost like suede. His broad nose was flattened, courtesy of one too many fists in the face, and he had eyes that missed nothing, dark glinting eyes that reminded her of a raven's.

Modal, that was his street name. She'd never known his real name, even when they'd been lovers in Tokyo five years ago. His rep as a runner had been just as drek-hot back then, and he'd worked as a personal expediter for many corps. She'd met him in a high-tone corporate bar in the Shibuya district, a weird little place called the Womb.

Officially speaking, they'd been on opposite sides of a run that had gone wrong. Sly's Mr. Johnson had been a mid-level exec for Kansei, a corp attempting some industrial espionage against a Kyoto-based multinational called Yamatetsu. The Johnson got what he wanted, then suddenly decided he didn't want it anymore. What he wanted was to get it back to Yamatetsu, *now*. (To this day Sly didn't know exactly what had gone down, but she could guess. Various shadowy characters had showed up at his house, maybe worked over his wife or threatened his kids. Hinted that things would only get worse if he didn't make restitution—*full* restitution—to Yamatetsu immediately.)

And that was where Sly had come in. She'd been running Matrix overwatch on the original raid, while a group of local shadowrunners had done the physical penetration into Yamatetsu's Tokyo facility. Then her Johnson had come to her, saying she was to deliver an optical chip plus a credstick—obviously part of the restitution—to a representative of Yamatetsu. Why couldn't one of the other runners from the raid do it? she'd asked. Because none of them were alive any longer, Mr. Johnson had told her.

The meet had been at the Womb, and the Yamatetsu contact had been a tall negroid elf with—paradoxically—a strong Cockney accent. (At the time, she'd assumed he was a legitimate employee of Yamatetsu, not a hired runner like herself.) It had been a civilized meet. If Yamatetsu knew Sly was involved in the original run, they'd obviously decided it wasn't worth zeroing her. All they'd wanted was whatever it was she'd taken, plus a massive payment for "damages." She'd handed over the chip and credstick, and gotten a receipt from the elf in return—*civilized*—and that was it. When Sly got up to leave, he insisted she at least stay to finish her drink. One drink had become several, and they'd spent that night—and several thereafter—together at Modal's doss near Shinjuku Station.

The meet at the Womb had signaled the end of Sly's employment in Japan, and she'd headed on home to Seattle. Modal had stayed in Tokyo for a few more years, but eventually he too had come home to the sprawl. They'd tried to renew their relationship, but it just wasn't the same. The spark had died, and each realized that the other was just going through the motions. It had depressed Sly a little at how easily they parted, for neither seemed to feel any particular emotion. It was indifference, not tears or anger or some other passion that marked the end of the affair. Is that all there is? Sly had wondered sadly.

And since then? Certainly, she and Modal had run into each other on occasion. News reports to the contrary, the shadow community in Seattle just wasn't that big. She knew that Modal had done the occasional run for Yamatetsu's Seattle operation, but to the best of her knowledge his association with the megacorp had ended a couple of years back.

And now here he is again, she thought. I make a run on Yamatetsu, my decker gets geeked, and up pops Modal. Coincidence? Coincidences did happen, she knew, but putting pure chance at the bottom of any list of possible explanations was a good survival tactic. She focused her electronic attention on the dark-skinned elf as he made his way through the tables.

Nimbly sidestepping an inebriated decker, Modal reached the bar and settled himself on a barstool. He raised a hand to Smeland in greeting. " 'Oi, T.S. 'Ow's it?''

Smeland greeted him with a smile. (So they know each other, Sly noted. Interesting.) "It's going. How about you?''

"Oh, not so worse." He glanced around, leaned closer to Smeland. With a mental tweak, Sly increased the gain on the nearest microphone. "Looking for a chum," he told her. "Sharon Young. Seen her about?''

Sly heard her gasp in her own ears, the sound somehow more immediate than the sonic data coming in through the datajack. So much for coincidence . . .

"She hasn't been around for a few days," Smeland answered smoothly, not missing a beat. "But who knows? Maybe you want to wait, she might be coming in later."

Modal shrugged casually, as though it didn't really matter. "Might just do that," he said. "I think I'll go pass the time with some old mates I see in back there." He smiled, showing brilliant white teeth. "A pint of your best ale, T.S., if you please."

Theresa chuckled. "Toff," she shot back, one of Modal's favorite expressions for someone putting on airs. (They know each other well, then, Sly realized. I'll have to ask her about that.) Smeland handed Modal a pint of draft, and he wandered off to sit with a couple of orks who Sly didn't recognize. Not Armadillo regulars. She mentally selected the microphone closest to that table.

And that, of course, was when her Mr. Johnson walked in. A short man—human, but not much above the height of a tall dwarf—dressed in a designer suit that must have cost as much as a small car. He stood in the doorway, looking around. Looking for Sly, of course.

"Frag," she breathed. This was going to be tricky. She didn't want Modal to spot her, but she had to meet with her Johnson. No meet, no payment. No payment, no contribution to the Sharon Young Retirement Fund. Frag it till it bleeds, she thought. Was there some way to send a message to Smeland, tell her to direct the Johnson back here? Dump a message onto the screen of the bar cash register, maybe? But no, the security system was just as isolated as Smeland had said. It didn't even hook into the other computerized equipment in the building.

She hesitated. Why? she wondered. Why am I afraid of Modal? And she *was* afraid, she realized with a touch of surprise. First, Smeland's story about the death of

Louis, and then the unexpected appearance of Modal—someone who'd worked for Yamatetsu in the past. But what does that mean, really? Frag, *I've* done a job for Yamatetsu Seattle. She remembered getting a call last year from the head of Yamatetsu's local operation, a contract to dig up background on some street op called Dirk Montgomery. Everybody works for everybody, right?

She'd been keeping tabs on Modal. Not seriously, not a full trace, but she was fairly sure she'd have heard if he was working for Yamatetsu again. Seattle wasn't a big town, not in the shadows. What were the chances, really, that Modal was working for Yamatetsu now? Slim. And what were the chances that it was Yamatetsu that had geeked Louis? Better, but still slim. So that meant the chances of Modal being after her for reasons other than past friendship were slim squared. Maybe she should just go back to the bar and meet Johnson, and to hell with Modal. If she was careful, maybe he wouldn't even see her. . . .

Movement. Fast movement in her "peripheral" vision, the part of the barroom she wasn't concentrating on. In the flesh, she'd have had her back turned, wouldn't have seen anything. But jacked in like this, she didn't miss it.

Someone surged to his feet, a table fell, drinks crashed to the ground. People yelled in outrage.

It was the fourth elf, the fourth member of the group discussing ghosts in the Matrix, the one who hadn't said anything. Faster than any metahuman had any right to move, he was on his feet, his right arm swinging up. He was pointing it straight at her Mr. Johnson, hand bent far back. And then a plume of fire burst from his wrist, the muzzle flash of an automatic weapon. A cybergun, implanted in a cyberarm.

Through the security system she could hear the bullets whip-crack across the intervening space, hear them slam into the chest, throat, and head of her corporate employer. Blood and tissue sprayed, the impact ripping a gurgling scream from the man's throat.

And then, even before Johnson had a chance to fall, the elf was moving again in a flickering dash toward the door. Slamming patrons aside, upending tables. Vaulting over the crumpling corpse of the corporator, flinging the door open and vanishing into the night.

Guns came out of holsters, sighting lasers flared. Slow, too slow. The deckers in The Armadillo were armed, ready to defend themselves. But though their reactions would have been as fast as thought in the Matrix, out here in the world of flesh and blood they were much too slow. One gun boomed, a heavy-caliber pistol, the bullet slamming into the door where the elf had been an instant before. It was Modal, she saw, bringing his Ares Predator back into line for another shot. Another shot that never came, because his target had vanished.

Only then did it begin, the confusion, the yells of outrage, the screams of horror. The aftermath of any assassination.

Moving slowly, Sly jacked herself out of the security system, sat back in the squeaking chair. Her Johnson was gone, the file on Morgenstern now nothing more than a waste of storage space. And Louis' encrypted file? Maybe, suddenly, it was even more important than she'd thought.

Maybe, she mused, it's time for a talk with Modal.

4

The pain had diminished slightly in Falcon's ankle. The ankle wasn't broken, but it was sprained, and pretty severely. He could feel it swelling up inside his high-top runner, pressing against the synthleather. Should he release the velcro straps holding the shoe closed, give the ankle more space to swell? No, he thought, it was better to keep the shoe tight as long as he could stand it. Doctors put tensor bandages on sprains, didn't they? The shoe would serve much the same purpose. But still it hurt, and it slowed down his progress back to his own turf.

The unwelcome attention of the Disassemblers had driven him a long way from home, and his detour to the park near the Renraku Arcology had taken him even further. Now it was a long walk back—much of it, unfortunately, through Disassembler turf.

Falcon sighed. He *could* take a detour, head east of Alaskan Way and loop out around the Kingdome, then approach his home turf through the Burlington Northern rail yards. But that would add kilometers to the trip, a very real problem considering the condition of his ankle. Besides, that route would take him into the territory of the Bloody Screamers, a gang with whom Falcon's First Nation was at war. If the Screamers recognized and caught him, even without his colors, they wouldn't be satisfied just giving him a beating. They'd tear him to pieces, then send him home to the First Nation as an "object lesson" not to stray.

No, the lesser of two evils was obviously the direct route, down along the docks, and to hell with the Disassemblers. If he was lucky, the ones who'd been chasing him would still be yarfing up their cookies anyway.

He headed west on King Street, intending to cut south on First Avenue. These were wide, well-lighted roads, offering him a good chance of spotting anyone who was potential trouble.

Of course, it'd give everyone else a good chance to see him, too. The Disassemblers rarely strayed as far north as King, but the stretch of First near the Kingdome went straight through the middle of their turf. Did it make sense to jander on through, perfectly illuminated by the sodium arc streetlights? Like frag it did. There was an alley—*another fragging alley*—to his left, leading south. Narrow, dark, and claustrophobic, it looked even more dangerous than the wide-open streets. But that's life, he thought. Appearances are lies. He turned into the darkness.

For a few moments his eyes, which had adapted to the bright streetlights, were blind. While taking a couple of tentative steps forward, waiting for his night vision to return, his right foot struck something. Something yielding.

"Hey!"

The grunt from the darkness was enough to scare the drek out of him. Falcon backed away a step.

His night vision was slowly returning. Sitting on the alley floor, leaning back against the wall was the vague outline of a human-sized figure. He'd stumbled into one of the individual's outstretched legs.

"Watch where you're walking, chummer," came the voice again. A deep male voice, resonant, but overlaid with a hint of fatigue. The figure moved, drew its legs under it, began to stand.

He was big, Falcon realized, taking a step back. "Hey,

sorry," he began hurriedly, "if this is your squat, you're welcome to it. I—"

The man cut him off. "I'm no squatter. Can't a man sit down and take a rest without someone calling him a squatter?"

Falcon could see the figure more clearly now. He was tall, close to two meters, almost two heads taller than Falcon, and heavily built; not fat, but bulky and muscular. Long, straight black hair pulled back from his face in a ponytail. High cheekbones, a strong, aquiline nose, and deep-set dark eyes. Falcon thought his complexion must be dark normally—maybe a little darker than Falcon's own—but at the moment the man looked somewhat pale. An Amerindian? Almost certainly.

The figure wore what Falcon thought of as a "business suit," the kind of close-fitting, dark jumpsuit that shadowrunners and street ops always wore on the trid and in simsense.

Falcon took another step back. "Sorry."

"Ah, forget it." The man sounded even more tired as he leaned back against the wall. With his right hand he reached around under his left arm, probing at his ribs. When he brought his hand back, the fingers were dark, shining with something wet. "Frag," he muttered. "It's opened up again. I guess you don't have a slap patch on you?" He snorted. "Didn't think so."

To his surprise, Falcon felt his fear slipping away. The squatter who wasn't a squatter was big enough to be daunting, and something about him hinted of lethal competence. But there was also something that convinced Falcon the man didn't make trouble just for the frag of it. Unlike the Disassemblers, for example. Give him reason to come after you, though, and may the spirits help you. "What happened?" he asked.

The Amerindian smiled grimly. "Didn't dodge fast

enough," he said. "High-velocity bullets always have the right of way."

Falcon looked at the stranger with increased respect. He'd seen someone take a bullet wound once—a First Nation member shot in the leg by a Screamer in a gang war. Just a scratch was all it had looked like, but what the trid called "wound shock" had really trashed his chummer out, knocked him flat on his butt. All he could do was lie there, staring dully at the blood seeping through his jeans. In contrast this guy had taken a bullet in the ribs—a nasty wound, judging by the amount of blood showing on his fingers—but he was handling it okay. Sure, he was tired, probably from blood loss, but he could still joke about it.

"You . . . like, you want some help?" Falcon asked tentatively.

The Amerindian snorted. "From you?"

Falcon drew himself up to his full height. "Yeah, sure. Why not?"

"Why not?" A weary smile spread across the man's face. "Don't sweat it, chummer, I'll take care of myself. But . . . good thought, you know? Good offer. Thanks." He gestured down the alley in the direction Falcon had been heading. "You've got to be somewhere, right?"

Falcon hesitated, then nodded. "Yeah. Yeah, I . . ."

A deep-throated yell cut him off. "*There* 'e is," a booming voice announced. "*Told* you I seen 'im!"

Falcon spun in horror. Four figures stood in the mouth of the alley, silhouetted against the streetlights. Huge, asymmetrical shapes. Even though he couldn't see the colors, Falcon knew they wore gray and white leathers.

The four Disassemblers stepped forward into the alley. "Led us a merry fraggin' chase, dintcha?" one of them snarled. "I seen you limpin'. Let's see you do it again now."

For a moment, Falcon considered running. But he

knew with sick certainty that the troll was right. His ankle was fragged; they'd catch him before he'd gone a dozen meters. He looked around desperately for a weapon of some kind—*anything*.

The Amerindian casually stepped away from the wall, into the path of the trolls. "Leave him be," he said calmly. "He has my protection."

Falcon saw the eyes of two of the trolls widen in surprise. There was something about the man's calm, measured manner that made him seem suddenly like a force of nature—lethal and implacable.

The troll leader didn't have the sensitivity to pick up on that. Or if he did, he ignored it. "Move it, you scroffy breeder," he snarled. He reached out an arm thicker than Falcon's thigh to push the man out of his way. Large though the Amerindian was, a hard shove from a troll would still be enough to fling him back into the wall.

But the Amerindian's chest wasn't there to receive the shove. At the last moment he'd twisted out of the way, grabbed the troll's wrist with both his hands, and pulled. Off-balance, the troll lurched forward. The Amerindian kept on turning. His back to the troll now, he had the creature's huge arm locked against his body. He repositioned his hands, *twisted*.

The sickening crack of breaking bone sounded loud as a gunshot in the alley. The troll bellowed his agony. Not for long. The Amerindian released the troll's broken arm, made another half-turn and slammed the heel of his right hand up under the Disassembler's chin. The troll's teeth slammed together with a clearly audible clash, his eyes rolled back in his head, and he collapsed in a boneless heap.

Two of the three remaining trolls leaped forward, roaring in anger at the fate of their leader. The third, the smaller, backed away from the incipient melee, his eyes bugged out in surprise and fear.

The two larger trolls reached the Amerindian at the same instant, a solid onrushing wall of flesh that would have been enough to smash the man from his feet. Even worse, Falcon saw the glint of steel in one troll's massive fist. A knife? It had to be. If they'd had guns, they'd never have rushed him. The Amerindian disappeared under the trolls. That's it, Falcon thought.

But no, it wasn't. One of the trolls howled in torment, a soprano whistling cry that made Falcon's thighs tense in unconscious sympathy. Light flashed, and something clattered to the ground at Falcon's feet. The troll's knife.

One troll was down, unmoving. The other was swinging a brutal haymaker at the Amerindian's head, but it didn't connect. The Amerindian ducked low, let the momentum of the troll's swing carry him on around, then fired two brutal short-arm jabs into the exposed kidneys. Bellowing, the troll arched back.

The Amerindian took a step and kicked the Disassembler's legs out from under him. The ganger went over backward. As the troll fell the Amerindian threw his own weight on top of the massive body, riding it down. The first part of the troll to hit the ground was the back of his skull. A loud crunch. The Disassembler convulsed once, then was still.

A tiny dot of ruby-red light appeared on the Amerindian's shoulder, tracked up to his head. Falcon spun.

The sole remaining troll stood in the mouth of the alley, a pistol dwarfed by his huge hands. The sighting laser was burning, and Falcon could see his finger beginning to squeeze the trigger.

Falcon stooped, snatched up the knife lying at his feet. Threw it, a desperate underhand toss.

The troll must have seen the knife out the corner of his eye. He twitched, just as the trigger broke. The pistol spat once, then the knife struck him in the head. It was a lousy throw for a real knife expert—the hilt hit first, and the razor-sharp edge did nothing more than nick the troll's chin—but considering the circumstances it was pretty fragging good.

Not good enough, though. Snarling with anger, the troll brought the gun back onto line, tightened down on the trigger.

And magically, the hilt of a knife seemed to sprout from his throat. Gurgling and spraying, he went over backward. He scrabbled desperately, then was still.

The Amerindian was still lying over the body of the second troll he'd felled. His left arm, the one he'd used to throw his knife, was still outstretched toward the gun-toting ganger. He'd made an underhand cast, much as Falcon had tried to do, but the fact that he was prone made it even more difficult. Difficult or not, the throw was perfect.

Slowly, the Amerindian pulled himself to his feet, groaning with the effort. For the first time, Falcon saw that the big man's right arm hung limply at his side. It didn't take long to understand why: the troll's bullet had ripped a couple of nuyen's worth of hamburger from the Amerindian's biceps. Blood poured from the wound and down his arm, dripping from his fingertips to the alley floor.

"Drek-eating fragging son of a *slitch*," the Amerindian grated. "Two in one day." He turned tired, pain-dulled eyes on Falcon. "Your offer of help still good?" he asked. "Know anything about first aid?"

Falcon looked askance at the make-do field dressing he'd bound around the Amerindian's arm. He'd torn the cloth from his own shirt, and the gray fabric was already staining dark. At least he'd slowed the bleeding, of that much he was sure. Otherwise the man would already be dead.

He walked slowly beside the Amerindian, ready to offer a shoulder if needed. But his companion seemed able to walk on his own, albeit slowly. Again, Falcon was amazed at how much punishment the big man could absorb. He'd sat still while Falcon bound his new wound, but as soon as the job was done he went right back to business—scooping up the troll's pistol and checking its action, then stashing it and his knife in his jumpsuit. When he got up to get moving again, Falcon had insisted on coming along. The Amerindian had protested, but not too hard. Since then, they'd walked maybe fifteen blocks, all through back alleys, heading into the heart of downtown.

"My name's Dennis Falk," the youth said to fill the silence. "My chummers call me Falcon."

The Amerindian glanced down at him, was silent for a moment. Then he said, "John Walks-by-Night. They call me Nightwalker."

Falcon considered shaking hands, but Nightwalker didn't make any move to offer his. "What tribe?" he asked.

"Tribe? No tribe."

Falcon looked up at him in surprise, briefly studying the big man's strong profile, his complexion, his hair.

Nightwalker didn't look at him, but spoke as though he could read the young ganger's mind. "Yes, I'm Amerindian. But I'm not tribal." Still without looking down, he smiled. "What tribe are *you*?"

"Sioux," Falcon answered, then corrected himself in a quieter voice. "My mother was Sioux."

"Matrilineal descent's okay with most tribes," Nightwalker said. "So Falcon's your tribal name? Given to you by the chiefs?"

"No," Falcon said slowly.

"Have you been officially recognized by a Sioux chief, by any Sioux band?"

"No."

"So, officially speaking, you have no tribe," Nightwalker said. "Like me. Right?"

Falcon was silent for a few long moments. "Yes," he said grudgingly. Then he added fiercely, "But I will have."

"No Sioux chiefs in Seattle, chummer."

"I'm going to the Sioux Nation."

Nightwalker looked down at that, quirked an eyebrow. "Oh? When?"

Falcon clenched his teeth, swore to himself. "When I'm ready," he growled.

"Oh?" repeated Nightwalker. "Something holding you back? Family, maybe? Your gang?"

Falcon wanted to tell the Amerindian to just frag off, but he couldn't do it. There was something compelling about the big man, some strange kind of charisma that captured his imagination. "Vision quest," he mumbled.

"What?"

"Vision quest!" Falcon almost yelled. He glared up into Nightwalker's face, daring the man to make fun of him.

But Nightwalker just regarded him placidly. An eyebrow quirked again. "Tell me about a vision quest," he said quietly.

Falcon snorted. You know what I'm talking about, he thought, but didn't say it. Instead, he explained what he'd learned from Langland's book.

When he was finished, Nightwalker seemed to consider his words before speaking. "So when the spirits call you, you'll go?" he said at last. "Then and only then?" He shook his head. "I don't think I believe that." He quickly raised a hand to still Falcon's incipient objection. "I'm not calling you a liar," he explained. "I just don't buy the philosophy. Your destiny's your own, that's what I think, your life's your own responsibility. And the way I see it, a man's a fool if he gives up that responsibility to *anyone,* even the spirits.'' He shook his head again. "But hell," he went on with a sudden grin, "I don't drek on anyone else's religion or philosophy. It isn't healthy, and who knows? They may be right. More power to you, Falcon, and I hope you hear the totems' song.''

They walked in silence for a few minutes, Falcon watching the big Amerindian obliquely. Even though the other man didn't complain, he saw that Nightwalker was in serious pain. And, worse, he was obviously weakened by the blood loss from his two bullet wounds. His face was pale, his skin stretched-looking. His eyes were sunken and glittered with fever. Though he maintained the same pace, his gait had changed from a walk to a kind of shamble. Falcon could tell that it was becoming harder and harder for the man to keep his body under control.

"Where are we going?" he asked eventually.

Nightwalker didn't answer immediately. Then he shook his head slightly, like someone fighting his way back from the verge of sleep. He turned a haggard smile on Falcon. "*We?*" he asked. "*I'm* going for a meet with my comrades. You're going back to wherever it is you came from.''

Falcon shook his head firmly. "You need me," he said.

Nightwalker laughed at that. "Don't flatter yourself. So you're fast with a knife and competent with a field dressing. That doesn't mean you can play in the same league as us. Maybe in ten years, but not now.''

"You're shadowrunners."

The big Amerindian glanced down at him again, this time appraisingly. After a moment, Falcon could see him make a decision. "Yes," Nightwalker said.

"What happened?"

Nightwalker thought about it, then shrugged. "I guess it doesn't matter if I tell you," he said finally. "It's not like there's much to tell. A run went bad. We were waiting for one of our team to finish her part of the job, but''—he shrugged again—''she never came back, let's put it that way. And then the other team hit us.'' He grunted. ''Another shadow team. The corp we were hitting on had hired shadowrunners of their own to protect them. We never expected it, but it makes sense. Set a thief to catch a thief.'' His voice trailed off, his face went blank, slack. For a moment he looked like a sleepwalker, his body continuing the motions of walking although his consciousness had faded.

''So what happened?'' Falcon prompted.

Nightwalker's head jerked like someone being awakened suddenly. ''I'm drifting,'' he said quietly. ''Blood loss, wound shock. Maybe you should keep me talking.''

''So what happened?'' Falcon asked again.

''They hit us hard,'' Nightwalker told him, his voice emotionless. ''There was me and . . . and my friend, plus the rest of my team from Seattle. And then six more from out of the sprawl.'' He glanced at Falcon, lips twisted in a grim smile. ''Real tribal types, you'd probably have lots to talk about.'' Then the smile faded. ''It was their run. They brought me on board as tactician and because I know the sprawl. The tribals were good, but only in small-unit actions. They needed me to coordinate the multiple teams. Marci—my friend—and the rest of my team were just guns in case things went bad.'' His eyes were slightly glazed, his gaze distant. Falcon knew he was replaying events like a trideo show against the screen of his mind.

''They took Marci out,'' the big Amerindian went on quietly. ''One slug: in through her upper lip, blew out the whole back of her head. A bunch of the others bought it too, I think.'' He shook his head. ''Or maybe not, maybe they were just wounded. Anyway, we were split up and had to bug out or they'd have geeked us all.''

''That's when you were hit?''

Nightwalker nodded slowly. "I guess so. I didn't feel it when it happened. Sometimes you don't. It was later I felt my ribs were numb." He glanced down at Falcon. "That's what a bullet wound often feels like: numb and dead. It only starts hurting later."

"So what do you do now?"

"Contingency plans," Nightwalker said slowly. "We got back-up meeting places, times, procedures. We regroup, see if there's anything we can do to pull the run out of the fire."

"That's where you're going now," Falcon stated.

"Uh-huh," Nightwalker answered dully.

Suddenly concerned, Falcon looked up at his companion. The big shadowrunner's voice had been sounding more and more listless, the pitch lower and the words less clearly enunciated. "You okay?" he asked sharply.

Nightwalker didn't answer immediately. Then all he said was, "Huh?"

Falcon stopped, felt his worry escalate as the Amerindian took another couple of steps before noticing and stopping too. "You okay?" he asked again.

Again a pause before Nightwalker answered. "No," he said slowly. He shook his head, as if to clear it. "No," he said again, his voice more definite now. "Frag, I'm fading."

"How far's the meet?"

"Denny Park. How far's that?"

Falcon looked around. They were near Sixth and Pine. "About a klick, maybe more," he guessed.

"Frag!" Nightwalker hacked a cough and spat on the ground. Falcon saw that the dribble of saliva on the Amerindian's lips was dark with blood. The big man leaned back against a wall, closed his eyes for a moment, his face haggard with exhaustion and pain. When he opened his eyes again they were feverishly bright, fixed on Falcon's face. "You said 'we' a while ago," he began quietly. "*We*. You still want to help me?"

Falcon hesitated, but only for a moment. "Yeah." He tried to keep his voice cool, conceal the excitement he felt. "Yeah, I want to help. What do you need?"

The shadowrunner shot him a smile, tired but knowing. "Get me to the meet," he said. "I'll make it, but I won't have much left, you know what I mean? I want you to cover me. Watch my back, watch out for my interests. You understand?"

"You don't trust your partners?"

Nightwalker's chuckle became a painful, wracking cough. He spat again, wiped a dribble of bloody saliva from his chin. "Trust isn't a common thing in the shadows, chummer. We've got to get you a gun."

Falcon weighed the pistol in his hand. It was heavier than he'd expected, and it felt cold and lethal. A Fichetti Security 500, the ork gunlegger had called it. A light pistol, chambered for fairly light ammo, just one step up from a hold-out. But in his relatively small hand it felt bulky.

He'd never bought a gun before. Truth to tell, he'd never used one or even held one. Not a real pistol. Like most of the First Nation gangers, he'd bought himself a "Saturday night special"—a jury-rigged, single-shot zip gun, picked up for about twenty nuyen from a bartender in a dockside tavern. But—again like most of his First Nation colleagues—he'd never used the weapon, never *intended* to use it. Owning a zip gun, carrying it in his waistband, wasn't much more than macho posturing. He knew that a few of the gang leaders had real guns; one had even put a slug into the leg of a rival ganger. For most of the others, a gun was more a prop, like a jacket with the gang colors, not a tool to be used.

The gunlegger had only smiled when Falcon asked for a pistol. But he'd stopped laughing quickly enough when the youth pulled out the certified credstick Nightwalker had given him. He took Falcon's hand, examined the size of his palm, then pulled out the Lightfire. "Not much gun," the ork grunted, "but this should do you well." The gun had cost 425 nuyen, which Falcon had paid without trying to bargain the gunlegger down. No time. He knew for sure he'd over-paid when the ork threw in an extra ammo clip as part of the deal.

Now he held the gun out toward Nightwalker.

The Amerindian looked like drek, his complexion sallow, eyes red and sunken, forehead pricked with beads of sweat. He was sitting on the roadway, back against the wall of a building, looking for all the world like a half-dead rubby. This was exactly where Falcon had left him before heading for the gunlegger's doss, and it didn't look like the runner had moved a hair in the meantime.

"So you got yourself a toy, huh?" Nightwalker's smile and voice were both dull, exhausted.

"I got you something, too," Falcon told him. "Here." He tossed a small package into Nightwalker's lap.

With clumsy fingers, the Amerindian opened the package, pulled out a small circular patch sealed in a plastic pouch. He shook out the other contents of the packet onto his palm: three small octagonal pills, a bright warning red in color. He looked up at Falcon. "Stimpatch?" he asked.

Falcon nodded. "And those are metas. Metam . . . something."

"Metamphetamines," Nightwalker finished. "The runner's friend."

"The gunlegger said they'd pick you up."

"Pick me up?" Nightwalker grunted with amusement. "Yeah, pick me up, take away the pain, make me invulnerable . . . or at least make me *think* I'm invulnerable. And then when they wear off, I crash, and I crash *hard*."

Falcon glanced away. "I thought they'd help."

"They will help," Nightwalker confirmed. "You did good. If I take them, I'll hate life tomorrow." He laughed. "But if I don't take them, I won't *see* tomorrow." He grinned. "I guess you didn't bring a glass of water too, huh?"

Nightwalker still looked like drek, Falcon thought, but at least he didn't look like he was going to croak any moment. Falcon had applied the stimpatch to the ugly puncture wound in the Amerindian's ribs, a wound that looked even worse than Falcon expected. And then Nightwalker had swallowed the metas, coughing painfully as the dry pills caught in his throat.

Fascinated, Falcon watched for a reaction. If the metas were as powerful as Nightwalker said . . . He didn't have to wait long. Like a spreading flush, the blood returned to the Amerindian's face. His eyes, formerly glazed, cleared visibly. With a grunt of pain, he forced himself to his feet. He still looks like drek, Falcon thought, but at least he doesn't look dead.

Carefully, Nightwalker stretched, testing the mobility of his body. He twisted at the waist, hissed with pain as the movement stretched the wound in his side.

"How're you doing?" Falcon asked.

"Good as can be expected," Nightwalker said, "which is pretty fragging lousy. What I really need's some magic. I don't suppose you're a shaman? Didn't think so." Slowly he did a deep knee bend. "Okay, I can move. Not fast, but I'll make it." He grinned at Falcon, slapped the ganger on the shoulder. "You want to lead?"

5

What is it about elevators and public stairwells that
makes men want to void their bladders? Sly wondered,
smelling the miasmic air. (And women too, she thought,
remembering the wasted-looking bag lady she'd once seen
squatting down on the open platform of the Westlake
Center monorail station.) In cynical moments she wondered whether it was the same instinct that made wolves
and dogs mark out their territory. In her mind's eye Sly
could see a go-gang filling their bellies with water before
the nightly cruise of their territory. She chuckled quietly,
then forced the vagrant thoughts from her mind. Time to
concentrate on biz.

She was near the northern end of Alaskan Way, down
by Pier 70, across the road from the newly renovated
Edgewater Inn. A strange part of town, paradoxical, almost schizoid, she thought. On the west side of the road
were flashy hotels like the Edgewater, expensive restaurants catering to rich visitors, tourist-trap stores selling
Seattle souvenirs and "genuine Amerindian artwork"
produced on computer-controlled lathes and extrusion
machines. Bright lights everywhere, high-tone cars being
tended by chromed-up valets who doubled as sec-guards.
And on the east side of the road . . .

Deepest, darkest scum-land. Rusting railroad tracks,
deserted warehouses. Burned out or stripped hulks of
cars. Reeking dumpsters. And rats, both the four-legged
and two-legged varieties. It made for a weird ambiance,

the juxtaposition of tourist-land and the urban realities of all too much of the sprawl.

Sly leaned against a ferroconcrete wall, in the shadows of a warehouse doorway. Disused, derelict, the place was boarded up, probably condemned for demolition when the city engineers got around to it. The doorway where Sly sheltered had once been sealed up too, but someone had torn off the plastisheet, probably an enterprising squatter who'd used it to construct some stinking hovel in the squat-city that had sprung up at the south end of the docks. The walls were liberally spray-painted with graffiti, and on the door behind her was the spray-painted notice—"Do not enter or you'll die." The trash and empty drug ampoules strewn all around said that not too many people took the warning seriously.

Sly checked her watch—twenty-three forty-three. She'd been here an hour, and the air was chill with gray drizzle. She shivered. How much longer?

As soon as the ruckus at The Armadillo had settled down, she'd slipped out the back way and started to track Modal. Not too tough a job for somebody with her range of contacts. Just spread the word, hand out her cel phone number (the number her phone was currently jury-rigged to accept, to be precise), and wait for some response. Questioning a couple of squatters just outside Smeland's establishment, she'd learned that "the black elf with the big fragging gun" had taken off on a big black BMW Blitzen bike. The same make and model Modal had ridden during the time he and Sly were trying to rekindle their affair. He'd always been a man of habit—a real risk in the biz—and she'd often ragged him about it. Now, of course, she was glad he was a man of unchanging patterns; it made her job so much easier.

She hadn't expected instant response. Usually it took hours or days for her information network to pull in pay-data. Tonight she'd lucked out. The first call had come in after less than an hour, followed immediately by independent confirmation. Someone had spotted Modal jandering into Kamikaze Sushi at the old Washington State Ferries pier—Pier 68, was it?

Sly knew Kamikaze Sushi, had been there a few times herself. It was another of the contradictory aspects of the north pier area, seemingly out of place on the west side of Alaskan Way. A small and rowdy restaurant, it was known for its all-night parties (in blatant defiance of licensing laws) and for the fact that it featured classic rock music at brain-numbing volume. *Old* stuff—the Rolling Stones, the Doors, Genesis, Yes—bands that had kicked off half a fragging century ago. The owner of Kamikaze Sushi was a big Japanese guy who called himself Tiger, and when it was him working behind the sushi bar, he was the restaurant's biggest draw. Cybered reflexes made Tiger the fastest sushi chef in the plex, but his habit of matching customers drink for drink—even trolls who outmassed him by fifty kilos—tended to take the edge off his skill. Thanks to "minor accidents" while under the influence, four fingers on his left hand and two on his right were cyber. (One recurring rumor claimed that the day he lopped off his left pinky he'd served it to an inebriated customer on rice with a dab of *wasabe* . . . and said customer promptly ate it.) But none of that seemed to slow Tiger down.

It had taken Sly about half an hour to get from Puyallup to the piers, worrying that Modal would have moved on by the time she made it. But no, when she took up her position across the road from Kamikaze Sushi, his big Blitzen was still parked out front. For the past hour she'd been cooling her heels in the doorway, waiting for the elf to reappear. Listening to the music, which she could hear clearly even at this distance, she fantasized about warming herself with a thimble-cup of hot *sake*. Impossible, of course. The whole purpose of this exercise was to cut Modal out of the pack, drag him off somewhere quiet, and ask him some probing questions. (She suddenly shivered again, but this time not with cold. An image of little Louis flashed through her mind, Louis screaming his way through an interrogation. With an effort, she pushed the picture back into the furthest recesses of her brain.)

This whole thing really had her going. She needed to know what Modal was up to, had to know what he knew about Yamatetsu and the hit on her Mr. Johnson, had to know why he was trying to find her. If he was working for the other side—assuming she wasn't just being paranoid—things could get dicey. Modal was quick and dangerous; she'd seen ample evidence of that a few hours ago. She was fairly confident that with the element of surprise on her side she could take him out quick and clean. But that wasn't what she wanted. She needed him alive, unhurt and able to answer questions. And if it turned out he didn't have some nefarious purpose for trying to find her, she had to avoid hurting his pride or enraging him so much he wouldn't reveal what she needed to know. She sighed. Nobody said this would be easy. She checked her watch again. Come on, Modal. Hurry up . . .

As though the thought had been a charm to summon him, the familiar figure of Modal in his blue leathers suddenly appeared in the restaurant doorway. He paused briefly, apparently letting the cool night air clear the fog of *sake* fumes and smoke from his head. Then the elf jandered over to his bike, swung one long leg over, and settled into the saddle.

Sly held her breath. The next moments would make all the difference. The elf had held tenaciously to one pattern—the big bike he used to love so much. Would he hold to another as well?

Yes! Instead of simply firing up the bike and taking

off, he reached deep into a pocket, searching for something. Sly knew what it was, the small computer module that controlled all the sophisticated functions of the Blitzen. Preferring not to depend on alarms and other theft-deterrent devices to protect his bike, Modal had modified the control panel so that the computer module fitted into a shuttle-mount, just like those used for car stereos. Whenever he parked the bike, he removed the module and slipped it into a pocket. Without it, the bike was inert, dead. A thief couldn't even start up the ignition, let alone control the mass of metal whose stability relied so much on the computer-controlled gyroscope mounted below the engine block. Unmounting and re-mounting the computer module took several seconds—seconds that could mean the difference between life and death in a scrape—but Modal had decided the risk was worth safeguarding his beloved bike.

That meant she had a few precious seconds while the elf brought the Blitzen back to life. She'd chosen her position with that in mind, and the gamble had paid off.

Head up, eyes still on Modal, Sly burst from her hiding place and sprinted across the road. She was behind him, out of his range of vision . . . or so she hoped. This was probably the biggest risk. If he caught even a flicker of movement in his peripheral vision, if he turned to look, his reflexes could bring his Ares Predator out of the holster to drop her in her tracks even before he recognized who she was.

Luck was with her, again. By the time she hit the other side of the street, the elf had extracted the computer module from his pocket, but was fumbling with it as he tried to slide it into its mount. Drunk? she wondered. Possibly, considering he'd been in Tiger's place for more than an hour. And if Modal was a friend, the sushi chef would have pushed several drinks on him. From everything she knew about him, the elf would hardly have refused them.

She slowed her pace from a dead sprint to a more normal brisk walk. The Ruger Super Warhawk heavy revolver with its shortened barrel was a reassuring mass in her coat pocket. She tightened her hand around the grip, made sure the safety was off.

Almost there. The elf hadn't looked up, hadn't noticed her. He was still fumbling with the module, muttering Cockney oaths under his breath. Five meters, three . . .

She was still a pace away from him when his instincts—honed by years on the street and only slightly dimmed by alcohol—finally kicked in. As he snapped his head around, she saw his dark eyes widen in recognition. Then his hand shot under his jacket, reaching for the Predator in its shoulder holster.

But too late. Sly was already lunging forward, flinging her left arm around his shoulder while grinding the barrel of her Warhawk into his right kidney. "Don't!" she whispered harshly into his ear.

His hand stopped, centimeters short of his weapon. For a moment she could feel the tension of his muscles under her arm as he debated. Then he relaxed with a sigh. He was fast, she knew, but not that fast, and he'd recognized and accepted the fact.

She let herself relax minutely, too. The fear had been very real, the fear that he'd try his modified reflexes against her flesh-and-blood ones. He wouldn't have made it, lived to tell about it, of that she was sure. Her only choice would have been to put a bullet into his spine, even though he was no use to her dead. Her other problem would have been the urgent need to escape from the well-patrolled pier area—a murderer with her victim's blood still on her clothes. Not a pleasant concept. (Less pleasant was the idea of killing someone she'd once cared for as more than a friend . . . but she couldn't dwell on that now.)

Modal sighed again. "A face from the past," he said lightly, conversationally. "How is it, Sharon Louise?"

To her surprise—and horror—she felt a stab of emotion at the sound of his voice. Sharon Louise. She'd gone by her real name back then, back in Tokyo, before she'd taken Sly as her street moniker. Just Sharon. But once Modal had discovered her middle name, he always called her by both. *Sharon Louise.* He was the only one who'd ever called her that. Even now, the name brought back memories—his mellow voice in the dark, the feel of his body against hers . . .

"Sly," she snapped, resisting, but only just, the temptation to reinforce the word by jabbing the revolver deeper into his kidney.

He shrugged, seemingly unconcerned. "As you like," he said reasonably. "It's been quite some time, mate."

She shook her head irritably, more to herself than to him. "We're taking a walk," she told him.

He was silent for a moment. "If you're going to do me," he said finally, "do me now and get it over."

That shocked her into silence. Not the words, not the sentiment. The idea wasn't alien. She'd have probably felt the same if the tables were turned. If she thought somebody was going to geek her, those last moments would be the worst kind of torture imaginable—the slow walk across the road into the shadows of the warehouses, and then, only then, the bullet into the head or the throat. No, it wasn't the words that got to her.

It was the tone of his voice, the calm, unemotional, almost placid way he spoke them. And the fact that she felt no tension at all in the shoulders under her arm. He was discussing his own death as if it made no more difference than . . . than where they'd go for a drink, than whether they'd sleep at his doss or hers. And that was, on some deep level, incredibly disturbing.

Brutally, she suppressed her reaction. "Your gun," she said flatly.

He hesitated for another second, and she could almost feel his thoughts as he calculated odds. Then he shrugged. "If that's the way you want it." Slowly, with his left hand, which she knew was his off hand, he reached under his jacket and pulled the Predator from its holster, gripping the butt with two fingers.

She took it with her own left hand, quickly concealing it under her coat. Then she stepped back, opening a gap of more than a meter between them. From what she knew of him previously, Modal had had his reflexes juiced, but never had any cyber weapons implanted. No spurs, no razors. That had been years ago, though. Sly didn't *think* he'd have gone under the laser in the interim—implanted weapons weren't really his style—but she wasn't going to bet her life on it. She tightened her grip on the revolver in her coat pocket, shoved it forward a little so the barrel made the fabric bulge. Just for a moment, a reminder that she could still geek him before he could close with her if she had to.

He nodded, acknowledging the wordless communication. "So what now?" he asked quietly.

"We're taking a walk," she said again. "Across the street, behind the warehouse. And no fast moves, okay? I don't want to geek you, but I will if you force me."

He nodded again. "I know," he said calmly. "Okay, it's your party." He swung himself off his bike, calmly started to jander across the road. A little belatedly, she followed, keeping some distance between them.

Halfway across, he turned back. For a hideous moment she thought he was going to try something; she tightened her grip on the revolver. But he just smiled. "I could blow the whistle on you, you know," he remarked, his tone still conversational. "Raise a bloody riot, yell, 'The slitch behind me's got two bloody guns.' "

"But you won't," she said, injecting more confidence into her voice than she felt.

He walked on, thinking about it for a few moments. Then, "No, I won't," he shot back over his shoulder.

In the relative darkness behind the warehouse, out of sight from the street, Sly began to feel more secure. She pulled her Warhawk from its pocket, trained it on the back of Modal's head.

He turned to face her, eyes steady on the massive revolver. "So you *do* have your own gun," he said. "I was starting to wonder."

She touched the Warhawk's trigger, activating the sighting laser, positioned the ruby dot on his forehead. "Kneel down," she told him coldly, "hands behind your head."

He didn't move. "I don't want to go on my knees."

"I told you I wasn't going to geek you," she snapped. "Get down."

He shrugged, as though it didn't really matter. But he obeyed.

Sly let herself relax a little more. With his wired reflexes, the elf was still hideously dangerous—particularly if he thought she was about to pull the trigger—but at least in this position he'd be slower to move. She released the revolver's trigger, and the laser died.

He looked up at her, smiled. "I guess you want to have a little talk."

She took a deep breath, trying to control her emotions. There was something very wrong here, but she couldn't figure what it was. Modal was just too calm. Not relaxed, for she could see the tension in his body. But it was the tension of readiness, like a panther poised to spring, not the tension of fear. His eyes were fixed on her like gun sights, but they revealed no obvious emotion.

It doesn't really matter, she told herself firmly. I've got the drop on him. I'm safe.

She forced her voice to sound equally calm. "Tell me about Yamatetsu," she said.

He nodded, almost to himself. "You know, then."

Know *what*? she wondered, but tried to keep the puzzlement out of her face. Maybe if he thinks I already know, he'll tell me more.

"I know some of it," she told him. "And I suspect more. I just need to confirm it."

Modal smiled at that. "I always did like your moves . . . *Sly*," he said—his purposeful hesitation over the name striking home. "Good interrogation technique. Don't let the subject know how much you've already got."

"Yamatetsu," she reminded him. "Are you working for them?"

He hesitated, eyes searching hers for some clue. "Yes," he said finally. Then added hastily, "But not in the way you probably think."

"Tell me," she pressed. "And don't lie to me. If you lie, I'll drop you right here."

He nodded. "Yes," he said slowly, "you would, wouldn't you? Okay, the truth. Yamatetsu's after you. Searching the shadows with a fine-tooth comb. They've got operatives out—their own people, plus maybe a dozen hired runners."

"And you're not one of them?"

He shook his head with a smile. "Not directly," he said. "I don't run the shadows anymore. It's a young mug's game, you know that. There's bold runners, and there's old runners. But there's no *old, bold* runners."

She grimaced at that. He's younger than I am, she thought with disgust. "So how come you're involved?" she asked harshly.

"What do retired shadowrunners do?" he asked rhetorically. "Open a bloody boutique? Sell ladies' hats?"

"You're a fixer." To her own ears, the words sounded like an accusation.

"On the bloody nose," he said with a grin. "I'm still in the game, I can use all my old connections, but I don't have to hang my arse out and wait for somebody to shoot it off."

She nodded slowly. "So Yamatetsu came to you to hire street ops." She thought out loud. "Who's Yamatetsu Seattle? Jacques Barnard, still?"

"You're out of date. Barnard got bumped upstairs three months ago. He's in Kyoto now, no doubt living in the lap of bloody luxury. It's Blake Hood. A dwarf and a real charmer. Blakey makes Jacques Barnard look like a nancy-boy."

"How many runners?"

Modal shrugged. "Blakey likes to share the wealth. He never gives everything to one fixer."

"How many contracts did he offer you?"

"Eight. And he was offering top brass, too."

Sly could hear her pulse in her ears. Eight high-priced runners. She probably knew some of them. Like they said, Seattle wasn't a big town, not in the shadows—and that made it worse. No pro was going to let sentiment get in the way of biz, and the people who were after her might know her habits, know where she dossed down. Frag, she thought, I could have talked to one of them tonight. Quickly she reviewed what she'd said on the phone to the members of her information net. Too much, probably.

Who the frag am I going to trust? she asked herself, feeling her fear like a dirty snowball in her belly. Nobody! Tox!

She glared down at Modal. "And of course you filled those eight contracts," she accused bitterly.

"Of course," he answered reasonably, "It's biz, isn't it? And even if I didn't, Blakey would just go to another fixer, wouldn't he?"

She had to accept the truth of what he was saying, but that didn't make her feel any better. "You were looking for me yourself, weren't you?" she grated.

His eyebrows rose at that. "So you *were* at The Armadillo. I thought you were."

"Why?" she growled. "What were you going to do? Scrag me yourself? Pocket the bounty?"

Modal was silent for a moment. "I don't know what I was going to do, and that's gospel." He shook his head. "The bounty would have been nice. Ten K's a lot of scratch, and times are lean. But god's truth, I don't know what I'd have done. Scragged you? Warned you? I don't know."

Sly found herself staring into the depths of those black eyes. They were still clear, showing not the slightest trace of fear or of any other emotion. He could be lying, but she didn't think so.

But . . . drek, ten K. A ten-thousand nuyen bounty. Somebody wants me bad.

"Why?" she demanded again, but this time the word was a different question. "Why's Yamatetsu after me?"

He shrugged.

Anger flared in her chest, almost, but not quite, over-powering the fear. "Aren't you at least curious?"

"Not really." Modal's voice was calm, uninflected. "It doesn't really matter. There're dozens of people on the street looking for you. Whatever the reason, they'll find you soon enough, and you'll go down."

She stared at him again. With a different intonation, those words could have been a threat. But the way Modal said them they were merely a bald statement of fact. Which only made them more terrifying.

"Do *you* know?" Modal's question was mildly curious, nothing more.

I *think* I do, Sly thought, imagining she could feel the weight of the two datachips—the one containing Morgenstern's personnel file, and the other one containing Louis' encrypted file—in her pocket. Imagination, of course; each chip, even in its carrier, weighed less than a feather. For an instant, she felt an almost overwhelming impulse to confide in Modal, to bounce her suspicions off him. But of course that made no sense. He could just as easily turn round and tell Yamatetsu how much she'd figured out. She shook her head.

"Oh, well." He shrugged.

And that, of course, brought her to another question. Just what the frag was she going to do about Modal? Turn around and walk away? Possibly. But she'd confirmed to him, accidentally and indirectly, that she was pretty tight with Theresa Smeland. That meant he could pass that gem on to Yamatetsu. And how would they handle it?

Probably the same way they'd handled Louis. She couldn't do that to Theresa. Sly could drop out of sight; there wasn't anything—not really—holding her to Seattle. But Theresa had The Armadillo, no doubt had much of her net worth sunk into the bar. Doing the quick fade would, for Smeland, be the same as Sly leaving behind her "retirement fund." That would leave Smeland with only what she could carry, plus whatever liquid assets she had, while the business she'd built up would be gone. Great way to reward a friend for being a friend, huh?

And Modal himself. Frag it.

His eyes were still on her—steady, untroubled. But there was something else in them, even if she couldn't discern any emotion. A look of awareness, of understanding.

He knows, she thought. He knows what I'm thinking. She couldn't meet his gaze, looked away. Looked at the rough ground, covered with garbage. Looked at the back of the disused warehouse, up to the lights of the city that showed above the hill leading to Elliot Avenue. She tightened her grip on the Warhawk. Frag it till it bleeds. . . .

"Geeking me would be the easy way out," the black elf said evenly, echoing her deep, painful thoughts. "But it's not the only way."

She looked at him again knowing that her silent entreaty, her inner plea for him to explain another way out showed in her face. "Talk," she said roughly.

"You can't just let me go free," he said, his voice as calm as if he were discussing the weather. "You think I'll go to Yamatetsu with what I know. I know your moves, Sharon Louise, I know where you hang. I know a lot of your mates. And I know you're here. If you let me walk, even if you take all my gear, I can get to a phone in two minutes. Yamatetsu could have this place flooded with street ops in another five. And how far could you get in seven minutes? Not far enough. Right?"

She nodded miserably. He was just reciting the reasons why she *had* to kill him. Was he depending on any feelings she might still have for him to keep him alive? (Were there any feelings? Yes, frag it, there were.) But if he was, he was misjudging her. She'd hate herself afterward if she had to kill him, but she *could* do it. If necessary. And she *would*. Her finger tightened on the trigger. The laser dot trembled on the kneeling elf's chest.

"But there's another way." Even this close to death, his voice gave away nothing, neither fear, nor supplication.

"Talk," she demanded again. This time her voice was a whisper.

"*Use* me, Sharon Louise," he said, the name paining her like a knife twisting in her gut. "Turn me. Make it so I can't work with Yamatetsu. Make it so I don't have any choice but to work with *you*."

"How?" The plea almost caught in her throat.

"I could say, 'Trust me'," he said with a chuckle. "But I know what that'd get me." He looked down meaningfully at the laser dot. "Trash me with Yamatetsu. Compromise me, make it look to Blakey like I've sold him out to you. He'll buy it. He doesn't trust anybody, and he knows we were . . ." He let his voice trail off.

She was silent for a moment. She couldn't feel her hands, was numb from the elbows on down, but she could see from the movement of the sighting dot that they were trembling. *It makes sense,* she thought. *What he says makes sense.* She wanted to believe him. She wanted . . .

"I'll tell you how. It'll work, Sharon Louise."

"Sly!"

"It'll work, Sly."

Suddenly, rage flared up inside her, a consuming fire of overpowering anger. She moved the gun off-line, pulled the trigger. The big revolver boomed, kicked hard in her hand. She heard the bullet slam into the ground beside Modal. He jumped at the report, at the sound of the heavy slug splitting the air near his ear. But his gaze remained fixed on her face, his eyes and face showing . . . *nothing.*

"*Feel* something!" she screamed at him. "Feel *something*! It's like you're a fragging *zombie*! What the frag's *wrong* with you? I could *kill* you!"

"I know." Still not the least trace of emotion.

She forced the rage down. Painted the bridge of his nose with the laser, knowing it must be flaring in his eyes. His pupils contracted, but that was the only reaction. "What is it?" she whispered. "Tell me."

"Always emotional, Sly," he remarked conversationally. "Always letting emotions get in the way. Just like I used to. Don't you get tired of it? Doesn't it slot you

up sometimes?'' He didn't wait for her answer, asked another question. ''Ever hear of 'deadhead'?''

Taken off balance by his query, she shook her head wordlessly.

''It's a drug,'' he explained flatly. ''It decouples the emotions. They're still there, but your conscious mind can't access them. When you're taking them, you can't *feel* your feelings. No fear, no anger. Most of all, no sadness. Can I?'' He moved his left hand slightly.

She tightened down on the trigger, felt it move. Another bit of pressure and it would break, putting a bullet into his head. She nodded.

Slowly, carefully, he reached down and extracted something from the outside pocket of his leather jacket. Held it toward her. A small plastic vial, containing dozens of small black pills. ''Deadhead,'' he explained needlessly. He set the vial down on the ground, put his hand back behind his head. ''I've been taking them for three years.''

She stared at the pills, then looked back into his eyes. ''When did you start?'' It was an effort to force the words out.

''Soon after.''

''And what . . .'' She couldn't finish the question.

''At first it was just what I needed,'' he explained. ''Everything's still there, all the sensations. Senses are unaffected. But the emotional reactions are just . . . tuned out. I can do anything, without emotions getting in the way. Just the thing for a shadowrunner, yes? That's what I thought. No pain, no regrets, no torturing yourself after the fact for the decisions you've made, for the mistakes.'' He shrugged again. ''Of course, it cuts out *all* emotions. I can't feel sadness, but I can't feel joy either. Not unless I take another kind of pill.

''And there are side effects. There always are with something that affects you this . . . *profoundly*. It feels like there's a band around my forehead, sometimes tight, sometimes loose, but always there. And if I misjudge the dosage, people's voices sometimes take on a . . . a kind of metallic ringing. But it's a small price to pay, don't you think?''

No! she wanted to yell. It isn't right. It isn't life. Emotion's what separates us from the animals, isn't it? We don't just act, we feel. But . . .

But wasn't there something attractive about it, too? An end to emotional pain. To those nights when you wake up in the dark, and you're tortured by all the might-have-beens and the never-weres? To the fear that loosens your bowels, twists you up inside? To those dark midnights of the soul when it just doesn't seem worth the effort to go on?

She shook her head. No. Sometimes the emotions weren't pleasant. But frag it, they were *her* emotions.

"Why don't you stop?" she asked, then came the question she'd really meant to ask. "*Can* you stop?"

He smiled up at her. A smile she now knew was a mask, an empty facade. A habit he'd acquired and hadn't lost yet, like an amputee trying to scratch at the leg that isn't there anymore. "The street doc who turned me on to these things said they were habituating," he said quietly. "Just habituating. I found out later they're physically addictive. More addictive than heroin, than nicotine, than cram. . . . No, Sly, I can't stop. And I wouldn't want to if I could.

"I said the emotions are still there, I just can't access them. Would you like to face a three-year supply of emotions? Emotions you haven't processed? All at once?" He shook his head. "I'd rather you pull that trigger, thank you very much."

She glanced down at the gun, realized she was still a hair short of firing. With an effort, she released the pressure on the trigger. Looking down at Modal, she saw not

the slightest trace of emotion, of relief, as she lowered
the weapon. Disgust twisted in her belly.

"I'll rat you to Yamatetsu," she said harshly. "Tell
me how to do it."

6

0230 hours, November 13, 2053

As they walked, Falcon toyed with the Fichetti pistol.
It felt solid, slightly heavier than he'd expected, a well-
machined chunk of metal and ceramic composite. Its
lines were smooth, business-like, with no odd protru-
sions to catch on a holster or the inside of a pocket. Even
the bulge of the laser sight, mounted under the barrel,
was rounded, streamlined. The weapon felt somehow reassuring in his grip, much different from his jury-rigged
zip gun. The zip gun should have been more lethal because
the round it fired was much bigger than the Fichetti's,
but Falcon had always suspected that the jury-rigging
would make using the zip gun even more dangerous to
him than to his target. Not so the Fichetti.

"Never been heeled before, huh?"

Falcon turned. Nightwalker was watching him with a
faint grin. Condescension?

The young ganger felt a tingling in his cheeks, knew
he was blushing. "Sure I have," the lie came quickly.
"All the time."

The shadowrunner didn't say anything, just watched
him steadily. His smile didn't change, but Falcon's inter-
pretation of it did. It wasn't condescension he saw, but
understanding. There was a difference.

"No," Falcon corrected quietly. "Just a zip gun. I guess that doesn't count."

"You got that," Nightwalker agreed. "Zip guns are for street punks." Before Falcon could bridle at the remark, the runner extended his hand. "Give it here."

Falcon looked at him in surprise and with a twinge of suspicion. "Why?"

Nightwalker sighed. "I just want to check it out," he said patiently. "Make sure you weren't ripped off. What'd you pay for it?" When Falcon told him, the big Amerind shook his head. "Premium price," he announced, "but don't sweat it. You didn't have time to shop around. Learn from it, though, and remember next time."

The ganger nodded, and handed over the pistol. I knew the scuz gouged me, he thought.

Without breaking stride, without even seeming to look at the gun, Nightwalker field-stripped the weapon. Worked the action, examined the chamber, checked the barrel for obstructions. "Mint, or close to it," he remarked, reassembling the piece. "Fired just enough to work the parts in. You got a good deal after all, chummer." He checked the load, his big hands dwarfing the magazine. Then he slammed the clip back into place. "Ever fire that zip gun of yours?" Falcon shook his head. "Ever fire *anything*?" Another shake of the head, this time more hesitantly.

"Don't sweat it," Nightwalker told him smoothly. "The best run's the one where you come back with no ammo spent." He handed the Fichetti back to Falcon, stuck his hands into his pockets. He stopped, and leaned casually against the alley wall. "I want you to try it now."

"Huh?" Real intelligent, Falcon, he chided himself, real frosty thing to say. But the runner's suggestion had taken him by surprise. "Here?"

"Why not?" Nightwalker shrugged. "Better to get used to it now than when the drek hit the fan, right?"

"What about the noise?"

"We're in a fragging alley in downtown fragging Seattle," Nightwalker said wearily. "You think anyone's going to come a-running if you cap off one lousy little round? Do it."

Falcon looked into the older man's face. His eyes were serious, but his lips were quirked in a half-grin. *Does he think I haven't got the balls to do it?* the ganger wondered. He shrugged, trying to emulate Nightwalker's cool manner. "Yeah, why not? What's my target?"

Nightwalker pointed with a thick forefinger at a dumpster a dozen meters further down the alley. "That'll do," he said drily.

Another fragging dumpster. It looked like it was gonna be one of those nights. Falcon didn't comment out loud, just raised the pistol and steadied it in what he thought was the proper two-hand posture. He settled his finger on the trigger—at the last moment remembering to flip the safety off—and applied pressure. The laser lit, painting the dark blue dumpster with a red dot. The aiming spot trembled, then steadied as he tightened his grip on the butt. He took a deep breath, held it. Pulled the trigger. The gun barrel jerked to the left.

But it didn't fire. No report, no kick, just a sharp metallic *clack*.

Before he could move, Nightwalker's hand flicked out, apparently from nowhere, and grabbed the gun, holding it totally steady in its new position. "Hey!" Falcon shouted.

"You missed, chummer," Nightwalker told him flatly, still holding the gun immobile. "Look where the target point is."

Falcon looked. The laser spot quivered on the building a meter up and at least a meter over from the dumpster.

"See that?" Nightwalker stressed. "You anticipated the recoil, you took the gun off-line when you tensed up. See?" He released the gun.

"It didn't fire," Falcon said accusingly.

Nightwalker just chuckled. Reached into his pocket and grabbed something, then held his hand out toward the ganger. Ten caseless rounds rolled around in his big palm.

He'd palmed them when checking the gun, Falcon realized. "Why?" he snapped.

"Two lessons in one," Nightwalker said, his voice serious now and his smile gone. "One, nobody thinks they anticipate the recoil, but they won't stop until they realize they're doing it. This was the best way of showing you. And two, never—fragging *never*—believe anyone who tells you, or even implies, a gun is loaded or unloaded. Check for yourself, always. You hear me?"

Falcon nodded slowly, watching the Amerindian runner with new respect. He'd obviously done this drek before. "Thanks," he said quietly.

"Null perspiration. All greenies make the same mistakes." Nightwalker slapped Falcon firmly on the shoulder, robbing the words of any offense. He handed over the loose rounds. "Reload your weapon, and let's roll."

Falcon followed the big man, trying to slip the slightly greasy-feeling caseless rounds into the magazine by touch. There's more to the shadows than I thought, he mused, a realization that was distinctly unsettling.

It was well after oh-three hundred hours by the time they reached the corner of Eighth and Westlake. Denny Way was two blocks north, Denny Park, where the meet would go down, another block west.

The Amerindian wasn't complaining, but Falcon could tell that Nightwalker was in bad shape. The big man's breathing was rapid and shallow, and the brittle gleam of fever was back in his eyes. He was slowing down again, nowhere near as much as right after the encounter with the Disassemblers, but still noticeably. He kept his left arm tight against his ribs, apparently applying pressure to the wound to slow the bleeding. The gray cloth dressing on his upper right arm was already completely dark, saturated with blood. The stimpatch and the metas were keeping him going, but for how long? Falcon couldn't help but wonder.

"Can we take a break here?" the young ganger asked, careful not to meet the runner's gaze. "I need a breather."

If Nightwalker knew he was lying—and why—he made no comment. The runner just leaned back against the building and closed his eyes. "I'm getting too old for this drek," he sighed. "I should have come into the light a long time ago."

Falcon didn't recognize the idiom, but assumed it meant retiring from the shadows. He watched as his companion forced himself to take deeper breaths, saw the man's mouth tighten with pain.

They rested for a few minutes. Then Nightwalker pushed himself away from the wall, passed a hand over his face. He needs more rest, Falcon thought, more time. But it was the Nightwalker's operation, Nightwalker's call. He walked close alongside the Amerindian as they started off again, always ready to offer a supporting shoulder if necessary. But apparently the proximity of their goal had given the runner more energy. His pace was still slow, but he didn't show the same tendency to stumble.

"What is this meet, anyway?" Falcon asked.

"Regrouping," Nightwalker replied. "Meet up, then bug out. Over the wall, out of the sprawl. We've got a safehouse set up in the Salish-Shidhe lands, somewhere I can hang and where I can mend.''

Falcon nodded. ''Anything I should watch out for?''

That earned him a sharp look. ''What do you mean?''

The ganger shrugged. ''You said I needed heat,'' he reminded the runner. ''Like, you don't really trust the others.''

Nightwalker gave him a tired smile. ''Yeah, well . . .'' He thought for a moment. ''I guess I don't really expect trouble. Just be cautious. Stay close to me when we get there,'' he added firmly. ''Let the others know you're with me.''

Falcon nodded, feeling a sudden chill, realizing that if he didn't, the others might geek him on sight.

Denny Park was about five blocks from Seattle Center. As they approached, Falcon could see the lights of the Space Needle reaching up into the sky. Though nowhere near as tall as the corporate skyrakers of downtown, its slender, graceful construction made it *look* taller.

The park itself was an oasis of green in the ferrocrete desert of the sprawl. It was about two city blocks in size, enough space for a couple of little copses of trees, some greensward, and even a fish pond. The landscaping had been part of the spate of urban renewal that had swept the city a few years back. Obviously designed by someone who didn't know the ugly realities of the sprawl, the intention had apparently been to create a place for kids to play, lovers to stroll, all that kind of drek. But it wasn't the kids and lovers who moved into the park. It was the squatters, the gangers, the drug and chip dealers, the chippies, the street apes, and the gutterpunks. And that fragging fish pond—within months, Seattle's hard rain had made the water so acidic that all the fish kicked off. These days Falcon would have feared dipping even a finger into the pond, afraid all he'd pull back would be bone.

They approached from the east, along Denny Way, which was mostly deserted at this time of night. Bikes rumbled by in groups, but the go-gangers seemed to have too much on their minds to hassle a couple of pedestrians. As they stepped off the pitted sidewalk onto the muddy greensward, Falcon kept close to Nightwalker, so close that his left shoulder brushed the Amerindian's right biceps, evoking a grunt of pain. Quickly, he backed off a step, but tried—by his body language, by just *thinking* as hard as he fragging could—to communicate the fact that they were together.

There were no lights in the park. (Once there had been, but playful locals had quickly shot them all out, and the city engineers hadn't bothered to replace them after the fifth or sixth time.) They weren't really necessary. The lights of the nearby buildings illuminated the area enough for Falcon to see that the greensward was empty. The nearest copse of trees was directly ahead of them, about thirty meters away, beside the acidic fish pond. Two meters into the park, Nightwalker stopped and waited.

Falcon looked around him. We're really exposed, he thought. Right out in the open. That's dumb. . . .

But it *wasn't* dumb, he realized after a moment. Sure, there wasn't any immediate cover other than a couple of parked cars on Denny Way behind them, but neither were there any hiding places for enemies nearby, nor any way someone could sneak up on them unobserved. Falcon stuck a hand into his jacket pocket, felt the reassuring weight of the Fichetti pistol.

For more than a minute, there was no movement. Nightwalker stood beside him, apparently relaxed. But no, even though his body was still, the runner's eyes were flicking around ceaselessly, looking for anything out of the ordinary.

And then the figure emerged from the copse next to

the pond. Another Amerindian, Falcon thought, or so the man's straight black hair might suggest. He wore the same dark clothes as Nightwalker. Another of the runners?

"Cat-Dancing," Nightwalker murmured under his breath, apparently naming the figure.

It *is* one of his comrades, Falcon thought, some of his tension leaking away. Nightwalker took a step forward, and the ganger followed him.

Cat-Dancing raised his right hand, made a beckoning gesture. His left hand was at waist-height, and it moved, too, making a quick brushing gesture in front of the man's belly.

Nightwalker stiffened as if from a taser hit. "Setup!" he barked at Falcon. "Break!" Simultaneously, he threw himself aside, turned and bolted for the street.

Falcon was frozen. Just for a moment, but long enough to see a flash of fire from within the copse, to see Cat-Dancing's skull burst under the impact of a bullet. Then the darkness of the copse lit up with muzzle-flashes—three, four, more. Bullets whip-cracked around the ganger, slammed into the ground around him, kicking up divots. With a yell of fear, he turned and ran, out of the park, back onto Denny Way.

Where was Nightwalker? The Amerindian was just *gone.*

Falcon reached the street, sprinted for the nearest car, a decrepit-looking Ford. A bullet slammed into the vehicle, punching a hole the size of a man's thumb in the door. Another shot blew out the passenger-side window. Something plucked at the shoulder of his jacket, something else buzzed past his ear. Falcon threw himself forward, into the shelter of the Ford, trying to tuck his shoulder under him for a landing roll. Not quite making it, he landed heavily enough to knock most of the air out of his lungs. He lay on the road for a moment, partially stunned, hearing bullets thudding into the car's body-work. A round passed through the car, shattered the driver-side window, showering him with fragments of glass.

His lungs were working again in a second, forcing air through his throat, suddenly tight and dry. He forced himself to a crouch, careful to keep his head below the level of the car's body. Pulling out his Fichetti, he looked around wildly for Nightwalker.

The big runner squatted in the cover of another car, a dozen meters away. He had a gun in hand, a big automatic, but he wasn't firing it. The sparks from high-velocity bullets striking off the car's coachwork told the ganger why. Even through his fear, he could see from the line of Nightwalker's body that he was in agony. Another bullet wound? No, the runner had moved so fast it was doubtful he'd been hit. But having to run and then dive for cover had probably reopened his wounds.

Another volley of shots hammered into Falcon's car. A tire exploded with a loud concussion, and the Ford started to settle at the rear.

Taking a deep breath, he risked a look, popping his head up quickly. Red light flared in his eyes. A *laser*! Instantly he dropped again, and not a microsecond too soon. A bullet roared over his head, so close he could feel the wind of its passage. His stomach knotted with fear, and he was wracked with nausea. Oh, spirits and totems . . .

He heard barked orders, but they were too far away for him to make out the words. More bullets pounded the car. Two more windows blew out, another tire. They were taking the car apart!

Why aren't they advancing? The thought was cold as ice, horrifying. Maybe they are . . .

He had to look. He couldn't stand the not knowing. Besides, if he didn't look, he'd only know what the gunman was up to when he eventually came around the car to paint the street with Falcon's brains. He raised his head again. Not over the hood of the car this time, but looking through the shot-out driver-side window.

Another laser spot, this time on the doorpost next to his head. Before he had time to react, three bullets slammed into the post, each within a hair-breadth of the ruby dot. *Fragging drek*! He dropped down again, panting, but not before he'd capped off two shots—blindly, wildly—in the general direction of the copse.

Nightwalker was firing too, his big pistol roaring, and with more effect than Falcon's pop-gun. A high-pitched shriek of agony rang out from the park as the runner scored. Then Nightwalker was also forced to drop as a continuous fusillade of shots almost took the car apart at the seams.

Falcon watched as the runner rolled, poking his head and shoulders around the rear of the car for another shot, then dropping back to avoid the answering bullets, then popping up somewhere else to let loose another couple of rounds. Even wounded, the runner was faster than any human being had a right to be.

Encouraged by the big man's example, Falcon raised his head again.

Just in time. There was a dark shape racing toward him, the red beam of a laser lancing through the darkness, probing for him. Only twenty meters away. The attacker would be on him in seconds.

Screaming in terror—and in a sudden, blazing rage—Falcon brought up his own gun, squeezing the trigger again and again. Dazzled by his own muzzle flash, he couldn't see the charging figure anymore. But it didn't matter. He fired blindly toward where he guessed the figure would be. Kept firing until the gun clicked empty. Desperately searched his pockets for the second clip. Realized, with numbing horror, that it must have fallen out when he'd ducked for cover.

But he popped up again anyway, squeezing the trigger to activate the laser. Remembering the chilling terror he'd felt when the red beams had flashed near him, he hoped, beyond hope, that his own sighting laser would make the attacker freeze long enough for Nightwalker to finish him.

But it wasn't necessary. The man was down, sprawled boneless on the sidewalk, obviously dead, no more than three meters from Falcon's car. So close . . . Falcon's stomach knotted again; he wanted to wretch. But with an Olympian effort he forced himself to keep control.

There were no more muzzle plumes from the treeline. For the second time, Falcon heard a shouted order. But now he made out the words. "Pull back!"

One last shot from the copse, a last futile gesture. The bullet plowed harmlessly into the car that sheltered Nightwalker. Then there was silence.

No, not quite. In the distance Falcon heard sirens, Lone Star patrols coming to check out the firefight. They had to get out of here, now. He looked over at Nightwalker.

The big runner was still crouching behind the car. His head and arms hung limply, and he looked unutterably tired. Falcon wanted to run to him, but fear rooted him to the spot. What if it was just a ruse? What if the others were waiting for them to break cover?

He *had* to go to Nightwalker. The Amerindian needed help. And runners helped each other when they could.

Wasn't Falcon a shadowrunner now? At least, in some small degree? He'd been in a firefight. He'd made his first kill. . . .

And it was that thought, that reminder of what he'd done, that broke the thin veneer of his control. The muscles of his stomach wrenched, twisted. He bent forward and emptied his guts onto the ground. Vomited again and again, until there was nothing left to bring up but dark bile.

After an unmeasurable time he felt a gentle hand on his shoulder. He looked up, wiping his mouth with the back of his hand.

It was Nightwalker, looking down at him. The Amerind's face was etched and tired, pale. His eyes were shadowed with pain and exhaustion . . . and maybe something more.

"We gotta go, chummer," the big man mumbled, barely enunciating the words. "Let's roll."

"Who were they?"

Nightwalker didn't answer, seeming to consider the question. Or maybe he's just drifted off again, Falcon thought with a chill.

They were sitting in the loading bay of a derelict store, somewhere along Denny Way, half a dozen blocks from the park.

They almost hadn't made it, not because of any hostile action, but because Nightwalker had barely enough energy to move. His left side was soaked with blood, right down to his leg. The dressing on his right arm was still in place, but it too was saturated, and the arm hung like a slab of meat.

Falcon had tried to hurry him along, supporting him when necessary. He'd tried to keep him talking, too. Somewhere he'd read that was a way of handling shock: don't let the victim slip into the darkness. *Keep him talking and you'll keep him alive.*

Maybe it had helped, maybe not. Nightwalker's voice had been almost lifeless when responding to Falcon's comments and questions. Sometimes he'd called him by other names—Marci, Cat-Dancing, Knife-Edge . . . They'd made it this far—just!—but it was obvious that

Nightwalker wasn't going to make it any further without a rest. And maybe not even then. The runner had lost a lot of blood—more than Falcon thought anyone could lose and not die—and was losing still more. Falcon had to do something about that, but wasn't exactly sure what.

"Who were they?" he asked again, making his voice sharper to cut through the fog that seemed to be invading the big Amerindian's mind. "Your chummers?"

Nightwalker opened his eyes, looked blankly at the ganger for a moment as if unsure who he was. Then, with a visible effort, he brought his wandering thoughts back under control.

"No, not them," he said slowly. His voice was still flat, numb, but at least his brain seemed to be tracking again. "They caught Cat-Dancing, used him to draw me in. Cat gave me the wave-off, saved my life. Paid with his own."

Falcon nodded. That was the way he'd read it, too. But . . . "Then who?" he pressed. "Who's 'they'?"

"The corp. Had to be."

"The corp you made the run against?"

"Had to be," Nightwalker repeated.

"Which corp?"

The runner regarded him steadily. His eyes were still clouded with pain and shock, but the spark of intelligence was definitely still there. "Oh, no," he said quietly. "That's 'need to know.' And you don't."

Falcon snorted. "Drek. I helped you, you owe me. . . ."

Nightwalker cut him off. "And that's why I'm not telling you," he explained. "You know who, and you'll wind up as dead as Marci and Cat. I owe you my life, sure, I know that. And I'm not going to pay off that debt by getting you greased. *So ka*?"

The ganger was silent for a moment. "Okay," he allowed eventually. "But look. Tell me about the run. What happened? What's it all about, huh? Cat got geeked saving you, didn't he? That means it's important." He leaned forward intently. "*What's* important?"

"You don't need to know," Nightwalker said flatly. "End of discussion."

"*Drek!*" Falcon spat. "Fine, don't tell me the corp you ran against. That I can understand. But tell me the rest. Leave out the names, but tell me what this biz is all about. You owe me that, Walker. You owe me."

Fighting the urge to press harder, he watched silently while Nightwalker thought it through. Eventually the runner nodded wearily.

"Yeah, maybe." Nightwalker sighed, coughed, his face screwing up with the pain. "Maybe I do owe you." He rested his head against the wall behind him, closed his eyes again. For a moment Falcon thought the Amerindian had drifted off again, faded away into whatever was going on in his mind.

But then he spoke. Quietly, so Falcon had to lean closer to hear. "You ever heard of the Concord of Zurich-Orbital?"

Falcon thought for a few seconds. He'd heard of Zurich-Orbital. Who hadn't? The oldest and most important of the NEOs—Near Earth Orbit habitats—spinning through space a hundred klicks above the upper fringes of the atmosphere. Zurich-Orbital. Home of the Corporate Court, the ruling and appeals body that handled relationships between the world-girdling megacorporations. Home of the Zurich Gemeinschaft Bank, the financial center of the megacorporate world. But the *Concord* of Zurich-Orbital? "No," he admitted.

"Didn't think so. Not many have. And that's the way the *zaibatsus* want it." Nightwalker breathed deeply for a few moments, as if accommodating his wounded body's demand for more oxygen. "You need a history lesson.

"Way back, in the nineteen-eighties, I think it was—

maybe the nineties . . . or the seventies; I'm not slick on ancient history—the world started swinging over to fiber optics for communication. Before then, everything was transmitted by radio or by electrons flowing through copper wires. Barbaric," he pronounced, "and risky. If you broadcast something, anyone can pick it up, maybe break your code and know what you're sending. If you put it through wires, people can read the data flow by induction. You scan?"

Falcon thought he did. A chummer in the First Nation gang was into electronics, and she'd tried to teach Falcon something about physics. "Electricity flowing through wires makes magnetism, right?" he ventured, parroting words he'd heard, but not really understanding them.

Nightwalker opened his eyes and looked at him in surprise. "Yeah, right," he agreed. "You can detect the magnetic field at a distance, and by measuring how it changes, you can figure out the electric flow in the wires. If it's data being sent down those wires, you can read it. And with the right gear you can change it. You following me?"

Falcon nodded.

"So when fiber optics came along," the runner continued, "everybody jumped aboard. Light flowing in a fiber isn't like electricity in a wire. There's no magnetic field. You can't read it, you can't tap into it, you can't change it. Totally secure.

"Or so everybody thought. Then some big-dome scientists figured something out. They worked for one of the big corps back then—3M, or 4F, or something like that, I think it was. They figured out there was a way to read fiber-optic communication. You could read it from a distance, you could even diddle a few bits here and there, change the information that's going through the light pipe." He chuckled. "'Course, it wasn't too practical. From what I hear, it took two Cray supercomputers, *big* electronic brains, the biggest they'd made to that time, plus a semi-trailer full of other high-tech drek, *plus* a fragging platoon of big-domes to run it all. I don't know how it works, I'm no technoweenie. But, frag if it didn't work.''

''No.'' Falcon shook his head. ''That's not possible,'' he said slowly. ''You *can't* read fiber-optic stuff. You *can't*. Everybody knows that.''

''Uh-uh. Everybody *thinks* that. Everybody wants to *believe* that. But those 4F guys, they did it.''

''So what happened?'' Falcon asked. ''If that's true, how come the corps all use fiber optics and think it's safe?''

''The crash of twenty-nine, that's what happened,'' Nightwalker said. ''Some kind of computer virus got loose, got into the global computer network. It crashed a lot of systems, blew away a lot of data, fragging near crashed the whole global economy. Right?''

Falcon nodded again. *Everyone* had heard horror stories about the crash.

''So the way it turned out,'' Nightwalker went on, ''parts of the viral code had the greatest effect on highly encrypted data, stuff that was protected by a lot of security. It invaded the security systems, so nobody could copy the important data to somewhere safe, and then it corrupted the files the security was supposed to protect. That's why the crash was as bad as it was. Most of the stuff that went forever, that nobody could ever recreate from the trashed files, was the most important stuff, the most secret. All the corps' biggest secrets, all the real cutting-edge tech the R and D big-domes were working on.'' He laughed bitterly. ''Why do you think the world's not as technically advanced as it should be?''

That shocked Falcon. You mean we should be *more* fragging advanced? he wanted to say, but didn't.

If Nightwalker noticed his surprise, he didn't remark

on it. "None of the corps talked about the black data they'd lost," he continued. "Of course they wouldn't. They didn't want to give anyone ideas, to have anyone beat them to the prize while they tried to replicate all the lost research." He paused and smiled. "Any guesses about what was in some of the black data that got itself lost?"

Of course. "That fiber-optic stuff," Falcon answered at once.

"Right in one. The guys who'd come up with it in the first place had put a lot of work into it during the fifty years before the crash. Other corps too. They'd got it a lot smoother, so you didn't need the two supercomputers and the drekload of other stuff. The way I hear it, they got it down so one tech could run it, and all the hardware would fit in one big van. Then *poof*! The virus blows it all away. Maybe the guys who'd actually done the research were killed in the rioting, or maybe the corps had already 'vanished' them. Whichever, they weren't around to tell anybody what they'd done.

"So that takes us to the year twenty-thirty," Nightwalker went on. "The crash virus is gone, and the corps are rebuilding the global network into what we call the Matrix. Some of the other *zaibatsus* get wind that 4F—or whoever'd bought them out—was trying to recreate the lost technology, trying to figure out how to tap into fiber-optic lines all over again. As you might imagine, that idea made a lot of the high-level suits drek all over themselves. They went to the Corporate Court in Zurich-Orbital and demanded that somebody put a stop to it. And the court did."

"The Concord of Zurich-Orbital?" Falcon guessed.

"That's it," confirmed Nightwalker. "All the big corps signed it. They agreed that none of them would ever try to reconstruct the technology. And, if any other corp—one of the smaller fry, maybe—tried to do it, all the Concord signatories would come after them and stomp them flat.'' The runner laughed. ''You can bet that all the signatories were running off to their private labs even before the ink was dry, trying to beat all the others to recreating the tech. But the Concord still did some good. Because of it nobody could put too many resources into the search without somebody else finding out. And then there'd be fragging hell to pay. No corp—not even the big boys—wants to slot off the Corporate Court. Not unless they've got a big fragging stick to threaten Zurich Gemeinschaft with.''

Falcon was silent for a few moments as he thought about it all. It made sense, kind of. . . . But then another concept struck him. ''Hey, what about magic?'' he asked. ''Why can't you read the fiber-optic stuff with magic? Why do you need the lost tech at all?''

Nightwalker smiled. ''I wondered if you'd pick up on that.'' He shook his head. ''Magic's not like that, it doesn't interact well with tech. If a shaman or a mage is trying to assense astrally, all he can pick up is the emotional content of any communication he taps into. And what's the emotional content of your typical data transfer?''

''Zero,'' Falcon answered at once.

''That's it,'' the big Amerindian agreed. ''Not particularly useful, right?''

Falcon nodded, but he was still confused. He'd understood Nightwalker's story, most of it, anyway, but one thing he still couldn't figure out. ''What's that got to do with your run?'' he asked.

''Can't you guess? The guys who hired my team, they'd found out that one of the local megacorps was *this close* to replicating the 4F tech. Our job was to bust into their research park, get the tech files, toast the lab and all the records, then bring the paydata back to the Johnsons who'd hired us.''

''So they could use it themselves?''

Nightwalker shook his head firmly. "No way. This is"—he hesitated, then laughed harshly—"this is Something Man Was Not Meant To Know, you get me? Any one corp gets this, it's going to destabilize *everything*. Frag, it's going to make the chaos after the crash look like a fragging tea party. No, my Johnsons were going to destroy the data, keeping just enough for proof when they ratted the corp doing the research to the Corporate Court and everybody else. Then they'd just sit back and watch the fun. No matter how big and tough a corp is, there's no way it can survive if every other major megacorp in the fragging world comes after it with knives."

Falcon was silent for a moment. What Nightwalker was saying made sense, sort of. But he knew something about the way Johnsons worked. Johnsons *were* corps, weren't they? And what corp would spend good credit hiring shadowrunners to *destroy* data that would make them trillions of nuyen?

But Nightwalker *believed*, didn't he? He bought the idea that his Johnsons were actually doing something for the good of the world and not thinking only of their own bank balances.

Well, frag, why not? Stranger things happened in the world, didn't they? And Nightwalker was more experienced with the shadows. He knew the way things shook. Maybe he was right.

"So what happened?" the ganger asked. "Did you get the data?"

"I don't know. Like I told you, I was physical support. We sent a decker into the system, but she didn't come back. Not before we got bounced by the other shadow team." The Amerindian shrugged. "We got hosed. I don't know whether the runner got the paydata or not. That's why I need to meet with the others."

"If they're still alive." The words were out of Falcon's mouth before he could stop them.

Nightwalker was silent for a moment. Then he nodded. "If they're still alive. But I've got to know for sure. This is too important to just let it hang."

Falcon sighed. I *knew* he was going to say that, he thought. "So what's your next move?"

"Another meet, another back-up location." Nightwalker looked at him appraisingly. "Can you get me there?"

Falcon didn't even ask where the meet was. "I can get your *corpse* there," he said flatly. "That's all that's going to be left unless we do something *now*." He forced firmness into his voice, deciding on the right course of action at the same moment he spoke. "I've got to get you to a street doc."

Nightwalker argued. But not too hard.

7

1100 hours, November 13, 2053

Sly thought the stretch of Broadway near Pine had gone downhill noticeably since the last time she'd been there. More chippies huddled in doorways or even squatting out in the steady rain, oblivious to everything but the simsense fantasies playing in their minds. More homeless, dossing down wherever they could find space. More orks and trolls swaggering around in their gang colors. If it's this bad during the day, she thought, what's it like at night?

The buildings reflected the changes in the neighborhood as well. Most of the store windows were bolted over with latticeworks of reinforced bars, and the rest were boarded up. One establishment—a little independent stuffer shack—had a rather pathetic sign posted in its front window: "Please don't break my glass again." The window was, of course, broken. Graffiti was everywhere, mainly spray-painted gang colors, slogans, or symbols. A rather talented spray-paint artist had covered some walls with abstract, almost cubist paintings, signing "Pablo Fiasco" at the bottom.

Seattle Community College, across Broadway from Sly's destination, looked like a war zone. The entire building had not a single intact window. The neon sign that had stood on the corner of Pine and Broadway, advertising the College, was nothing but a twisted and scorched wreck. Grenade? Sly wondered, seeing other scorch marks here and there. Security personnel were about—private guards hired from Hard Corps Inc. But there weren't many, maybe a half-dozen or so. They didn't look as though they liked their duty, shifting nervously from foot to foot and scrutinizing everyone who came within twenty meters.

Sly found the changes depressing. From what she knew of Seattle's history, this area hadn't been a good place to be after dark around the turn of the century. It was the haunt of drug-users then, not simsense addicts, but the risks were the same—militant kids who'd do anything to get the money to buy what they needed to feed their heads. Then, sometime around 2010, the money had started to flow downhill, north along Broadway. Just a few blocks away was "Pill Hill," the location of many of Seattle's best hospitals. The infrastructure necessary to support those hospitals—labs, restaurants, good-quality housing, various suppliers, and so on had moved into the Pine and Broadway region, squeezing out the gutterpunks and street apes.

Sly wasn't sure what economic changes had reversed the neighborhood's fortunes—didn't really want to know;

it probably would have been depressing. But the changes
were undeniable. The stretch of Broadway between Pike
Street and Denny Way had definitely started its slide back
down the socioeconomic curve. It had been going on for
some time, but Sly couldn't help but be surprised, and a
little disturbed, by how far the area had descended in
only a few months.

Enough of the civics lesson, she told herself as she
pulled her bike up outside her destination. It was an old
building, maybe as much as a hundred years old—on the
east side of the road just north of Pine. A weird, anachronistic shape among the plasteel and construction composite buildings that surrounded it, her destination was
built from red and white blocks of stone—*real* stone, not
some ersatz façade—with little towers, or maybe turrets,
on the corners, and a central steeple. Graven in the stone
over the front door was the building's original identity—
the First Christian Church—but Sly knew that it hadn't
been a place of worship for at least two decades. Now it
was the home and base of operations of her friend Agarwal.

As she killed her bike's engine and swung out of the
saddle, she thought about what she knew of Agarwal. He
had a monster rep on the streets and in the shadows, was
one of the few shadow deckers who'd really hit it big,
then managed to leave the game with most of his black
earnings intact. That was obvious from the place he chose
to live. Even with property values dropping in this part
of town, the church must have cost him a few million
nuyen, and that didn't include the extensive modifications
he'd made after moving in.

Most runners never got out of the biz, Sly knew. Not
alive, that is. And those that did either didn't have much
credit saved up or else they took what they'd scammed
and faded from sight to avoid unwanted attention from
the corps they used to run against. Agarwal was the ex-

ception, living happily—and apparently safely—within a
few klicks of the corps he'd taken for millions. She wondered how he did it. The buzz in the shadows claimed
he'd built himself some unassailable "life insurance"
over the years. That he'd gathered devastating information on all the corps who'd like to see him flatlined, all
of it set up with a "dead man's switch." If Agarwal ever
got geeked or if he neglected to communicate daily with
his sophisticated computer "watchdogs," all those tera-
bytes of damaging data would be dumped to public sec-
tions of the Matrix for everyone to see. No corp, it
seemed, wanted to risk that kind of exposure just to settle
an old score with Agarwal. So far, the aging decker had
been able to live in relative security.

Relative being the operative word, of course. Even with
the attentions of the corps averted, there were others
who'd just love to pay Agarwal a visit. After all, his home
looked like a security nightmare, virtually impossible to
defend against a group of determined thieves.

But appearances were deceiving. Aren't they always?
Sly thought. Agarwal's home was as secure as a couple
million nuyen's worth of high-tech defense systems could
make it. Again, judging by the street buzz, no fewer than
four major B and E gangs had made moves against Agarwal's place over the last few years. None had succeeded,
and none had survived to dissect their failure afterward.
None. No bodies, no clues as to what happened, *nothing*. They'd just disappeared. (When Sly had once asked
Agarwal about it, he merely shrugged and smiled. After
knowing him a while longer, she decided she really didn't
want to know.)

Sly had met Agarwal five years ago, soon after her final
Matrix run. She'd been trying to get her brain back together, and her fixer, a chummer named Cog, had found
it in his heart to help her out, to put her together with

someone who understood the trauma she'd experienced. That someone was Agarwal.

Cog had been right in thinking that talking to Agarwal would help. It was Agarwal who convinced Sly that there was life after punching deck, and who helped her through the nightmares and terrifying fugues of those first few months. Of course he understood what she was going through. He'd suffered in much the same way, his own crash having been the stimulus for finally retiring from the shadows. Even after eight years he still had fugues from time to time, but he managed to control them, minimize their impact on his life. That had given Sly hope that she could come back fully as well. Which was the way it had turned out, of course. She'd done even better than Agarwal, her younger brain bouncing back faster. Her last fugue—a minor one that snipped no more than two minutes out of her life—had been more than two years ago.

She climbed the stone steps to the front door, pressed the intercom button. No response for a few seconds, but Sly knew she was being scanned by a sophisticated suite of sensors. She smiled up at where she guessed the vid camera to be, opened her leather jacket to show she was unarmed.

The door buzzed, swung open of its own accord. She stepped into the front hall.

Agarwal's modifications to the inside of the church had left almost nothing of the original structure. In contrast to the anachronistic exterior, the inside revealed the cutting edge of contemporary decor. Concealed indirect lighting, flooring that looked like gold-veined marble but gave under her feet like plush carpet. Furniture in the modern reductionist school of design. And everything in off-white, eggshell blue, or iridescent mother-of-pearl. Sly felt as though she'd stepped into an image from Interior Design datamag. She crossed the hall, passed through the other door.

Agarwal was waiting for her in his library, a high-ceilinged room, every wall lined with tall bookcases. (Real books. Even after knowing Agarwal for years, coming in here was always a shock to Sly, reminding her of just how rich her friend was.)

"Sharon," he greeted her warmly in his precise Oxford accent. "A pleasure to see you again, a pleasure. Come, I want to show you my latest project."

With a smile, she followed him out of the library toward the stairs.

Agarwal was in his late forties, about Sly's height, slender and with narrow shoulders and hips. He had a long, thin face, dominated by a hooked nose. His skin, the color of milked coffee, was rough, with large pores. He wore his thinning hair combed straight back from his face, showing the single datajack in his right temple. He always wore wire-framed spectacles—a strange affectation in these days of permanent-wear contact lenses and corneal surgery—behind which his brown eyes looked soft and weak. Every time Sly had ever seen him, he'd been wearing a two-piece suit, always new, always impeccably tailored, but several years out of style, and a tie. Doesn't he ever dress casually? she wondered.

He led her downstairs into his workshop, a large, open area that took up the entire lower floor of the building. This was one of the most significant modifications he'd made to the old church. He flipped on the lights.

The large room was filled with cars, an even dozen of them, Sly counted. Half were in various states of disrepair; the others looked in mint condition, like they'd just rolled off the assembly line. Which was impressive in and of itself, since not one of the cars was less than fifty years old. She let her eyes wander over the rows of vehicles. She'd seen most of them before, but the sight of so many antique vehicles—some of them unique in the world—was awe-inspiring. Right next to her was a Rolls Royce Silver Cloud, model year 2005, she thought. And over there an Acura Demon, the fastest production car built in 2000. And her favorite, somewhat out of place among the speed and luxury machines that surrounded it, a lovingly restored 1993 Suzuki Sidekick 4x4. As always, Sly tried to estimate just how much Agarwal's collection was worth, but gave up after she reached ten million, with half the cars still to go.

Agarwal touched her arm, ushered her across the workshop toward the three up-and-over doors that opened onto the sloping ramp leading up to the back alley. "This," he said, pointing, "is my latest acquisition."

She looked at the car. Black, sleek, and low-slung, it reminded her of a shark. Its long, sloping hood bulged a little strangely, hinting at a massive power plant. It looked vaguely familiar; Sly knew she'd seen something like it before, probably in some historical drama on the vid. "A Corvette, isn't it?" she guessed after a moment.

If Agarwal's smile had been any broader, he'd have swallowed his ears. "A Corvette, yes, Sharon. But a very special Corvette, a modified Corvette. This is a Callaway Twin Turbo." He caressed the sleek black hood. "A wonderful car, built in 1991, if you can believe it—sixty-two years ago. The engine is a five-point-seven V-eight, producing four-oh-three horsepower at forty-five hundred rpm, and five hundred seventy-five foot-pounds of torque at three thousand rpm." The statistics rolled off his tongue easily, almost lovingly. Sly knew how much joy he got from memorizing such minutiae. "Zero to a hundred kilometers per hour in four-point-eight seconds, lateral acceleration zero-point-ninety-four gravities, top speed"—he shrugged—"Well, I don't know that, but probably almost three hundred kilometers per hour. A marvelous car. An absolute joy to restore."

Sly nodded. This had been Agarwal's hobby, his vocation, since he'd left the shadows a few years back. He was as knowledgeable about vintage cars, about internal combustion technology and automotive engineering, as anyone in the plex, maybe in the country. He could, if the project interested him, strip a car down to the nuts and bolts and then rebuild it better than it had ever been before. She glanced over at him. As always, his area of interest just didn't match his appearance. Does he take off his suit when he's grubbing under cars? she wondered with concealed amusement. Or is that why he's always wearing new clothes every time I see him?

"Looks wiz, Agarwal," she told him. She grinned wickedly. "How does it handle?"

He smiled mildly. They both knew that Agarwal never drove any of his cars. The sport, to him, was taking a drek-kicked rustbucket and restoring it to pristine glory, then simply enjoying the knowledge that he owned something of beauty. Actually driving the cars once he was done with them held no interest for him whatsoever.

After giving Sly another couple of minutes to silently contemplate his vehicular "babies," Agarwal led her back upstairs to his study. This was a small, cozy room on the upper floor, with windows that looked west toward the skyrakers of downtown. He seated her in a comfortable armchair, put a cup of Darjeeling tea on the table beside her. Then he settled down in his high-backed desk chair, steepling his fingers in front of his face.

"I understand life has been . . . interesting . . . of late, Sharon," he remarked.

Sly nodded, smiling at her friend's understatement. She thought back over the last twenty-four hours. Her visit to Theresa Smeland. The assassination of her Johnson. The hard meet with Modal. Sending a copy of Louis' encrypted file to Agarwal over the phone lines. And then the multiple phone calls—all from different pay phones, all to different corporate and shadow contacts—to rat the black elf to Yamatetsu.

Is it going to work? she wondered for a moment. It seemed like it would. Modal's cunning, and his understanding of corporate psychology and human nature seemed unchanged since the old days. Improved with practice, if anything. The body of rumors, evidence, lies and wild speculations that he'd concocted certainly seemed to paint the picture of someone who'd sold out his corporate masters to an old lover. Unless there was some angle that she was missing, Modal's name had to be worse than drek with Yamatetsu, and the corp would probably have soldiers out gunning for him as well as for her. And that was the goal, of course, to remove any possible benefit Modal could gain from killing her or turning her in. Sure, down the road apiece he might try to buy his way back into the Yamatetsu fold with her head, but any move like that would be very risky. The Yamatetsu reps he contacted would be more likely to set up an ambush than a clean meet.

Yes, she thought, I can trust Modal . . . for the moment. That conclusion hadn't made it easier to leave him behind this morning, but there was no way she'd take him along to her meet with Agarwal.

The ex-decker was watching her silently, giving her time to decide what to tell him and what not. His mild smile was unchanged.

"It's been an interesting twenty-four hours," she allowed at last. "Did you have a chance to work on the file I sent you?"

"Since your call, I have worked on nothing else, Sharon," he told her. She felt a twinge of guilt at that. Any time he spent helping her was an hour he couldn't devote to his beloved cars, but this was important.

"Did you learn anything?"

Agarwal nodded. "First of all, I conclude that something very important, and very unusual—unheard of, I might say—has been happening in the corporate culture. For one thing, the activity on the stock exchange has been . . . abnormal, to say the least. Over the last two days, perhaps more, there has been a great deal of re-shuffling of corporate affiliations. Megacorporations have been attempting hostile takeovers of smaller corps that had been, until now, considered off-limits because of their associations with other megacorps. Do you understand the significance of that?''

After a moment's thought, Sly had to shake her head. ''Not really,'' she admitted. ''Economics isn't my strong suit.''

He sighed. ''Economics is *everything* in this world, Sharon, you should know that.'' He paused for a moment, re-ordering his thoughts. ''All the major corporations walk something of a tightrope when it comes to competition. Each megacorp is competing with every other corp for market share, for money it can extract from the market. Since the market is, in most sectors, mature, that means that we have a zero-sum game. Any gain by one corporation is a loss for a competitor, or competitors. Thus, success comes to the corporation that can compete best.

''Unfortunately, there is a downside to, shall we say, *overzealous* competition. If one *zaibatsu* were to openly war on another, the aggressor might improve its market share considerably. But the chaos such major conflict would cause in the financial markets and elsewhere would mean that the potential market was reduced. As an analogy, the aggressor corporation might get a bigger slice of the pie, but the pie would be made smaller by the disruption. On an absolute level, the aggressor's revenue would be diminished.

''That's why the megacorporations play by the rules of

the Corporate Court and by the unwritten laws that all successful executives understand instinctively.''

"But corps do pull raids on each other," Sly pointed out. "Frag, Agarwal, you did enough of them."

Agarwal chuckled. "So true," he agreed. "But the shadowruns that one corp commissions against another are small matters.'' He waved his hand airily, indicating the building around him. "Oh, not for the likes of me or you. But for a *zaibatsu* with annual revenue in the trillions of nuyen, our efforts are no more than a pinprick to a dragon."

Sly digested that in silence for a moment. "Those 'unwritten laws' you're talking about," she said finally, "they're being broken? That's why those takeovers are important?"

"Exactly. Something has happened to spur the megacorps into more direct competition. There are even reflections of this on the street. Have you noticed an increased presence of corporate security forces in the metroplex?"

"Not really," she said. "I guess my mind's been on other things."

"Yes, quite. And very understandable. My searches through the databases show that there are many people looking for you, my friend. Denizens of the shadows, informants, street ops, and the assets of several corporations."

That shook Sly. "Several?" she blurted. "Not just Yamatetsu?"

Agarwal's face grew serious. "Several," he repeated. "Granted, Yamatetsu seems at the forefront, but there are others. Aztechnology, Mitsuhama, Renraku, DPE, plus other smaller players. All are interested in learning your whereabouts." An edge of concern came into his voice. "I trust you are taking adequate precautions?"

She nodded distractedly. "I'm taking care of myself."

She paused for thought. "What's going down, Agar-wal?"

"It seems like the prelude to a corp war," Agarwal intoned grimly, "an all-out corp war. Though I pray not, for the concept terrifies me."

"What's that got to do with me?"

"I could say, a lot, as it will affect everyone in Seattle. But I understand your meaning. My guess would be that one of the corporations—perhaps Yamatetsu, perhaps one of the others—has lost something. Something of immense value, not only to them but to all the other corporations in Seattle. Of so much value that they're willing to risk corporate war to get it for themselves.

"Further, I would suspect that the corporations have somehow decided that you have what they seek or know where it can be found." His voice was suddenly impersonal, totally noncommittal. "Would you have any idea about that, Sharon?"

Involuntarily, Sly shot a glance at the sophisticated computer sitting on Agarwal's desk—the machine he'd have been using to decrypt the file she'd sent him. He saw the movement of her eyes, nodded gently to himself.

"Did you crack the encryption?" Sly was disgusted to hear a faint quiver in her voice.

"Have you kept current on the mathematical theories of data encryption?" Agarwal asked elliptically.

"Some," she answered.

"Then you understand public key encryption?"

"A little. Enough to get by. That's what was used on the file?"

"In part. There are multiple levels, which leads me to believe that the file is something highly significant. The primary level of encryption uses the Milton paradigm and a seventy-five-bit key."

Sly pursed her lips, whistled soundlessly. "How fast's your computer?"

"On the close order of five hundred teraflops."

Five hundred teraflops. Five hundred *trillion* floating-point operations per second. A very fast machine. She closed her eyes, ran through the math in her mind. Then she cursed under her breath. "It's unbreakable, then," she pronounced. "Even at five hundred teraflops, that machine's going to have to chew on it for a thousand years before it can break the code."

"Closer to *fifteen* thousand years," Agarwal corrected gently. "*If* I use simple brute-force computation. Are you aware of Eiji's research into recursive series?"

She shook her head, then said quickly, "Don't bother to explain it to me. Just cut to the chase."

He bowed his head with a smile. "As you wish. Eiji developed techniques that can be applied to public key encryption, and yield certain . . . short cuts."

"You can break it, then?"

"I believe so. It will take time—a day, maybe more— but significantly less than fifteen thousand years."

"And the other levels of encryption?"

He shrugged. "I doubt they would be anywhere near as complex as the primary level."

She nodded. A day, maybe a couple of days . . .

"What will you do in the interim?" he asked, echoing her own thoughts.

"Pull a fade," she answered immediately. "Keep my head down and wait." She paused. "Maybe do some digging on Yamatetsu, find out if there's anything in the Matrix . . ." She saw his eyes widen in alarm, quickly reassured him. "I wouldn't ask you to do that, Agarwal, you know that. I'll find somebody else."

The tension melted from his face. "Yes," he said quietly, "yes, of course. Forgive my reaction, but . . ."

"Nothing to forgive," she told him. "Remember who you're talking to."

He sighed. "Of course. I . . . of course."

"Do you have the time to work on it now?"

Her friend nodded. "I've already put aside all my other projects. There will be no distractions."

"About payment . . ."

He raised a hand to stop her. "If we are seeing the prelude to a corp war, averting it would be payment enough."

She nodded, reached out impulsively to squeeze his hand. Friends. Rare in the shadows, but more precious than anything else.

8

2100 hours, November 13, 2053

Falcon shifted on the tattered vinyl couch, tried to find a position where the broken springs didn't poke into his back and ribs. Mission fragging impossible, he told himself with a snort. More fragging comfortable on the floor.

Regardless of how uncomfortable was the couch, he had to admit that he *had* slept on it. Fitful snatches, but sleep nonetheless. His body still needed more after the long, tense night, but now that his mind was working again he knew he wouldn't be able to drop off anymore. He looked at the clock on the gray wall. Only nine o'clock? It couldn't be, he'd only gotten here at about seven. . . .

Then he realized the clock was the old twelve-hour variety, not the twenty-four-hour style he was used to. That meant it was twenty-one hundred, halfway into another evening. He'd been asleep longer than he thought.

He swung his feet to the floor, rubbed at itchy eyes

with the back of one hand while glancing around at the waiting room he'd staked out as his flop.

Pretty slotting lousy, he thought. Yellowing linoleum tile on the floor. (And what did that say about the age of the building? How long ago did people use *linoleum*?) Gyproc walls that might once have been white. The torture device disguised as a couch. A telecom with its screen broken and outgoing circuits disabled. *Just charming.* The air was sharp with an assortment of disturbing smells, mostly what Falcon classified as "medical," but with an unhealthy underpinning of rot. I should have taken him to a real doctor, he berated himself for the dozenth time.

But that was the last thing he *could* have done. Nightwalker was suffering from bullet wounds, and Falcon knew that by law the doctor would be forced to report the matter to Lone Star. Obviously, legal entanglements were the last thing the big Amerindian needed right now.

Then there was the problem of identity. Falcon was willing to bet that, as far as the establishment was concerned, Nightwalker didn't have one. Like Falcon himself, he probably was one of the SINless—an individual who had no System Identification Number, the official identity code by which the government, the medical system, and every other facet of society recognized its own. Had he taken Nightwalker to any hospital or to just about any licensed physician, the drek would have hit the fan as soon as the receptionist asked to see the runner's credstick with his SIN stored in its bubble memory.

And even if he'd managed to get around those two problems, there was the problem of credit. Runners didn't have health insurance, that was for fragging sure, and neither he nor Nightwalker had enough on their credsticks to pay emergency-room user fees.

So what did that leave? A free clinic, like the ones run by that touchy-feely Universal Brotherhood outfit. But there were problems with that idea, too. Falcon wasn't sure that they didn't buy into the same "gunshot wound, call the Star" drek as the real hospitals. And anyway, the ganger didn't think he could drag the fading Nightwalker all the three or four klicks to the nearest clinic.

The one option left was a street doc, a shadow cutter. At first Falcon thought he was fragged there, too. This wasn't his patch, and street docs didn't advertise in the public datanets.

But then he remembered hearing one of the First Nation "elder statesmen"—a tough-talking Haida who must have been at least nineteen—bragging about how he'd been stitched up after a rumble by a shadow cutter who worked out of a defunct restaurant near Sixth and Blanchard. That was enough to get Falcon started, and a few cautious queries made of some squatters he'd almost tripped over helped him find the spot.

Just in fragging time, too, he thought, remembering how Nightwalker had looked when he'd finally dragged him into the shadow clinic. Another few blocks and he wouldn't have made it.

For a moment, his fear for the runner's life, pushed into the background temporarily by his faith in medical tech, rushed back. Was Nightwalker going to make it?

Then another question struck him. If he didn't, what did it matter? Nightwalker wasn't a chummer, he wasn't in First Nation. And he was so fragging old . . .

But he was a shadowrunner, and that had to count for something. A runner, and an Amerindian—even if he claimed not to have a tribe. And, most important, he'd trusted Falcon, depended on him for help. And *that's* why it matters, he told himself.

Falcon looked at the clock again. Twenty-one-ten. Fourteen hours since he'd dragged Nightwalker into the decrepit building. Thirteen since the doc had disappeared into the treatment room with him. Was she still operating, or stitching, or whatever it was docs did? Or had Nightwalker croaked on the table, and she just wasn't telling him? He stood up, took a step toward the door into the treatment room. Stopped in doubt. He'd never been very good at waiting—particularly if he couldn't sleep through it.

As if on cue, the door opened and the doc walked out. She'd introduced herself as Doctor Mary Dacia, but Falcon knew the street had mangled her name to Doc Dicer. She was small and thin, with short-chopped red hair and big expressive eyes. Kinda cute, Falcon thought, particularly with those bodacious rockets. Or she *would* have been cute if she hadn't been so *old*—easily more than twice his age.

"You finished with him?" he asked.

Doc Dicer looked tired. She'd been wearing some semi-fashionable face paint when they'd arrived, but now she'd scrubbed it off, leaving her face pale and wan. She raised an eyebrow expressively. "I finished with him a while ago," she said in her throaty voice. "Looked out to see how you were going. You were catching zees big time."

"So how is he?"

The doc's expression became more serious. "As well as can be expected, which is not fragging very. I put everything back in the right places, made sure nothing too vital was missing, and patched all the bigger holes. If he wasn't so tough, he'd have flatlined hours ago, or as soon as I put him under, but he's lost a lot of blood. His heart's under major stress. I almost lost him when he had a cardiac arrest on the table." She looked at Falcon sharply. "Did you give him metamphetamines?"

Falcon swallowed hard. "Yeah, but he . . ." He cut off the justifications before they could get flowing. "Did they hurt him?"

Doc Dicer shrugged. "Can't say," she told him.

"They stressed his cardiovascular system like you wouldn't believe, but maybe they stopped him from arresting earlier. Even money either way."

That let Falcon breathe a little easier. "Can I see him?"

He could see the doc mull that over for a moment. Then she nodded and led him into the treatment area.

Nightwalker looked almost small lying in the bed surrounded by high-tech monitoring equipment. His face was nearly the same color as the grimy walls and his closed eyes seemed sunken. He looks a hundred years old, Falcon thought. Prematurely aged. For an instant he thought about his mother, then forced the image away.

Falcon glanced around at the tiny "ward," which was only marginally bigger than the bed. The gray walls, the monitors, anywhere but at Nightwalker's face. Weak! he raged at himself. You're weak! He forced his eyes back to the Amerindian. This time the images of his mother didn't recur. He felt his breathing slow, his muscles relax.

Doc Dicer had been watching him, but quickly looked away when he shot her a glare. "When will he wake up?" he asked.

"I *am* awake." The runner's deep voice startled Falcon. "Just drifting, you know?" He opened his eyes, looked around. "Where is this?"

Quickly, Falcon brought him up to date.

Nightwalker looked at the street doc, then back at Falcon. "You did this for me, huh?"

Falcon nodded.

"Sure you did," the Amerindian said, almost to himself. "You had to. Runner's code of honor, right?"

Falcon knew that was all the thanks he'd ever get from Nightwalker. But it was plenty, better than the cliché words that were so easy to say. For the first time he felt that Nightwalker was accepting him, maybe not as an

equal, but at least as a comrade. He nodded again, not trusting himself to speak.

"What time is it?" the runner asked. Falcon told him.

"Frag!" Nightwalker spat. "The second back-up meet's at twenty-two-thirty. Gotta move." He tried to sit up.

Doc Dicer put a hand on his chest, pushed him down. Falcon knew that the Amerindian could have thrown her across the room one-handed if he'd wanted to, but he obediently settled back again. His dark eyes were fixed on hers.

"You're not going anywhere," she told him sharply.

"I feel good enough," he answered. "This is something I've got to do." Gently but firmly, he took her hand, moved it off his chest. Falcon could see the doc's muscles tense as she tried to pull her hand from his grip, but she couldn't move it a millimeter.

"Look," she snapped, "maybe you don't hear too good, or maybe you got brain damage from anoxia when your heart stopped." She spoke slowly, with the kind of tone people reserve for congenital idiots. "Yes, you feel good. Because you're jazzed to the eyeballs on painkillers, energizers, and don't-worries. If I take away the painkillers and the tranqs, you'll know just how bad you feel. If I take away the energizers, your heart'll stop just like *that*." She tried to snap her fingers but it didn't work.

She went on firmly, overriding his attempt to reply. "You haven't croaked—*yet*—because I happen to be damn good at my job." She sighed. "You don't know how bad you're hurting," she said more quietly, "how bad the damage is. If you were a car, I'd say you were firing on only one cylinder, had only one gear—the rest are stripped—no brakes, doubtful steering, and three flat tires. Do you hear what I'm saying to you?

"You're alive. Now. If you stay here, I can keep you alive for a day or two for sure, maybe longer if we're both lucky. If you go to a hospital, a *real* hospital, they'll be able to put you back together properly, and odds are you'll live. But''—her voice grew harsh again—''if you think you're going to be able to walk out of here, forget it. You'll make it to the front door—*maybe*—before your heart stops, and that's only because you're a tough moth-erfragger.'' The diminutive doctor pulled her hand back from the big man's grip, and glared down at him.

Falcon watched as Nightwalker's eyes closed and his breathing slowed. Was he thinking? Deciding? Or maybe consigning his spirit to the totems . . .

After a few seconds, Nightwalker opened his eyes again, looked up at the street doc. Falcon saw those eyes were clear, untroubled—calm. The eyes of someone who'd made the big decision.

''I'm on energizers, right?'' he asked gently. ''What energizers? Turbo, right?'' He named one of the designer drugs originally created for medical purposes but that had found an even bigger market on the streets.

Unwillingly, Doc Dicer nodded. ''Turbo,'' she confirmed.

''What dosage? About fifty milligrams?''

She nodded again.

''So two hundred mil would see me through the night.''

''And kill you by the dawn,'' she snapped.

He nodded acceptance. ''But I'll be able to function tonight.''

''Yes. If I gave you that dosage. Which I won't.''

Nightwalker was silent for several seconds. Falcon could hear Doc Dicer's rapid, angry breathing, could hear his own pulse in his ears.

Finally Nightwalker said quietly, ''There's something important that I have to do, Doctor. I can't tell you what it is, but I've sworn my life to seeing it through. Do you understand? I need two hundred milligrams of turbo.''

"It'll kill you," the doctor said again. "I can't do it. . . ."

"You can't *not* do it," the runner pressed. "Everyone has the right to choose the time of his own death, the right to give his life as he sees fit. Who are you to take that right away from me?"

There was silence in the room for almost a minute. Nightwalker just lay there on the bed, watching Doc Dicer with almost inhuman calm. The doctor couldn't meet his gaze. Falcon's eyes flicked back and forth between the two of them.

Finally the doc moved. Reached down into her belt pouch to pull out a hyposprayer and a small ampoule of violet liquid. She still couldn't meet Nightwalker's gaze as she fumbled the ampoule into place, adjusted the hypo. "Two hundred milligrams," she rasped.

Falcon turned away as she administered the drug.

"What do you expect to do?"

Nightwalker turned at Falcon's question, looked down at the young ganger.

"What do you expect to *do*?" Falcon asked again. Before you die, he wanted to add, but didn't. "What if this meet's a setup too?"

The runner just shrugged. They'd taken an autocab, one of the cybernetically controlled vehicles just beginning to proliferate in the sprawl, to Boren and Spruce, and were now walking the last couple of blocks to Kobe Terrace Park.

Nightwalker was having no trouble keeping up with Falcon's purposefully fast pace. He moved so smoothly, so easily, that the ganger could almost forget how injured the runner was, about the drug coursing through the other man's veins, burning up his body from the inside. Nightwalker seemed young again, almost as young as Falcon himself. In some way, maybe that was appropriate for the night before he died.

"And so what if it *isn't* a setup?" Falcon pressed. "What the frag can you do?" *Before you die.*

Nightwalker answered calmly, ignoring the anger in the young man's voice. "With Marci and Cat-Dancing gone, there's just the tribals left. They don't know the sprawl. I can tell them how to make it back to the Salish-Shidhe lands without getting stopped—either by the Border Patrol or the corp armies. I can give them some contacts."

"What if they've already gone?"

"They won't be."

Falcon shook his head angrily. "Then what if the corp already got them? You've killed yourself for nothing."

"Then I die," the Amerindian answered simply. "The decision's made, why torture myself about roads I didn't take?" He looked up at the clouds reflecting the lights of the city. From the runner's expression, Falcon might almost have thought Nightwalker was looking *through* the clouds, at the stars. "Tonight is a fine time to die."

At twenty-two thirty hours, the downtown core was humming. The suits and the beautiful people were out to see and be seen, eating and drinking, catching a show, cruising the clubs. The energy was high; the night almost buzzed with it.

Not in Kobe Terrace Park, though. The ground rules were different here. By day it was a safe place—as safe as anywhere could be in the plex—a spot to sit out on the grass on the rare sunny day, to eat lunch, to relax. Like so many other parks it became a war zone after dark. Two-legged predators prowled the concrete terraces, lying in wait behind bushes and trees for any prey foolish enough to wander into view. Lone Star—all too often outgunned by the first-tier gangs who used the park as a venue for settling scores—left the place alone once the sun went down.

Falcon didn't know the park well, having been there only once by day. Never at night. Only gangs like the Ancients and the Tigers, the heavy-hitters of Seattle, came out to play there after dark. The First Nation wasn't anywhere near their league—being second-tier, or even third.

These and other uncomfortable thoughts rattled around Falcon's mind as they reached the park. Nightwalker seemed totally unconcerned, jandering south from where Tenth Avenue ended at the park proper. (And why the frag not? Falcon asked himself bitterly. He's got nothing to lose.)

The young ganger tightened his grip on the butt of his Fichetti, which was reloaded, cocked, safety off, ready to party. (He was still somewhat surprised that it was Doc Dicer who'd sold him two clips of ammo. Shadow cutter and gunlegger?)

"What if it's another setup?" he hissed to Nightwalker.

The runner just shrugged. "If it is, it is."

Just fragging chill, Falcon thought bitterly, stepping up his scrutiny of the impenetrable shadows around them. Right now he was wishing for eyes in the back of his head.

It was Falcon who spotted the figure first. A patch of deeper blackness in a pool of shadow. The ganger stopped dead, nudging his larger companion with an elbow. "There," he whispered, indicating the direction with a jerk of his chin.

He felt the runner tense up beside him. Nightwalker brought his left hand up to his waist, made a quick, curious gesture. The shadowy figure responded with another, similar gesture—not the wave-off that had cost Cat-Dancing his life, Falcon was glad to see. Nightwalker relaxed, strode forward to join the figure. Belatedly, Falcon scurried to keep up with him.

Now that he was closer and his eyes better night-adapted, Falcon could better make out the figure. His first impression was that the man looked a lot like Nightwalker. He was big too, maybe even broader across the shoulders than his comrade. He had the same straight black hair, the same aquiline nose, the same hard eyes. There was no doubt of his Amerindian blood.

The two men clutched each other's forearms. Falcon couldn't be sure, but he got the feeling Nightwalker was more pleased by this meeting than the stranger. "Hoi, Knife-Edge."

"Hoi, Walker. Thought you were hosed, man."

"Not yet." There was something about the runner's voice that made the stranger search his comrade's face.

But if Knife-Edge understood what he saw there, he didn't mention it. He flashed a hard glare at Falcon. "What's this?" Falcon bristled at the man's tone, but held his tongue.

"Stay chill, Edge," Nightwalker said quietly. "He's stone, chummer. He helped me out of heavy drek. We're tight."

Knife-Edge looked skeptical. "Tight with *that*?" He snorted. "Well, your funeral, *omae*."

"Yes," Nightwalker agreed simply, earning him a quizzical look from the other runner.

"Yeah, right," Knife-Edge muttered, turning away. "The others are here. Bring your chummer if you got to."

With a reassuring pat on the shoulder, Nightwalker led Falcon deeper into the shadows.

The "others." There were three of them, all big, all Amerindian, all with the same air of competence as Nightwalker and Knife-Edge. They were squatting under cover of a small copse of trees in one of the park's upper terraces. As Falcon followed Nightwalker into the tiny clearing, he felt their hard eyes appraising him. One of the tough-looking men flexed his right hand, and three wickedly sharp spurs snicked out from the back of his hand.

"Chill," Knife-Edge ordered quietly. "He's with Walker."

The cybered runner shrugged, and the spurs retracted into their sheath of flesh.

Nightwalker looked around at the faces. "This is it?" he asked quietly. "What about the others?"

"Gone," Knife-Edge answered simply. "When the run crashed, we all split up. Nobody from team one made it out. I saw Marci buy it, which means you were the only survivor of team two, Walker. Teams three and four . . . well, there's Slick, Benbo and Van"—he gestured to the other three runners—"and me, and that's it. I think Cat-Dancing made it out, but we lost track of him."

Nightwalker briefly filled the group in on the events of the previous night.

Knife-Edge nodded slowly when he was finished. "Yeah, that hangs together. We heard rumblings the meet was razzed, but of course we couldn't warn you. Or Cat."

"What about the Cowgirl?" Nightwalker asked. Falcon assumed he was talking about the decker.

"Never made it," Knife-Edge stated. "After we shook the opposition we checked out her doss. Found her still jacked in, dead as fragging meat."

Nightwalker seemed to collapse in on himself, the brittle, transitory energy lent him by the turbo ebbing away. "So it's over," he said quietly.

"Maybe not," Knife-Edge corrected him. "There's a strange buzz on the street—like, somebody else got hold of the paydata."

"*Our* paydata?"

"That's what the buzz says, Walker. Don't know how.

Maybe Cowgirl contracted herself some Matrix cover on the quiet.''

"Who?" Nightwalker demanded. "Who has it?"

"Don't got a name," one of the other Amerinds spoke up for the first time. "Some local slag. Some runner."

"Is that true?" Falcon could hear the desperation in Nightwalker's voice, the urgent need to believe.

"That's what the buzz says," Knife-Edge confirmed.

"So what are we doing about it?"

"Chill, friend." Knife-Edge laid a reassuring hand on the other runner's shoulder. "We got feelers out all over the plex, trying to get a line on the local. We can't do much till we get an identity, can we?"

"But you don't know the channels. . . ."

Knife-Edge cut Nightwalker off. "We may not be locals, but we know how to work the streets. We've got the angles covered. It's just a matter of time." He checked his watch. "Look, chummer, let's blow. We got us a safe place to hunker down." He glared at Falcon. "What about . . . ?"

"He comes with me," Nightwalker said harshly. "I said we're tight. I vouch for him."

For a moment Falcon thought Knife-Edge was going to object. But then the Amerindian just shrugged. "Your call, Walker." He looked the runner over again. "You want to sleep in the van? You look drek-kicked."

Nightwalker shook his head slowly.

"Later," he said, and only Falcon understood the meaning of his words. "I'll sleep later."

9

Is it starting? Sly sipped at her glass of scotch, staring out the window at the lights of downtown. Corporate war. Is it starting already?

It had been a strange day. A difficult one, a nerve-wracking one. She needed information on what was shaking on the street, what the corps were up to, and who was involved in the plex-wide search for her. But, of course, she was limited by the very existence of that search. How could she know which of her contacts, her erstwhile allies and comrades, had taken the megacorps' credit and had joined the hunt? She couldn't. Sure, there were ways of putting out feelers without identifying yourself, but that was nowhere near as efficient as personal contact with people who knew and trusted you. Within an hour of leaving Agarwal's place, she realized how isolated she really was.

That was when she'd remembered Argent. A heavily chromed street monster and the leader of a shadow team that called itself the Wrecking Crew, he'd worked with Sly on a major run a few years back. Since then she'd kept in intermittent contact with the big man. Though they never got close enough to consider each other chummers, they *did* share a healthy respect for each other's competence. It came as a disturbing shock to Sly to realize that Argent was the only runner in the entire sprawl she could trust, even marginally.

It had taken her a half-hour of hard thinking before

deciding to risk a call to him. What finally decided her
was the fact that Argent had a strong—Sly thought ob-
sessive—hatred of Yamatetsu, for some reason he never
discussed with anyone. That personal quirk should be
enough to stop him from ever getting involved in anything that might benefit the megacorp, she figured. Not
the best basis for trust, but better than nothing.

Argent turned out to be a good choice. He answered
her preliminary questions immediately, without having to
go to his contacts, as though he'd already picked up on
the changes happening on the streets. "Things are getting dicey," he told her, "in and out of the shadows.
Lone Star's out in force. More patrols, better armed.
Where there'd normally be a patrol of two Stars, there
are six; and when they'd normally be riding in a light
patrol car, they're packed into Citymasters. They're acting weird, too, like they know something's going down
but they're not sure what.

"Corp forces are also out," he went on. "Up-gunned
patrols, too, doing this strange kind of dance. Lots of
rumbles all over the plex. The media says they're gang-
related, but that's drek. They're not happening along turf
borders. My reading is that it's the corp soldiers scrapping it out." His face on her telecom screen took on a
worried expression. "Something *real* bad's going down,
Sly. I don't know what it is, and that scares me." That
comment had hit Sly hard. If his street rep was any proof,
it would take a frag of a lot to put a scare into Argent.

He'd also confirmed some of Agarwal's comments—as
if Sly had really needed confirmation. All the major
megacorps were in on it—whatever *it* was—but Yamatetsu seemed to be the key player.

"And they're all looking for *you,* Sly," he added without her having to ask. "Maybe not by name. I don't think
all the players have ID'd you yet. But they're all asking
the right questions on the street, and they're covering all

your usual haunts." He'd chuckled grimly. "I take it
you're not at home, or we wouldn't be having this conversation.

"I'll keep my eyes open and my ear to the ground,"
he said, "but until you hear from me you'd better find
someplace *real* secure to hunker down." He'd paused.
"Got a good spot, or do you want a suggestion?"

She took him up on the offer, and the suggestion had
been surprising. Innovative, and possibly the best idea
she'd heard in a long time.

Which was how she'd ended up at her present location.

The *Sheraton,* for frag's sake. One of Seattle's best,
and most expensive, hotels, across the street from the
exclusive Washington Athletic Club.

Sly would never have thought of it herself, but Argent's reasoning made immediate sense. First, who the
hell would look for a shadowrunner—particularly one
being hunted by the corps—in a high-tone hotel that
catered largely to corporate suits? The hunters would
be searching the shadows, the squats and grimy flops in
the rougher parts of town where the locals' hatred for
the corps would interfere with the search. And second,
once she'd checked into the Sheraton, the hotel's own
highly touted computer and physical and magical security would help shield her. The only difficulty would be
actually checking in.

Which, it turned out, wasn't hard at all, thanks to Modal. Over the last few years, he'd collected a wide variety
of fake identities—including names, histories, and even
SINs—for both males and females of almost all the major
metahuman races. Presumably he'd had a thriving business selling these to runners and others who found their
real identities something of a liability. As soon as she
mentioned the problem, the black elf had produced a
credstick for each of them, carrying all the data neces-

sary for an almost watertight cover. He didn't say where
he got them, and she didn't ask.

Then it had been only a matter of marching into the
Sheraton lobby, bold as brass, and taking two adjoining
rooms in the names of Wesley Aimes and Samantha Bou-
vier. Even though Sly was sure the clerk would hear her
heart pounding, the bored dwarf had merely slipped the
credsticks into the registration computer's slot. When
they read out as good, he issued them the magnetic cards
that served as keys, mumbling, "WelcometotheSheraton,
hopeyouenjoyyourstay."

While riding up in the elevator, they learned that a
convention was booked into the hotel tonight. A convention of representatives of private law-enforcement agen-
cies. Execs from Lone Star and that corp's equivalent
from around the world filled the rooms on the fifteenth
and part of the tenth floor. At first that had scared the
drek out of her. But then, on deeper thought, Sly realized
it *increased* the level of their security. What corp hunter
would expect his quarry to hole up in the midst of a
bunch of cops? And even if somebody *did* track her to
the Sheraton, they'd think twice about pulling anything
shadowy when a significant percentage of the hotel guests
were armed to the fragging teeth.

Once the initial fear was gone, she found the whole
concept funnier than hell. What do cops do for fun at a
convention? she wondered. Arrest each other? Beat each
other up? Sly relaxed so much that she had difficulty not
bursting out laughing when a British Alde Firm exec—a
dwarf wearing a bright scarlet jacket, a sash, and a kilt—
boarded the elevator on the tenth floor on his way up to
a hospitality suite on the fifteenth.

So here she was, in room 1205, looking out the window and enjoying a glass of single malt from the minibar.
She looked over at Modal, who was sprawled on the bed,

looking indecently comfortable as he idly zapped through the channels on the trideo.

She didn't like having him here. It didn't matter that she was confident—as confident as she could reasonably be—that any attempt to sell her out to the corps would just get him whacked. But his involvement made her seriously uncomfortable.

Why? she asked herself. He was a skilled street op, a good, steady gun to have at your back. He'd be an asset no matter what she finally decided was the best course.

Was it just that they used to be lovers? She chewed on that for a few minutes, taking another swallow of scotch to turbocharge her brain.

No, not really. It was just . . . just that he reminded her of a zombie. Modal had always been so passionate about things. Not just about her, or about sex. But he'd always seemed personally involved, *deeply* involved, in everything he did, even though he didn't let emotions interfere with a run. And now?

No emotion at all, courtesy of the violet pills he was popping every couple of hours. And that was it. He *looked* like Modal, he *talked* like Modal. But it was like he *wasn't* Modal. He reminded her of the horror trids that had scared her so as a kid, the ones where the walking dead came to hunt the living. It was almost as though Modal were one of those animated corpses, brought back to only a semblance of life. She shuddered.

Sly looked at her watch, saw it was oh-one hundred. Time to call Agarwal for an update. She wished there was some way to relay incoming calls to room 1205, but she couldn't think of one. Cellular phones had locator circuits in them—otherwise how could they register with the cel network?—so she'd ditched hers hours ago. Some electronic genius might have been able to kluge together some untraceable relay, but she knew it was way beyond her capabilities. She walked through into the adjoining room, closing the connecting door behind her. Settled herself down on the edge of the bed and placed the call.

Agarwal answered immediately. His face on the telecom screen looked tired, his soft brown eyes bloodshot behind his glasses, as though he'd been staring at a computer screen for hours without a break. Which he probably had. The background was out of focus, but she could recognize the decor of his study.

"Sharon." He gave her a tense, worried smile. "Are you all right, Sharon?"

She nodded with a smile, tried to make her voice reassuring. "I'm still kicking, chummer. No hassle. Did you get anything?"

"Several things. But it may not be anything you want to hear."

Her mouth went dry, but she kept her smile in place. "Did you break the encryption?"

He bobbed his head nervously. "Some of it. As I suspected, there were multiple levels, with differing degrees of security on different portions of the file. I broke enough to understand the importance of what it is you have . . . and enough to scare the fragging drek out of me."

Sly had never heard Agarwal curse, had thought the ex-decker didn't have it in him. Perhaps more than anything else that was what bothered her now. Unable to keep her feigned smile in place, she let it fade. "What is it?"

"I think this is lost technology, Sharon. Do you know what that means?"

She paused, marshaling her thoughts. "The crash of twenty-nine," she said. "The virus took down the network, and some data got trashed. Is that what you mean?"

He nodded again. "In essence, yes. There's still much we don't understand about the virus that caused the crash.

Was it self-originating? Was it released into the network accidentally? Or was it a case of core wars?''

"Hold the phone,'' she said, raising a hand. "Core wars?''

"Computer warfare, Sharon. Warfare between corporations, waged by releasing tailored virus codes into a competitor's system. Some technohistorians suggest that the crash virus might have been designed for such a task, judging by its preference for highly encrypted files.'' He paused. "In any case, it seems undeniable that your file contains research into technology lost in the crash. And that, of course, might explain the megacorps' sudden activity. If one *zaibatsu* has recovered important lost technology, it might represent a sufficiently great competitive advantage that other megacorporations would risk corporate war to get it for themselves.''

Sly nodded slowly. This latest bit of news tied in well— too well—with Argent's comments.

"I set up a second computer to monitor the datafaxes and corporate databoards,'' Agarwal continued. "My watchdog program found some highly disturbing news.''

"What?''

"The Corporate Court in Zurich-Orbital has noticed the goings-on in Seattle, and seems to have come to the same conclusion about the possibility of a corp war,'' Agarwal said. "The court ordered an official cooling-down period, a temporary cessation of all unusual corporate activity in the metroplex.''

"The court's got the clout to do that?''

"Not directly,'' Agarwal explained. "The court has no enforcement arm. The megacorporations follow its decrees because the alternatives are unthinkable.'' He paused, and his expression sent a chill up Sly's spine.

"*Were* unthinkable,'' he amended. "To my knowledge, at least three of the major megacorps have totally disregarded the court's edict.'' He took off his glasses, rubbed at his red eyes. "This is unheard of," he said softly, "and immensely frightening. It implies that full corporate war is closer than ever."

Fear clenched Sly's stomach. Her mouth was so dry she had to swallow before she could speak. "You're saying all the corps are after *me*?"

"After *this*," Agarwal corrected, "after this file. And there might be more. There's some evidence that the UCAS government is involved too. Hints that federal teams are also operating in the sprawl."

"The feds? Why?"

The ex-decker shrugged. "To gain an advantage over the corporations perhaps? The government has definitely been seeking an edge in the past few years. Or perhaps to gain an advantage over its own competitors—the Confederate American States, the Native American Nations, California Free State, maybe even Aztlan and Tir Tairngire."

Sly shook her head slowly. This was getting too big, too fast. "And they all want the file? They're all after me?" Suddenly she felt very alone, very small. "What the frag am I supposed to do, Agarwal?"

Her friend's face was expressionless. "Yes," he said finally. "That is the question, isn't it?"

10

0145 hours, November 14, 2053

Falcon wandered around the old building, a condemned bowling alley in the Barrens, that Knife-Edge called his safe house. With the electricity cut off, the

only light came from portable lamps that the runners had
set up around what used to be the restaurant. All the
furniture was gone—either moved out when the place
closed or else "acquired" by neighbors afterward—
and the far ends of the lanes were gaping holes, showing
that the automatic pinsetters had been stripped out as
well. Though the lanes themselves were the worse for
wear, their woodgrained plastic scratched and stained
here and there, they were still generally intact.

Knife-Edge and his "boys" were sprawled around the
restaurant, eating some rations they'd brought with them.
Falcon's belly growled at the smell—How long since I've
eaten? he wondered. Twenty-four hours?—but his pride
wouldn't let him ask for handouts. Nightwalker lay
propped up against a wall. He was starting to fade. The
other runners seemed to assume it was just exhaustion,
but Falcon knew better.

Knife-Edge had vanished for almost an hour after they'd
first arrived at the safe house, presumably working the
shadows for information. Now he was back again, talking
through his options with the other runners. The tough-
looking Amerindians kept shooting Falcon hard looks,
making it plain they thought he didn't belong. But so far
Nightwalker's voucher had kept them from kicking him
out . . . or worse. But what happens when Nightwalker's
dead? he thought grimly.

"I think I got a line on the local who's got our paydata," Knife-Edge was saying to his comrades. "Still no
name, but I think I got a communication channel."

"What channel?" It was the one called Slick who
spoke. He'd finished his rations, and was casually strop-
ping a throwing knife against a leather strap. In the lamp-
light, the knife's edge looked already razor-sharp.

"Another local runner," Knife-Edge explained.
"Used to work with a chummer of my brother's, before
he got geeked."

"So's this local got a location?" This from Benbo. He was the largest of the team. A human, but with enough mass and bulging muscles to be mistaken in poor light for a troll.

Knife-Edge shook his head. "No, or if he does he isn't telling. But he'll pass a message if I ask him."

The last runner, the one called Van, nodded. He was the smallest, but even so he had to mass a good fifteen kilos more than Falcon. His gray-blue eyes were always steady, seeming to glint with an understanding that he was disinclined to share with anyone else. "You're thinking of setting up a meet, aren't you?" Van said in his quiet voice.

"Yeah, seems like the best way to go." Knife-Edge turned to Nightwalker. "Hey, Walker, give us a good location for a shadow meet." He paused. "Walker?"

Falcon snapped his head around. Nightwalker had slumped down further, his head hanging limply. His eyes were still open, but Falcon knew they weren't focusing on anything. "Oh frag . . ." He ran over to the big Amerindian, crouched beside him.

He's dead. But no, he wasn't. He was still breathing—shallow, fast-paced breaths, almost like panting. Falcon grabbed his shoulder, squeezed. Nightwalker jerked his head up, looked at the young ganger, tried to focus. But Falcon knew that whatever the runner was seeing, it wasn't him. He looked closer into his chummer's eyes. By the yellow light of the lamp, he could see that one pupil was contracted almost to the size of a pinprick while the other was dilated so much there didn't seem to be any iris around it. What the frag did it mean? Whatever it was, it wasn't good.

"What's wrong with Walker?" Knife-Edge asked sharply.

"He's hurt," Falcon answered quickly, "hurt *bad.* I tried to get him patched, but he's starting to go." He stood up, facing Knife-Edge, pulling himself up to his full height. He swallowed hard, tried to force a tone of confidence, of command, into his voice. "Look, I've got to get him to a clinic."

"Huh?" Benbo grunted.

"He'll die if I don't."

Knife-Edge thought about that for a few moments. Finally he shook his head. "No clinic."

"He'll die!" Falcon almost shouted.

The eyes of the four Amerindians were cold, predators studying their prey. Slick held his knife by the blade in a loose, three-fingered grip. The grip of a knife-thrower, Falcon knew.

"No clinic," Knife-Edge said again, his voice like cold steel.

"He's your *comrade,*" Falcon grated. "What about the shadowrunners' code of honor?"

Benbo barked with laughter, a harsh sound that echoed back from the lanes. Falcon saw Knife-Edge glance over at Slick, saw the knife-man slightly shift his grip on his weapon.

I'm going to die, Falcon thought, but the idea didn't bring the fear he might have expected. All he felt was anger. "By the fragging totems, he's your comrade!" he yelled. He searched his brain for anything Nightwalker had told him, anything he could use to save both their lives. "He's your fragging *tactician!*"

Slick shifted his weight, readying for the throw.

But Knife-Edge raised a hand, made a quick gesture. Slick shot his leader a disbelieving look, but lowered his knife.

"Yeah," Knife-Edge said quietly. "Yeah. Get him patched, kid."

Benbo growled something under his breath, too low for Falcon to hear.

"He's an asset, Ben," Knife-Edge pointed out. "You

don't waste assets if you don't have to. Maybe once you've learned that, you'll be able to lead a team.'' The leader fixed Falcon with his cold eyes. ''Get him patched and then bring him back.''

Falcon felt his knees weaken, had to force himself to remain standing. *Now* the fear hit him, twisting his guts. ''I'll need the van.'' He struggled to keep his voice emotionless, knew from the runners' expressions that he'd failed.

''Take it,'' Knife-Edge said after a moment's thought. ''We've got other wheels.''

Falcon nodded, turning back to Nightwalker.

''We're expecting you back, kid,'' Knife-Edge said quietly, ''*with* Walker and *with* the van. Otherwise you and Slick here will have a real long talk about it.''

Slick chuckled quietly.

Falcon drove the van carefully through the streets of the Redmond Barrens. He'd learned to drive after joining the First Nation, had been trained by the gang's best, had even worked as wheelman on a couple of small operations. But even so he had to concentrate intensely to keep from getting into trouble. Despite the van's apparently trashed exterior, it was in excellent condition where it counted. The engine was perfectly tuned, and cranked out more horsepower than anything Falcon had ever driven. Too heavy a touch on the gas pedal and the thing had the tendency to get away from him, spinning its tires and laying rubber. Not the best way to avoid attention, and attention was the last thing the ganger wanted at the moment.

Nightwalker was slumped in the bucket seat beside him. *He looks like death,* Falcon thought, catching occasional glimpses of his friend in the illumination of the few streetlights that still worked. Eyes open but not really seeing anything, breathing shallow and fast. The Amerindian's broad forehead glistened with a sheen of sweat. When Falcon touched his chummer's hand, the flesh felt cool. Not yet the chill of death, but too close.

Falcon almost thought Nightwalker was going to kick off in the bowling alley when he'd tried to wrestle the big man to his feet. The runner had gasped, the breath rattling in his throat, then stopped breathing altogether. Just for an instant, but it was the longest moment Falcon had ever lived through. Knife-Edge and his men merely sat back and watched him struggle, both Slick and Benbo with nasty smiles. But then Van had taken pity on him, coming over to sling the much-bigger Nightwalker over his shoulder like he would a child, and carried him to the vehicle. Falcon wanted to thank him, but the runner had turned away and vanished back inside before he could get the words out.

Now Falcon was wracking his brains for a place to take his comrade. The regular hospitals were out. They might take Nightwalker in and treat him, expecting to squeeze their fees out of him after putting him back together. But they'd ask some hard questions of whoever brought in somebody in his condition. Falcon couldn't afford that.

So that left the free clinics. Of those, the ones run by the Universal Brotherhood were the best bet. From what he'd heard, they had a "no questions asked" policy, at least with regard to the people dropping off patients. For all he knew, they might be required, by law, to report gunshot wounds to Lone Star, but that wouldn't affect him. Nightwalker might have to face some uncomfortable scrutiny, but that was better than being dead, wasn't it?

For a moment he felt pangs of guilt. He told me not to take him to a clinic, Falcon remembered, and I promised I wouldn't.

But did that promise still count? No, Falcon told himself, it ended as soon as Nightwalker's condition got this bad.

Now the only question was, where was the fragging UB clinic? Falcon knew there was one in Redmond, but where? He cruised aimlessly for a few minutes, hoping to spot something that would either jar his memory or give him some clue. First Nation turf had more than a dozen billboards advertising the Brotherhood, all of them showing the address of the local chapterhouse. But here in the Barrens, it seemed that billboards doubled as target flats for heavy ordnance. If the Brotherhood had ever put one up here, people had long ago shot it to bits.

Then a thought struck him. This van had some heavy mods. Maybe . . . He pulled over, examined the complex dashboard.

Yes, the spirits were with him tonight. The van's electronics suite included a Navstar satellite uplink and a nav computer. Shouldn't the computer's database contain useful information such as the location of medical clinics?

It took him a few long moments to make sense of the computer's interface, which wasn't too complex because it was designed for use by a driver while on the road. He punched in his request, and the computer had the answer in an instant: Universal Brotherhood Redmond Chapter, corner of Belmont and Waveland.

He hit another button to bring up a map of Redmond. Frag, it was further away than he thought. When you were used to the downtown core, it was easy to forget just how big the suburbs were. He traced out the best route, then pulled away from the curb. Fortunately there was almost no traffic at this time of night, and seemed to be no Lone Star presence at all. He let the van's speed creep a little higher.

Nightwalker shifted next to him, groaned something. Falcon reached over, laid a comforting hand on his shoulder. The Amerindian mumbled again, rolled his eyes as though he couldn't quite control them. But then he seemed to focus on the ganger's face.

"That you, Falcon?"

"Yeah."

"Whuzzapnin'?" His voice was slurred, like that of a drunk about to pass out in the gutter.

"Taking you to a clinic," Falcon said firmly. "Knife-Edge ordered it." He figured that was the best way to avoid argument. "He said you don't waste assets."

"Yeah." His voice trailed off, his eyes half-closed. But then, a few seconds later he roused himself again. "I feel like drek, chummer." In the flash of a streetlight, Falcon could see his friend's mouth twist into a tired smile.

"You'll be okay." Falcon gave the van more gas, felt it leap forward.

Nightwalker was silent for a few minutes. Although that worried Falcon deeply, he took advantage of the silence to concentrate on his navigating. Okay, here's Belmont. So hang a left and boot it for Waveland.

The Amerindian runner stirred again. "I'm Salish," he whispered.

"Huh?"

"I'm Salish," he said louder. "I told you I had no tribe. But I'm Salish."

"Called by a chief?" Falcon asked.

Nightwalker shook his head. "Nah. But I'm Salish, just the same. Like you're Sioux." He paused, head bowing down toward his chest. "Never made a vision quest," he murmured. "Or maybe this is it."

"Yeah," Falcon growled. "Just hang on, okay?" He stomped the gas pedal to the floor, fought with the wheel as the van accelerated like a race car.

He screeched to a stop at the corner of Belmont and Waveland, the van's front wheel bumping up onto the curb. The Universal Brotherhood chapterhouse looked like it had once been a four-plex movie theater, with two floors of offices above the main level. The marquee was still in place. "The Universal Brotherhood," it declared, "Come in and find the power of Belonging." (Yeah, right, Falcon thought.) The front doors were closed, and most of the lights were off. But what else could you expect at two in the fragging morning?

So where the hell was the clinic entrance? If it wasn't at the front, it had to be back in the alley. He booted the van again, bumping off the curb, throwing the vehicle into a screaming bootlegger turn. Pointed it down the dark alley behind Belmont.

He flicked on the high-beams as he slowed the van back to a crawl. Where was the clinic entrance? The quartz-halogen headlights made the alley noonday-bright, showing him the rear of the Brotherhood chapterhouse. Above the single door was a sign reading, "Universal Brotherhood Soup Kitchen."

Soup kitchen? Where was the fragging clinic?

He cruised slowly down the alley. The entrance to the soup kitchen was locked, secured with a gate of heavy metal bars. No way in there. Frantically, he kicked the van forward. There was another door at the other end of the building. No sign above that one. But again the door was shut, another gate locking it tight. *Oh, spirits and totems* . . .

Doesn't this chapterhouse have a clinic? Falcon thought desperately. I thought they all did.

He stopped the van, punched another query into the nav computer's database. This time he requested not just the location of the Brotherhood chapterhouses, but whatever information the computer had on their facilities.

He felt his body chill as the data scrolled across the small display screen. There were four chapterhouses in the plex, as he'd thought. But according to the computer, only two of them had free clinics: the Octagon, in central Seattle, and the smaller chapterhouse, in Puyallup. The Brotherhood ran two other clinics, one in Everett and one down by the Tacoma docks. That brought the number up to four, which was why Falcon had assumed all were connected with chapterhouses. Frag it to hell! He punched more queries into the nav computer. The nearest clinic was the one downtown, at Eighth and Westlake, two fragging blocks from fragging Denny Park. At least a half-hour drive, even with the van's powerful engine and the light traffic. Could Nightwalker hang on that long?

He looked over at his friend. (Friend? Yes!)

In a sudden panic Falcon reached out to grab the man's shoulder, then pulled his hand back at the deadly chill of the flesh under the Amerindian's jacket.

Nightwalker's eyes were still open, but Falcon knew they saw nothing. His face was slack, pale as bone. His posture, his body, looked no different. But Falcon knew— *knew*—that the man's spirit had fled.

He killed the van's engine, rested his forehead on the steering wheel. What do I do now?

Nightwalker was dead. He could do no more for him. Or could he?

Falcon remembered what the Amerindian had said about the lost technology, the ability to tap into fiber-optic communications. He hadn't understood everything—hadn't understood *much* of it, to be honest—but he remembered how serious the runner had sounded. Nightwalker knew so much more about the way the plex worked, how the megacorps interrelated, and he'd thought the search for the lost tech was significant. Maybe the most important thing he'd ever been involved in.

Could Falcon just turn his back on that? Could he just walk away, leaving Nightwalker's task uncompleted?

Could he leave it up to Knife-Edge and his men? And

could he trust the other Amerindians to do the right thing
with the prize if they ever did get their hands on it?

What the frag am I doing? he berated himself. I'm
nobody, just a punk ganger. I'm not a shadowrunner.
Didn't Nightwalker tell me I'm not in his league?

But he also said I was his comrade. He said we were
bound by the shadowrunners' code of honor—even if
Benbo laughed at that. Didn't that mean that Falcon had
an obligation to see his friend's task through?

This is a chance to make a difference, he told himself,
to do something important. Not just scrabble through the
sprawl for my own benefit. I could never make a difference with the First Nation. I never thought I'd ever have
the chance. How can I turn away now?

He sighed, rubbed at his eyes. He'd been thinking so
hard that they'd started to water. That had to be the reason. He looked over at his friend.

"I'm in," he said to the lifeless Nightwalker. "It
scares the drek out of me, but I'm in."

Falcon had just dumped Nightwalker's body in the alley
behind the Universal Brotherhood chapterhouse. It bothered him, on some deep level, but what the frag else
could he do? He wished he knew more about the traditions of Nightwalker's tribe. How would the Salish handle the body of a friend? From Langland's book, Falcon
knew that burial traditions varied. Some tribes interred
the bodies with great ceremony and reverence, singing
songs to guide the spirits of the dead to the land of the
totems. Others seemed to have no such traditions, just
dumping the bodies without any ceremony. The spirit
was gone, these tribes seemed to believe, leaving the
dead body only an empty shell. Why treat it specially
when the person was not there anymore? He didn't know
to which group the Salish belonged, but he told himself

that Nightwalker's spirit—wherever it was now—would understand.

He drove back to the safe house slowly. Meeting with Knife-Edge and the others without Nightwalker to protect him scared him drekless, but his decision left him no choice. At least he thought he had a way of handling it.

There were new faces in the restaurant when he walked in. Five of them, all orks, wearing gang colors that identified them as members of the Scuzboys. He knew the gang by their rep, a real hard group that hired themselves out as muscle to various shadow teams.

The biggest of the five orks, probably the leader, bared yellowing tusks in a snarl as he spotted Falcon. ''Who's dis fragger?'' he demanded.

Knife-Edge didn't answer him, just regarded Falcon levelly. ''Where's Nightwalker?'' he asked, his voice cold.

''At the clinic, where else?'' he replied, trying to keep his fear under control. ''He's too trashed to move. The docs say he'll be down a couple of days. He sent me back here. Said he'll keep in touch through me.''

Falcon held his breath as Knife-Edge thought about that for a moment. He relaxed as the runner nodded.

''Which clinic did you take him to?'' Van asked.

''The Universal Brotherhood free clinic,'' he answered smoothly. ''Nightwalker told me he didn't have the credit for anything else.''

That seemed to satisfy Van, who turned his attention back to field-stripping and cleaning the large rifle that rested in his lap.

Falcon decided that now was the time to say what he had to say. ''Nightwalker says he wants me along on the meet. That way I can report back to him what went down.''

One of the orks hawked and spat on the floor. "Don't need no breeder kid," he snarled.

From their expressions, Falcon could see that Knife-Edge and the other Amerinds thought the same way. "Nightwalker's the tactician," he said, struggling to keep his voice calm. "He said I'd be an *asset*" —he stressed the word—"to scope out the meet."

Again he watched Knife-Edge's face as the runner gave it some thought.

"I know the sprawl," Falcon added.

"So do we," the Scuzboy leader snapped.

After a few moments, Knife-Edge shrugged. "Yeah, why not?"

Slick shot his leader a disgusted glance, but didn't say anything.

"Does Walker have a spot for the meet?" Knife-Edge asked.

Falcon nodded, glad he'd figured it out on the drive back. "He says Pier Forty-two, the Hyundai terminal. With the dockworkers' strike, it'll be deserted till dawn."

He glanced over at the Scuzboy leader, saw the ork nod in agreement. "Yeah, dat's good."

"That'll do," Knife-Edge concurred. "Now let's talk tactics.

"I'll specify that the local's supposed to come to the meet alone, but there'll probably be back-up anyway. Benbo, you and I'll do the face-to-face drek. Van, you take the god spot. Any back-up shows, you take them down."

Van caressed the stock of his weapon tenderly. It was a sniper rifle, Falcon now realized. "Baby'll do the job. What about the local?"

"Once I know where the paydata is, I want a clean head-shot."

Van nodded. "Null perspiration."

"And Slick, I want you to . . . *bodyguard* the kid."

The knife man smiled, showing yellowed teeth. "You got it, chummer."

"What about me and da boys?" the Scuzboy leader asked.

"Perimeter support," Knife-Edge replied. "Secure the area, sanitize it. And if back-up shows, scrag 'em."

The ork gave a phlegmy chuckle. "Sounds like a party," he growled, fingering one of his chipped tusks.

Falcon scanned the faces around him, wondering what the frag he'd gotten himself into. It wasn't a meet they were planning. It was an ambush. But what could he say? If he raised any objections, he was sure Slick would stick a knife through his throat. Which was probably what he'd do once Knife-Edge had what he wanted.

"Okay," Knife-Edge said, flowing to his feet in one smooth motion. "Gear up and into the van. I'll make the call once we're rolling."

11

0230 hours, November 14, 2053

The telecom in the adjoining room rang. Sly answered it at once. Only one person had the direct-connect LTG number, or only one she knew about, that is. And anybody else who knew where she was holing up sure as drek wouldn't be phoning first.

Argent's face filled the telecom screen. "Hoi, Sly. What's up?"

"Whole lot of nothing here," she told him. His expression said he knew she was lying, wordlessly asked her to confide what was troubling her. Best to keep it quiet, she decided. The fewer who know, the better. She shook her head in answer to his unspoken question.

He shrugged. Message received and understood, she thought. "Got word someone's looking for a solo meet," the chromed runner told her.

"Who?"

"Don't know for sure," he said. "The contact came from an old associate of Hawk's, but I don't know if he's the principal."

Hawk? Sly wracked her brain for a moment, trying to place the name. Then memory returned. Hawk had been Argent's closest chummer, combat shaman and second-in-command of the Wrecking Crew. He'd bought it almost a year ago, under circumstances Argent never talked about. Sly suspected the big shaman had gotten scragged on the run that had turned Argent so solidly against Yamatetsu.

"Did you find anything?" she asked.

"Not much," he admitted. "Most of my contacts are lying low because of the corp heat wave. What buzz I *did* hear says it's a team of out-of-plex runners."

"Where from?"

"Don't know, except that it's not Seattle and not UCAS. Cal Free, maybe, but it's anybody's guess."

Sly thought about that for a moment. Out-of-plex, out-of-country. That sounded promising. It was possible these people would have associations with the local corps, but not so likely. "Has the corp war spread?" she speculated out loud.

"Not yet," Argent said slowly, "but my guess is it's only a matter of time."

Sly nodded to herself. That was good; it cut the odds still further that these out-of-town runners had been hired by Yamatetsu or any of the other big local players. "So they want a meet," she said slowly. "Why?"

Argent shrugged again. "The contact didn't say much.

Just that he knew you had some information that interested them. Something important.''

Again Sly saw the unspoken question on his face. She just smiled and shook her head.

The big man sighed. ''Okay, your biz,'' he conceded, ''but sometimes keeping it too close to your chest can get you ripped, Sly. But you know that.''

Her smile grew warmer; his concern touched her. ''Do they want this . . . *information*?'' she asked. ''Are they looking for a deal?''

''No,'' Argent said, surprising her. ''The way I read it is they'd be just as glad if you keep hold of it.'' And take all the heat, was what he didn't have to add. ''They just want to discuss it with you, and maybe have some say in its disposition. They're interested in figuring out the best way to handle it, to realize maximum profit for you and them. Does that make sense to you?''

Sly nodded slowly. ''It makes sense. Where do they want the meet?''

''South harbor.'' He flashed an address, plus map coordinates, onto her screen.

''When?''

''They say time's of the essence. Oh-four-hundred.''

''Today?'' She looked at her watch. It was already oh-two thirty-eight.

''Yeah. Tight timing.'' He paused. ''Gonna go, Sly?''

''I don't know,'' she answered honestly. ''Have you got any reading on these guys at all?''

''Nothing solid,'' he admitted, ''either negative or positive.''

She tapped a fingernail against her front teeth. Which way to jump? This could be a setup, or it could mean another group to work with, allies. Which way?

''What would you do?'' she asked.

Argent's face went totally expressionless. ''Your run,'' he said flatly.

She snorted. "I *know* it's my run. I'm not asking you to take responsibility, Argent. I'm no newbie. I'm just asking for your reading, friend to friend. It's my decision, and I'll make it no matter what you say."

He relaxed. "Yeah. The buzz on the street's freaking me." Sly knew that was the closest he'd ever come to an apology, but the sentiment was there and that was all that mattered.

She watched him as he thought it through. "Tough call," he said at last. "It could go either way. I don't want to influence you and get you killed."

"But *you'd* go for it, wouldn't you?" she pressed.

"Yeah," he said after another pause. "Yeah, I'd go. But you can bet your assets I'd take back-up. Lots of back-up."

"You said they wanted a solo meet."

"Since when do you let the other team call all the shots?"

"Good point," she acknowledged.

"So, have you got back-up? Or are you totally cut off?"

She glanced through the connecting door, into the other room where the black elf was sprawled on the bed. "Minimal back-up," she admitted.

"Modal," Argent said sourly. "The street says you got him to sell out his Johnson. Do you trust him?"

She didn't answer immediately, which she knew was answer enough.

"Yeah, I thought so." Argent frowned. "I can send you two guns if you want. You know Mongoose, I think, and I'll send his street brother Snake."

Sly considered it. She'd met Mongoose, a razorboy with reflexes chipped even higher than Modal's, on a run the year before. Later she'd heard that he and another sammy called Snake had signed on with Argent to replace Hawk and Toshi, the two men who'd died on a run toward the end of 2052. Mongoose was competent, she knew. Snake had to be too. Argent didn't hire hacks.

She nodded. "Thanks, I'll take them. Standard rates, but"—she smiled—"you might have to wait a while for payment."

Argent waved that off. "Just pay their per diem and forget my cut. Want them to meet you down there?" He chuckled. "I think the Mongoose and the Snake would look a little out of place in the Sheraton lobby."

That brought a smile. She remembered Mongoose's scraggy reverse-mohawk, the angular tattoos on his cheeks, his polished-steel incisors. "Have them meet me at the Fourth Avenue South monorail station." She checked her watch again. "Can they make it by oh-three-fifteen?"

"If *you* can," he confirmed. "Briefing when they get there?" She nodded. "You got it, Sly." He hesitated. "Wish I could do more."

"You're doing plenty, chummer," she reassured him. "Thanks for the assist. It's what I need."

To her surprise, the heavily chromed shadowrunner seemed embarrassed by her gratitude. "Clear it," he said, waving his hand as if to erase something. "Slot and run, Sly. The boys'll be with you. Give me the scoop later." And he was gone.

She rolled her head to release the tension in her neck. Later, she thought, if there *is* a later.

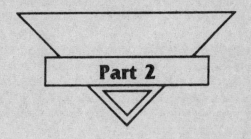

Part 2

Intersection

Part I

Interlection

12

It was cold down on the docks. Falcon zipped his leather jacket shut, turned up the collar. Wished he could have afforded a fleece-collared coat like the ones the Scuzboys sported.

The orks seemed warm enough—or if they weren't, they were too proud to bitch about it. As for Knife-Edge and the other runners, they had to be toasty-warm in those insulated jumpsuits. Besides, the bulky body armor they wore on top would keep the chill out. The night wind gusted again from Elliot Bay, bringing with it the tang of salt overlaid with the reek of oil and a dozen chemical contaminants. Falcon crossed his arms over his chest and tried to stop his teeth from chattering.

Getting into the Hyundai pier area had been routine. Like all the Seattle docks the Pier 42 section was surrounded by a high fence topped with three strands of cutwire. Private security guards patrolled the perimeter, but it was so long and the security presence diminished so much by corporate cost-cutting, that the odds were very low of actually meeting the sec patrol.

The Scuzboys had handled the fence. One of the orks had scanned it with some kind of hand-held sensor, confirmed it wasn't electrified and that the alarm would sound only if the wires were actually cut. Another had scrambled up the fence, to sling a flexible blanket of woven Kevlar fibers over the strands of cutwire. Then the rest of them were able to clamber over the fence, and drop safely inside the compound.

To Falcon's surprise the Hyundai compound *wasn't* full of cars. Got to be the dock workers' strike, he figured. Huge areas were completely empty, deserted parking lots under the carbon arc lights. Down by the pier itself, and around the periphery, huge shipping containers were stacked in long rows. They had to be at least ten meters long by four wide and maybe three high. For a moment, Falcon wondered what was in them. Not cars, he decided. Probably spare parts or something.

Slick jabbed the ganger's shoulder with a knuckle, pointed toward Knife-Edge, who was already leading the group toward the water. The runner was using the stacked containers as cover from any security guards who happened to be wandering around the area. Rubbing his shoulder, Falcon followed.

The section called Pier Forty-two was actually two piers, extending almost due west. They were newer than the areas of the docks further north, less decrepit and drek-kicked. Falcon assumed they must have been destroyed when this portion of Elliot Bay caught fire three years ago—ah, the wonders of water pollution—and had recently been rebuilt. On each pier was a mobile gantry crane, huge red-painted structures that Falcon thought looked big enough to lift a small building.

Knife-Edge stopped in an open area between two rows of containers. He looked around, apparently estimating distances and sight-angles. After a moment he nodded. "This is it. Ground zero." He grinned nastily.

Falcon made his own inspection, had to admit that it was a good place for a meet. Or for an ambush. The open area was roughly square, maybe fifteen meters on a side, and could be reached by following one of four "lanes" between stacked containers. (For a moment, he wondered how the local runner would know where, in the entire Hyundai compound, the meet would take place. But Knife-Edge would have that figured, wouldn't he? Maybe he'd send out the Scuzboys to leave markers—symbols scratched on shipping containers, perhaps—identifying the specific location.)

Knife-Edge pointed up at the gantry crane looming over the open area. "How's that for the god spot?"

Van considered it, cradling his sniper rifle like a baby in his arms. Then he nodded. "I'll take the catwalk there," he stated, indicating an accessway about halfway up the crane's structure. "It gives me cover *plus* a three-sixty degree field of view." He squinted his eyes, estimating distance. "About sixty meters to ground zero, give or take." He smiled. "From that range, you tell me which eyebrow hair you want me to hit."

Knife-Edge slapped him on the shoulder. "Set up an open perimeter, but stay hidden," he told the orks. "Anybody who wants to come in, let 'em. But watch them close. If I squawk three times"—he held up his microtransceiver, pressed a button, causing a muffled electronic buzz from everyone else's radio—"take down any back-up you've got spotted. Understand?"

The Scuzboy leader nodded. "Null persp," he drawled. "Me and da boys done this before." He gestured to his chummers, barked something unintelligible in what Falcon assumed to be some kind of gangspeak.

As the orks dispersed into the night, Knife-Edge pointed to a container on the south side of the open area.

"Benbo and I will hang up top," he said. "When the trogs report the local's arrived, we'll make the meet." He patted the microtransceiver, which was now clipped to his belt. "I'll keep a channel open so you can all hear what's going down."

"What about me? And *him*?" Slick demanded, glaring at Falcon.

"Up there." The leader pointed to another container on the north side of "ground zero." The killing zone, Falcon thought uncomfortably. "Belly down on top of the container, and just hang. When the drek comes down, you'll know what to do, Slick."

The Amerindian chuckled, a sound that chilled Falcon to the bone. "Yeah, I'll know what to do." He prodded Falcon in the shoulder again. "You heard the man. Let's move." He adjusted the sling on his assault rifle and headed for the spot Knife-Edge had indicated.

As he climbed the ladder welded to the outside of the container, Falcon saw that the orks had already disappeared, presumably setting up a loose perimeter around the area. Van was clambering up the ladder leading to his sniper nest, while Benbo and Knife-Edge were checking the area one last time before taking their own positions.

Falcon didn't like what was going down. He was convinced that if Nightwalker were here, the runner would insist on a fair meet rather than this ambush. But Nightwalker can get away with that drek, he told himself. I can't. Raising any kind of objection would be the quickest way of getting himself killed.

With a sigh, he swung himself onto the top of the container, took up his position next to Slick. He stuck his hand in his pocket, felt the reassuring heft of his Fichetti. (To his surprise, the Amerindian runners hadn't asked about a weapon, and he sure as frag wasn't going to volunteer the information.) The metal container was cold, leeching from his body what little heat remained. He arranged himself into the least uncomfortable position and settled down to wait.

He didn't have to wait long. It was oh-three-forty according to his watch when he heard Slick's radio crackle. "Dey're here," an ork voice whispered. "Da scag an' two back-up. Comin' from da east."

"Two?" Knife-Edge's voice over the radio sounded skeptical. "That's all?"

"Dat's all we seen," the ork confirmed.

"Nobody could have leaked through?"

The Scuzboy snarled wordlessly. "We know our biz, Mr. fragging Tribal."

"Check the perimeter," Knife-Edge insisted.

The ork was silent for a moment, and Falcon thought he was going to refuse. But then he growled, "Okay, youse guys, sound off. Position one?"

"Yeah."

"Two?"

"Check."

"T'ree?" Silence. "T'ree?" the ork demanded again. Beside Falcon, Slick moved nervously, flicked the safety off on his AK-97.

"Position t'ree?" There was real tension in the Scuzboy's voice now.

"Three here." The reply was a disgusted whisper. "Fraggin' radio's futzin' up on me."

Falcon heard the ork leader snort. "Position four?"

"Check," the final ork answered.

"Perimeter confirmed," the Scuzboy boss concluded. "And dere's *still* just da two back-up. Razorboys, botha dem. Still coming from da nort'. *Hold it.*" There was silence for a moment, then the ork spoke again. "Okay, we got da scag coming on alone. Da razorguys is splitting up ta cover."

"Can they spot your boys?" Knife-Edge asked.

The ork laughed harshly. "If dey do, it's gonna be da last t'ing dey ever see."

"I got a sighting." The voice was Van's. "The subject's about thirty meters out, coming slowly."

"Armed?" demanded Knife-Edge.

"Nothing heavy," the sniper said. "Personal weapon only." He hesitated. "I can take the shot now . . ."

"Maybe the paydata's hidden somewhere," Knife-Edge told him. "I'll give you the signal. Okay, chummers," the runner's voice came a little louder. "Show time. I'll keep an open channel."

Falcon saw two dark figures drop from the top of a container across the open space. Knife-Edge, who seemed to have removed his plated vest, and the heavily armored Benbo. Neither had any obvious weapons, though Falcon was sure they had holdouts of some kind hidden somewhere on their persons. Not that they really needed them, with Van the sniper and with Slick ready to rock and roll with his AK assault rifle. Edge and Benbo positioned themselves near the southwest corner of the open area, facing the "lane" down which the local runner would be coming, but well out of Slick's line of fire.

The local runner emerged into the killing zone, then stopped and coolly surveyed the area. Falcon stared, unabashed.

She's beautiful, he thought. The woman was tall and slender, with dark wavy hair. Good curves, too, shown off nicely by her street leathers. She moved with confidence and grace, a hint of controlled power. Like a martial artist, Falcon noted. He wished he could see her face better, but the light wasn't good enough. There was the hint of an olive complexion and high cheekbones, but he couldn't be sure.

But what did it matter anyway? he thought with a

twinge of sadness and guilt. Won't be much left of her face after Van's put a bullet through it. In his mind's eye he saw the sniper carefully aligning his scope's crosshairs with the woman's head.

The Amerindian leader stepped forward, stopping ten meters away from her. Benbo followed a step behind and to the right, his heavy armor making him look grotesque in comparison to the slender woman.

"I'm Knife-Edge." Falcon heard the words from two sources—from Slick's radio, and an instant later directly from the killing zone. The minuscule time lag added a dreamlike element to the scene.

The woman nodded. "Sly," she said, introducing herself. "I got word you wanted to talk."

"*We* got word you've got something we're interested in," Knife-Edge countered. "We made a run against Yamatetsu Corporation, but we got hosed. Somebody else got the paydata. Buzz on the street says that's you. Have you got it?"

The woman shrugged. Falcon thought he could see a smile. "My biz," she stated.

Knife-Edge nodded in acknowledgement. "Your biz," he concurred. "We don't want it. We just want to make sure it's disposed of properly. The drek's really going to come down if it gets loose, you know that."

Sly was silent for a moment, apparently considering the Amerindian's words. "Maybe," she admitted finally. "How do you plan to dispose of it?"

"Uh-uh." Knife-Edge shook his head. "First I've got to know if I'm talking to the right person. Have you got the paydata or haven't you?"

Next to him, Falcon felt Slick tense, saw him shift his grip on the AK. He could imagine Van taking aim, tightening his finger on the trigger.

Sly drew breath to answer.

And then all fragging hell broke loose.

Something slammed into Benbo's chest, lanced through the armor as if it didn't exist. Blew out most of the Amerind samurai's back. Benbo spun, arms flailing, head flopping loosely now that most of his spine was missing. For a terrible moment, Falcon could see *right through* the man's chest—a gaping hole, with little flames licking around the ragged edges. The samurai flopped to the ground in a messy heap. Magic! Falcon thought. What else could it be?

"Holy fragging drek!" That was Sly, the female runner. She flung herself back and to the side, rolling toward the cover offered by a cargo container.

Knife-Edge snarled. A pistol had appeared in his hand, apparently out of thin air. He raised it, leveled it at Sly.

Something punched through his stomach, low and on the left side, spinning him wildly and flinging him from his feet. Whatever it was slammed into the container behind him, blowing a hole the size of a man's fist in the thick metal. What the frag was *that*?

Falcon heard a vicious spit from above and to his right. Van with his sniper rifle was getting into the act. The bullet spanged off the container beside Sly. She rolled again, trying to bring up the weapon that was suddenly in her hand. But before she could bring it to bear, the sniper's second round grazed her arm, and the pistol flew from her grip.

Then automatic fire spattered and clanged against the catwalk where Van had his nest, striking blue and white sparks from the metal. Falcon heard a scream, saw the sniper rifle fall from the crane to crash out of sight among the containers.

The previously silent pier was suddenly alive with gunfire and muffled explosions. A spray of tracers, yellow dashes of light, arced wildly into the sky. Falcon couldn't see any possible target. Possibly the gunner had been hit, and his dying reflex had squeezed off the burst as he fell. In the chaos, it was impossible to count how many distinct firefights were actually going down, but there certainly seemed to be more shooters than the five Scuzboys and the two razorguys they'd seen arrive with Sly.

Falcon looked down into the killing zone again. It was empty except for what was left of Benbo. He knew Sly's wound hadn't been mortal, and it looked like Knife-Edge had survived whatever had cored him front-to-back. But what the hell *was* that thing?

He heard a growl beside and behind him. He turned.

It was Slick, of course, his face ugly with rage. "You fragging sold us out!" he snarled. "You're gonna die, pudlicker!" He started to bring his assault rifle up, slowly, as if to draw out his enjoyment.

Too slowly. With a panicked yell, Falcon dragged the Fichetti from his pocket.

As soon as he saw the pistol emerge, Slick tried to snap the rifle onto line. But he was still too late. Falcon saw the Amerind's eyes widen as the Fichetti's laser painted his forehead. And then his face simply disintegrated as the ganger pulled the trigger again and again.

Nausea knotted Falcon's stomach, threatened to make him spew. He turned his face away from the smashed ruins of Slick's head.

Bullets slammed into the container from somewhere, ringing it like a gong. Apparently even the relatively quiet shots from his pistol had attracted unwanted attention.

He started to roll toward the north side of the container, the side away from the killing zone, then hesitated, glancing down at the pistol. The Fichetti was a convenient weapon, and it had already saved his life twice. But it was like a peashooter next to the *thing*—magic, rifle, artillery, whatever it was—that had blown a hole right through the heavily armored Benbo. He needed more firepower.

He rolled back, tugged the AK-97 from Slick's nerve-less fingers. Even coming that close to the corpse turned his stomach. But he needed the weapon. He checked that the safety was off and that there was a round in the chamber. That was just about as far as his knowledge of automatic weapons extended. Fortunately the AK was a recent model, with a digital ammunition counter just below the rear sight. It read twenty-two, which looked good to Falcon. He stuffed the Fichetti back into his pocket, slipped the AK's sling over his head and right arm, and crawled to the north edge of the container.

There was a ladder on this side, too. The barrel of the assault rifle clanged against the container halfway down, and Falcon braced himself for some kind of impact. But nobody shot at him. When he was less than two meters from the ground, he jumped.

Forgetting, of course, about his bad ankle. He howled with agony as he hit, keeping his feet only with difficulty. Muffling his curses, he unslung the AK and looked around him.

The lane between the containers was dark. And—thank the spirits and totems—empty. He paused for a moment. What the frag do I do now? he asked himself.

A long burst of autofire, punctuated by a scream of mortal agony, answered the question for him. *Just get myself the frag out of here!* He looked around again, getting his bearings. Okay, he thought, the crane's to the west, so the way out is *that* way. He started off in a limping run. Reached an "intersection" where two lanes met, hung a hard right.

And skidded to a stop. The female runner—Sly—was a couple of meters ahead of him. As he rounded the corner, she'd dropped into a combat crouch. In her hands was the weapon she'd dropped in the killing ground—a brutal hogleg of a revolver. She held it steady in both hands, aiming it directly at Falcon's heart.

13

Another Amerind, Sly thought. Part of the same gang?
He had to be. Smaller than the others, but armed with a
fragging AK-97. Sly started to squeeze the trigger. The
laser sighting dot touched the center of the man's chest.

He didn't try to bring the assault rifle to bear. Instead
he held it in his left hand, pistoned both arms out to the
sides. "No!" he gasped. She tightened down on the trigger. Another couple of grams and the trigger would
break, sending a bullet slamming into his heart.

And that was when she realized just what she was seeing. He's a kid, she thought in astonishment. Big for his
age, but no older than sixteen, maybe seventeen. Old
enough to carry an AK, old enough to kill her. . . .

But he wasn't *trying* to kill her. She held her fire, emotions warring within her. The trigger was just a hair short
of breaking. There was no way she'd fail to get the shot
off before he could bring the AK onto line.

"No . . ." More of a moan this time.

She couldn't grease him, not like this. "Drop it!" she
screamed. "Drop it *now*!"

He dropped it. The assault rifle crashed to the ground.
In his eyes she saw terror, confusion, a whole suite of
other emotions.

Not a pro, then. And what did that mean? The Amerinds who'd faced her at the meet—the unarmored one and
his back-up—were cool, controlled. Pros, definitely pros.
The sniper up on the crane, him too. He almost got her

before someone else took him out. All pros, all experienced runners. Why would they have this greenie kid along with them on a run? If he was with them at all . . .

Frag it, what was she supposed to do now? What do you do with prisoners in a firefight? Damn it, this had never happened to her before. When the lead started to fly, you flatlined the bad guys and got the frag out. Anybody you didn't know to be a friend was a target, plain and simple.

But she couldn't bring herself to geek this kid. Not like this, not in what currently served for cold blood. If he made a move for another weapon, she could do it in an instant, no worries, no second thoughts, no guilt. But not now.

And she couldn't just leave him behind. He could have any number of holdouts, ready to put a slug into her skull the instant she turned away from him. Frag it!

Modal would drop him in his tracks, she knew, just to be sure. It was the only logical thing to do, and his violet pills would guarantee that no confusing emotions got in the way.

But *I'm not Modal,* Sly thought.

"Hands behind your head!" she shouted, her decision made. "Move it!"

The kid laced his fingers behind his head. There was a plea in his eyes, but he kept silent.

"Turn around," she told him. He obeyed instantly. "Look back and you're dead. Move your hands and you're dead. Now *move.*"

The kid started forward along the lane between the stacked containers. She saw that he was limping slightly, favoring his left leg. She rose from her combat crouch, her own left knee feeling like it was on fire. Great, two cripples. Club Gimp. She kept her pistol trained on him, her laser dot on the back of his neck. She started after him, keeping a good three meters back. Too far for him to be able to jump her before she could put a couple of rounds into him. When she reached the dropped AK, she crouched and scooped it up with her left hand, without letting her eyes or her laser sight waver from her prisoner. Quickly, before the kid could react, she shoved her Warhawk into her pocket, settled the AK against her hip. It had a laser sight, too. The assault rifle's targeting spot replaced her pistol's on the young Amerindian's back. With the weight of the AK in her hands, she felt confidence flooding back into her. Her knee hurt like drek, and the wound she'd taken in her left forearm from the sniper burned and dripped blood. But with the additional firepower she thought she had a better chance of getting out of this intact.

"Keep walking," she ordered.

They reached an intersection. "Stop!" The kid froze in his tracks, didn't look back, didn't shift his hands a millimeter. She hesitated for a moment, getting her bearings. Fortunately the crane made a good landmark. "Turn left," she instructed, "and move faster."

The kid picked up his pace down the new lane. From his limp, she new that the faster gait must be hurting him severely, but he didn't make a sound. She followed, keeping the three-meter separation constant.

Multiple firefights were still going on around her. She could hear the sporadic chattering of autofire from at least four directions, but nothing sounded near enough to worry about. Not for the moment. From the sound, she figured all the firing was coming from SMGs or maybe light carbines. Her armor jacket would stop SMG rounds at any reasonable range, but what about that monster weapon, whatever it was—the thing that had gutted the Amerindian razorguy? What the frag was it? And how *portable* was it? Could the gunner be stalking her right now? She felt the muscles of her back and belly tighten.

"Faster," she commanded. The kid obeyed without a

word, speeding up to a shambling run. The AK's sighting dot bounced around as she matched his pace, but it never left his back.

Another intersection. If she remembered correctly, the rendezvous spot she'd arranged with Modal should be to the left. Will Modal be there? she wondered. Or is he already down? Am I alone? One way or another, worrying about it wasn't going to help. You made a plan and stuck to it, changing it only when you knew it was hosed.

"Turn left," she snapped.

This new lane was narrower, the shadows deeper. She was moving away from the carbon arc lamps that illuminated the wharf area. The containers that made up the lane walls weren't jammed together nose-to-tail like they were closer to the cranes. That meant there were gaps between them, gaps easily big enough for a gunman to hide in. She scanned from side to side, but it was useless. The shadows were impenetrable. The first clue she'd get that a shooter was there was when the first rounds hit. "Faster," she shouted.

Where the frag was Modal?

A laser dazzled her left eye. She spun, trying to bring the AK around, knowing she'd never make it. She tensed for the hammering impact as the first bullet shattered her skull.

No impact. She continued her turn, about to clamp down on the assault rifle's trigger.

"It's Modal." The elf's voice sounded from the gap to her left. The laser painting her face died.

She released the trigger, lowered the AK's barrel to point at the ground.

Modal stepped out of the darkness. He had his Ares Predator in his left hand; a silenced Ingram SMG filled his right. "What's this?" He gestured at the Amerindian kid with the heavy pistol.

"Prisoner," she told him.

He scowled at that. She could tell what he thought of the idea.

"We take him with us," Sly said forcefully, her voice brooking no argument. "Maybe he can tell us what's gone down."

"*I* can tell you that," the elf grunted. "It's totally *fugazi*, that's what it is. There were four orks on the perimeter. I took one, borrowed his radio. Now they're fighting with somebody else. One group, maybe even two. They act corp." In his eyes were questions he obviously didn't want to voice just yet.

Sly knew she wanted answers to the same questions. "Maybe *he* can tell us," she suggested, inclining her head toward the kid. He was standing as still as if he'd been petrified, every muscle in his body rigid as they argued his fate behind his back.

Modal considered that for a moment, then nodded. "It's your call."

"Where's Mongoose and Snake?"

"I saw Snake go down. He's dead. Mongoose?" He shrugged.

"Then just get us the frag out of here," she told him. "I think the meet's adjourned."

Sly peeled back the protective cover of the slap patch, applied it to the bullet wound in her left forearm. The patch stung for an instant, the way it always did. Then the sting faded, taking with it the sharp, throbbing pain. Thank god for slap patches, she thought, pressing on it to make sure the adhesive held. Already she could taste the familiar flavor of olives as the DMSO—dimethyl sulfoxide—in the patch absorbed into her bloodstream, bringing with it the painkillers, energizers, and antibacterial agents that would start the healing process. She hated the taste in her mouth—always had—but she'd certainly gotten used to it over the years.

They were in the shadows of the Alaskan Way viaduct, about level with University Street. The Renraku Arcology separated them from Pier 42 and the fragged-up meet. Sly knew that it shouldn't make her feel any safer, because Renraku was after her too, but it did.

She glanced at her watch. It was oh-four-twenty—only twenty minutes after the meet was supposed to have started. Busy morning, she told herself with a wry grin.

Modal was crouching in the shadows next to her. The kid—now wearing a set of plastic restraints, courtesy of the elf—huddled against a concrete pillar a couple of meters away. Modal was examining the Fichetti Security 500 he'd taken from the kid's pocket.

"Good piece for a gutterpunk," the elf remarked to Sly, slipping the gun into his own pocket.

She knew that Modal was actually saying the boy wasn't as innocent as he looked, but decided to ignore him. For the first time since they got to the viaduct, she spoke *to* the kid, not *about* him. "What's your name?"

"Dennis Falk," the kid answered. "Falcon."

She looked at his leather jacket. No gang colors, but something about him told her he had to be a ganger. "Who do you run with?"

"First Nation," he mumbled.

That made sense. The First Nation was a low-level Amerind gang that claimed the dock area near the Kingdome. Was that how he'd come to be at Pier 42? Out on gang biz and he stumbled into the meet from hell? "What were you doing at the pier tonight?" she asked. "And where did you get this?" She patted the assault rifle that rested across her knees.

He looked up into her face, his dark eyes steady. The terror was gone, replaced now by intelligence. He was trying to figure out just what, and how much, to tell her.

"Don't lie to me," she said quietly. "Remember, you don't know how much I know. And if you do lie, I might decide that Modal here is right about what to do with prisoners." Playing along with the game, Modal bared his teeth at the kid in a feral smile.

Good cop, bad cop. It always worked. She saw the potential resistance vanish from Falcon's eyes. "What were you doing there?" she repeated.

"I came with *them*," he muttered. "The Amerindian runners."

Modal shot her a sharp look. So he *is* an enemy after all, Sly thought. She saw Modal slip his finger onto the trigger of the kid's own Fichetti.

The kid was still talking. "I found out it was a setup. It was never a meet, it was always an ambush. But I couldn't do anything about it, they'd have geeked me."

"Hold the phone," Sly said, more to Modal than the kid. Looking a little disappointed, the elf lowered the Fichetti. "Get your story straight here. What—exactly— is your connection with the Amerinds who set me up?"

Falcon launched into a weird, scattered story about meeting a wounded Amerindian shadowrunner, helping him get to a rendezvous with his chummers after a hosed run. When the runner croaked, the kid had thrown in his lot with the others to make sure that the dead runner's last wishes were carried out. Or something.

Modal caught her eye, shook his head. The story didn't sound credible. People didn't get involved in major shadowruns just because some stranger flatlined in their arms.

No, that wasn't necessarily true. *Kids* might. Kids whose only ideas about shadowrunning came from the trid or from simsense. She looked into Falcon's eyes again. She thought he was telling the truth.

The kid still hadn't finished. "The meet was an ambush from the start," he repeated. "Then the drek hit the fan, and the runner 'bodyguarding' me thought I'd sold them out. He was going to geek me. So I shot him and took his AK. Then I just wanted to bug out. I was heading for the fence when I met you.''

That hung together too, Sly thought. When she'd first seen the kid, he didn't seem comfortable or familiar with the assault rifle, as though he'd just picked it up a few seconds before.

''So just what happened when the meet crashed?'' she asked.

Falcon shrugged. ''First thing I knew, something blew the drek out of Benbo.'' (That had to be the heavily armored samurai guarding the leader.) ''Slick thought it was something you'd set up, but I saw your face when Benbo keeled. You were as surprised as anyone.'' He hesitated, then asked, ''What the frag was that? Magic?''

''I think I got it figured,'' Modal answered. ''It took me a while, Sly, you ever hear of a Barret?''

She thought for a moment, shook her head.

''It's old,'' the elf continued, ''maybe nineteen-eighties or nineties. But it's the ultimate sniper rifle.

''It's a *big* thing. Bolt action, single-shot. But it's chambered for fifty-caliber rounds. Bloody fifty-cal *machine gun* rounds, mate. It'll take any standard MG ammunition—military ball, tracer, explosive, SLAP, APDS, white phosphorous—and it's accurate at a klick and a half. A good sniper can squeeze off three shots before the first hits.''

She remembered seeing the gaping hole blasted right through the Amerindian samurai. She shuddered. ''Fifty-cal explosive rounds . . .''

''I don't think those were explosives,'' Modal corrected. ''More like APDS tipped with depleted uranium. The ultimate anti-armor round. The slug hits anything solid—like armor—and the kinetic energy pushes the uranium over the activation threshold. It catches fire, and it

burns at more than two thousand degrees Celsius.'' He
grinned nastily. ''Enough to bloody well ruin the day of
any street sammy, if you ask me.''

In her imagination, Sly could still see the fireball burning in the Amerindian's chest before it burst out of his
back. ''That's serious drek,'' she murmured. With an
effort she turned her attention back to Falcon. ''So who
was it took out your chummers?''

''They're not my chummers,'' he corrected her quietly. Then he shook his head. ''I don't know.''

''Corp teams,'' Modal put in. ''Like I said.''

''Let's get back to the Amerindians,'' Sly suggested.
''I don't suppose they told you why they were after me.''

''Sure,'' Falcon said, nodding his head vigorously.
''Nightwalker told me. Lost tech, from the crash.''

Sly and Modal exchanged glances. She hesitated, afraid
to ask the next question—the *key* question. ''Did he say
what lost tech?'' she inquired slowly.

''Sure,'' the kid repeated. ''Fiber optics.''

The kid continued to explain for several minutes. When
he was finished, Sly found herself just staring at him.
Shocked. Tox, she thought. No wonder the corps are going to war. The ability to tap into a competitor's suppos-
edly secure communications. More than that, to *change*
the flow of data. She knew how prevalent was fiber-optic
communication. *Everything* used it. The LTG system, the
Matrix. Dedicated corporate and government datalines,
too, because light lines were supposed to be immune to
tapping. Even *military* channels, for frag's sake, because
fiber optics would be unaffected by the electromagnetic
pulse if anyone set off a nuke in the upper atmosphere.

How many *trillions* of nuyen had been invested in this
''ultra-secure'' technology? There was no way that the
megacorps, the governments, could switch everything to

another medium of communication, not immediately. And during the transition phase, whoever had the technology Falcon described could quite literally control *every facet* of a competitor's communications. To gain that kind of advantage—or to avoid that kind of *dis*advantage—the corps would do anything. Even go to war.

She looked over at Modal. He understood the enormity of it, too. She could see it in his eyes. "Jesus," he breathed. "Sharon Louise . . ."

"I know." She stared at Falcon for a few more moments. The kid met her gaze steadily.

"I want to work with you," he said at last. He was obviously trying to keep the fear and tension out of his voice, but wasn't doing a very good job.

Modal snorted. Sly ignored the elf. "Why?" she asked.

"Nightwalker wanted to do the right thing with the information when he got it," the kid explained. "He wanted to destroy it so nobody could use it. He wanted to rat the corp that was doing it to the Corporate Court in Zurich-Orbital.

"I think Knife-Edge had other ideas," Falcon went on. "I think he wanted to keep it for himself. Use it himself, maybe, or sell it to the highest bidder." He shook his head. "Nightwalker didn't want that.

"You've got the information," he said quietly. "What are you planning to do with it?"

And that was the big question, wasn't it? Sly thought. Destroying the encrypted file and all the information it contained—that was obviously the best choice on the global scale. But on the *personal* level it was no answer at all. *She'd* know she'd destroyed the file, but how would the corps know? I could tell them, and *of course* they'd believe me, yeah, right. No, with a prize this important, even the slightest chance—no matter how remote—that she hadn't destroyed the file, that she'd kept a copy, and the corps would stay on her trail. Eventually they'd grab her and torture her to death to confirm to their own satisfaction she was telling the truth. And even if they *did* believe she'd destroyed it, they'd *still* keep after her for much the same reason. When suitably "motivated," maybe she could remember some details from the file that might let them steal a march on their competitors.

No, destroying the file wasn't the obvious solution it seemed.

"What are you going to do?" Falcon asked again.

"I don't know," she admitted. "I haven't found the answer yet."

"I want to help you find it."

Modal snorted again. Again Sly ignored him. "Why? It's not your fight."

Watching the kid's face, she could see the real answer that was ringing in his head. Because his friend Nightwalker would have wanted it this way. Fuzzy-headed, sentimental, over-emotional drek!

At least the kid didn't say it out loud. He shrugged. "Because it's important," he said slowly. "And because you'll need all the help you can get."

A laser painted the side of Falcon's face. Modal had the Fichetti raised, ready to blow the kid's head off.

"No, Modal," she snapped, forcing the whip-crack of command into her voice.

He didn't lower the gun, but neither did he pull the trigger. "He's a liability, Sly," the elf said emotionlessly.

"No. I'm an *asset*." The kid jumped on the last word like it had some real significance to him.

And Sly had to agree with him. "Leave him," she said quietly to Modal. "Until I say otherwise, he's with us."

"You're making a mistake."

"It's mine to make."

"Not if it gets me scragged, too," Modal said. But he

lowered the pistol, slipped it into his pocket.

That was one advantage of the pills, Sly had to admit.
No bulldrek male ego, no worry about saving face. "I
want to get out of here," she said. "We need wheels.
Modal, can you boost us a car?"

Driving the stolen Westwind back to the Sheraton, Modal groused about leaving his bike behind, but Sly knew
he was just blowing off steam. He understood as well as
she did that going back to pick up the bikes would be too
much of a risk. She'd wondered idly whether Mongoose
had ever made it out of the killing zone. She'd have to
call Argent when she got a chance to update him on what
went down. And to tell him that at least one of his boys
wasn't coming home.

The kid who called himself Falcon had ridden in the
back with her. Grudgingly, Modal had followed Sly's instructions and cut off the restraints, but only after sub-
jecting the Amerindian to something only one step away
from a strip search.

Now the car was abandoned in the underground par-
kade of the Washington Athletic Club, across the street
from the Sheraton, with the AK-97 in the trunk. Modal
had bitched about that, too, but hadn't had an answer
when Sly asked him how he expected to smuggle the
assault rifle into the hotel. He knew as well as she did
that the Sheraton's weapons detectors would pick up their
handguns, Modal's Ingram. As in most better-class hotels, the security personnel would simply have recorded
that the guests in rooms 1203 and 1205 were carrying
"personal defense devices." But the matter wouldn't be
so routine if the electronics suite were to pick up the AK
concealed under somebody's coat.

The clock on the bedside table of room 1205 read oh-
four-fifty-one. Only two hours since they'd left the hotel
for the meet. It felt more like days.

The kid, Falcon, flopped down in an armchair. In the brighter light, he looked younger than she'd originally thought, no older than fifteen. And he looked tired, like he hadn't slept in days. His face was pinched, his olive complexion pale.

"You want to crash out?" she asked. "Use the bed in the other room."

He nodded, then asked hesitantly, "Is there anything to eat?"

She glanced over at Modal. "Why don't you call room service?" she suggested. "Get some food up here for all of us. I've got to make a call."

She could see that Modal wanted to argue—he obviously still thought the kid was a liability—but he held his tongue. She shrugged. As the elf had said, keeping the kid with them was her mistake to make. Despite his misgivings he was going along with her.

She sat down on the bed of room 1203, keyed in Agarwal's LTG number.

"Have you seen the news?" was the ex-decker's first question when he answered the phone and saw who it was.

"Not really." Modal had turned on the radio in the stolen car, but Sly hadn't really given the news report much attention. She wracked her brain, trying to remember what the significant stories had been. Gang clashes, random street violence . . . But what had Argent said? The gangs *weren't* involved, and the violence was neither random nor unmotivated. She felt cold. "It's starting, isn't it?" she asked Agarwal.

Agarwal didn't answer her question directly, but his serious expression was communication enough. "As of about five minutes ago," he said quietly, "there have been no more reports of anything that could be corporate violence in the news media. *And* any descriptions of such events in the current affairs databases were erased. What does that tell you, Sharon?''

A lot. Fear twisted within her, but she forced a chuckle. "I guess it doesn't mean it's all over, huh?"

"What it tells *me*," Agarwal went on, as though she hadn't spoken, "is that the metroplex government—possibly backed by the federal bureaucracy—has issued a 'D Notice', an official gag order. Add to that the fact that just before your call, a voice-only announcement from Governor Schultz was broadcast on all trid and radio channels, and posted in all datafaxes and newsbases." He snorted. "At five to five in the morning, I assume the voice was synthesized. The illustrious governor is rarely known to rise before ten."

"What did Schultz say?" Sly asked.

"That all of the untoward gang and street violence has come to an end," Agarwal said bleakly. "That the government has stepped in. That everything is back to normal, and that no citizen of the metroplex should fear for his or her safety." He snorted again. "As if the government could guarantee that in a corporate war." He shook his head. "All members of government are liars. They are consummate liars, they lie continuously. *They* know that *we* know that they lie, but they lie just the same. And then they talk about their *honor*."

The ex-decker chuckled wryly. "Forgive me my political digressions." He sighed. "I blush to inform you I have yet to break the file completely."

"I don't know that it matters so much anymore," she admitted. "You were right, it's lost tech. And now I know exactly what." As efficiently as possible, she briefed him on what Falcon had told her.

When she was finished, Agarwal looked pale, shaken. "So the Concord of Zurich-Orbital is about to collapse?"

She shrugged. "It didn't seem to do much good," she

said. "Yamatetsu was still working counter to it, and I guess the rest of the corps were too."

"Yes, yes," Agarwal brushed that off. "But there is more to the Concord than just the matter of fiber optics, Sharon. Much more. It is perhaps the most wide-ranging agreement the megacorporations have ever entered into with each other.

"The Concord has provisions covering most facets of communications technology," he went on. "You know that most of the *zaibatsus* have their own satellites, communication and otherwise? Well, many of those satellites are thought to have sophisticated jamming circuits, or even anti-satellite—ASAT—capability, to destroy the communication assets of a competitor. Similarly, many megacorporations still carry out research into 'core wars'—which, as I mentioned to you earlier, is viral warfare against a competitor's computer systems.

"Of course, if any corporation were to use any of these capabilities—jamming, ASAT, or viral—there would be reprisals. Followed by counter-reprisals, followed by escalation. Followed by a level of—shall we say—'digital bloodletting' that no corporation would wish to even contemplate.

"*That* is the importance of the Concord, Sharon," Agarwal concluded, "to prevent that. And it has worked, for more than twenty years. In 2041, an Atlanta-based corporation called Lanrie—a small player, its influence limited to the Confederated American States—infected a competitor in Miami with a tailored computer virus. Somehow the major *zaibatsus* found out about it. Under the terms of the Concord of Zurich-Orbital, and with the sanction of the Corporate Court, the megacorporations totally destroyed Lanrie. Shattered its financial structure. Destroyed its facilities and assets. Executed its Board of Directors. All as an object lesson. Since then nobody has actually practiced viral warfare."

Sly was shaken to the core. Her skin felt as cold as if an icy draft were blowing through the room. "And the corps are ready to break the Concord?"

Agarwal nodded. "The Corporate Court is trying to call them back," he explained, "like hunting dogs to heel. To remind them of the Concord, no doubt, and its importance. But—as I told you the last time we talked—the *zaibatsus* are ignoring the Court's edicts. The potential benefits of the prize—the lost technology—outweigh the potential dangers of breaking the Concord. Or so the megacorporations see it."

She thought it through for a few moments. "Have they crossed the line yet?" she asked. "Has anybody passed the point of no return?"

"Not yet. But all are perilously close to the line. The situation is more unstable than ever before."

"Can it be stabilized again?"

"Up to the point that one megacorporation makes a substantive, direct attack against significant assets of another," Agarwal pronounced, "yes."

"How?"

He fixed her with his tired eyes. "If we assume that the corporations remain on the precipice, and don't go over before you can act," he said slowly, "I think it all rests in your hands. In how you deal with the information you hold.

"The way I see it," he continued, "you have two choices. The first is to destroy the information."

That suggestion wasn't new; she'd already considered it and discarded it. "It won't work," she told Agarwal. "Nobody would *believe* I'd destroyed it."

"As you say," he agreed.

"And the second choice?"

"If you can't make sure that *nobody* gets the information," he said, "then make sure *everybody* gets it. Disseminate it, publicize it, so that every megacorpora-

tion has equal access to the information. The only answer
is to keep the playing field level and to make sure everyone *knows* it's level. When one corporation, or faction of
corporations, has an advantage—or is *thought* to have an
advantage—*then* things are unstable. Do you understand,
Sharon?''

She nodded slowly. In concept, it made perfect sense,
it was simple. But . . . "How?" she demanded.

He spread his hands eloquently. *Search me* . . .

"And what if I don't manage it?"

"Corporate war," Agarwal stated positively. "The
collapse of the world's economy within a few days of its
start. The first food riots probably wouldn't occur for at
least a week. The big question is whether civilian governments would have time to launch military action before they collapsed. I think any nuclear exchange would
probably be quite limited. . . .''

He kept talking, but Sly had stopped listening.

What the frag am I going to do? she asked herself
again and again.

14

0515 hours, November 14, 2053

Falcon ate like a starving man, which was exactly what
he was. The woman, Sly, had said to get enough food to
feed them all. The black elf—Modal, Falcon thought his
name was—had gone a little overboard. Three burgers—
real beef, not soy filler—pasta salad, bread, cheese, salad
. . . more food for the three of them than Falcon would
have picked out for six of his gang chummers. He scoped

out the hotel room. Of course, anybody who could afford
this kind of doss wasn't going to skimp on food.

No skin off my butt anyway, he thought, and no cred
off my stick. With that established, he set to with a will.

By the time he'd polished off a burger, two cheese
sandwiches, an apple, and some strange star-shaped fruit
he didn't recognize, Falcon was starting to feel a little
better. Modal was sprawled on the bed watching him.
The elf had polished off his own burger quick enough,
and now he was sucking on a beer he'd pulled from the
room's minibar.

Thinking that a beer would go down just wiz, Falcon
glanced at the elf, at the beer in his hand, raised an eyebrow questioningly. Modal's expression and body language didn't change. He'd still rather see me flatlined,
Falcon thought. Which means he's not likely to offer me
a drink. He hesitated, then crossed to the minibar and
fished out his own beer. An import, he saw, in a real
glass bottle. Modal was scowling fiercely, but at least he
hadn't shot him. Falcon twisted off the top, sprawled back
in his chair, and gave the brew the attention it deserved.

A few minutes later, the door to the adjoining room
swung open. Falcon had heard Sly carrying on a phone
conversation, but the door's sound insulation was enough
to keep him from making out any of her words. It must
have been bad news, he thought. She looked like hell,
face pinched and white, eyes haunted.

Modal sat up, put his beer down. "Bad news?" he
asked in his weird accent.

Sly nodded, slumped down on the bed next to the elf.
Modal handed over his can of beer. The dark-haired
woman took a healthy pull on it, smiled her thanks.

"Things are definitely . . . what you said earlier, fugazi," she told the elf. Then she interrupted herself.
"What does that mean, anyway?"

"Totally fragged up," the elf explained. "It's slang from the Smoke." He paused. "It's happening?"

"Looks like it," Sly admitted unwillingly, then went on to discuss something about the Concord of Zurich-Orbital. Apparently there was more to it than Nightwalker had told Falcon—or perhaps more than Nightwalker had *known*. The young ganger didn't understand all the strange corporate maneuvering and backstabbing Sly described, but he *did* understand the bottom line. It's like the gangs, he thought. As long as a truce benefits everyone, there's peace. But when somebody sees an advantage, there's a turf war. Apparently the megacorps worked on the same principle, and were now readying for their own kind of war. Though he couldn't see how a corp war could hurt him personally—or the two runners, either—their sour expressions told him they thought it was serious drek. And they understand this high-level stuff better than I do, he had to remind himself.

"So what did the man suggest?" Modal asked.

"Nothing concrete," Sly said. "Good concepts, but no suggestions about what to *do*."

"I've got a suggestion if you want to hear it," the elf put in. "Just get on your fragging bike and go. Hit the Caribbean League or anywhere else that strikes your fancy." He shrugged. "Okay, I know you don't have the credit to come into the light completely, but why not take your retirement in bloody installments? Let the corps bugger each other blind, and serves them right. When everything's settled down, you can get back into the biz.

"I'm bloody serious," he pressed, as Sly shook her head. "Just toddle off into the sunset. It's better than getting splattered—which is what'll happen if you stick around; you know that, Sly. Travel light, get rid of all liabilities"—the elf glared at Falcon, and the young Amerindian knew exactly what he was getting at—"and *go*."

Sly was silent for a moment. Watching her eyes, Fal-

con could almost see the thoughts moving behind them
as she considered Modal's suggestions. "Maybe," she
mused softly.

A knock sounded on the door. "Room service," came
a muffled voice from the hallway.

At the first sound, guns had almost magically appeared
in the hands of both runners. Now Falcon saw them both
relax.

"Probably come to collect the plates," Modal said.
He slipped his pistol back into its holster, then smoothly
swung to his feet and headed for the door.

Danger.

Who said that? For a moment, Falcon glanced around
looking to see who had spoken. The voice had been so
clear. . . .

But it hadn't been a woman's voice, and it hadn't been
the elf's strange accent. It sounded more like . . .

My voice? An icy chill shot up Falcon's spine.

Modal was almost at the door.

Shockingly, for just a split instant, Falcon's ears
seemed to ring with the crash of gunshots, the echo of
screams. When neither of the others reacted, he realized
the sounds were only in his mind.

Modal reached for the door handle.

"No!" Falcon shouted.

The elf froze, turned and glared at him.

"No," the ganger said, trying to fill his voice with a
control he didn't feel. "Don't answer it. It's a setup."
As he spoke the words—and *only* then—he knew them to
be the truth.

"Oh?" The elf's voice dripped with scorn. "And just
how the bloody hell do you know that, eh?"

Falcon couldn't say, except that he *did* know. The
knock on the door sounded again, sharper, more insis-
tent.

And accompanied by another sound—a sharp click of

metal on metal. At first Falcon thought that was in his head as well, but then he saw Modal tense.

"Bloody hell, he might be right." The massive pistol was back in the elf's hand. He looked around him, apparently sizing up the tactical situation. "Get into the other room," he ordered quietly.

Falcon had already come to the same conclusion, and was heading for the connecting door. Sly joined him in the second room, followed by Modal. The elf partially closed the connecting door, leaving a tiny gap. The two runners had their weapons at the ready. Falcon felt helpless, vulnerable, wishing for his Fichetti or even his old zip gun. Give me *something*.

"Do they know about the two rooms?" Sly asked quietly.

Modal shrugged. "We'll know in a minute." He put his back against the connecting wall, so he could watch the front door to this room *and* clearly hear what was happening next door. Falcon heard the metallic snicks as both runners flicked the safeties off their weapons. Then they waited.

Not for long. Another sharp rap on the door of room 1205. A few more moments of silence.

Then all drek broke loose. Somebody or something smashed into the door, tearing it off its hinges. Falcon heard the muted spits of silenced gunfire, then the dull crump of an explosion that shook the wall. Holy frag, he thought, a grenade!

Silence again. The raiders next door would know that the room was empty; their prey wasn't there. How would they respond?

Sly and Modal didn't give them time. "Cover," the woman whispered, as she sprinted toward the door to the hallway. Modal nodded, edged closer to the door connecting the two rooms. Falcon could see the strategy. Sly would hit them from behind, from the hallway, while

Modal came at them from the front. Make them pay for their mistake, their ignorance about the two rooms.

But what the frag do *I* do? he thought blankly. Unarmed, without so much as a knife . . .

He didn't have long to worry about it. Sly silently opened the door, slipped into the hall. A moment later, Falcon heard her heavy pistol crash.

On cue, Modal kicked open the connecting door, spun—inhumanly fast—around the frame, his heavy pistol already roaring and bucking in his hand. Falcon heard a scream of agony, a scream that trailed off into a moan, and then a gurgle. Score one kill.

A burst of autofire chewed into the door and the frame. But Modal wasn't there anymore. His chipped reflexes had flung him aside, darting into the cover of a heavy armchair. More screams as his pistol spat flame again. And then he was out of Falcon's field of view.

The firefight continued, but there wasn't anything he could do to help the runners. A wild burst of fire stitched through the connecting wall, smashing the trideo set. He threw himself to the floor, then crawled toward the connecting door. He couldn't stand not knowing what was going on, even if taking a look might cost him his life. He poked his head around the door frame.

Room 1205 looked like it had been decorated in Early War Zone, the grenade having blown the drek out of everything. Small fires were burning where hot shrapnel had lodged in flammable material, and Modal and the others were making short work of whatever had survived the blast. Near the connecting door one of the attackers was down, and decidedly dead. He wore what looked like a high-tone corp suit, probably armored, though it hadn't done him any good. Modal's bullets had blown away most of his head. The figure still clutched a tiny, lethal-looking machine pistol in its lifeless hand.

There was matching carnage in the rest of the room.

Three more attackers—a man and two women, all wearing corp fashions—were sprawled here and there, in various states of disassembly. Blood and tissue were everywhere, and the room smelled like a slaughterhouse. Falcon swallowed hard, trying to keep his stomach where it belonged.

Modal was in the doorway, firing out into the hall. Probably taking out stragglers, Falcon surmised. The elf's lips were drawn back from his teeth in what looked like a smile of inhuman glee.

He'll kill me, too. The thought struck Falcon with an impact like a bullet-train. *He thinks I'm a liability, he's said it often enough. He wants to get rid of me.*

And what better time than now? One shot, and all Modal had to tell the woman was that Falcon had stopped a round fired by one of the attackers. No more liability. No more Dennis Falk.

The young ganger looked at the machine pistol in the hand of the nearest corpse. *It works both ways,* he thought fiercely. *I can kill him before he kills me, and blame it on the raiders.*

If he was going to do it, he had to do it *fast*. The sounds of the firefight were dying down in the hall outside. He pried the dead man's fingers from the weapon. Rose to a crouch, leveled the weapon at the elf's back. Started to squeeze the trigger, then froze in mid-movement.

What was he doing? He wasn't a murderer. Sure, he'd killed—first the slag in Denny Park, then Slick at Pier 42. But both of them had been trying to kill *him*. It had been pure self-defense, him or them. But now? He couldn't shoot Modal in the back. He couldn't.

He lowered the gun.

Modal turned, as if sensing something behind him. Looked back over his shoulder.

Falcon had the machine pistol still gripped in both hands, the barrel pointing at the floor behind the elf.

Their eyes met for a moment.

And Falcon knew—*knew*, beyond a shadow of a doubt—that Modal realized what had almost happened. For a moment the elf stood, stock-still. Then his lips twisted in a wry half-smile.

"Let's get the frag out of here," he said. "And bring your toy along."

15

0531 hours, November 14, 2053

"Who the hell *were* they?" Sly said.

They were driving along in another car, one stolen from the Sheraton's underground parking lot. They'd sprinted down the fire stairs from the twelfth floor before the hotel's security response—probably massive, considering the mayhem that had broken loose—could arrive on the scene. Modal wanted to grab the same car they'd had earlier (his Ingram and the AK-97 were still in the trunk) but Sly convinced him that risking the security in the Washington Athletic Club garage was too much of a gamble. Besides, the Sheraton lot was such easy pickings that it took him only a minute to bust into and hot-wire the ignition of a sleek Saab Dynamit. Now they were cruising south on I-5, out of the downtown core.

"Who?" Sly asked again.

Modal pulled something out of his pocket, tossed it into her lap. "Here," he said, "the previous owner doesn't need it anymore."

Sly flipped on the map light, examined the item. It was a synthleather wallet that was once light tan but now was stained dark with its owner's blood. She flipped it open, glanced through the contents. Laminated hard-copy printouts of the personal drek found on anybody's credstick—driver's license, DocWagon contract, gun license, etcetera drek etcetera—all in the name of Lisa Steinbergen. Probably an alias, Sly thought.

But then she found something that changed her mind. A corporate ID card, with a small holo showing a petite redhead about Sly's own age. (She remembered spotting the small woman, seeing her go down as one of Modal's shots punched through her throat.) If the name on that card was not an alias, what did that mean?

She put that thought aside for later consideration. In the upper-left corner of the card was a full-color holo of a corporate logo—a stylized Y.

"Yamatetsu," she said flatly.

"I knew they were corp," Modal remarked. "I guess they expected to take us without any problem."

Sly nodded. Why else carry your ID to a job?

Unless it was some kind of trick to make them *think* it was Yamatetsu, when it was actually someone else. . . .

But that didn't hold together. For the theory to make sense, the bosses who'd sent the team would have expected Sly and her chummers to dice up the hitters. By all rights, she, Modal, and the Amerindian kid should be either dead or captured. The corp team had come in smart. Sure, they'd made one big mistake—they didn't know that Sly and crew had two rooms—but even so, it had been a close call. If not for the kid . . .

She glanced back over her shoulder. Falcon was sitting in the back seat of the Dynamit. Lost in his thoughts, he hadn't said a word since they left the Sheraton.

It surprised her to see him toying idly with the machine pistol he'd taken from one of the dead hit men. She didn't know why Modal had let the Amerindian keep the weapon. Then again, there was some kind of weird dynamic going on between the elf and the kid, something she didn't understand.

"How did you know?" she asked.

Falcon looked up, startled. "Huh?"

"How did you *know*?" Sly repeated. "We'd have opened the door. We'd have got ourselves scragged but good. You knew it was a setup. How?"

The ganger didn't answer right away. Sly saw his eyes go blank as he retreated back into memory. "I don't know," he said at last.

"You heard something?" she pressed. "Saw something?"

He started to shake his head, then hesitated.

"You heard something?" she repeated.

"I heard . . ." His voice trailed off.

"You heard what?"

"Nothing." Those sharp black eyes were seeing something, something that confused him or scared him. But she knew right then that he wasn't going to talk to her about it. Not now, maybe not ever.

She shrugged. "You saved our lives," she said. "You've got our thanks for that." She let him sink back into his silent study, turned to face the front again. There was little traffic on I-5. That would change in the next half-hour, but for the moment the roads were as clear as they ever got.

But to take advantage of clear roads, she thought, you've got to know where you're going.

As if overhearing her thoughts, Modal spoke up. "So, what now?"

"I don't know," she confessed. "I've got to do *something.*"

"Why not do what I suggested?" the elf said. "Drop

out of sight. Slip the border, and just keep your head down till the drek stops flying.''

It was an attractive idea, but . . . She shook her head. ''I can't.''

''Why the frag not?'' he demanded. ''Because of the bloody corp war?'' He snorted. ''Who named you as responsible for the whole bloody world? And anyway, what good can you do if you get the chop?''

She sighed. ''That's part of it,'' she admitted, ''but just a small part. You say I should take my retirement in installments, right? Well, what kind of retirement is running for my life? Knowing that every fragging megacorp in Seattle—and the rest of the world as well—wants to wring my brain out? No matter how low a profile I keep, no matter how good my security, how soon before *somebody* scores? What are the odds I'll last a month? Two months? A year? Sooner or later my luck will just run out.'' She shook her head. ''I couldn't handle just *waiting* for it. Could you?''

Sly could see Modal still wanted to argue, but he didn't have a logical comeback. He drove in silence for a few minutes. Then, ''So what did the toff have to say?'' he asked. ''Argybargy, or whoever?''

''Agarwal.''

''Whoever.''

''He said I've got two choices,'' Sly explained. ''One is to destroy the file—''

''Sounds good to me,'' Modal cut in.

''—and *prove* to everyone that I destroyed it,'' she finished. ''Doesn't sound so good anymore, does it?''

''Not bloody likely,'' the elf conceded. ''How do you *prove* something like that? What's the second choice?''

''Disseminate it, make sure *everyone* gets the information. That way nobody gets an advantage. There's nothing to go to war about and no percentage in scragging us.''

Modal nodded slowly as he thought it over. "I like that one better," he mused. "Did he say how?"

She shook her head. "Any ideas?" she asked him with a wry smile.

"Hmmm." Again Modal was silent for a time. "You've got to make sure everyone gets the data at the same time," he said finally, thinking out loud. "If you tell corp A before you tell corp B, it's a bloody certainty corp A will try to geek you before you can tell anybody else.

"And there's something else," he added pensively. "It's like destroying the file: you have to make sure everyone *knows* what you've done. Every corp has to know that all the rest got the same paydata, right? That's the only way to persuade them there's no margin in coming after you."

"You're saying I can't do it privately," Sly pointed out. "My only choice is to do it openly, publicly."

"I guess that's what I'm saying." Modal paused. "So that answers your question, doesn't it? You've got to *post* the data. Post it publicly, on some kind of electronic bulletin board system. A BBS."

A BBS. Yes, that was logical. "But *which* BBS?" she asked. "All the big ones are owned, directly or indirectly, by some megacorp. As soon as I post something like this—assuming I can even log on—the system operator's going to snatch the data and erase my posting. It'll be like giving the data directly to one corporation, the one that owns the BBS."

"What about Shadowland?" Modal asked.

Shadowland. That was the name of the most famous clearinghouse for "black" or "shadow" information in North America. Its services included bulletin boards that contained the most astounding variety of dirt on governments, corps, and individuals (some of it even true); on-line, real-time "conferences" where deckers and others argued over just about *anything;* "virtual" meeting places where deckers could conduct business safely; and much more. The governments of North America—particularly the more secretive ones like the Pueblo Corporate Council and Tir Tairngire—hated Shadowland with a passion, as did the megacorps. The shadows were full of rumors concerning attempts to compromise or crash the system. According to conventional wisdom, the only reason that Shadowland still existed was that its central data core—its hub, known as the Denver Data Haven—was located somewhere in the contested territory of Denver. So edgy were all the governments that had divided up the city under the Treaty of Denver that none could organize a campaign to ferret out and eliminate the Shadowland service. From that standpoint, Modal's suggestion made a lot of sense. *But* . . .

"But what corp runs Shadowland?" she asked.

"Huh?" Modal grunted in shock. "Shadowland's independent, everyone knows that."

"Sometimes I get suspicious about things that 'everyone knows,' " Sly said quietly. "What *is* Shadowland? It covers the continent, right? Headquarters in the Denver Data Haven—wherever the frag *that* is—but it's got local 'floating' servers in every major city in North America. Right?" Modal nodded, troubled. "And all those servers connect back to the Denver hub, right?"

"What are you getting at?" Despite his emotion-deadening drugs, Modal sounded surly, as though Sly's questions were starting to undermine some cherished belief. And maybe that's just what I'm doing, Sly realized.

"Nobody's ever compromised those data channels. Isn't that what everybody says? Nobody's ever found the links between the floating servers and the hub; nobody's ever broken them. No government, no corp." She could hear the intensity in her own voice, recognized that the ideas she was pursuing disturbed *her* as much as they did

Modal. "Secure channels—that many of them, and that secure . . . Doesn't that require one frag of a lot of resources for a scroffy bunch of shadowrunners?"

Modal didn't answer at once. But when he did, his voice was totally under control, its usual emotionless self. "So what are you saying?" he asked.

"I'm asking, who runs Shadowland? Wouldn't controlling it secretly be a real coup for some megacorp? Total control over one of the biggest communication resources for the shadow community in North America. And, who knows, maybe even the rest of the world. The corp can monitor *everything* that's going on out of the light. It can spread whatever information—or *dis*information—it wants. It can eliminate speculations that harm its interests. It can manipulate every fragging shadowrunner who depends on Shadowland for *anything*."

Modal whistled tunelessly. "That is one twisted bloody concept, mate," he said at last. "Do you really believe it?"

She shrugged. "I don't know," she admitted. "But it makes sense, doesn't it?"

"Too *much* bloody sense," Modal agreed.

"And even if I'm wrong," Sly went on, pursuing the logic to its conclusion, "I still don't think I can trust the data to Shadowland. So far, nobody's crashed the Shadowland hub, mainly because it hasn't been worth the cost to do it. But now . . . Do you see what I'm getting at?"

Grudgingly, Modal nodded. "Now that we're looking at a corp war, all bets are off."

"Let's say Mitsuhama's the first corp to spot the posting on Shadowland," Sly said. "They download the data . . . and suddenly it's in their best interest to make sure nobody else gets it—*no matter what the cost*. They've got to take down Shadowland. So what if they have to use up ninety percent of their private army and blow up half of Denver to do it. If it guarantees they're the only ones with the lost tech, it's all worthwhile, isn't it?''

''It wouldn't be that easy . . .''

''Wouldn't it?'' Sly demanded. ''Shadowland has serious resources, but compared to the entire, worldwide resources of Mitsuhama Computer Technologies? And its subsidiaries? *And* whatever other companies it's got its hooks into? Come on.''

''All right,'' the elf conceded after a few more klicks had hummed under the Dynamit's wheels. ''Shadowland's out. So what else? I still think the BBS is the only way to go. So pick a private BBS with the clout to fight off a major megacorp.''

''Yeah, right,'' Sly snorted.

''I don't know,'' Modal mused. ''What about a government system? Mitsuhama's tough, but I'd like to see them try to scrap it out with the UCAS government.''

''The governments want the lost tech, too.''

''Huh?'' That shocked Modal, she could see.

''Why not?'' She repeated what Agarwal had told her about the federal teams operating in the sprawl.

When she was finished, he sighed. ''Every time we turn around, the bloody box is smaller. So the governments are out. What about systems that the megacorps wouldn't want to crash, for their own reasons?''

''What reasons?'' Sly demanded. ''Name one.''

''The Zurich-Orbital Gemeinschaft Bank.'' The voice came from the back seat.

Sly turned, stared at the kid who called himself Falcon. No longer lost in his own thoughts, apparently he'd been listening and coming up with his own conclusions.

''What about the bank?'' she asked.

''It's where the corps keep their money, right?'' the ganger said. ''What corp's going to blow up its own bankroll?''

Sly was silent for a few moments. The kid probably

thinks the Z-O Gemeinschaft's just one big vault full of gold, she thought, but it doesn't work that way. High-level banking's not about money as such, or gold. It's about *information*. Agarwal had taken pains to explain this basic truth to her. The Z-O Gemeinschaft was just a bunch of big computers, a massive exchange for financial information.

But the kid's idea still makes sense, doesn't it? she thought. Any financial transaction is just an exchange of data. But you've got to have a safe channel to exchange that data. That's why the Gemeinschaft's important. Falcon was right. The Gemeinschaft was much too important for any corp to trash it, or even threaten it. All she had to do was get the data from the encrypted file into the Gemeinschaft's information system.

All. *All?* The Gemeinschaft was a bank. And not just any bank, it was the megacorps' bank. What kind of security would it have on its datafiles, on its communication channels, on every node in the system? Black ice all the way, no doubt about it. Killer black ice—the best that almost unimaginable sums of money could buy.

"You okay, Sharon Louise?" Modal had slowed the car, was watching her with some semblance of concern.

She was shivering, her hands were shaking, and her skin felt cold.

"Are you okay?" the elf asked again.

"I'm all right," she said, trying to keep her voice calm and controlled. Trying to force the fears to the back of her mind. "I'm just thinking, that's all." She took a slow, deep breath, let it out quietly, imagining the tension leaving her body with the air. *Better.*

"The Gemeinschaft's a no-go," she pronounced firmly. "Too much security. No decker would ever be able to penetrate it." She saw Falcon slump with disappointment. "Good idea, though."

Then another thought struck her. "Not the bank," she mused, "but what about something associated with it? What about something else that's in Zurich-Orbital?"

"You're not talking about the Corporate Court. . . ."

She patted Modal on the shoulder. "But *think* about it," she said, enthusiasm growing. "For one thing, what corp is actually going to make a move against the Corporate Court?"

"They're already ignoring the Court," the elf pointed out.

"Ignoring it and acting directly against it are two different things," Sly reminded him. "And it's in the same orbital habitat as the Gemeinschaft Bank. Who knows, maybe they even share computer resources. Nobody would dare slot with the Court, because they might crash the bank."

"And there won't be as much security, maybe," Falcon added from the back seat.

"That might be the way to go," Sly concluded. The kid was right. Unless the Court was totally paranoid—possible, but not certain—a decker would have a better chance of penetrating that system than the bank. . . . And living to talk about it afterward.

Modal looked sour. "You're assuming the Court has some kind of BBS," he reminded her.

"It makes sense that they would," she said.

"You've got to make sure."

Sly nodded, then gave it some thought for a few minutes.

"Head for Puyallup," she told Modal.

Theresa Smeland's apartment was only a few blocks from The Armadillo, on 123rd Street East, half a block off Intercity 161. Sly had never been there before, but she knew that Smeland owned the entire upper floor of the small building, while the ground level was occupied by an electronics supply shop.

In her mind, Sly had always pictured a clean, well-maintained building—maybe one of the few heritage buildings that the corrupt Puyallup municipal council had actually bothered to preserve. As Modal stopped the Dynamit outside, however, she drastically revised her estimate of Smeland's finances.

The building looked like pure drek. The pseudo-stone facade was cracked and coming away in chunks. The acidic hard rains had discolored the walls and awning of the electronics store, turning both a gray-blue reminiscent of corpses. As for the store itself, it had definitely seen better days. The windows were cracked and starred, the security bars rusting and pulling loose from the walls under their own weight. Beside the closed door, no doubt locked this early in the morning, was a small sign reading, For Service Push Buzzer. Beneath it was the spot where the buzzer had presumably been mounted before someone had thoughtfully stolen it.

At the far left side of the building was another narrower doorway, with a door made of heavy, quite possibly bulletproof, metal. That had to be the way to Smeland's place.

Sly climbed out of the Saab, hesitating at Modal's questioning look. "Come on," she told them, "both of you."

She walked up to the metal door, looked for a buzzer or bell or maybe an intercom. Nothing. But, as she took another step closer, a small red light flicked to life above the door. Proximity sensor, she guessed, triggering a vid camera, plus maybe other systems as well. It was a good thing she'd called ahead using the Dynamit's phone. (A potential risk if the car had already been reported stolen, of course, but a calculated one.) She smiled up at where she thought the camera probably was.

"I see Modal finally found you." Theresa Smeland's voice sounded—tinny and electronic—from above the door.

Sly glanced back over her shoulder, saw the elf and the Amerindian standing behind her. She smiled up at the camera. "It's a long story, T.S.," she said. "Can I bring them up?"

Smeland hesitated a moment, then assented. With a click, the metal door opened.

Sly stepped through, saw a staircase ahead of her. The walls on either side looked to be made of reinforced ballistic composite, and the stairs were narrow enough that the extended shoulders of her jacket brushed both sides. At the top of the staircase was another reinforced metal door, but no landing, and the stairs themselves were steep. Which meant that anybody who wanted to smash down the door would have nowhere safe to stand. Certainly, a minigrenade or a rocket launcher would make short work of the upstairs door, but Sly was certain the staircase area itself would have security systems in place to take care of anyone who would try to bring such a weapon into the building. (Weapon detectors and gas systems? Almost certainly. Automatic gunports designed to hose down the stairway? Quite possibly.) There wasn't much doubt that Smeland was making her home as safe as humanly possible.

With Modal and Falcon close behind her, Sly climbed the stairs. Before she reached the top, she heard another click, and the upstairs door swung open. She stepped through into a tiny anteroom, facing yet another door. Then that, too, opened.

Standing in the doorway was Theresa Smeland, wearing a pale blue floor-length housecoat. She looked tired, which Sly thought was probably because she'd closed the club only a few hours ago, but alert. She smiled a greeting at Sly, stepped back to let her three visitors enter the apartment.

Never judge a chip by its slipcover, was the first thought that passed through Sly's mind. From the condition of the building's facade, she'd expected Smeland's place to be comfortable enough, but with most of the decor designed to cover up the building's structural shortcomings.

Dead wrong. Everything—the furniture, the carpeting, the lighting, the works of art on the walls—was absolutely top-of-the-line. The decor didn't seem to follow any formal school of design, at least not one that Sly was aware of—neither nuevo-industrial, or East African, or semi-gothic. But everything fit—there wasn't any better way of saying it—contributing to a single, congruous whole.

Smeland chuckled throatily. "Like it, Sly?"

Sly shook her head slowly. "The club's more of a money-spinner than I thought."

"This didn't come from the club," Smeland explained. "This was personal. I did a favor for . . . for a chummer of an old comrade," she said carefully, "and this is what he did for me in return."

"Too bad about the building," Modal threw in.

"Oh, the building's structurally sound, better than most in the neighborhood. When work's necessary I get it done, but I decided not to do anything about the way it looks." Smeland shrugged. "Why draw attention? What B and E gang's going to hit a place that looks like it'll fall down if they talk too loud?"

"There's that," Modal conceded. "May I?" He waved toward one of the room's silk-upholstered armchairs. "It's been a long, tiring night."

Smeland nodded. "Sit down, all of you."

Sly watched as Smeland settled herself gracefully in an armchair, tucking her feet underneath her. Modal slumped down in another chair, instantly relaxed, while Falcon sat—rigid, nervous—on the couch. Sly picked a spot on the other end of the same couch, allowed herself a few moments to relish the opulence surrounding her.

Then she began, "I need your help, T.S."

Smeland nodded with a wry smile. "I kind of guessed that. I don't get too many social calls this time of the morning. What do you need?"

Sly took a deep breath. "I need some information on the Corporate Court."

Smeland's eyes opened wide. "In Zurich-Orbital?" she asked. "Since when have you been playing in the big leagues?"

"It's not by choice, believe me," Sly assured her friend.

"So, what do you want?" Smeland asked. "A personal meeting with the Supreme Justice? Printouts of Aztechnology's balance sheet? Or do you want something *really* tricky?"

"Nothing that fancy," Sly assured her friend. "I just need to know if the Court has some kind of BBS—some system designed to disseminate information to all the megacorps."

"That's all, huh?" Smeland snorted. "I'd guess there would have to be something like that. But you need to know for sure?"

Sly nodded. "And I need to know how to access it."

Smeland shot her a startled look. "You want to read the Corporate Court's BBS, is that what you're telling me?"

"I want to *post* something."

"What?" Smeland demanded. "Your resumé, your brag-sheet? Are you looking for a fragging job, Sly?"

Sly just shook her head. She could see her friend was rattled. But she also knew Theresa would get her control back soon enough.

In fact, it happened within a few seconds. Smeland smiled, a little shamefacedly. "Sorry," she said quietly. "I'm just not used to working at this level, you get my drift?" She was silent for another half-minute or so, then said, "Relatively speaking, it shouldn't be that tough."

"Relatively speaking," Sly echoed.

Smeland nodded. "*Anything* to do with the Corporate Court isn't going to be a no-brainer, you know that, Sly. But I don't think this will be impossible. What is it you want to upload?" Hastily she raised her hands, palms out. "Don't tell me exactly, I don't want to know. But is it a text file? Or something else?"

"Text only."

Sly could see Smeland relax a little. "That makes it easier," the ex-runner allowed. "Security on a BBS is always going to be tougher if you're trying to upload an executable program code, because it can contain computer viruses. That's not a danger with simple text files."

Sly nodded; she understood that. "So how does this work?" she asked, wording her questions exceedingly carefully. "What's the best way of finding out, first, whether the Court has a BBS, and second, how to deck into it?"

"There's only one way," Smeland stated firmly. "The Court's got a system access node in the Matrix. You just crash into that SAN, and you scope out the Zurich-Orbital system"—she smiled grimly—"while making *fragging* sure you stay away from anything even peripherally related to the Gemeinschaft Bank. That's up there, too, you know."

"We've discussed that," Sly said drily. She paused, getting her thoughts and her words in order. The next question was the key. "T.S.," she began, "I—"

But Smeland cut her off. "I know what you're asking," she said sharply. "Am I willing to go in, right?"

"Not all the way." Sly felt cold, numb. She clenched

her hands into fists in her lap to stop them from shaking. "I need you to run cover for me, T.S., that's all. I'll do the main penetration. I just . . ." She stopped for a moment, struggling to keep her voice calm and reasonable. "I just need an escort," she went on, "somebody to watch my back. I don't think I can do this alone."

Smeland was staring at her, hard. "I'm surprised you can contemplate even doing it at all," she said honestly.

So am I, thought Sly. "Will you help me, T.S.?"

Sly watched as the older woman stood up, drifted to the unidirectionally polarized window that looked down into the street. She wanted to press her case, add more reasons why Smeland should help her out. But, tough as it was to hold her tongue, she recognized that her silence was the most effective persuader she had. She glanced over to Modal and Falcon. Both were watching Theresa, but neither seemed to feel the urge to say anything.

"It's got to be important, right?" Smeland spoke quietly, almost to herself, without turning away from the window. "Otherwise you wouldn't be doing this." She was quiet for another couple of minutes.

"All right," she said at last. "I'll run cap for you. To the Z-O SAN, and along the uplink into the habitat's local system. But no further, Sly. I'll just lurk at the top of the uplink." She shrugged. "Most of the heavy ice to be cut should be in the SAN, and on both ends of the uplink, right? I'll get you through that. Once you're in, there shouldn't be much ice . . . unless you trigger the Gemeinschaft Bank's security. And if you do that, all I could do would be die with you."

Sly let a lungful of air hiss out, realizing only then that she'd been holding her breath. "That's all I need, T.S.," she reassured her friend.

"When do you want to do this?" Smeland asked.

Sly wanted to say she didn't want to do it at all, but what she did say was, "As soon as you can do it, T.S."

Theresa turned from the window. "How about now, then?" Her expression was grim. "I suppose you need a deck."

Sly ran her fingers over the cyberdeck Smeland had loaned her. She recognized the enclosure—a simple, straightforward Radio Shack box. But the electronics, the actual guts . . . The Shack wouldn't have recognized any part of this. Custom work, all of it. And good custom work, too. Sly wondered if T.S. had built it.

Smeland had pulled her own deck out of its reinforced Anvil case, and had it across her lap as she sat, in half-lotus, on the floor. It was a custom job, too, Sly could see. The enclosure had come from a Fairlight Excalibur, but she could tell from the key layout and the port configuration on the rear plate that Smeland had made enough modifications to turn the unit into a virtually new deck.

Both decks were connected to a splitter box, and from there to a telecom jack in the wall. Sly stared at that connection. That was the way to the Matrix. The thought tolled in her head like a great bell. *The Matrix . . . the Matrix . . . the Matrix . . .* She picked up the deck's "skull-plug"—the small F-DIN-style connection designed to be inserted into the user's datajack. So innocuous-looking, and yet so dangerous. Through that tiny connection, a decker could project her consciousness into cyberspace. But, also through that connection, any of the multiple threats of the Matrix could worm their way directly into her brain. Sly was shaking again.

Out the corner of her eye, she saw Smeland watching her. "Sure you want to do this?" Theresa asked.

Those were the words, but Sly knew the real question was: Are you capable of doing this, or are you going to fold on me when the going gets tough? "I'm up for it," Sly said. Quickly, before she had time for second thoughts, she slipped the deck's plug into her datajack, heard and felt it seat positively into the chrome-lipped socket.

She settled her fingers on the keys, powered the deck up. She felt the almost-subliminal tingle in her head as the link between brain and deck was energized. The link wasn't active yet—no data was flowing, either way—but she could tell, without having to look at the deck's small display, that it was positively established. She punched in a command for the deck to run a self-diagnostic, saw the columns of data superimpose themselves over her visual field. Unlike when she was actually in the Matrix, she could still see the "macro" world around her, but, being jacked in, the diagnostic data seemed more real, more immediate than the "real" world.

"Fast deck," she remarked to Smeland. "Good response."

"One of my protégés juiced it as a kind of practicum," Smeland said. "My payment for training her was that I got to keep the deck afterward."

Sly nodded. It was well-known in certain circles that Theresa Smeland frequently took promising young deckers under her wing, and taught them what they needed to know to survive in the biz. Shared with them the technical skill and the professional world view she'd developed over her long career. Some people claimed that Smeland had connections with organized crime, that she was a recruiter who turned over her most promising "protégés" to the Mafia dogs. But Sly had never seen the slightest bit of evidence to support this accusation.

"Do you want a practice run?" Smeland asked. "Just to get the old reflexes back? I've got a drek-hot Matrix simulation I can run on my telecom."

"No," Sly said, more sharply than she'd intended. "Let's get going." *Before I lose my nerve,* she didn't add—and, judging by Theresa's understanding expression, didn't have to.

"Fine," Smeland acknowledged. "Let's do it."

Sly took a deep breath, hit the Go key.

And the consensual hallucination that was the Matrix blossomed in her brain.

I'd forgotten how beautiful it is, was her first thought. *So beautiful and so terrifying.*

It was as if she hung in space, hundreds of meters above a sprawl of city lights. Above her was a blackness deeper than midnight, the blackness of infinite space. Here and there strange "stars" hung in the sky—system access nodes for the local telecommunications grid—and other constructs that blazed with the brilliant colors of lasers and neon. Below her, datalines—looking like crowded freeways turned into rivers of light—crisscrossed a landscape made up of countless glowing images and constructs. Some loomed large—the neon-green Mitsuhama pagoda, the Aztechnology pyramid, the Fuchi star—while others were just dots of color from this apparent "altitude." The tapestry of light faded off into the distance, eventually reaching a "vanishing point" on the electron horizon.

The icon that represented Theresa Smeland in the Matrix—a large, anthropomorphic armadillo with T.S.'s dark, intelligent eyes—blinked into existence beside her. For an instant, Sly wondered what her own icon looked like. Obviously not the familiar quicksilver dragon, the shape she had formerly used to run the Matrix. Now her icon would be whatever Smeland's protégé had programmed into the deck's master persona control program—its MPCP. Well, it didn't really matter anyway. What a decker's icon looked like didn't make any difference to his or her performance—except, perhaps, psychologically.

"Ready to go?" It was Smeland's voice, but sounding

flat and anechoic. Sly knew that T.S. was sending her
words electronically, directly into her brain, rather than
speaking them out loud for Sly's meat ears to pick them
up.

She answered the same way. "I'm ready. Which node
is it?"

The armadillo looked up, pointed with a forepaw. A
bright red circle flashed into existence, ringing one of
the brighter "stars" above. "That's it," Smeland announced.

"So let's do it."

Sly *knew* that, in reality—whatever reality was—she
was sitting in Theresa Smeland's apartment, tapping on
the keyboard of a cyberdeck. But that wasn't the way it
felt. According to her sensorium—the sum-total of the
sensory data received by her brain—she was hurtling upward into the black sky of the Matrix, faster than a semi-
ballistic rocket plane. Her chest felt tight with the terrible
thrill of it; her heart beat a triphammer rhythm in her
ears.

The node that was their target grew larger, changed
from a dimensionless spot of light into a rectangular slab
about four times as wide and nine times as long as it was
thick. The two large, flat faces looked like they were
made of polished, blued steel like gunmetal. The smaller
faces burned brilliant, laser-bright yellow. The massive
construct, many dozens of times larger than the two
deckers' icons, spun in space, a complex motion as it
rotated at different rates around its three axes. Along the
construct's edges, the burning yellow shifted in intensity,
constantly flickering, hinting at the huge quantities of
data flowing through this gateway to the telecom system.

Smeland's armadillo icon was hurtling directly at one
of the LTG SAN's large faces, Sly close on her tail. Without slowing, they both plunged into the seemingly solid
surface. The universe twisted in on itself, flipped inside

out around Sly. She knew she'd experienced this shift
hundreds of times before, but the last time had been five
years ago, and the emotions forget. Fear knotted her
stomach, squeezed a low moan from her throat. Then
they were through, into a different section of the Matrix.

Just for a moment. Another transition, as they plunged
through another system access node into the regional
telecommunications grid—the "long-distance" trunks of
the world's telecom systems. Again the universe flipped
and spun.

And they were out, rocketing over a black plane. A
part of the Matrix without constructs? Sly wondered.

But no, there *were* constructs, just not many of them,
and in unfamiliar locations. In the Matrix she was used
to, the "ground" was covered with system constructs
and datalines. In this strange "world," however, the
constructs hung overhead. Maybe two dozen of them, no
more, too distant for her to make out any details other
than their colors. By the intensity of their light, she
guessed at the immense power of the computers they represented.

She looked to the horizon, at first unable to see any
dividing line between the "ground" and the "sky." But
then her brain made sense of what she was seeing. There
was a horizon, invisible, but defined by the massive, in-
conceivably distant constructs it partially occulted. They
looked like fortresses, huge, blocky things, brutal in their
simplicity of design, but, if this had been the "real"
world and the horizon at its normal distance, those constructs would have been many times the size of the largest mountains.

"What *are* they?" From the tenor of her voice in her
own ears, Sly knew she'd spoken out loud.

Smeland's reply, direct into her mind, was calm, reassuring. "They're major military systems, government
systems, the UCAS Space Agency . . . the big boys."

"We're not going near them, are we?"

Her friend's chuckle sounded clearly in Sly's mind. "Not a chance. Our destination's just ahead."

With an effort, Sly tore her attention away from the massive, distant system constructs. Contrary to her initial impression, there were a few constructs on the "ground"—small, dimly illuminated, probably shielded as much as possible from prying eyes. Smeland's armadillo icon was leading her directly toward one of these, a blue construct that looked like a radio telescope or large satellite dish.

"That's it?" Sly asked, ringing the construct with a circle of light the way Smeland had done.

The armadillo nodded. "Doesn't look like much, does it? But that's the SAN leading to Zurich-Orbital." Smeland paused for a moment as they hurtled on. "Have you ever done a satellite uplink before?" she asked.

Sly shook her head, then quickly remembered Smeland wouldn't be able to see the gesture. "No," she answered. "Anything I should watch out for?"

"Time lag's the big thing," the decker answered. "Light speed delay. As little as a quarter of a second if we've got a direct line of sight from the satlink station to Zurich-Orbital. As much as half a second—or even more—if we have to sidelink to other satellites to make the connection."

Half a second? In the Matrix that was forever. "Okay . . ."

Smeland picked up on the hesitation in Sly's voice. "It's not that bad," she said reassuringly. "Both these decks have chips to compensate for the delay. It's there, but you won't notice it unless you get into a scrap. In cybercombat, no utility in the world's going to help. You still won't feel the time delay as a delay; it's just that your reaction time will be for drek."

They began to slow as they neared the satlink system construct. It looked more like an impressionistic rendering of a satellite dish, Sly saw now, rather than the real thing. Its structural members glowed dimly with a deep blue verging on ultraviolet. Individual elements flickered as data passed through the system.

But there was something else there, as well. Small, dark spheres glided back and forth along some of the structural members, like beads on the wires of an abacus. When she watched individual beads, their motions seemed completely random. But when she expanded her attention to include the whole system, she couldn't escape the feeling that there was some pattern to their movement. "What are *they*?" she asked.

"Ice," Smeland said flatly.

The word felt like a cold dagger, slipped deep into Sly's abdomen. "Gray?" she whispered. "Or black?"

The armadillo shrugged. "I can't tell from here." Smeland paused. "Do you want to go on?"

Black ice. Killer ice. Images flashed through Sly's mind—memories of claustrophobia, of choking, of a cramping pain in her chest.

The last time I faced black ice, I *died*. It stopped my heart, suppressed my breathing . . . If somebody hadn't jacked me out—immediately, without a second's delay— I'd have flatlined for sure.

Five years old the memories were, but still as vivid as if it had been only yesterday. This is what I've got in common with Agarwal, she told herself. We both faced the gorgon and lived . . . but just. They'd both come away with their lives, and with the unshakable belief that they were living on borrowed time. That the next time they faced black ice, they would surely die.

Sly felt pressure on the back of her skull and neck, like somebody had placed a hand there and had begun to squeeze gently. She recognized the feeling. It was her body's warning of the onset of a fugue—a pseudo-epileptic seizure, where her brain temporarily went into cold shutdown. She forced her body to relax, to breath slower and deeper, drawing in the life-giving oxygen her brain needed. Slowly the pressure on the back of her neck began to recede.

Smeland's armadillo icon was watching her. "You okay?"

"I'm frosty," Sly answered brain-to-brain, knowing her voice would contradict her words all too clearly.

"Your call," Smeland said again. She turned back to the satlink construct. "Let's see what we can do about getting past these buggers."

The armadillo opened its arms in a slow, sweeping gesture. Dozens of tiny, mirror-bright spheres appeared—icons representing some kind of masking utility, Sly thought—and drifted toward the construct.

The small beads that were the intrusion countermeasures programs changed their pattern of movement, speeding up so that they became blurs. The mirror spheres drifted closer.

And gradually, the ice beads slowed down, resumed their regular slow motion. Sly felt a strange tightness in her shoulders, knew that the muscles of her meat body were rigid with stress.

The masking utility seemed to have worked; the ice beads showed no unusual activity whatsoever. Side by side, the two icons moved closer to the system construct behind the screen of mirror spheres. Still nothing. They were close enough to reach out and touch the midnight-blue construct.

"Ready?" Smeland asked. And then she grunted, "Uh-oh."

Before Sly could respond, the ice beads picked up their pace again, flashing back and forth along the structural members of the construct. Faster and faster they moved. An electronic whine rose in pitch and intensity, climbing the frequency spectrum, driving into Sly's ears like an icepick.

A dozen of the ice beads burst free from the construct, hurtled toward the two deckers.

Sly didn't even have time to scream before they struck.

16

0717 hours, November 14, 2053

Falcon was bored.

At first the concept of watching two deckers at work had fascinated him. Like everybody who'd ever watched the trideo, he knew *something* about the Matrix, but had never hung with anyone who dived brain-first into it for biz. He'd imagined it would be exciting, tense, with the dedicated decker hunched over her deck, while her friends kept nervous watch, wishing they could help but knowing they were unable to do so.

At least, that was the way it looked on the trid. But of course, on the trid there was always the tense soundtrack, the fast-paced camera cuts back and forth between the decker's sweating face and the anxious expressions of her chummers.

In real life, without the cinematic tricks, it was just two women tapping away at keyboards. About as exciting as watching people in a word-processing pool, the ganger quickly decided.

Well, maybe not *quite* that bad. Now and again one of the women would grunt or mutter something to herself or to each other, Falcon wasn't quite sure which. But an electrifying high-energy media extravaganza it wasn't.

Modal seemed to have the right idea about how to handle things. The thin elf was slumped bonelessly in a chair, one leg dangling over the chair's arm, fast asleep.

That's what I should be doing, Falcon told himself. He was exhausted; his muscles ached, his skin was sore, and his eyes felt gritty.

How long since I've slept? he wondered. Not that long actually. He'd crashed out at Doc Dicer's body shop, waking up at around twenty-one hundred hours the previous night. That meant he'd only been awake for—he checked his watch—a little more than nine hours.

A very busy nine hours, of course, which went at least some distance in explaining why he felt so drek-kicked.

He looked back at the two deckers. How long was this going to take?

Suddenly, shockingly, the two women jerked violently as though they'd been poked in the solar plexus. Sly fell back in her chair, mouth hanging open. Her eyes were half-open, but rolled so far back that Falcon could see nothing but the whites.

Smeland slumped over to the side, the thick carpet cushioning her deck as it slipped to the floor. The woman moved sluggishly. Her eyes were open, too, but definitely not focusing. Her mouth was working, and she was making garbled "whurr" noises.

So fast that Falcon didn't even see him move, Modal was beside Sly's chair, cradling her head gently in his hands. Falcon jumped from the couch, knelt beside Smeland.

The decker was starting to return to some semblance of consciousness. Her eyes were rolling wildly, but Falcon could tell she was at least trying to focus. No such attempts at control from Sly. She was out—dead?

Smeland covered her face with her hands, rubbed at her eyes. Then, with an obvious effort, she forced herself back to a sitting position. She looked like hell, Falcon thought, face pale and sheened with sweat, eyes blood-shot, chest heaving.

"What the bloody hell happened?" Modal demanded. His voice crackled with tension.

"Ishe," Smeland mumbled. Then, making a concerted attempt to articulate more clearly, she repeated, "Ice. Gray or black, I don't know. We got dumped." She pulled the deck's plug from her datajack, with a metallic snick that made Falcon's skin crawl.

The ganger saw Modal peel back one of Sly's eyelids with a thumb. "She's not dumped," he snapped.

"Huh?" Smeland was trying to push herself to her feet, wasn't making it. Falcon offered her an arm. She took it, steadied herself. "Not dumped?"

"That's what I said. She's acting like she's still jacked in."

Smeland walked unsteadily over to Sly, looked into her face then down at the deck. "That's not possible," she muttered.

"Well it's bloody happening, isn't it?" Modal grated. He reached for the optical fiber lead socketed into Sly's datajack. "Shall I jack her out?"

"Wait a tick," Smeland said sharply. She punched a few commands into Sly's cyberdeck, examined the display. Falcon looked over her shoulder, but the scrolling digits and symbols meant nothing him.

They obviously meant something to Smeland, though, and just as obviously she didn't like it. She frowned, chewed on her lower lip.

"Shall I jack her out?" Modal repeated.

"*No!*" Smeland grabbed his wrist to reinforce her words.

"Why not?"

"She's in a biofeedback loop with the deck," Smeland explained. Her voice had a quiver to it that Falcon hadn't heard before.

"So it's black ice that's got her," Modal said. "Then I *should* jack her out."

"No," Smeland repeated. "Normally, yes. But not now. It's the biofeedback that's keeping her alive," she explained. "The ice—or whatever it is we hit—shut down her heartbeat and her breathing. And now *it's* the only thing keeping her alive."

Modal shook his head. "I don't understand."

"It's like she's hooked up to a respirator in a hospital," Smeland said. "Jacking her out is like unplugging the respirator. She'll die."

"Then what do we do?" Falcon demanded.

"Nothing." Smeland's voice was flat, almost emotionless. "Anything we try will just kill her. Whatever did this, it has to be doing it for a reason. When it's finished, maybe it'll let her go."

"And if it doesn't?"

Smeland's only answer to Modal's question was a shrug.

Just fragging great, Falcon thought, looking down into Sly's face. Her eyes were still half-open, the lids quivering. Pale skin was tightly stretched over her high cheekbones. She looked half-dead.

There was a sound from outside—a screech of brakes. Inhumanly fast, Modal was at the window, looking down into the street. "Oh, frag," he muttered.

Falcon joined him at the window. A large car had pulled up behind the stolen Dynamit. It disgorged several large figures—large figures bearing large weapons. Four of them, two trolls, two humans. And probably another four around back, Falcon thought, if this was the attack it looked like.

"T.S.," Modal said urgently, "how good's your security?"

Smeland looked up from Sly's deck. "Good enough to stop a small army," she answered. "Why?"

"I just hope that's going to be enough," Falcon said
quietly.

17

0719 hours, November 14, 2053

Fear wrenched a scream from Sly's lungs as the ice
beads struck. But the scream sounded strange to her
ears, as if it hadn't happened anywhere but in her own
head. The Matrix faded around her, leaving her in darkness. There was a wrenching pain in her chest, a terrible
feeling of chilling numbness from her body. No! she
screamed inwardly. Not again.

A moment of disorientation, as though she were tumbling wildly through space. She was still surrounded by
darkness—no, not darkness, nothingness—and her other
senses also seemed to have failed her. No sensations came
from her body; the pain in her chest was gone as if it had
never been, and she couldn't hear or feel her heartbeat
or her breathing. For an immeasurable time she tumbled
through the void. Or maybe she wasn't tumbling; maybe
it was just her brain—starved of sensations—feeding her
false stimuli to fill the nothingness.

I can jack out. . . . She tried to break the connection
between her and cyberspace. But nothing changed.

Panic coursed through her. I *can't* jack out! And then
a chilling thought bubbled up from the deep recesses of
her mind.

You can't jack out from death. . . .

And then, as suddenly as it had vanished, sight returned.

At first, she thought that somehow she was outside the
Matrix, magically transported, perhaps, to an environment
that was, in its very familiarity, disturbing. Chilling.

She was standing in an executive office. Rich, neutral-
tone carpet on the floor, sourceless lighting illuminating
objets d'art on the windowless walls. The room was
dominated by a large desk of dark wood, clear except for
a pen and pencil set and what looked like a clock-
calculator. Behind it was a comfortable-looking leather
chair. It was the kind of office that might be found on
the upper floors of any corporate or government edifice,
anywhere on the continent—or in the world, for that matter.

The office door had to be behind her. Sly turned. No
door.

And it was then Sly realized the true nature of where
she was. As her point of view had moved, reality around
her had broken down—momentarily, almost sublimi-
nally—into individual pixels, picture elements, revealing
itself as only an illusion of reality. Only when she
stopped, when she looked straight at something—the
wall, an abstract painting, whatever—did it appear solid.

But not quite. Now that she knew what to look for,
she could spot the individual pixels that made up every
element of her environment. The resolution was incredible, much better than anything she'd ever seen in cyberspace, but it was all a program construct of some kind.
Which meant she was still in the Matrix.

But how? This wasn't the way things were supposed to
work. When you got hit by black ice, you beat it in cybercombat, or you got dumped out of cyberspace back
into the "real" world. Or you got killed. That was the
way of things, the nature of black ice. Somehow, however, she'd found herself in a *fourth* option.

Was T.S. here, too? In an analog of this place? Or was
Smeland dumped, possibly flatlined?

Just what the frag was going on?

She heard a sound, like that of a man clearing his throat, but with the flat, anechoic tone that told her the "sound" had been injected directly into her sensorium through her datajack. She turned back to the desk.

The high-backed swivel chair was no longer empty. Sitting there was a man of medium height, with short-cropped gray hair and icy gray eyes. For a moment she tried to guess his age, confused by the conflicting clues of his hair color and the absence of wrinkles around his eyes, then gave up the effort as meaningless.

He isn't real, she recognized, noticing that the resolution in this portion of the Matrix, incredible though it might be, wasn't quite up to defining individual hairs on the man's head. Another construct. A decker's icon.

She remembered the time and effort she'd put into "sculpting" her own icon when she was a working decker. Remembered the programming effort and the computing horsepower required to animate a construct with a resolution orders of magnitude worse than what she was looking at now. This kind of animation took huge amounts of programming and processing resources. Where am I? she thought desperately.

The man—the construct, Sly had to remind herself— regarded her steadily. He seemed to be waiting for her to start the conversation. But she wouldn't oblige him.

Finally he nodded and said, "You are Sharon Louise Young." His voice was strong, the voice of a young man. But, she had to remind herself, since nothing here was actually "real," that didn't tell her anything she could depend on.

Again the man waited. "That's me," Sly said at last. "And you are . . .?"

"Jurgensen, Thor. Lieutenant, CSF, UCAS Armed Forces." He smiled ironically. "I think we can dispense with the serial number."

UCAS Armed Forces. Sly remembered the massive constructs beyond the horizon of cyberspace, the data fortresses larger than the largest mountains. She felt as if a chill wind was blowing right through her.

"CSF, what's that?" she asked, although she thought she already knew.

"Cyberspace Special Forces," Jurgensen answered, confirming her guess. He leaned forward, intertwined the fingers of both hands on the desk in front of him. "You have some information, Ms. Young," he said quietly. "We would like you to hand it over to us."

"What information?"

Jurgensen shook his head. "Don't insult my intelligence," he said. "I assure you I don't underestimate yours. You know exactly what I mean. The datafile you . . . *acquired* from Yamatetsu Seattle. The datafile describing the corporation's research into the interception and manipulation of fiber-optic data transmission. The 'lost tech,' to use the common argot. We know you have it. We also know that various other . . . um, factions . . . have tried to relieve you of it."

"So now it's *your* turn, is that it?"

The decker construct chuckled dryly. "If you like," he conceded with a shrug. "There's a difference, though. My colleagues and I wish to give you the chance to voluntarily hand the information over to us."

"Why should I?" Sly demanded.

Jurgensen shrugged. "Various reasons," he answered calmly, then began ticking off points on his fingers. "One, enlightened self-interest. Who could protect you from the other factions better than the military?

"Two, bringing the megacorporations back under the control of the civilian government. You've worked for and against the *zaibatsus*, Ms. Young. You know how far they can go, how much they can get away with, without the slightest fear of governmental action. With the infor-

mation you acquired, we can . . . um, bring the mega-corporations to heel, to some extent, at least, and return to the electorate some semblance of control of their own lives.

"And three, patriotism." Jurgensen grimaced wryly. "I know, it's an outmoded term, an unfashionable concept. But it's still worth considering. Countries on this continent and around the world are in competition—for resources, for markets. They compete through trade controls and tariffs, through technological and industrial efficiency, and through more . . . *obscure* . . . means. Though nobody would expect you to buy into the old fallacy of 'my country, right or wrong,' we do hope, Ms. Young, that you'll consider the personal advantages of being a citizen of a competitively successful country."

"That's it?" she asked after a moment. "That's your pitch?"

"That's it," Jurgensen confirmed. "Consider it, please."

"Now?"

The lieutenant spread his hands, palms up. "Why not?" he asked reasonably. "I can guarantee you won't be interrupted or disturbed."

In other words, you're not going to let me go until you get what you want. "I don't have what you want with me," she told the military decker.

Jurgensen shrugged. "Tell me where in the Matrix it is," he said. "I'll send a smart frame to get it."

A smart frame—a semi-autonomous program construct. That told her they weren't going to let her out of here, even if she gave them what they wanted.

So what? she suddenly asked herself. Maybe Jurgensen was right. He made a reasonable case for an alternative she hadn't really examined before. If I can't destroy the data, and if I can't make sure everyone gets it simultaneously, I can always choose the best person to give it to—the lesser of all available evils. Minimize the disruption, the danger.

And then depend on the faction I choose to protect me from the rest.

How well did the UCAS government fit the bill? The concept of bringing the megacorps under some degree of control was definitely attractive. Ever since the Shiawase Decision granted extraterritoriality to multinational corps back in 2001, the civil government had lost most of its influence. *The governments handle all the drek jobs the corps don't want,* Sly thought, *and that's it. It's the megacorps that call all the shots.*

And what about that nationalism drek? Null program . . .

Or maybe it wasn't. Sly had never kept a close eye on international affairs—except as they directly impacted the shadows, of course—but she couldn't help but pick up rumblings here and there about what was happening on the international front. There was continuous squabbling between the UCAS and the Salish-Shidhe nation about the status of Seattle. Some hotheads on the tribal council wanted to usurp control of the city. And, since that would deny the UCAS its last port on the Pacific Coast—and its sole gateway to Japan and Korea—the boys and girls in D.C. were scrabbling for a way to stop that from happening.

And then there were the ongoing border "disputes" between UCAS and both the Sioux Nation and the Confederate American States. Despite the federal government's vociferous claims to the contrary, the fed seemed to entertain some pretty fragging extensive territorial ambitions. The way things stood at the moment, however, not much ever came of them. The contenders seemed too evenly matched in capabilities.

But that'd change right fast if UCAS got hold of the lost tech, wouldn't it? With that kind of advantage, wouldn't the federal government be tempted to step up the—what did Jurgensen call it?—the "obscure means" of competition between nations? And how destabilizing would that be to the political climate of North America?

Corp war or conventional war? Is that what I'm looking at here?

Jurgensen was watching Sly steadily. "Where is the information, Ms. Young?" he asked quietly.

Maybe the best thing she could do at the moment was explore the parameters of her choices. "What if I don't want to tell you? Are you going to threaten me?"

"Threats?" The decker construct's eyes opened wide as if the idea hadn't occurred to him. "You mean, like this?"

Suddenly, Jurgensen was flanked by two hulking figures, figures out of nightmare. Sly jumped back with a cry of alarm.

The creatures, or whatever they were, stood almost three meters tall—if scale meant anything here—their deformed heads brushing the ceiling. They were roughly humanoid in shape, but were not flesh and blood. Instead, they seemed to be pure darkness, coalesced into physical form. They were regions of nothingness, of nonexistence, precisely bounded but with no surface, no texture, no features. They had no visible eyes, yet Sly could sense that they were aware of her, studying her, scrutinizing her, evaluating her as an opponent or as prey.

"What *are* they?" she asked. She heard the fear in her own voice. *Why did you ask, Sly? You know what they are.*

Jurgensen glanced to his left and right at the two massive figures. "They're ice, what else? Our latest revision of 'golem class' black IC, driven by high-level expert system code." He smiled coldly. "So, you see, I *could* threaten you. The golems could hurt you seriously— without killing you, of course—and you wouldn't be able to jack out to escape them."

He paused. "But that's simply too brutish," he went on more gently. "I'd much prefer that you didn't force me to take that course." He looked at the two ice constructs again. "Do you think we'll be needing them?"

Sly couldn't bring herself to speak, just shook her head rapidly. Jurgensen smiled, and the two nightmare figures vanished. The knot in Sly's gut seemed to loosen infinitesimally.

"Answer my question, please," Jurgensen continued. "Where in the Matrix is the information?"

"It's not *in* the Matrix," she answered, lying smoothly. "It's in an isolated system, a fully shielded system."

"Tempest-shielded?" Jurgensen asked, naming the military designation for a system completely isolated from all electromagnetic tampering.

Sly nodded. "And it's keyed to my retina print," she added. "If anybody else tries to access it, the data's erased."

The military decker was silent for a moment. "Why don't I believe you?" he asked finally.

Sly just shrugged.

"If it *is* in the Matrix, I can find it."

You're bluffing, Sly thought. The optical memory chip containing the datafile was installed in the chip slot of the cyberdeck Smeland had loaned her. If you could find it, if you could trace back into my deck from wherever the frag we are, you'd already have it. She fought to keep a triumphant smile off her face, glad that the resolution of her icon wouldn't be enough for Jurgensen to read her expression.

Jurgensen drummed his fingers on the desktop. Sly thought she understood his dilemma. *You've got some very real restrictions, haven't you? You can keep me here, stop me from jacking out. But if you do, that means I can't get you what you want.*

Unless Jurgensen could trace her physical location,

send a team over and capture her meat body as effectively as he'd caught her consciousness. But *could* he do that? And if he could, why hadn't he done so already?

"Look," she said, "I'll make you a deal. You get the data, I get protection. But I'm physically in Everett, the data's in Fort Lewis. I've got to go get it. Which means you've got to let me go." She held her breath. *I'm in Puyallup, not Everett—my meat body, at least. Will he pick up on the lie?*

Jurgensen was silent for almost a full minute, almost as though he was consciously drawing out the tension. But then he nodded.

"How do I get back . . . here?" she asked.

"The easiest way is to try to reach Zurich-Orbital," the military decker told her. "We're watching all access routes. You'll automatically get diverted here."

"I'll be back," she lied. "Now, can I . . .?"

"You can jack out."

Again, Sly tried to break the connection. This time it worked. She felt the momentary disorientation as her real sensorium replaced the construct that was cyberspace.

And suddenly she found herself in a world that seemed to be blowing itself apart. . . .

18

0727 hours, November 14, 2053

Falcon ducked as another burst of gunfire from the street blew out what little glass was left in the window. He wanted to run, to get out of this trap. But run where?

The Smeland woman probably had some secret back

way out—Falcon certainly would if it were his place—
but she hadn't told anybody about it.

According to her, they couldn't move Sly, though Falcon didn't fully understand why. Something about Sly
being linked to the Matrix and that she'd die if anybody
jacked her out. That meant they didn't have any choice.
If they wanted to keep the attackers from getting to Sly,
they had to do it here. They'd done the best they could
to shelter her from stray gunfire, laying her down on the
floor between the heavy couch and a wall, but their options were limited by the length of the cable connecting
Sly's cyberdeck to the splitter box and from there to the
wall outlet. Falcon had asked if they couldn't unplug the
deck from the wall but keep Sly jacked into the deck,
but both Modal and Smeland had looked at him like he
was an idiot. Just asking, he'd thought bitterly at the time.

He also wondered why the frag Smeland and Modal
were still hanging. Modal he could almost understand;
apparently he and Sly had some kind of history together,
though it was hard to understand how someone as vibrant
as Sly could have feelings for a person as cold and emotionless as the black elf. And vice versa.

And what about Smeland? Sure, she and Sly had been
chummers. But you don't put your life on the line for
every chummer, do you?

And then there was him . . . He *couldn't* bail out,
which relieved him of making any decision. If there was
a back way out, Falcon didn't know about it, and the
front door wasn't an option. But, he found himself wondering, even if there was another way out, would I take
it?

Falcon crouched down beside Sly, looked into her pale,
drawn face. No change. If it weren't for the rhythmic
movement of her breast, he'd have written her off as flatlined.

He twitched reflexively as Modal squeezed off another

high-velocity greeting to the gunmen in the street. The
elf was moving like a chipped jack rabbit, popping up at
one window for a quick shot, then ducking down again
before anybody could return fire. Repeating the process
at another window. Sticking his own head up for a look-
see didn't seem like the healthiest thing to do, so Falcon
didn't know if the elf was scoring. At the very least Modal's shots would be forcing some of the attackers to keep
their heads down.

The fire from the street had taken out all the glass,
leaving the windows perfect targets for grenades. At first
the ganger hadn't understood why nobody took advantage
of the opportunity. One frag grenade lobbed into the
room from down below would have splattered all of them,
at no risk to the attackers.

But then he'd realized that's not what the raiders, whoever they were, wanted at all. The odds were that they
wanted to take Sly alive, and keep her alive long enough
to squeeze from her the location of the datafile on the
lost tech. So that meant no grenades. It also meant that
when the attackers finally made it up the stairs and
through the front door they'd be very careful about confirming targets before opening fire. That might make all
the difference in the world for Falcon, Modal, and Smeland, who would have no problem identifying anybody
coming in from outside as a bad guy. The attackers,
meanwhile, would have to hold their fire long enough to
figure out who was who, which would cost them.

As it was, though, nobody had made it up the stairs.
Smeland sat cross-legged in a corner, jacked into her
cyberdeck, directly controlling the security systems that
protected her home. Early on in the assault, Falcon had
heard the muffled boom as the attackers blew open the
street-level door. Smeland, already jacked in, had drawn
her lips back from her teeth in a grimace that was as
much snarl as smile . . .

And that's when the firing had begun, the terrible rip of ultra-high-speed autofire, from just outside the upper door. It had gone on and on—for five seconds at least, much longer than it would take to empty any normal weapon's magazine. The noise of the extended burst had been almost loud enough to mask the horrible screams from the stairwell. Almost.

"Frag me," Modal muttered. "Gun port?"

But Smeland didn't answer him.

The autofire weapon, which she was apparently controlling, had opened up twice more since then, presumably clearing the stairway of anyone trying to reach the upper level.

Falcon saw Modal pop up again, fire off a couple of shots from his heavy pistol, then drop back into cover. Automatic fire from the street stitched the window frame and the opposite wall. "Where the frag's Lone Star?" the elf demanded of nobody in particular. "They should be here by now."

To Falcon it seemed that the strange, almost tentative firefight had been going on for hours. Glancing at his watch, he was astonished to see that only eight minutes had passed.

But eight minutes could be a fragging long time. The elf had a point: where was the Star? Normally a patrol car would be on the scene of gunfire within a couple of minutes, usually backed up all too soon by an armored Citymaster or maybe a helicopter gunship. Why not now? Unless it was because these slags had the clout to tell Lone Star to keep out of it? And with that kind of influence, they had to have other resources as well. Like maybe a mage or shaman on call. The way Falcon figured it, the only reason he and Modal weren't already being chewed up by a spellworm was that the attackers had known—before they made their assault—that Sly and company had no magical assets. But now that the assault was stalled, he could picture somebody yammering into a radio, whistling up someone to remedy that oversight. And when that spellworm arrived, then the drek would really hit the fan.

Smeland cursed viciously, jerked the deck's lead from her datajack.

"What is it?" Falcon asked.

"They found the last of my sensors and took it out," she snarled. "I'm blind."

Modal looked over at her. "That means they'll be coming."

She nodded. "I've got one last surprise, but I'm going to have to guess on the timing." She shrugged. "And who knows if it'll be enough."

"Explosives in the stairs?" the elf guessed.

"Flechette grenades in the ceiling."

"Ouch," Modal said.

"*If* I blow them while somebody's actually there. After that . . ." Smeland shrugged expressively.

Something slammed hard into the door at the top of the stairs. Falcon saw the heavy metal shake with the impact, almost tearing loose from the hinges. He looked expectantly at Smeland.

From somewhere the woman had acquired a small machine pistol. But she wasn't paying it any attention. Instead, she was focusing on the door, her finger poised over a key on the cyberdeck.

Do it! Falcon wanted to shout.

"Not yet," she muttered.

A fusillade of bullets slammed into the door, but did no harm. It would take a lot more than that to penetrate so much metal, Falcon knew, but it was certainly the prelude to a renewed assault. The ganger checked the load of the machine pistol he'd picked up from the dead corporator in the Sheraton room. Fourteen rounds. That'd have to do; he didn't have any spare clips.

Another burst struck the door while a massive volley from multiple weapons came in simultaneously through the windows. Falcon ducked low as ricochets whined around him.

"Holy *frag*. . . ." It was Sly's voice.

Falcon spun. The runner's eyes were open, and she was struggling to focus. With a shaking hand, she reached up and tugged the plug free from her datajack. She started to sit up, but Modal was instantly beside her, pushing her down. "Keep your bloody head down if you don't want it shot off," he growled.

"What's happening?"

"Later," the elf told her, "if there *is* a later." He turned to Smeland. "Where's the back door?"

The decker keyed a quick command into her cyberdeck. With a click and a whir, a section of the wall near one corner swung open like a door. "There's a ladder, then a concealed door to the alley."

"T. S., you go first," Modal ordered. "Get out, and just keep on going. You're next, Sharon Louise. And you"—he stabbed a finger at Falcon—"you get her down and out right fragging quick. I'll cover."

Falcon could see that Sly wanted to protest, but he grabbed her shoulder and started dragging her to her feet. "Move," he snapped. Almost as an afterthought, he snatched up the cyberdeck, tucked it under his arm.

Smeland's finger punched down on a key, and the room rang with multiple explosions from the stairway. Explosions, and more screams. A rain of splinters spattered off the metal door. Falcon cringed, imagining the whirling storm of metal darts filling the stairwell, flaying flesh from bone.

While the overpressure from the grenades was still echoing from the walls, Smeland darted through the concealed door. Falcon followed, dragging Sly through the door.

There was a small anteroom, a circular hole in the floor leading down to a similar room on ground level. Smeland was already at the bottom of the metal ladder, beckoning for them to hurry.

"Go," Falcon told Sly. *"Move it!"*

The runner still looked partially stunned—dump shock, wasn't that what deckers called it?—but she still moved fast. She swung halfway down the ladder, then dropped the last meter and a half to the floor.

His turn. "Catch." He dropped the cyberdeck down to Sly, didn't wait to see whether she caught it safely. He grabbed the sides of the ladder, pushed his feet against the outsides of the vertical bars, then let himself slide down. As he hit the bottom, Falcon heard another explosion and the chatter of gunfire from the room above.

Something suddenly blocked the light, plummeting toward him. Falcon flung himself back, just in time to avoid Modal. The elf had decided to jump down, not even bothering with the ladder. "Get the frag out of here!" he screamed. To punctuate his words, the elf raised his pistol, emptied the clip up the ladder. A shriek from above confirmed his marksmanship.

Smeland was opening a door in the wall facing the ladder. Sly was right behind her, Falcon ready to follow the two women out. He looked back over his shoulder at Modal. In the gray light of dawn flooding in from outside, he saw blood pumping from a gaping wound in the left side of the elf's neck.

Smeland darted through the door, Sly close on her heels. Falcon hesitated. Modal had ejected the spent magazine from his pistol, was trying to fish a replacement out of his pocket. But his left arm was virtually useless, seeming to refuse the orders his brain was sending to it. He's dying, Falcon realized. Now he's dying, too.

"Modal!" he shouted. When the elf turned, Falcon

tossed him the machine pistol. Modal dropped his own gun, plucking the new weapon out of the air with his good right hand. Turning, he triggered a short burst up the ladder. No cry this time, but Falcon could hear the bullets slamming into flesh and bone.

"Come on!" It was Smeland's voice, from outside. Falcon turned and ran, Modal close behind.

Emerging into a wide alley, he was startled to see sitting there a big old Ford, vintage twenty-thirties, its engine running. Smeland was behind the wheel, Sly beside her. The back door was open.

Falcon flung himself into the big rear seat, then reached out to help the wounded Modal in after him.

But Modal had turned back to face the building, machine pistol raised.

The elf's instincts were right on. An instant later, a figure appeared in the doorway, a heavy shotgun braced against his hip.

Modal fired first, a long burst that blew the figure's throat open and turned his face to a pulpy mass. Already dead, the attacker's final spasm made his finger clench around his weapon's trigger. The big shotgun roared.

The blast caught Modal full in the chest, hammered him back into the car. He remained upright for an instant, then slumped to the ground.

"Frag!" Falcon scrambled across the car seat, leaned out and grabbed the elf under both arms to drag him bodily into the Ford. He couldn't reach the door to shut it, but who gave a frag anyway? "Boot it!" he screamed at Smeland. With a squeal of tires, the car took off, the acceleration throwing Falcon against the seat.

From behind them he heard a yell, the words lost as they sped away. From ahead came gunshots. Something slammed into the metalwork of the car, but whether it was a bullet or a gunman who didn't get out of the way fast enough Falcon couldn't be sure. Sly returned fire, the reports of her big revolver punishingly loud inside the car. Then the immediate emergency seemed to be over. The ganger debated doing something about the door. But then Smeland threw the car into a screeching left turn, and the door slammed shut under its own weight.

"How is he?" Sly had turned and was leaning over the back of the passenger seat.

Falcon didn't have to reply; she could see the answer as well as he could. The elf's entire chest was a mass of blood and torn flesh. He'd been wearing a padded jacket, perhaps armored enough to stop rounds from a light submachine gun. But against a blast from an assault shotgun—at less than ten meters? Not a fragging chance. The elf might as well have been wearing a T-shirt for all the protection the jacket gave him. He was dead, Falcon knew, if not now then soon. And whatever time he had left wasn't a blessing.

It turned out that Modal was still alive. The elf's chest heaved. He coughed, blowing pink spray from his lips. Falcon wanted to turn away, wanted to vomit, but with an ultimate effort of will, he controlled both impulses.

Sly *knew*. The ganger could tell from her face. She reached down, grabbed the elf's hand, squeezed it hard.

Modal's eyes flickered open, focused on Sly's face. "How is it, Sharon Louise?" he asked. He coughed again, bright arterial blood leaking from his mouth.

Falcon could see Sly blinking back tears. "Good," she said huskily. "Good."

"I'm not afraid, Sharon Louise." Modal's voice had a terrible bubbling tone to it. "I'm not afraid, and I'm not sad. I should be, don't you think? Isn't that part of it, after all?" He took a breath as if to say something else. But a sharp spasm convulsed his body, and the air hissed wordlessly from his lungs.

That's two. The thought was enough to chill Falcon to the marrow. Two people dead, dying in my arms like the old fragging cliché. How many more before this is fragging over?

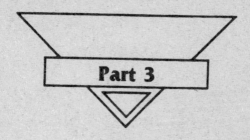

Part 3

Out of the Bucket

19

0850 hours, November 14, 2053

They were alone now, just Sly and the kid Falcon. T. S. had offered to help her out, to see her through this, more for old times' sake than anything. Though Theresa had tried to hide it, Sly knew she was relieved when Sly refused the offer.

Smeland had driven her to a particularly unpleasant part of south Redmond, where she claimed to have a good place to hole up until things settled down . . . if they ever did. When T. S. pulled up at the curb, Sly was searching for the words to ask the last big favor she needed from her chummer. Fortunately for her, T. S. beat her to it.

"You can have the car," Theresa said quietly. "It'll be hot. Whoever those gunners were will have the tag number. They'll get the word out, but it should be able to get you far enough to boost another ride.

"And I can handle . . . him," she said, indicating Modal with a jerk of her head. "I've got friends who can take care of it."

Sly nodded wordlessly, not knowing what she would have done with the body. She wouldn't have wanted to just dump Modal's lifeless form, but what other choice would she have had? She was relieved when Smeland solved the problem for her.

Smeland's destination turned out to be an ork "hall," an old store that had been "remodeled" into communal housing. Theresa had gone into the building, to emerge a couple of minutes later accompanied by three burly male orks. All three were wearing gang-style leathers, but Sly didn't recognize the colors. (He probably knows, she thought, with a glance at Falcon, but didn't bother to ask.)

The orks opened the back door and dragged Modal's carcass out. Totally unconcerned about the other people on the street, mostly orks, the biggest of the three had slung the elf's bloody body over his shoulder, then carried it into the hall. Sly was looking around nervously, waiting for some bystander to react, to interfere, maybe to run off to call Lone Star. But, if anything, the general reaction was complacency, if not utter boredom. And that, she thought, is about the scariest comment on the Barrens that anyone could make.

Another of the orks had climbed into the back seat with a towel to wipe away the worst of the blood. After tossing the soaked cloth out to his chummers, he spread another piece of fabric—almost like a dropcloth—over the stains.

And that had been that. He bared his chipped fangs at Sly in a quick grin, then he and his "stymates" disappeared back inside the hall.

To Sly's mixed disappointment and relief, Smeland had not reappeared. No goodbyes, no temptation to tell T. S. something that might get her greased. Sly gestured for the kid to join her in the front seat, then got behind the wheel and pulled away. She rolled down a window, hoping the wind of their speed would dilute the cloying smell of blood and death.

She knew they had to ditch the car, ditch it and steal another one.

But then what? The question was doubly chilling because she didn't have a good answer. Hole up and wait for everything to blow over?

But it *wouldn't* blow over, would it? The corp war would start. And eventually, someone would track down Sharon Louise Young, torture her until they knew everything she did, and then kill her. Sooner or later it would happen, no matter how deep into the shadows she tried to hide. Sooner or later someone would get lucky . . . and probably sooner rather than later. So what other options did she have?

She glanced down at the cyberdeck lying on the front seat beside Falcon. The kid had rescued it from Smeland's place while Sly had been in a daze of dump shock. And a fragging good thing he had. The optical chip containing the lost tech datafile was in the deck's chip slot.

Maybe I should cut a deal with Jurgensen, she reflected. Some of his arguments made sense. The UCAS military definitely had the resources to protect her from the corps. If they stuck by their agreements, she amended silently. And if they don't geek me themselves, just to keep the fact that they've got the tech secret.

Trust. It all came down to trust. How far did she trust Jurgensen? Did she trust him to keep his word? To keep her alive? To use the tech in ways that didn't destabilize the whole fragging continent?

No, she thought, with a pang of physical pain. I *don't* trust him. How can I?

So what did that leave? Hadn't she just eliminated all her alternatives?

Sly shook her head slightly, struggled to enforce a brittle sense of calm. Deal with the immediate, she told herself, worry about the eventual later. At the moment, the immediate involved getting another vehicle.

And Falcon. She turned to the Amerindian. "Where do you want me to drop you?" she asked

His head jerked around. "Huh?"

"I'll drop you off somewhere," she said patiently. "Where?"

He was silent for a moment, but she could almost feel his racing thoughts. "No," the kid said at last, his voice little more than a whisper. There was fear in his eyes as he looked into her face, but his expression was set, determined. "Nowhere."

Sly wanted to rage at him, but forced herself to speak calmly. "This isn't your game."

"Maybe it is."

"Why?"

Sly watched his face, saw from his expression that he had an answer. She could also see just as clearly that he was struggling hard to formulate it in words she could understand—that he could understand. She didn't push, but didn't give him an easy out either. Let him figure it out, she told herself.

After more than a minute, he shrugged. "It's my choice," he said quietly, evenly. "It's my life, I can do with it what I want."

"It's my life, too, chummer."

He nodded in acknowledgment. "If *you* want to get rid of me, you make the call, you say so. But unless you've got a good reason, I want to stay in."

It was her turn to think it through. She pulled the Ford over to the side of the road, put the car in neutral. She stared into the young Amerind's face, into his eyes, but she couldn't read this kid. There was fear there, but it was mixed with many other emotions. Plenty of determination too.

"What are you going to do?" he asked her.

That was the question, wasn't it? "I don't know yet," Sly admitted. "What do you think I should do?"

"Get out of the plex," he answered immediately. "All this corp drek is limited to Seattle, to the UCAS, isn't it?"

"For the moment."

"So get out," he repeated. "Slip the border, go someplace quieter. Give yourself time—give us time—to figure out our next move. And if you're planning to handle it with this"—he patted the cyberdeck—"you can do it from anywhere, right? So why be a fish in a bucket when you can get out of the fragging bucket?"

From the expression on the kid's face, a tinge of embarrassment overlaying his earnestness, she knew the analogy wasn't his, was probably something he'd heard on the trideo. But it hit home all the same.

Why *not* get out of the bucket?

"Where would you go?" she asked slowly.

"Sioux Nation." Again he answered at once, as if he'd figured it all out some time ago. "Fewer corps, less drek going on behind the scenes. The Council of Chiefs keeps tight control over that kind of thing."

That's not what I've heard, Sly thought. But . . . "You've been there, then?"

Again that tinge of embarrassment crossed the kid's face. "No," he admitted unwillingly, "but I know about it. It's a good place."

Maybe. She couldn't be sure how much of the Amerindian's enthusiasm was based on fact and how much on sentimental fantasies.

But there was still something in his suggestion. Getting out of the plex—out of the bucket—did sound like a good idea. The obvious choice was the Salish-Shidhe Council, because it involved crossing only one border. Wasn't avoiding needless complexity one of the first rules of any operation?

Still, S-S might not be the *best* choice. No matter how vociferously the intertribal council denied it, events in Seattle had a big effect on what went down in S-S territory. As the corp war continued to heat up, the news would leak into the Salish-Shidhe nation first. It was highly likely that any megacorps with a presence in S-S were already maneuvering as actively as they were in downtown Seattle.

So where else? Tir Tairngire? Forget it. The corps had almost no presence in the elven nation; the elves wouldn't let them in, pure and simple. But the same territorial paranoia and isolationism that kept the megacorps out meant that the Tir borders were even harder to penetrate than those of the Pueblo Corporate Council—and that was saying something. What difference would it make to her if she got geeked by a corp hit team or a Tir border patrol? Dead was dead.

Tsimshian? Strange things were happening up there. Both the shadow buzz and the newsfaxes agreed on that. Apparently some faction—the Haida National Liberation Army or some such overblown drek—was trying to overthrow the government—*again*. Jumping into the middle of civil unrest and retaliatory repression didn't seem like such a swift move.

So that left the Sioux and Ute nations, if she wanted to deal with the minimum number of illegal border crossings. To be honest, Sly didn't know enough about either place to make an intelligent choice. So why not go with the kid's hunch?

"Where in Sioux would you go?" she asked.

"Cheyenne, I guess. It's the capital, the biggest city." He grinned—a real grin, not something faked to cover his fear. "More shadows to hide in, right?"

What the frag, anyway? "Why not," she said, a statement rather than a question.

"I'm coming along, right?" he asked urgently.

Who else could she turn to for help? No one.

Sly nodded. "Why not?"

Sly stopped the car in the alley behind Agarwal's house, beside the wide ramp leading down to the ex-decker's garage/workshop. She killed the engine, started to get out.

"Why are we stopping here?" Falcon asked.

"We need another car," she explained.

"We can get one here?"

She smiled at the kid's doubting tone. "You better believe it," she told him. "And if we're lucky we can get some fake datawork to pass us through the border checkpoints." She swung out of the car. "Wait here, I'll be back. . . ." Her voice trailed off.

"What is it?"

She stared at the back of the old church. The rear door was open a crack. A cold tingle of apprehension shot through her. She reached under her coat, patted the butt of her revolver in its holster. "Stay here," she told him.

"Frag that." The Amerindian clambered out of the car, flipping the safety off the machine pistol he carried. He slung the strap of Smeland's cyberdeck over his shoulder.

For a moment she considered ordering him to stay with the car. But what authority did she have anyway? As much as he wanted to give her, no more. So why push it over something that didn't really matter? And anyway, an extra gun couldn't hurt.

She led the way up the steps to the door. They stopped for a moment while she listened.

Nothing from inside the building. With the toe of her boot she swung the door open slowly, let it bump against the wall. Drawing her pistol, she stepped inside.

From what Sly knew of Agarwal's security system, her

weight on the floor should have triggered some kind of
alarm even if the door were open. That implied that all
the interlocking systems were probably down. Which, in
turn, implied that either Agarwal had turned them off
personally, or that whoever had left the door open had
managed to defeat some of the most intense security in
the plex. Not a reassuring thought.

She stopped again to listen. More silence.

The house *felt* empty, lifeless. Her apprehension grew,
turning to a twisting knot in her belly. Gesturing for Falcon to follow, Sly crept deeper into the house, looking
for Agarwal.

She found him in his study, but he was dead, undeni-
ably and messily so. He was sitting upright in his high-
backed desk chair, upright because long velcro straps had
secured him in that position. One strap around his waist,
another around his neck so he couldn't slump forward.
One around each forearm, holding them to the chair's
arms. Another around his legs, bending them back under
the chair and securing them around the swivel pedestal.
Someone had cut away his clothes—and then cut away
more than just his clothes. His face was slack, expressionless, white as parchment. His eyes were open, because two of the things they'd cut away were his eyelids.
Like twisted claws, his hands gripped the ends of the
chair arms, the knuckles white as ivory. Under the chair
was a plastic drop cloth that someone had spread to catch
the blood—and more than blood—that had fallen from
their work. It was a meaningless, macabre touch of neat-
ness.

Agarwal had lingered. Sly didn't know how she knew,
but she did. They had been professionals, skilled in their
craft. He hadn't died quickly.

She closed her eyes, looked away.

Heard a sound behind her. Spun, revolver coming up.
It was Falcon, of course, the sound a choking gag. The

youth's eyes bulged, his face almost as white as Agarwal's. He dropped his machine pistol, turned aside. Noisily spewed the contents of his stomach onto Agarwal's expensive carpet.

She turned back to her friend, her mentor. I'm sorry. She mouthed the words silently. So sorry.

I did this. I didn't wield the knife, the pliers, the probes. But I did this to you just the same. Because I came to you for help, before I knew the magnitude, the importance, of the game I'd got myself into.

"Who?" Falcon's voice was a croak, the word forced through a tight, hoarse throat.

"I don't know."

The kid wiped his mouth with a sleeve, spat to clear his mouth.

"They're not watching the place," Sly said. If they were, she thought, we'd be dead. Or worse.

"Why not?" he demanded.

"I don't know."

He spat again. "We've got to go. Maybe they'll be back."

"Yes."

But she didn't move. She couldn't leave Agarwal. Not like this. She had to do something. . . .

"We've got to go," Falcon said again.

He was right, she knew. There wasn't anything Sly could do for her friend now.

She forced herself to speak. "Downstairs," she told him. "We'll take one of his cars."

He hesitated.

"Come on," she said, pulling the kid by the arm. "He won't be needing them anymore."

20

Falcon stared in stupefaction at the rows of cars. They were beautiful. He'd never seen anything like them. He ran a hand, tentatively, almost tenderly, along the hood line of a 9-series BMW. Thirty years old—twice as old as him—but it looked like it had just rolled off the assembly line. Any one of these would be worth more money than his whole family would see in their whole lifetime. And there were, what, a dozen of them? He shook his head in awe at all this high-speed engineering in one place.

But they didn't save their owner, did they?

He felt rather than heard Sly come up behind him.

She was taking the death of the old slag really hard. No surprise there, of course. It had trashed Falcon out, too, and he hadn't even known the bugger. Bad enough to see anyone who'd gone that way, let alone if he was a chummer.

But even though Sly was emotionally drek-kicked, she still seemed to be tracking okay. Her face was pale, her eyes haunted, but it looked like she was still with it. She had a set of car keys in her hand, a bulky-looking portable computer under her arm.

"What's that for?" he asked, pointing at the computer. "We've got this." He patted the cyberdeck slung over his shoulder.

"We still need passes to get over the border." Her

voice sounded flat, emotionless. "I think I can rig something up with this."

He nodded. He hadn't really thought about the actual logistics of slipping the border. When he'd envisioned himself ducking out of the plex and heading southeast into Sioux, the daydreams had never included any details of border posts, immigration, and all that associated drek. He'd just *done* it. But this was reality, not daydreams. "Good thinking," he said.

She threaded her way through the nearest cars, heading for a low-slung monster near the big up-and-over doors. Unlocked the driver's door.

He examined the car as she stashed the computer in the luggage space behind the front seat. It was almost five meters from bumper to bumper, he guessed, and not much more than a meter high, the top of the Targa-style roof only coming up to his belly. The strangely contoured hood hinted at a beefy power plant. It looked blindingly fast, even standing still. He kicked at one of the fat tires. "What is it?" he asked.

"It's a Callaway Twin Turbo," Sly answered dully. "A modified Corvette, built in nineteen-ninety-one. It's . . ." She hesitated, and he heard her swallow hard. "He told me all about it, but I don't remember what he said. Get in."

Falcon nodded. He walked around the sleek machine and opened the passenger door. The seats were low, almost like fighter plane combat couches he'd seen on the trid. There was no rear seat—and no room for one—just a small, carpeted space behind the two front buckets. He stashed Smeland's cyberdeck there, trying to arrange it so it wouldn't rattle around too much. Then he slipped inside, the seat almost wrapping around him, supporting him from the sides as well as the back. He shut the door.

Sly was sliding into the driver's seat, arranging her

long legs under the steering wheel. She shut her door, too, with a solid thud-click.

He looked around the car's interior, staring in un-abashed amazement at the wraparound dash, the complex stereo mounted in the center above the gearshift. (A six-speed gearbox, he noted.) They built this in nineteen ninety-one? he thought in wonder. Tech wasn't this advanced sixty years ago, it couldn't have been. *Could it?* He remembered Nightwalker's comments about how technological advance had been slowed by the crash of twenty-nine. Maybe it could. . . .

He saw Sly looking with befuddlement at the instrumentation, the steering wheel, the stick shift. Craning down to look at the pedals.

"What's the matter?" he asked.

"No rigger controls," she muttered, almost to herself.

Well, of course not, not in 1991. "So?" he asked.

Then he looked at the datajack in her forehead and understood. She couldn't drive something that was manual.

"Want me to handle it?"

She looked across at him, doubt in her eyes. For a moment, he felt a flare of anger. *She's still thinking I'm a kid,* he realized, *just a fragging kid.*

"You can drive something like this?" she asked skeptically.

"This? Null perspiration, chummer." His anger injected a touch of scorn into his voice.

She hesitated.

"It's me or nothing, isn't it?" he added, more reasonably.

Another moment of hesitation. Then she nodded. "Do it."

They changed places. The driver's seat was even lower than the passenger side, the pedals way forward, right against the fire wall. Falcon searched for the seat adjustment, found the small panel of buttons. With a little jockeying around, he set the right position, tilted the wheel down so it almost touched the tops of his thighs. Then, shooting Sly a smile expressing more confidence than he actually felt, he reached forward and turned the key. It was a twin turbo. Even sixty years old this thing was probably a rocket.

The engine caught at once, a low, full-throated rumble. The instruments came alive, the gas gauge creeping up until the needle sat steadily on the F. *At least I don't have to worry about that.*

He blipped the throttle, watching the needle on the tach jump responsively. A six-grand tach, with the red line plainly marked at fifty-five hundred rpm. The speed was marked in miles per hour, graduated up to 210. He ran the conversion in his head. That was what, three hundred twenty-five klicks? No, more. Probably full of drek. But then he glanced at the big turbo boost gauge, the six-speed stick.'Ninety-one? Wasn't that before most of the heavy emission-control legislation came down? Maybe it wasn't drek after all.

He depressed the clutch, which was smooth as silk, and tested the throw of the shift. The gearbox was tight, precise, much better than anything he'd ever driven. He was starting to doubt whether he could handle this thing at all.

But then he forced the doubts out of his mind. Like he'd said, it was him or nothing. "What about the door?" he said.

Sly reached up to a small box clipped to the sun visor, pushed the button on it. The big door directly in front of the car silently rose.

Checking the gearbox pattern on the shift knob one last time, Falcon slipped the car into first. He gave the engine a little gas, watched the tach needle rise to about fifteen hundred revs. Then—carefully, almost gingerly—

he began to let the clutch out, paying attention to exactly where it began to catch. Smoothly, the big car pulled out and cruised up the ramp to street level.

The Callaway was a pure joy to drive. Now that he'd gotten the feel of the pedals, Falcon's fear of the big engine had turned to unadulterated admiration. The torque was incredible. Even though he knew the car would be much happier cruising faster than safe city speed, the application of power was smooth and well-mannered enough that he never had the feeling the vehicle was trying to get away from him. For the first couple of blocks, he kept one eye on the boost gauge, nervous that he'd accidentally rev high enough for the turbos to kick in. But then the car started to feel like an extension of his own body, of his will. He didn't think it was going to do anything that would surprise him.

He glanced over at Sly, glad to see she'd released her white-knuckled grip on the door handle. "Where to?" he asked casually.

"The east route," she answered after a moment. "Highway Ninety. But go *around* Council Island," she added quickly.

He snorted. "I can figure *that* out for myself."

She reached behind the driver's seat to pull out the computer she'd acquired from the dead man's place. Set it on her lap and opened out the keyboard. Then, as if second thoughts had hit her, she shot a doubtful look at Falcon.

He grinned broadly. "Chill, Sly," he told her. "You do what you got to. The wheels are totally under control."

As if responding to the confidence—real, this time—in his voice, she nodded with a quick smile. Then she busied herself powering up the computer and unrolling the fiber-optic lead.

Let her play with her toy, Falcon thought, still grinning like a bandit, and I'll play with mine.

Highway 90, but bypassing Council Island. The quickest way was north on I-5, across the Highway 520 floating bridge, and then south on Route 405. All freeways. Which was just fine with Falcon.

He cruised the Callaway south along Broadway, then hung a right on Madison, heading southwest toward I-5. As he pulled up the on-ramp, he saw that the freeway traffic was relatively light. His grin broadened. Why not? He pushed down the gas pedal.

Even though he was watching the boost gauge and anticipating the extra power, the sudden added thrust as the twin turbos kicked in caught him by surprise. The big rear tires chirped, and the car surged forward, throwing Falcon and Sly back in their seats. The car wobbled alarmingly for an instant before Falcon got her back under complete control. Sly yelped in fright.

"Null persp, chummer," he crowed as he threw the Callaway up through the gears. "Just seeing what this baby can do." He could feel her eyes on him, but didn't take his gaze from the road and traffic ahead. "I could get *used* to this." He took the car up to 115 mph—more than 180 klicks!—before he backed her off to a more moderate speed. The machine felt as smooth and steady, as much under precise control at speed as it did cruising at fifty klicks on back streets.

Yeah, he could really get used to this.

21

I feel like drek, Sly thought. I need to sleep.

She reached down, played with the buttons controlling the power passenger seat. Tilted the back a little further down, adjusted the lumbar support slightly.

The seat was comfortable, as comfortable as any car seat could be after six hours of solid driving. And the low, steady hum of the engine, the thrum of the tires on the road, should have been soporific, but Sly couldn't drop off even though she was physically and emotionally exhausted.

She'd come close a couple of times, drowsing off, but as her thoughts began to range free, beyond her conscious control, the terrible images came back. Modal blowing bloody foam with his last breaths. The horribly abused body of Agarwal. She'd jolted awake, her muscles rigid, like she'd been hit by a taser dart.

They were out of Seattle, out of the UCAS. Shouldn't that make a difference? But of course it didn't.

Crossing the border into the Salish-Shidhe lands had made for a few tense minutes. Sly had been pretty sure that the data she'd manufactured on Agarwal's portable computer and then downloaded into the optical chips of two credsticks would pass all but the most intensive scrutiny. But being pretty sure and *knowing* were two very different things. While Falcon—now traveling under the name of David Falstaff—handed the two credsticks to the alert Border Patrol guards, she'd felt serious fear twisting

her insides. If they didn't accept the false identities and passports for David Falstaff and Cynthia Yurogowski, they'd hold Sly and Falcon until they dug up their real names. And when those *real* names come over the Matrix, who else might be taking an interest?

But all had gone well. The Border Patrol officer had slotted the credsticks one by one into the reader on his belt, scanning the information they contained via the connection to his datajack. He'd asked a couple of routine questions—reason for travel (even though that was, by law, included on the travel permits), home address (ditto)—but Falcon had answered them smoothly enough. (He fragging well *should* have, after the way she'd drilled him.) Then, just when she thought they were through, the patrol slot had wanted to talk about the fragging car.

Sly forced herself to relax. That was all past now. After the border guard had asked a couple of technodweeb-type questions about displacement and horsepower, to which Falcon invented answers on the spot, he'd simply waved the Callaway through and gone on to the next vehicle.

There'd been almost no traffic on Highway 90 as they began to climb into the Cascade Mountains, driving through what used to be the Snoqualmie National Forest. The sky was heavy with grayish-black clouds, but the rain was holding off.

Though the road was wet, the only real snow was in the dispirited-looking patches on the grass verges of the highway. That was unusual for the Cascades in mid-November, Sly knew. Seattle never got even the slightest touch of snow anymore—thanks to its "industrial micro-climate" and localized greenhouse effect—but the mountains often got several meters. The roads through the high passes like Snoqualmie were often closed, particularly since many of the tribal factions making up the Salish-Shidhe council seemed to consider snow plows to be "inappropriate technology.'' The unseasonable weather was a piece of luck for which Sly was grateful. A relatively light car like the Callaway would probably not handle snow very well.

The forest-clad mountains of the Cascade Range rose around them. Because of the restricted view, it was easy to forget that Snoqualmie Pass was at an altitude of more than a thousand meters, and that the peaks surrounding them were up another thousand meters higher than that. Every now and again, Sly caught a glimpse of Mount Rainier rising like a giant, head and shoulders taller than the flanking mountains. Rainier had lost its actual peak in 2014 when the land had responded to Daniel Howling Coyote and his Great Ghost Dance, but it was still more than four thousand meters tall.

Except for short-term business trips like the one that had taken her to Tokyo, Sly had never left Seattle, never even visited the Cascades lying only a few hours east of the sprawl. She'd always imagined them to be like the Rockies, huge, majestic, rugged peaks of bare rock and snow, which she'd seen once when biz had taken her to Banff and Lake Louise, further north in what used to be the border between Alberta and British Columbia. (It was the preserve of Dunkelzahn the great dragon, although that august personage had had nothing to do with her run—thank whatever gods there happened to be.) She'd loved the Rockies, found them beautiful, overawing, even terrifying in a way.

She remembered being driven along Highway 1, heading roughly north from Banff to Lake Louise. To the left of the highway was a seemingly unbroken row of shattered-looking peaks, clawing at the underbellies of the low clouds. She recalled one in particular—Mount Rundle?—a massive upthrust of rock with a perfectly flat upper surface, angled upward at about forty-five degrees. At the time she'd thought it looked like a paving stone,

one section of a roadway to the gods, smashed and driven upward by an unimaginable force. At the left and southern end, it terminated in a jagged cornice, from which the steady wind blew a long pennon of snow that had made her think of tatters of cloud-stuff hooked on the sharp rock. She was sure that, volcanically and geologically speaking, the Banff area had probably been ''dead'' millennia before mankind first appeared on the scene. But the area still possessed an aura of newness, of immediacy, of violent forces currently—but not permanently—held in check.

These Cascade peaks seemed older, more weathered, softened somehow by their covering of trees.

She glanced over at Falcon. If the kid was feeling any strain from driving or from the border crossing or from anything else, it didn't show in his face or posture. He looked relaxed, even had a smile on his face as he steered the powerful car around the tight corners of the pass road.

''When you're tired, tell me and we'll stop,'' she said.

He nodded.

Shifting around until she found the most comfortable position, Sly closed her eyes and tried to sleep.

To her surprise, it worked.

The coastal mountains were long behind them, replaced by the arid semi-desert of southeastern Salish-Shidhe. They'd left the clouds behind with the mountains, and the early evening sky was a clear and infinite blue. Here, too, there was no sign of snow, and Sly knew that meant the climatic changes weren't limited to the Seattle area. The way it used to be, when she was a kid, November would always have meant snow around Sunnyside and the Columbia River. At the very least, the ground should have been iron-hard with frost.

But here it was, well past seventeen hundred hours,

with the sun sinking toward the horizon, and the temperature was still well above freezing. Maybe even as warm as ten degrees Celsius. Sly wondered idly if the Salish-Shidhe lands might have maintained the archaic Fahrenheit system, which would have made it about fifty degrees. Unseasonably warm no matter what system you were using. The temperature would probably drop like a rock after dark, but Sly still doubted they'd have to deal with any snow.

They'd needed to gas up soon after hitting the plains, which had made Sly somewhat nervous. Most service stations dispensed only methanol and natural gas because petrochem vehicles weren't all that common, particularly in the tribal lands. To make it worse, Falcon was convinced that the Callaway needed high-octane unleaded, a specific type of gasoline that might not be available everywhere.

As it turned out, they needn't have worried. They were still on Highway 90 at this time, the major connector between the Salish-Shidhe Council and the Algonkian-Manitou Council nation. As such, it probably had more traffic—and more long-haul petrochem vehicles—than any other route within a thousand kilometers. The first service station they'd pulled into had the fuel the Twin Turbo needed. (At an outrageous price, of course, but what choice had they but to pay the going rate.)

Not long after, they'd turned south on Route 82 and tooled through Yakima. The map that Sly had picked up at the gas station—a hard copy map, printed on real paper—helped them refine their route. The trick was to keep their average speed up by staying on the old interstates as much as possible, but to avoid getting detoured into either A-M Council or Tir Tairngire territory. (Granted, the former was nowhere near as serious as the latter, but the fewer border crossings they had to make, the better she'd like it.)

They would follow Route 82 south over the Columbia River until it hit Route 84. (According to the map, the meeting of the two highways wasn't more than a klick from the Tir Tairngire border. That was closer than either Sly or Falcon really wanted to get, but any other route would have added hours to the journey.) Then it was southeast on 84—but bypassing Boise if possible—and on to the Sioux border at Pocatello. From there, the only available major road would dip down into the Ute Nation, so they had to take to the "blue highways"—the secondary roads—until they could pick up Highway 80 at Rock Spurs. From there it would be a straight shot roughly east, through Laramie, until they hit Cheyenne.

And what then? Sly wondered. Was this journey really taking her closer to a solution, or was it just an elaborate way of avoiding the issues?

No, she scolded herself sharply. She mustn't think like that.

She looked over at Falcon. "Can't we go any faster?" she asked.

His only answer was a grin as he pushed down on the accelerator.

22

0010 hours, November 15, 2053

The drek-eating motel was too close to the drek-eating highway, and Falcon's drek-eating bed was too close to the drek-eating window!

Every time one of those big, long-haul trucks thundered by, he thought the clamorous roar of the engine was going to shake his teeth loose. And then the shock wave as those countless tons of metal hurtled through the night would slam into the window and wall, making them shake as though a grenade had gone off outside. *And we're supposed to sleep through this?* Falcon groused inwardly

He glared over at the other bed, where Sly lay curled up in fetal position. For a moment, he was almost angry enough to boot her bed as hard as he could. If he wasn't getting any sleep, why the frag should she? They'd tossed a coin for who got which bed, but it had been her fragging coin, and she who'd fragging tossed it!

But then the anger faded away. Did he really think it would make a difference being only a few steps further away from the highway? Get real, he told himself.

Maybe they shouldn't have stopped at all. When Sly had pointed out the motel sign ahead, he'd been tired enough to think it was a good idea. In retrospect, though, the whole thing was turning out to be a royal pain in the butt.

The Crystal Springs Resort. He snorted. Resort? *Last* resort was more like it. And the only springs he'd encountered were the ones that creaked whenever he shifted his weight on the bed. The old slag at the front desk hadn't even glanced at the personal data scrolling across his computer screen when Sly slotted their credsticks to pay for the room. (They'd kept their new identities—David Falstaff and Cynthia Yurogowski—but Sly had changed things so they both hailed from Bellingham now.) Falcon thanked the spirits they both looked Amerindian—or sort of. People were less likely to question them.

People like the desk man, for one, but his leer told Falcon what he thought about why a woman would be getting a motel room with a guy half her age. That had stirred up an interesting mess of emotions, of course.

Part of him wanted to punch the slot's lights out; another part had kinda wished he were right.

He wasn't, of course. They'd tossed for the beds, then settled down for a couple of hours sleep.

That was when the first of the trucks had passed by.

Thinking about it logically, Falcon was glad they'd decided to stop. His first encounter with one of the huge multi-trailer "road trains" had fragging near scared the wits out of him. He'd been blasting along at the Callaway's comfortable cruising speed of about two hundred klicks per hour, the road ahead looking totally empty. Of course, that had been judging by the lack of headlights from oncoming vehicles. (At two hundred klicks per hour, he was overdriving the car's own headlights; if there'd been anything on the road that didn't have its own lights, he'd probably have hit it before his brain even registered seeing it.) For an instant, Falcon thought he'd seen a constellation of tiny lights up ahead, but dismissed it as no more than a mild hallucination. Then a great, roaring mass of metal loomed up in the oncoming lane. It blasted by before he could even react, leaving the Callaway bucking wildly in the *thing's* slipstream. With a chuckle he remembered how that had awakened Sly from her slumber mighty pronto. (The thing was gone, just a couple of small red lights in the rearview mirror before she'd even finished her first yell.)

Maybe ten minutes later he was ready for the next one. Letting up on the gas, he slowed the car down to less than a hundred-fifty klicks per hour so he'd have more chance to see it. This time he spotted it a couple hundred meters away. It was moving without headlights, blacked out except for an array of tiny running lights indicating its dimensions. He'd been able to make out more of the details as it hurtled by.

Falcon thought he recognized the tractor as a Nordkapp-Conestoga Bergen. With five huge, self-powered trailers in tow, it formed a massive, concatenated convoy almost a hundred meters from bumper to bumper. It was probably going at about a hundred-twenty klicks per hour, which would make the closing speed something like *two hundred-seventy* klicks. No wonder the Callaway had bucked like a plane trying to fly through a tornado.

Why the frag are they running without headlights? Falcon raged inwardly. Fragging idiots!

It was only then that the details of what he'd seen actually registered. Instead of windows, the big Bergen had the standard slit-like windshield, way the frag up there above the road. No driver could have seen where the hell he was going, what was on the road ahead while seated in that monstrous solid wall of metal. Then he remembered the strange, lumpy devices mounted all over the front of the tractor. And finally he'd understood.

Truckers in Seattle and the rest of UCAS were bitching like hell about these things. The trid reports hadn't made much impression at the time, but now it all came back to him. It seemed that some of the Native American Nations were experimenting with something the Australians had adopted for long-haul freight shipments through the Outback. Totally automated trucks using autopilots with expert systems and limited artificial intelligence that operated entirely via massive sensor suites mounted on the truck bodies. Blasting through the night without a single living person on board. Running without headlights because the sensors saw better in the dark than a meat driver would under noonday sunlight. Much more dependable, because autopilots didn't drink or do drugs or chips while on the job; didn't fall asleep; and—most important—didn't go on strike for higher wages or better working conditions.

Falcon found himself wondering just how effective those autopilots were. What if I'd drifted over the center

line? he thought. Would the big truck have dodged the
Callaway? Would it have hit the brakes? Or would it have
just blasted on through, turning the Twin Turbo into metal
confetti? Quite possibly the latter, he decided. Considering the difference in mass, a head-on crash would total
any oncoming car, but probably wouldn't leave more than
a scratch on the tractor. And the cost of touching up the
paint job was probably less than the cost of any delay.
The thought was chilling.

Another road train rocketed by, shaking the motel to
its foundations. Not a living thing on the freeway, but
the freight still moved.

"How did you know?"

He jumped at the voice, looked over at Sly. She was
still lying in her fetal position, face toward the far wall.

"Huh?" he asked.

She rolled over, sat up, resting her head against the
stained and scratched headboard. "In the Sheraton. How
did you know about the raid?"

It was the same question he'd been asking himself all
the while he'd herded the Callaway through the night. Sly
had been dozing in the passenger seat, leaving him alone
with his thoughts. He shrugged. "I heard something,"
he said uncomfortably.

"What did you hear? Somebody cocking a weapon?
What?"

He hesitated. If he told her the truth, would she think
he was losing it? Then he wondered if maybe he was. "I
heard a voice," he said slowly.

She shook her head in dissatisfaction. "We heard that,
too," she reminded him. "He said, 'Room service'."

"No. I mean, I heard that too. But . . ." His voice
trailed off.

She didn't press him, just watched him steadily. The
light from the motel's neon sign leaked in through the
badly fitted blinds on the front window, tracing straight

lines of yellow-red across the room, across the beds. Her eyes reflected the light, making her look like some kind of fire-eyed creature from a horror trid.

He tried again. "I heard . . . I heard my own voice, but it was in my head. I didn't hear it with my ears. My own voice . . . It said, 'Danger.' And I knew. I *knew* it was a setup."

To his surprise—and relief—Sly didn't call him a liar, didn't say he was a deluded idiot. She just nodded slowly. "Are you a mage, Falcon? A shaman?" she asked quietly.

He shook his head, chuckled wryly. "No," he replied. *Not yet.*

And then he hesitated. Did he know the answer? What was it really like when the totems called? Did you hear it as an outside voice? Or was it your own voice you heard? Was he now treading the path of the shamans, only he didn't know it? He shrugged, pushing the thought aside. He'd worry about that when this was all over. If it would ever be all over.

"Were you born in Seattle, Falcon?" Sly asked. Her voice was soft, relaxed. She seemed still half-asleep, calm and unworried for the first time since he'd met her. Her face was smooth, unlined. It made her look much younger.

"Purity," he answered, "out in the Barrens."

"I know Purity," she said. "What about your family? Are they alive?"

"My mother is, I know that."

"Still in Purity?" He nodded. "Why'd you leave?"

He was silent for a while, remembering. Remembering the woman who'd raised him and his brothers, who'd taken care of them, who'd worked herself to a nub, prematurely old, to try to give them what they needed, to give them a better chance than she'd ever had. Remembering the guilt he'd felt when he first realized just how much it was costing her to feed another mouth, to provide for another person. "I needed to get away," he said at last, disgusted by the note of suppressed emotion in his voice—the sound of weakness. "I just wanted my own life, you know?"

He lay there tense, waiting for her to probe for more information, to open up painful topics, to bring up painful thoughts, with her questions. But she remained silent. He looked over at her. There was a gentle smile on her face, a smile of sadness. Of understanding.

"Your father?" she asked gently.

He shrugged again. "He . . . he went away when I was young." To his surprise, it didn't hurt as much to say it as he'd expected. "He was a shadowrunner."

"Did you know him?"

"No. He went away when I was six, and he wasn't around much before then. But my mother talked about him a lot."

"What happened to him?"

"I don't know," Falcon answered honestly. "Mom— my mother—doesn't either. She said he went on a run but just never came back. She told us it was some big thing, a run on some major corp. She thought maybe he picked up too much heat and went underground to keep from bringing that kind of grief down on his family. She said when the heat was off, when the corps weren't gunning for him anymore, he'd come back to us. Take us away from the plex. That's what she said."

He waited for the next question—*Do you believe that?*—but she didn't ask it. Just watched him quietly, nodded.

So *do* I believe it? he asked himself. Did I *ever* believe it?

At one time, yes, of course. When you're young enough, you always believe your mother, don't you? When she tells you about Santa Claus, about the tooth fairy, about the Easter fragging Bunny. And about your dad the high-class runner making the big score against the corps.

So, was Rick Falk—who'd *also* used the street handle Falcon—hiding out in the lap of luxury somewhere? Waiting for the perfect time to come back to Purity— probably in a Rolls Royce Phaeton limo—to whisk his family away to a life they could never have dreamed? Was he thinking—every day and every night—of the wife and kids he left behind?

What were the fragging odds, huh? His dad had died nine years ago, that was the truth. He went up against a big corp, and the corp swatted him the way Falcon might swat a fragging mosquito. That was the truth.

Like father, like son?

"I'm tired," he told Sly, then rolled over and closed his eyes. Another road train hurtled by, its engine noise and shock wave seeming to shake the entire fabric of reality.

23

1945 hours, November 15, 2053

The city of Cheyenne, Sioux Nation, was larger than Sly had expected, but much smaller than Seattle, of course. The downtown core was about the same size, but the outlying areas were less extensive. No great, sprawling suburbs, decaying and going to hell in a handcart. As they cruised in on Route 80, then taken the Central Avenue off-ramp into downtown, she'd seen hints that there probably *had* once been the spread-out bedroom communities, the rows of car dealerships and fast-food restaurants, the strip malls and the bowling alleys. But all that had been before the genocide campaign, before the Great Ghost Dance and the Treaty of Denver. Now the Native Americans had torn down all those signs of "whiteskin oppression," and the land had returned to its natural state. Scrub grass and trees had grown over the remains of the razed buildings and their foundations.

The downtown itself was something of a contradiction. The buildings were tall, competently built, and much better designed than those of Seattle. There was a kind of coherence to the look of the city, a kind of totality, with each edifice playing its part. Instead of resembling some kind of architectural dog's breakfast, the individual structures meshed with one another, creating a sense of unity. Sly found it strange, and wondered if this was how cities were meant to be.

They'd cruised right through the core and out the other side. The city had a busy, bustling feel, its roads and sidewalks crowded. But somehow it didn't have the same kind of keyed-up, frenetic, on-the-edge feel that marked Seattle. Or Tokyo, for that matter.

They'd driven past the Cheyenne Municipal Airport, ducked onto Route 25 heading north. And there they'd found a place to set up a base of operations. A small motel just off the highway to the west, right on the edge of a massive military airbase. It used to be called Warren Air Force Base or something like that, Sly recalled, dredging that bit of trivia from the depths of her memory. Now, according to the big signs near the main gate, it was simply Council Air Base ("Peace through Vigilant Strength").

The motel was the Plains Rest, a two-story ferrocrete building constructed in a U-shape around a tree-shaded swimming pool. Most of its trade probably came from traveling businessmen who needed a place to flop near the airport but not too far out of town.

Checking in had been no problem. The woman at the front desk had been more alert than the slag at the Crystal Springs, actually reading the personal data from their credsticks when the computer monitor displayed it. The fake IDs and other documentation had stood up to her scrutiny, however. With that she'd handed over the passcard to room 25D, a "housekeeping suite" with a minuscule kitchen alcove, overlooking the pool.

Now Sly sat at the small table, plugging Smeland's cyberdeck into the phone jack, and powering up the system. Falcon was sprawled on one of the big double beds, playing with the controls for the massage system. He rolled his head from side to side, obviously trying to work a kink out of his neck.

"What now?" he asked.

Good question, Sly thought. "I'm just going to deck in and see what's buzzing in the Matrix," she told him, trying to keep the nervousness from her voice. "Keep an eye on me while I'm gone, okay?"

He nodded, patted the machine pistol he'd set on the bedside table. "Watch yourself," he told her quietly.

Yeah, watch myself. She snugged the brain plug into her datajack. Hesitated for a moment. I'm not going in deep, she reminded herself. Just a surface scan. There's no ice on public datanets. Nothing to sweat over. Then, before she could have any second thoughts, she hit the Go key.

Half an hour later Sly unplugged the lead from her datajack, sat back in the uncomfortable chair and stretched. More creaks and clicks from her back. Drek, she was getting too old for this.

Falcon was watching her from the bed. "What gives?"

"Nothing," she said, extending the stretch a touch more, wincing from the pain of misused tendons. "We're in the clear. No wants or warrants out for Sharon Young or Dennis Falk. Or for Cynthia Yurogowski or David Falstaff either, for that matter."

The kid looked surprised. "You expected there to be?" he asked in disbelief. "The UCAS and Sioux are too busy drekking around on each other's borders to have any kind of cooperation."

She nodded. "Yeah, I know. Officially, no extradition treaty, only limited diplomatic relations. But I was worried about *un*official cooperation. As in some Seattle-based megacorp makes a *big* donation to the Sioux Policemen's Benevolent Fund—contingent on them scooping up those desperadoes Young and Falk, of course."

"They could do that?"

She wanted to chuckle at his naïveté, but didn't let her amusement show. "They could do that," she replied levelly. "The fact that they *didn't* probably means they don't know we're here."

"*Probably,*" he echoed.

"Sometimes that's as good as it gets."

He was silent for a few moments. "How long's that going to last?" he asked casually. Only his eyes betrayed the intensity of his concern.

"Before they track us here?" She shrugged eloquently. "Probably not long. At some point *some*body's going to notice that one of Agarwal's cars is gone, and then trace us through the borders."

"We should have stolen some other plates."

Now she did chuckle. "What good would that do?" she asked. "How many 1991 Callaway Twin Turbos do you think are out there?"

He sank back into morose silence. Sly left him to his thoughts.

"So what do we do now?" he asked eventually.

And, as always, that was the big question.

Sly knew what she *wanted* to do, which was head for the Caribbean League and leave the corps to frag each other blind. Maybe that was the only way out. Let the rest of the world go to hell in its own way, and hope no one decided to nuke Barbados. . . .

But the old problem *still* remained. She might decide to opt out of the whole thing, but how could she convince everyone who was after her of that fact? She couldn't. Which meant there was still only one way out, no matter how much she hated to even think about it.

"Are you going to try Zurich-Orbital again?"

She clenched her fists hard to stop the sudden shakes. Turned away, pretended to busy herself coiling up the cyberdeck's fiber-optic lead. "No," she said when she thought she had her reactions under control. "No, I don't think it's time for that yet." She glanced at him from the corner of her eye, watching his response.

He just shrugged, but she thought she saw a hint of something—understanding, maybe?—in his eyes. "The Matrix is *your* game," he said reasonably. "Your call."

Neither spoke for a few minutes. I've got to tell him the truth, she thought at last. I owe him that much.

"I'm scared, Falcon," she blurted out. "I'm scared of going back into the Matrix."

"Why?"

She looked away. "Five years ago, I fragged up. I fragged up really bad. Some black ice got me. It didn't kill me, but it came *this close* to frying my brain. It took years for the damage to heal.

"The *physical* damage," she stressed. "The psychological damage? A lot of it's still there. I'm convinced . . ." She stopped, consciously slowed down the pace of her words. "I'm convinced, deep down convinced, that the next time I hit black ice it's going to kill me. End of story."

"You went into the grid before," the ganger pointed out.

"With T. S. running top cover, yes." She suppressed another shudder. "And even then . . ." She forced herself to stop picturing the hulking shapes, the black ice constructs, flanking Jurgensen.

She paused. Falcon didn't say anything, just watched her steadily. Did he understand any of this? she wondered.

"I know I'm going to have to go back and take another shot at Zurich-Orbital," she said slowly, her own words chilling her to the core. "I don't have any other options. But I'm not ready yet.

"I need more equipment—some utilities for the deck. And maybe a phase loop recourser, some other toys." She paused, added quietly, "And I need to psych myself up for it. Do you understand?" She looked over at him.

He was still sprawled casually on the bed, but something about the line of his body had changed. His eyes were on her, steady, appraising. And comprehending. Accepting. "Your call," he said.

Then suddenly, as if trying to shake off an unpleasant thought, he rolled off the bed. "You do what you got to do," he said firmly. "But I gotta move, Sly. If I stay here I'll go squirrelly for sure."

She smiled in understanding. How long since she was like that, all energy and need to do something? Ten years? More? It didn't feel like it. "Take the car if you want," she said. "But be careful, okay?"

He shot her a rebel smile. "Hey, careful's my middle name."

Yeah, right.

He grabbed the keys from the table, headed for the

door. "Don't wait up, huh?" He paused. "And be careful yourself." And then he was gone.

24

2200 hours, November 15, 2053

Falcon walked slowly, enjoying the feel of the nighttime city around him. He'd parked the Callaway in a pay lot off Twenty-third Street, near the corner of Pershing Boulevard. Paying in advance with his credstick—David Falstaff's credstick, to be precise—he'd discovered something he'd never known about the Sioux Nation.

They still used hard currency for some things. Not just credit transferred electronically, but real, honest-to-god currency. Coins made of metallicized plastic, bills of coated mylar. The actual base currency was the familiar nuyen, like just about everywhere else on the continent. But it seemed that most minor transactions—like paying for parking and probably bribes—were conducted using coins and bills. When Falcon had pulled out his credstick, the parking attendant, a big slag with a dyed Mohawk cut, had gotten a mite testy. Falcon played the dumb tourist trip to the hilt, claiming he was fresh into the nation from Salish-Shidhe lands, quickly apologizing for his ignorance. In a flash of brilliance, he asked the attendant if he could rack up a larger bill on his credstick and take the change in coin. After a minute or so of bitching and whining, the slag had agreed, charging him a hundred nuyen for a five-nuyen parking fee, and handing him eighty-five nuyen in assorted coins and bills. (The extra ten nuyen was, of course, a "transaction fee," required by law.) With the coins an unaccustomed weight in his pocket, Falcon strolled away from the freelance entrepreneur, and started to cruise.

Pershing Boulevard seemed to be "the strip" in Cheyenne. Near the intersection with Twenty-third were some big, government-type buildings, including one that was billed as the Sioux National Theater. But further west along Pershing, more toward the center of town, the buildings were smaller and a little seedier. Lots of taverns and clubs, many with signs advertising LIVE NUDE ON STAGE, and others with more elaborate holo displays showing in almost clinical detail the attractions featured within.

At first he noticed that almost everyone he passed was an Amerindian. Most were wearing clothes that wouldn't look out of place on the streets of Seattle. But every now and again he'd spot someone in traditional deerskin breechcloths, leggings, beaded moccasins. The most common hairstyle was what most people in Seattle called the Mohawk—a fringe of hair down the center of the head, with both sides shaved.

A memory nagged at Falcon, something he'd read in that book by H. T. Langland. This style was never worn by the real Mohawks, he recalled, but by the Creek and some other tribes. According to Langland, the traditional Mohawks had traditionally shaved the *tops* of their heads, leaving a fringe around the sides and back. At the corner of Pershing and Logan he spotted someone with that shaved-top style: a *big* slag in a uniform that fairly screamed "cop," and with a huge fragging gun that looked almost a meter long in the holster on his belt. He hurried on by, averting his eyes, feeling the cop's gaze leaving cold trails down his back.

Strolling down another street of girlie bars, Falcon wondered what he was doing out here. The truth of the matter was what he'd told Sly: he had to get out or in another hour he'd have been chewing up the place. Besides, getting a feel for the city was worth *something*.

And what *about* Sly? Part of him was glad she'd confided in him, told him what was slotting her up. But another part didn't want to know that Sharon Louise Young, the competent, experienced, professional shadowrunner, needed to psych herself up to face something that scared her, just the way Dennis Falk had to. Firmly he put both thoughts aside. Worry about that drek later, he told himself.

He paused outside a particularly seedy-looking dive. Either it didn't have a name or else just didn't bother to advertise it. Its sole claim to fame, according to the holo outside, seemed to be a duo act, featuring two startlingly endowed blonde Anglos who apparently had a strange penchant for vegetables, flutes, and Ping-Pong balls.

He drifted inside, only to be stopped at the door by the bouncer from hell—an Amerindian troll whose asymmetrical head brushed the high ceiling of the entranceway as he demanded some ID. Falcon slotted his credstick, silently grateful for Sly's decision to make David Falstaff twenty-one years old, handed over a crumpled five-nuyen bill for the cover charge, and jandered inside.

The salad show was in full swing, the two blondes on stage looking cosmically bored by the whole production. There were a couple of vacant seats down in "gynecology row" bordering the raised stage, but he chose a small corner table near the rear, giving him a more strategic view of the whole establishment. When the waiter came by, Falcon ordered a shot and a beer, then continued splitting his attention between the show and the audience.

The place was busy but not packed. The guys down in gynecology row were paying rapt attention to the goings-on not two meters in front of their noses, but the rest of the crowd seemed more concerned with their own biz. The feel of the place reminded him of Superdad's, a real hole out in Redmond that catered about equally to blue-collar voyeurs and to street operators looking for a safe meet. With a quickening of interest, Falcon scanned the faces of the crowd a little more intently. If this was like Superdad's, a good percentage of the "audience" would actually be shadowrunners, trying to score some biz. (How active is Cheyenne's shadow community? he wondered. Then wondered some more about how to find out. Go up and ask someone? *Excuse me, sir, but are you a shadowrunner? Are you planning anything illegal in the near future?*)

When his drink order arrived, he paid with a fistful of coins. The waiter watched with exaggerated patience as Falcon had to hold up the individual coins to the stage lighting to read the denominations. Then, with a mutter of, "Tourists," the slag wandered off.

"Hoi there, honey. New to town, huh?"

Falcon turned. There was a woman standing behind him. Short and pleasantly rounded in all the right places, with frizzed auburn hair. She wore a short, low-cut dress in emerald green, off the shoulders, prevented from coming all the way off only by a generous expanse of bosom. Subtle face paint, in colors that accentuated both her hair and the color of the dress she almost wasn't wearing. Broad smile on a face that looked only a couple of years older than Falcon's. Bright green eyes, steady and appraising, that made him up his estimate of her age by more than a decade.

"Feel up to buying a lady a drink, huh?" she asked. Her voice had a musical southern lilt to it.

"Uh . . ." Falcon hesitated for a slow five-count. Then, "Why not?"

She pulled up a chair, settled herself comfortably close to him. Crossed her legs, showing a goodly expanse of pale thigh. Another Anglo, he couldn't help but notice. Falcon started to wave for the waiter, but the woman put a surprisingly large hand on his arm. "I'll get it, honey." And then she whistled between her teeth, painfully loud near his ear. When the waiter looked over, she pointed to the table. The waiter nodded and headed toward the bar. "Sammy knows what I drink," she explained need- lessly. I bet he does, Falcon thought.

They waited in silence until the waiter delivered her drink—a fruity-looking thing with a small paper parasol standing in it. She watched as Falcon fumbled with the bills, paid the waiter the ten nuyen he demanded. Only when Sammy had departed did she speak again.

"Have you got a name, sugar?"

"David Falstaff," he answered. "And you?"

"Bobby Jo Dupuis." She pronounced it "Doo-*pwee*," the second syllable pitched a major seventh above the first, and almost piercing enough to make his fingernails split. "Good ol' Bobby Jo." She laid a hand on his arm again, squeezed gently. "So, where you from?"

"Bellingham," he answered, "up in Salish-Shidhe." The woman's hand on his arm made him a little uncom- fortable, but he was too embarrassed to move it.

"Going to be in town long?"

"Maybe."

"Business or pleasure?" She began to massage his arm gently.

"Biz," he answered quickly. Then he hesitated. Maybe this was a chance to find out something useful about the shadows of Cheyenne. "I guess how long I stay in town depends on whether I find something to make it worth my while, you know what I mean? Something to keep me here." He shrugged, tried to sound nonchalant. "That's kind of why I came in here. Am I in the right place to find something that's going to keep me busy?"

She squealed with laughter. "Sugar, you sure as hell

found yourself the right place. And you found yourself the right person, too. Good ol' Bobby Jo's sure enough the girl for you if you want to keep yourself *real* busy, you get my drift?''

This was definitely *not* going the way Falcon had expected.

''Ya know,'' the woman went on conversationally, ''I really *like* this place, but . . . well, maybe it's not the best place for conversation, you know? Like, for two people to really get to know each other.'' She began to stroke his calf with the side of her foot. ''You got a place around here where we could, you know, *talk*, sugar?'' she purred.

A sudden feeling of panic bubbled up inside Falcon's chest. He looked around wildly for some way out, for some kind of help.

And that was when his eyes lit on a familiar face. On the far side of the room, a big man with broad, bulging shoulders was making his way through the crowd toward the front door. Apparently he'd just emerged from some back room behind the stage. He wasn't looking around him, apparently hadn't spotted Falcon. Frag it, Falcon thought, it's Knife-Edge. The leader of the Amerindian runners who'd tried to ambush Sly, the ones with whom Nightwalker had been working in the sprawl.

Falcon snapped his head around, away from the big runner. Ducked down low toward the table, grabbed his untouched shot glass and sucked back the contents. He tried not to choke at the fire in his throat. Keeping his hand, holding the glass, in front of his face, he watched Knife-Edge from the corner of his eye. The big man still didn't look around him, just worked his way through the crowd to the door, then disappeared outside.

Falcon jumped as Bobby Jo squeezed his leg, high up on his thigh. ''Honey, you look like you done seen a ghost.''

Not quite, he thought, remembering how the hidden sniper's shot—the one that had blown Benbo's chest apart—had cored Knife-Edge front to back. I wish he *was* a ghost. . . .

The runner was gone, the door swinging shut behind him. Falcon jumped to his feet. Bobby Jo, thrown off-balance because of her crossed legs, teetered for a moment, eyes wide, grabbing at the table to keep herself from pitching to the floor. *"Hey!"* she squealed in a teeth-hurting soprano.

"Sorry, Bobby Jo," he mumbled. "Gotta go."

Falcon hurried toward the front door, heard the woman hissing viciously behind him, "Pudlicker! Pudlicking hoopfragging pansy kid . . ." Then, thankfully, he was out into the night, the cold breeze blowing away the alcohol fumes, leaving his head clear.

Knife-Edge was already half a block away, heading east on Pershing, back toward Twenty-third Street. The big runner was walking quickly, but Falcon thought he could detect a trace of a limp. (Only a trace? After the hit he took? There had to be healing magic involved.) The ganger started after him, trying to look casual while also using knots of pedestrians to shield him from view in case Knife-Edge should glance over his shoulder.

It wasn't as easy as it looked on the trid, he decided, after catching the third hard elbow in the ribs when he accidentally bumped a passerby. Trying to keep concealed was slowing him down, and the large figure of Knife-Edge was already almost a block ahead. At this rate, Falcon would lose him before they'd gone another two blocks. What the frag should he do?

Knife-Edge didn't seem to be watching for tails. Since leaving the bar, Falcon hadn't seen him glance over his shoulder once, and the angles were wrong for the runner to use store windows and other tricks. After thinking about it for a moment, he changed his tactics, closing the distance until he was only about a half-block behind his quarry. At that range, it probably didn't matter that he wasn't sheltering behind pedestrians. If Knife-Edge ever did glance back, what were the chances he'd recognize one face in the crowd at a distance of fifty meters? Not good, he figured. On the other hand, Knife-Edge's size and his distinctive gait—thanks to the unknown sniper—made it unlikely that Falcon would lose sight of him.

They passed the Sioux National Theater again. A performance had apparently just ended, and a flood of men and women looking much better-dressed than the pedestrians further west on Pershing were crowding the sidewalk, signaling for taxis or retrieving their own cars from valets. For a single, tense moment, Falcon thought he'd lost Knife-Edge. He pushed through the crowd, winning some curses and another elbow in the ribs. *Where is he?* Falcon thought, then spotted his prey again. He wasn't more than forty meters ahead, still heading east.

On the other side of Twenty-third Street, the number of pedestrians began to diminish. A mixed blessing: the odds of losing Knife-Edge were greatly decreased, while the chance that the runner would spot his shadow were *in*creased. Falcon backed off as far as he dared, pretending to look in a store display until Knife-Edge had opened the gap by another twenty or so meters.

As the traffic on the sidewalk changed, so did the buildings that flanked it. The grotty bars were replaced by high-tone stores and boutiques, all closed at this time of night. Then, as Falcon hit a cross-street called Windmill Road, the buildings changed again to become tall office complexes mixed together with what looked like governmental structures. He glanced over at a large building across the street. *Bureau of Justice,* read the big brass letters beside the door. *Yep,* he thought, *we're into*

government-land. He swung his gaze back to the figure
of Knife-Edge ahead of him.

And couldn't spot him. The runner had vanished.

For a moment Falcon panicked.

Then he saw the large figure. The samurai had left the
sidewalk, was climbing a shallow flight of steps to the
door of a blocky-looking office building just ahead. Two
large bushes flanked the bottom of the stairway, which
explained why Falcon had momentarily lost sight of the
man. He dropped to one knee, pretended to busy himself
adjusting the velcro fastener of his runner, while actually
keeping his eyes on his quarry.

Knife-Edge stopped at the door, reached into his
pocket and extracted something too small for Falcon to
see. With whatever it was in his hand, he reached out to
the door. Then, with the other hand he pulled the door
open. A passcard, Falcon thought, what else? The big
man stepped into the building, the door shutting behind
him, and that was that.

Falcon didn't move immediately, still "adjusting" the
shoe's fastener. He couldn't imagine what he was supposed to do now. All Falcon knew was an overwhelm-
ingly important need to find out where Knife-Edge was
going and what he was doing in Cheyenne. But how could
he do that? He saw the runner disappear into an office
building, sure, but how many businesses would you find
in the average office building?

Was there any way of narrowing it down? It was obvious Falcon couldn't get into the building itself if Knife-
Edge needed a passcard. . . .

Maybe it would help to learn to which floor the runner
had gone. Which would require looking in through the
glass front door of the building, watching the indicator
over the elevator.

Which meant he had to hurry. Falcon jumped to his
feet and ran, stopping only when he reached the large

bush at the bottom of the stairs. Cautiously, he looked
around the bush.

Yes, this was the perfect vantage point. He could see
into the lobby, and had an uninterrupted view of the bank
of elevators. Even better, it looked like an elevator car
hadn't yet responded to Knife-Edge's call. The big runner was standing there, waiting, his back to the front
door and to Falcon. The ganger checked: yes, there *were*
indicators over each of the elevator doors, and yes, they
were big enough for him to read from this distance.

What building was this anyway? He glanced away for
a moment, checked the logo and the big letters mounted
over the door.

The logo was a stylized intertwining of the letters O, M, and
I, the words explicating what those letters meant.

Sioux Nation Office of Military Intelligence, they read.

Office of Military Intelligence. Oh holy frag. . . . For
a single instant, Falcon stood frozen there.

An instant too long. As if cued by some kind of instinct, Knife-Edge glanced back over his shoulder for the
first time.

Falcon felt the runner's gaze on him, saw his eyes
widen in recognition. Saw the man's hand come up holding something. No, not a gun: a tiny radio. Saw him start
to speak into it.

And suddenly Falcon was un-frozen, could move
again. Move he did. He turned and sprinted back the way
he'd come, back toward the crowds and the tacky neon
and the girlie bars and Bobby Jo Dupuis. Away from the
Office of Military Intelligence and the runner who *wasn't*
a runner after all and the official, uniformed skull-
crushers he must have at his beck and call.

He heard something behind him, the crash of boots on
concrete. Running footsteps—*heavy* running footsteps.
He risked a quick look over his shoulder.

And wished he hadn't. There were four of them after

him, Mohawked trolls in semi-military uniforms, heavy-duty handguns out. Where'd they come from? Falcon wondered. Had they been fragging summoned? But of course it didn't *matter* where they'd come from. They weren't more than twenty-five meters behind him, armed to the tusks, and coming like bats out of fragging hell. "Stop!" one of them roared. "Stop or we shoot!"

In your dreams, I'll stop. Falcon poured on the speed.

A gun boomed behind him, then a bullet smashed off the sidewalk at his feet. Fragments of concrete flayed his legs through his trousers. Warning shot? he wondered. Or trying to wing me? It didn't matter anyway, he realized. With Knife-Edge back there, capture was as good as death, wasn't it? Something went whirr-thup past his ear, the gunshot itself sounding an instant later.

Ahead he saw a narrow passageway between two boutiques. He took the corner at maximum speed, scrabbling for traction and almost losing it. Then accelerating for all he was worth down the narrow, echoing lane.

He had to get out of here *now,* he realized. With the unbroken walls on either side of him—ferrocrete, construction composite, or maybe something even more resilient—any bullets shot down the alleyway would ricochet wildly back and forth. Which, of course, increased the chance that they'd strike something valuable—namely, Dennis Falk a.k.a. David Falstaff.

Behind him, the parallel walls amplified the thundering bootsteps of his pursuers. Two guns spoke simultaneously, the bullets whining off into the darkness. Neither shot was close enough for him to feel or hear the passage of the actual round. But that wouldn't last, he knew. All the odds were with the trolls behind him, and nobody lasted long betting against the house.

But what were his options? Judging from the sounds, he thought he was opening up the gap. The troll guards were like greased hell on the straightaways, their long legs eating up the ground. But when it came to any kind of maneuvering, even their strength couldn't overcome their bodies' almost ludicrous inertia. When Falcon had taken the turn into the alley, he'd extended his lead by at least ten meters, maybe a lot more, which the trolls were currently regaining with every step they took.

So, was he supposed to turn now, try and gun them all down, the way the hero does it in a trideo show? Forget it! That might work on the trid, but in the past three days Falcon had learned a lot about just how much relationship the trid had to real life. Slim and none. If he stopped, if he tried to return fire, he might crease one or two of the trolls—if he was *real* lucky—before they reduced him to a cloud of airborne blood droplets and a smear of tissue on the ground. No, thank you.

A wider opening to the right. Without even looking, he blasted around the corner at full bore.

Another alley, wider, stretching off into the distance. This one was wide enough for trucks to drive down to collect garbage from the dumpsters that sat like sleeping beasts every block or two.

For a moment, Falcon could easily have convinced himself he was back in Seattle, back in the part of the sprawl he called home. The Kingdome would be that way, the Renraku Arcology over there.

And then, suddenly, time seemed to telescope, to collapse on itself. He wasn't in Cheyenne. The span of time that had taken him from Seattle to here might never have existed. He was back in the alleys of Seattle, with a pack of trolls on his tail, trolls who wanted to kill him. Sure, part of his brain knew they were military sec-guards. But, by the spirits and totems, they might as well have been the Disassemblers dogging him near the docks. For some reason, the sense of familiarity energized his body, gave him the juice to run even harder.

The way he'd lost the Disassemblers that time was by

wearing them down. In any straight race he would lose. So the trick was to throw a couple of cuts and turns into it.

To his left, he saw another opening, another alley. He almost laughed out loud as he cut hard left, every muscle in his body cooperating like parts of some perfect racing machine. Two more bullets went spang! off the concrete around him, but he didn't slow down. The trolls were already fifteen meters further back. Another opening yawned, this time to his right. As he rounded the corner, this time he *did* laugh out loud. Another fifteen meters.

He didn't know how long the chase went on, soon losing track of his direction or of how far back the pursuers were. He knew from the echoes of their pounding boots and once in a while the sound of a shot that they were still on him, but nothing got anywhere near him anymore. He was glad for the sounds of pursuit; without that to cue from, his random cuts and turns through the back streets and alleys of Cheyenne might accidentally have taken him straight back into their faces.

And then it didn't *matter* how long he'd been running. All that mattered was how much longer the chase would go on. The cold air was tearing at his throat, searing his lungs. The muscles of his legs burned like fire.

That was the difference between these slags and the Disassemblers, he thought, listening to the steady sounds of pursuit. These guys were in shape.

Maybe in better shape than Falcon. He might be opening the gap, but that was purely because of the speed differential. The further he ran, the more convinced he became that they'd be on him the moment he stopped. They'd be on him and they'd kill him. Or worse, he thought, remembering what was left of Agarwal.

He hurled himself around another corner, almost plowing full-speed into an open dumpster. He skidded to a stop.

Why not?

He vaulted into the dumpster, sinking calf-deep into the noisome contents. Reaching up, he dragged the heavy lid down. Unlike the ones in Seattle, these hinges weren't rusty; the lid was going to close all the way. Working quickly, he jammed something under the metal top, leaving an opening almost a hand's-breadth wide. Then he crouched low, put his eye to the gap, and waited.

What the frag am I doing? he thought suddenly, the answer hitting him as hard as one of those speeding road trains he'd passed on the nighttime highways. The realization was terrifying. He was acting as though his pursuers were the Disassemblers, him trying to repeat the same trick that had saved his hoop back in Seattle.

But these slags weren't the Disassemblers. They were trained fragging security guards, probably military-trained. And he thought he was going to shake them off as easily as some chipped-out homeboy trolls from the docks?

Falcon reached up, set his palms against the heavy metal lid, prepared to push it open. This fragging stupid detour had cost him too many seconds, too many meters. If he was *really* lucky, he'd be out of the dumpster with the same lead he'd started with outside the OMI building.

But he *wasn't* lucky. Before he could lift the lid a centimeter, the sound of boots against the concrete became louder, clearer. In panic, he peeked through the gap he'd left.

The trolls had rounded the corner, were no more than a few steps from his hiding place. All were breathing hard, but none looked trashed. Falcon guessed that, if necessary, they could keep up the chase as long as he could.

But they won't have to, will they? He ducked as low as he could and still watch the outside. He struggled to keep his labored breathing quiet.

The leader of the trolls didn't waste his breath in speech. In the dim light, his hand flashed through a quick sequence of complex gestures. They didn't mean anything to Falcon, but they were obviously expressive to his comrades. One nodded.

Then, to Falcon's horror, the troll walked straight to the dumpster. Reaching out with a hand the size of Falcon's head, he grabbed the edge of the metal lid.

25

2312 hours, November 15, 2053

Sly checked her watch. It had been a hard couple of hours. After Falcon left, she'd gone back into the Matrix, staying out of areas that probably had serious security, yet digging a little deeper than the first time.

It was an axiom of shadow work that the best way to find something hidden was not to look for it directly. Instead, you watched other things that might be affected by the item you were after. You looked for unusual reactions, strange perturbations that were not logical. And when you found the perturbations, the chance was good that what you were actually seeing was the effect your hidden target had on things around it. If you looked in enough areas, cataloged enough perturbations, you could often mentally calculate the exact location of your original subject. Someone had once told Sly that this technique came from astronomy, and was responsible for the discovery of one of the outer planets—Pluto, she thought it was. Astronomers had measured strange perturbations in the orbits of other planets, and postulated that they were caused by the gravity of another, as yet undiscovered, world. They calculated where that new world would have to be to cause the measured effects, pointed their telescopes to that part of the sky, and bingo.

Sly had done very much the same thing, but instead of planetary orbits, she examined the activities of local corporations, specific types of news reports, and activity on public computer bulletin board systems. She looked for patterns analogous to the slight wobbles in a planet's motion that the astronomers had noted, and she found them. What they told her was that something large and very influential was operating beneath the surface of Cheyenne business activity.

A large and active shadow community. It couldn't be anything else.

Where did the runners come from? she wondered curiously. Did they learn their chops here or were they imports? How many of the Seattle runners who'd dropped out of sight and who she'd assumed were flatlined had actually pulled a quick fade and reappeared in Cheyenne?

Once she had a sense of the size and activity of the shadow community, it wasn't too hard to plug in to it, at least peripherally. Large electronic credit transfers to various sources gave her the LTG number of a local "salvage consultant" and part-time fixer named Tammy. And from her, Sly purchased the LTG number for the local Shadowland server.

During her search, she'd come across something else, something she hadn't been actively seeking, but interesting just the same. A name kept popping up, apparently the name of someone who was occasionally active in the Cheyenne shadows, an infrequent player but very influential when he *did* play. *Montgomery*. No first name, and no further details. Could that be *Dirk* Montgomery? Buzz on the streets of Seattle said Dirk had made a really big score—*the* score, the Big One that every runner dreamed of—and had slipped into the light to enjoy his spoils in retirement. If that was true, why was he still hustling? And why was he in Cheyenne?

She shrugged, then put those speculations aside as irrelevant. It was probably a different Montgomery anyway.

Sly toyed with the deck's brain plug, glanced over at the bed where Falcon had been sprawled. To her surprise, she found herself wishing the kid were back. At least he would have been someone to talk things over with.

The idea of decking into the local Shadowland system frightened her, she had to admit, but she didn't know why. It wasn't as if she'd be going up against any ice. (There *was* ice associated with Shadowland, of course, to protect it from corp and government deckers who'd like to close it down. But as long as she didn't try anything drek-headed like commandeering the system or erasing important files, she wouldn't even know the intrusion countermeasures were there.) It was just that Shadowland was symbolic. It represented her old life, the life of the shadow decker. The life that had almost killed her, that had slotted up her mind for more than a year, and that still caused her occasional nightmares.

Stupid, she told herself. Logically there was no more risk in logging onto Shadowland than in making a phone call. She'd already done something much more risky by trying to hack into Zurich-Orbital.

Yes, another part of her mind replied, but then you had Smeland running cover, didn't you? This time there's nobody to watch your back.

She shook her head. She knew that she'd be able to find dozens of reasons—logical or emotional—why she shouldn't do what she knew she had to. So the trick is, don't think about it, she told herself. Quickly, before she could change her mind, she snugged the plug into her datajack and typed the first command string into the deck.

* * *

Erehwon, the place was called. It was a "virtual bar," something Sly had heard about but never experienced personally. Back when she'd been running the Matrix for a living, people had talked about creating "virtual meeting places" in the network. But if any such places had actually existed then, neither she nor anyone she'd known had ever visited one.

Of course, that was five years ago, an eternity when it came to technical developments. Virtual meeting places—forums, discussion groups, and so on—were commonplace, an accepted way of life. Instead of meeting physically around a conference table or using limited intermediaries like conference calls and two-way video, people with datajacks could meet *virtually*. All participants in a meet would project their persona icons into a selected locale in the Matrix, and then carry on their discussions there.

The advantages were obvious: no travel time or cost and total physical security (because the participants never had to leave their homes). Some technopsychologists were pointing at the phenomenon of virtual meetings as one of the most significant changes in human society since agriculture replaced early mankind's hunter-gatherer existence. These psychs believed that the Matrix would eventually spawn "electronic tribes" and "virtual nations." Membership in a particular social group would no longer depend on physical location, but more on channels of communication. Just as "telecommuting" had changed the work place in the late nineteen-nineties because knowledge workers no longer had to live within commuting distance of—or even on the same continent as—their employer, so this would change other facets of societies (or so said the pundits). While most people in 2053 still thought of "groupness" and "nationhood" in a geographical, location-based sense, virtual meeting places were starting to break this concept down.

Even with the proliferation of virtual meeting places, Erehwon seemed to be unique. According to the buzz on the Shadowland bulletin boards, it was a virtual *club*. Deckers could project their icons into the network nodes that made up Erehwon and interact with anyone else who happened to be there. Biz went down, of course, but many deckers from around the world seemed to like just hanging there, conversing with other patrons and simply enjoying themselves.

The virtual club was crowded as Sly's icon entered the node. She remained motionless for a moment, absorbing the scene around her.

According to the sensorium being fed into her data-jack, she was standing in a smoky, low-ceilinged tavern. The resolution was good enough that, for a moment, she could almost believe it was real. But then she looked closer at the crowd.

The patrons of Erehwon reminded her of a group of video-game characters who'd taken a night off and gone out for a beer. The decker icons that filled the place ranged from the innocuous to the threatening to the whimsical, and from the most mundane to the most outré and bizarre. A neon samurai rubbed shoulders with an anthropomorphic hedgehog, while a two-headed dog engaged an alabaster angel and a black gargoyle in conversation. Resolution varied from icon to icon. In some the individual pixels were large, creating a coarse, "jaggy" appearance, and the animation was jerky and imprecise. In others, the rendering was so masterful that they resembled state-of-the-art cinematic computer animation, looking more real than reality itself. Making a quick tally in her mind, Sly estimated the current clientele at about thirty-five deckers.

To her right was a long oak bar, "the juice bar," one

of the features that set Erehwon apart from other virtual locales. It was a Matrix construct, but it served a very real purpose. Deckers could send their icons up to the bar, where they could order "buzzers." In terms of icons, the drink icons appeared as beers, highballs, or shooters. In actuality, however, they represented small and simple utility programs that produced slight and temporary bio-feedback loops in the minds of the deckers partaking. These loops produced various psychological effects—generally a mild euphoria—that partially mimicked the effects of alcohol. Although Sly had no intention of experimenting with buzzers tonight, she had to admit the concept was attractive. One could get the pleasant buzz of drinking without any hangover, and theoretically, simply abort the utility at any time to be instantly "sober" again.

She started to circulate. Even though nothing here was "real," and individuals' icons could—if both wished it—pass through each other without interference, old habits died hard. She threaded her way through the crowd, careful not to bump anyone's elbow or tread on anyone's foot.

It took her a few subjective minutes to find the icon she was looking for. A bare-chested Amerindian warrior with the head of a pearl-white eagle, he was sitting at a small corner table. In front of him were three empty beer mugs, indicating that he'd been doing buzzers. He looked up as she approached.

"Moonhawk," she said.

The finely rendered icon blinked its eyes. "Do I know you?"

For a moment Sly wished she'd been able to visit Erehwon as her familiar quicksilver dragon icon. That icon had something of a rep, possibly even one that spread as far as Cheyenne. But of course she was limited to the icon in the MPCP of Smeland's deck—a rather uninspired female ninja.

"No," she answered coolly. "But there are people in Cheyenne who know *you*. They say you're good."

The eagle-headed warrior shrugged. "Good enough, maybe," he said laconically. "Who gave you my name?"

Sly smiled, shook her head. "That's not the way they want to play it."

Moonhawk shrugged again. "So talk. What do you want?"

"Tools of the trade," she said. "Utilities. A couple of pieces of hardware."

"Why come to me?"

"Buzz says you're the man."

"Maybe." Moonhawk studied her briefly. "Hypothetically speaking," he said after a moment, "if maybe I was able to help you out, you've got the nuyen?"

Now we get down to it, Sly thought. *"Hypothetically"*—she stressed the word ironically—"I'd have the nuyen." She ran a quick display utility that produced a wallet fat with banknotes. She waved the wallet-construct under Moonhawk's nose, then made it vanish again.

"So, again hypothetically, what're you looking for?" the fixer asked. "What utilities? What hardware?"

"For utilities, I want it all," Sly said firmly. "The full suite: combat, defense, sensor, masking."

Moonhawk chuckled. "You ain't wanting much, are you? What're you doing, refitting a whole slotting deck?"

That's just what I'm doing, she thought, but only smiled.

"Any particular style?" the fixer queried. "You into music, colors, what?"

"Doesn't matter to me. You give them to me, I can use them. They've just got to be hot. Hypothetically speaking, of course."

Moonhawk snorted. "What hardware?"

"A phase loop recourser." When the fixer didn't respond immediately, she added, "A PLR."

The icon's piercing eyes widened in surprise. "A *who*?" Then he laughed. "Chummer, you're out of date. *Way* out of date. PLRs don't do squat against the ice they're writing now. Any black ice worth its name's gonna go through a PLR like it wasn't there." He laughed again, a harsh bark of cynical amusement.

Right then she was thankful that her icon wasn't well enough rendered to show her embarrassment. "Then all I need is an off-line storage chip," she said, keeping her voice as level as possible. "Two hundred megapulses. And a microelectronics tool kit. And that's it."

"And that's it," he echoed. "Well, *omae*, it's your lucky day, considering we've just been talking hypothetically. I know a guy knows a guy who's got some utilities he'd be willing to part with."

"They've got to be hot."

"*Nova* hot," Moonhawk assured her. "It's all rating six and up"—he shot her a doubtful look—"if your deck can handle it. Class act all the way, all from IC Crusher Systemware. You *do* know ICCS, don't you?"

She didn't. Even the software companies had changed since her day, but nodded knowingly. "He's got the hardware too?"

The fixer nodded. "You interested?"

"I'm interested," she confirmed.

"Okay then," Moonhawk said briskly, suddenly all business. "How soon you need them?"

Sly hesitated. The sooner I get the utilities, the sooner I don't have any more excuses. She forced the thought away. "Soonest," she said firmly. "Tonight."

The hawk-headed icon hesitated. "Rush might cost extra."

"Bulldrek," she told the fixer firmly. "If your friend of a friend's got the stuff like he says he does, he'll want to unload it as soon as possible so he can get his hands on the nuyen, right? And if he doesn't have the stuff on hand, I'm going to go deal with a *serious* fixer. Do we understand each other, Moonhawk?''

The fixer glared at her for a long moment, then his expression cleared. He chuckled. ''Okay, okay, hang easy. It was worth a try, right? Give me a tick and I'll set up the meet.''

The icon froze, like a single frame in a movie. Sly knew the fixer had suspended his Matrix connection while placing another call.

It didn't take long. ''You've got a meet,'' Moonhawk announced. ''At oh-one-thirty. That soon enough for you?''

Sly nodded. ''Where?''

''Reservoir Park, at the Roundhouse. Head east out of town, you'll find it. The man's name is Hal.'' He hesitated. ''You sure you got the nuyen for this? Your shopping list is going to cost you a hundred-K nuyen and up.''

''I'm good for it, Moonhawk.'' She paused, drew her ninja icon's lips back from her teeth in what could—almost—be called a smile. ''Your chummer better have the goods, slag. Or next time we meet it's going to be in the flesh.

''Get my drift?'' she said before jacking out.

26

2320 hours, November 15, 2053

Falcon could smell the troll's foul breath even over the reek of the dumpster as the sec-guard's massive hand closed on the edge of the metal lid.

The young ganger ducked lower, heart pounding in his

ears, stomach in knots. He thought wildly about firing a long burst from his pistol into the troll's face the moment he opened the dumpster, but then what? There would still be three more of them.

With a creak, the heavy lid began to rise.

"Hey, you slots! Over here!" The taunting voice echoed from the concrete walls of the surrounding buildings. A male voice, young and dripping with scorn.

One of the troll guards cursed, and the lid banged down again. The chunk of garbage that Falcon had used to wedge the lid open was still in place, so it didn't close all the way. Confused, he peered out through the narrow slit.

The trolls had turned away from the dumpster, were starting off in hot pursuit of a figure heading back the way Falcon had come. A familiar-looking figure with straight dark hair, leather jacket, and velcro-strapped runners. It could have been Falcon's identical twin.

But there was something *strange* about the figure. Not just his appearance. He just doesn't feel right, Falcon thought, then realized he was shivering, and not only from fear. Something crazy was going down here.

One of the trolls snapped off a couple of shots at the fleeing figure. From his angle of vision, Falcon thought the shots had gone true, but the figure showed no reaction. A mocking laugh rang out—not Falcon's voice. Then the trolls were out of sight, the crash of their boot heels on the concrete soon fading.

Just what the flying frag was going on here?

Falcon pushed the lid open. He climbed out cautiously, dropping silently to the ground where he crouched in the shadow of the dumpster.

"It's okay, they're gone."

He spun at the voice sounding beside him. Dragged the machine pistol from his pocket, brought it to bear.

The weapon's sighting laser painted the face of a

woman standing near another dumpster. She hadn't been there a second ago, he told himself, I *know* it! She squinted her eyes against the glare of the laser, but made no other move.

She was Amerindian, with straight black hair gathered into a braid that hung halfway down her back. She wore what Falcon considered traditional Plains-tribe garb: a deerskin tunic over wrapped leggings and beaded moccasins on her feet. Feathers, beaded fetishes, and other talismans covered her clothing. Though she was small, almost tiny, something about her demeanor made Falcon feel more like she was looking *down* at him from some superior height. Frag that drek. *I'm* the one with the gun, he reminded himself.

He tried to guess her age, found it very difficult. Her hair was lustrous black without a trace of gray, her face unlined. And very attractive, he couldn't help but notice. Judging from those clues, he'd have guessed her to be about twenty. But again he came back to her manner, her obvious self-possession. Taking that into account blew his estimate out of the water. She could be any age at all.

Realizing that he still held his gun levelled between her eyes, he didn't lower the weapon, but backed off on the trigger so the sighting laser died. "Who are you?" he demanded.

"My name is Mary Windsong," the woman answered, her voice light, almost lilting. She dropped her gaze from his eyes to the weapon. "That isn't necessary, you know," she added. "I don't mean you any harm." Then she continued to merely watch him calmly.

Falcon felt his face begin to get hot. Was he blushing? He felt vaguely ludicrous, a big, tough shadowrunner pointing his heat at this unarmed, harmless-looking woman. "Sorry," he mumbled. He lowered the gun to waist-level, but didn't put it away. It stayed in his hand, the gun barrel not *quite* pointing at her.

"You know *my* name," the woman said pointedly.

The ganger hesitated, then thought, What harm would it do? "Falcon," he said, then went silent before asking what he really wanted to know. "What the frag was that a minute ago? I saw . . . I saw *me* running away."

Mary Windsong laughed, and Falcon was forced to knock a few years off his original age estimate. She's not much older than me, he realized.

"It was the best I could think up on short notice," she answered lightly. "I saw you duck into the trash, and I knew the OMI goons would look in there. So . . . just a simple illusion spell, but it did the trick."

"You're a shaman, then?"

She nodded. "I follow the path of the totems," she acknowledged.

"Which totem?"

"I sing the songs of Dog."

Falcon wanted to pursue that line of questioning further, but first he had to know some other things. "Why did you help me?" he asked. "What's in it for you?"

She shrugged. "Nothing, directly. But when I saw those OMI goons about to grab you"—she smiled broadly—"I figured, what the hell, eh?"

"What's *with* OMI, anyway?" he wanted to know. "Who are they? What's their game?"

Mary chuckled again. "You want I should give you a political science lesson right here and now?" she asked. "The trolls will have lost the illusion by now; they might be back any time."

Falcon hesitated. His first impulse was to get the frag out of there, to save his own hoop and let Mary go about her business. But, he had to admit, the young shaman probably had information that would be useful to him and

Sly. Like, what was the connection between Knife-Edge and this OMI thing?

"Is there somewhere we can go and talk?" he asked.

The tavern was called The Buffalo Jump. A small, smoky place, no tables, just a long bar, scarred and carved here and there with initials and bits of graffiti. There were only five patrons present, not counting Falcon and Mary. Amerindians all, and every one a tough-looking hombre, much more interested in their beers than the other patrons.

Mary led Falcon to two rickety stools at the far end of the bar, away from the front window with its flickering beer signs. The bartender, a mountain of muscle with a face that looked like a boiled red fist, apparently knew Mary. He greeted her with a warm smile—or his best approximation of same—and brought them each a half-liter of beer. He then lumbered down to the other end of the bar, and continued his task of using a gray rag to redistribute the grime on the counter top.

The shaman took a healthy pull on her beer. Then, "You want to know about the OMI, right?" she said. "How much do you know about Sioux politics?"

Falcon shook his head. "Not enough."

She chuckled. "You got that straight, particularly if you're on the bad side of the OMI.

"OMI's military intelligence," she went on. "They're supposed to work closely with the Sioux Special Forces—the Wildcats, you heard of them?"

Falcon nodded slowly. He'd heard stories about the Wildcats, the ultimate military hard cases, experts at black ops. A unit of heavily cybered warriors leavened with a platoon of shamanic commandos. "Real bad news, right?"

"Good understatement, chummer," she said. "OMI

also works with the rest of the military doing threat estimates, intelligence on troop movement, other support functions like that. At least, that's what they're *supposed* to be doing.

"Couple of years back, OMI got a new director, a real hag from hell called Sheila Wolffriend, who everybody just calls 'the Wolf.' Well, the Wolf started building OMI into her own private little empire. More assets, more resources. Looser ties with the Wildcats and less supervision by the Sioux Military Council. Instead of merely using them to get information and provide support for the other forces, she started running her own black ops from time to time. People kicked and screamed at first, particularly the Wildcats; they expected her to frag up big time, leaving them to clean up the drek afterward. But Wolf didn't just *think* she was good, she *was* good. All of her ops ran smooth as silk.

"The Wildcats approached the Military Council," Mary went on, " and tried to get OMI shut down. But the Council didn't go along. They backed the Wolf, and even cut back on the Wildcats' authority." Mary laughed softly. "A lot of people decided right then that the Wolf knew where some real important bodies were buried."

"Hey, wait a minute." Falcon held up a hand for silence. "How the frag do you know all this?"

"Where do you think OMI got its assets?" the shaman asked. "From the Wildcats? They'd like to see the Wolf burned at the stake. So where?"

Falcon thought for a moment, then smiled grimly. "From the shadows," he guessed.

"Right in one. She recruited some of Sioux's hottest runners. So of course some of the background leaked out into the 'shadow telegraph,' you know what I mean?"

Falcon understood. The shadow telegraph was the underground grapevine that carried the buzz about almost everything that happened out of the light—if you knew how to tap into it. "So what happened then?"

Mary shrugged. "That's when the telegraph kind of dried up. The Wolf's got *something* pretty heavy going on. What some people are saying is that OMI wants to mount a big operation against the UCAS. Other people say they'll be going after Pueblo. Me, I don't know: either one sounds like pure suicide."

"Do you know any of the people the Wolf recruited?" Falcon asked.

"Some. Anybody in particular?"

As accurately as he could, Falcon described the runner who called himself Knife-Edge.

When he was finished, Mary shook her head. "No bells," she said. "But you could have been describing any number of players in Sioux."

Falcon nodded, finished off his beer. "Yeah. Well, thanks, Mary. I owe you one." He started to get off the bar stool.

"Hold it." She grabbed his forearm in a surprisingly strong grip. "I've answered your questions; maybe I've got some of my own."

He resettled himself on the stool. "Shoot."

"What totem do you follow?"

He grimaced. "None." Then added fiercely, "Yet."

Mary looked perplexed. "No? But . . ." Her voice trailed off.

"But what?"

"But I felt . . ." She paused, apparently trying to order her thoughts. "I felt the power of the spirits."

"Huh? When?"

"When I cast the illusion of you running from the OMI guards. I felt the power in you, I felt you sense my song."

He stared at her. He remembered his reaction at the sight of his magical double across the alley. He *did* sense

something strange about it. It wasn't right, he recalled.
I *felt* it. Is that what she's talking about?

"I felt . . . something," he said quietly.

"You sensed my song," she repeated firmly. "Only
one who has heard the spirits could do that. But"—she
looked puzzled again—"you say you don't follow the path
of the totems."

"I *tried*," he told her, then quickly explained about
the book by H. T. Langland, about his attempts to hear
the call of the spirits. "I . . ." He hesitated, embarrassed. "I was on a vision quest." He glared at her chal-
lengingly, daring her to laugh or contradict him.

But Mary Windsong didn't do either. She just scruti-
nized his face. "A vision quest," she said slowly.
"Yes." She paused again. "Do you want to complete
your vision quest, Falcon? I think I might be able to help
you."

He didn't answer immediately, just stared at the young
woman. Is she serious? he wondered. Or is she just
stringing me along, taunting me because she does something I can't?

But Mary's face showed no hint of a mockery. She
only sat there, calmly watching him, waiting for his answer. "How?" he asked huskily.

Mary shrugged—a little embarrassed, Falcon thought.
"There are ways to . . . to aid a vision quest," she said.
"Techniques some shamans have developed. You can
help someone along, be their . . . their 'spirit guide,' I
call it, but that's not quite right."

"How does it work?"

She met his gaze, and he felt a tingle run through his
body—almost an electric shock. "I'll show you, if you
like," she said quietly.

He hesitated. "Does that mean I have to follow your
totem?"

Mary shook her head. "Not necessarily . . . All the

guide does is take you to the plane of the totems. Whatever happens after that"—she shrugged again —"that's up to you and the totems, not me."

"But how does it work?" he asked again.

She was silent for a moment, seeming to order her thoughts. "Sometimes the totems are speaking to you," she said slowly, "but your own mental walls keep you from hearing. A spirit guide can help break down those walls—help you hear the voice of the totems—if the voices are there to be heard."

"It's safe?" he asked.

She smiled grimly. "Safer than some other techniques people use," she answered.

"So it's safe," he pressed.

"I didn't say that," Mary corrected him. "The technique *itself* is safe. But sometimes people use it to hear the call of the totems when the totems *aren't* calling . . . if that makes any sense. *Then* there can be . . . problems. Do you want to try it? It's your decision. I can guide you, to the best of my abilities, but—"

"But if I'm wrong, if the totems *aren't* calling . . . what can it do to me?"

She looked at him steadily. "It can kill you," she said softly. "But I don't think that's a danger with you. I *felt* the Power in you, and I'm not usually wrong about these things."

Falcon stared at her. It sounded so enticing, so simple. Should he try it?

Walking the path of the shaman—it was what he'd always dreamed about. And here was this girl—this shaman—offering him a chance to realize that dream. She said I sensed her song, he thought. Did I? I sensed something. Do I risk it?

And what about Sly? Could he really make the decision in isolation? He and Sly were chummers, comrades.

If he died, she'd be alone. (And I'd be *dead*! he reminded himself.)

But what could he really do to help Sly anyway? She had to deck into Zurich-Orbital, and he couldn't follow her into the Matrix. She didn't need him to do what she had to do. If he failed—if he died—it wouldn't affect her that much.

And if I succeed, I'll be a shaman, Falcon thought. And as a shaman, I could help Sly a lot more after she's made her Matrix run. Afterward, when things are winding down, I'd be able to help her more, wouldn't I?

And I'd be a shaman.

He glanced at his watch. Midnight, or close enough. What had Sly said? That she needed to get some utilities and some tech toys before making her run on Zurich-Orbital. That would take some time, wouldn't it? *Time enough for me to do this. . . .*

Turning to Mary, Falcon swallowed through a throat suddenly tight. "Let's do it," he said hoarsely.

Mary led Falcon into The Buffalo Jump's back room, an airless, windowless broom closet furnished in Early Squalor. Following Mary's instructions, the ganger settled himself on the floor, forcing his legs into an approximation of the full-lotus position. The young shaman crouched facing him, placed a small metal bowl between them. Wordlessly, she opened the beaded pouch on her belt, pulled out various kinds of leaves and what looked like dried herbs, all wrapped in small swatches of velvet. Some she tossed right into the bowl, others she crushed between her palms before adding them to the mix. Sharp odors stung Falcon's nose, caught in the back of his throat.

From the bag, Mary also extracted a small fetish with a feather tied to it by a slender leather thong. It was the skull of a tiny animal—a mouse probably, Falcon thought. She closed her eyes, passed the fetish over the bowl. Then she set it down on the floor, opened her eyes again.

Mary looked searchingly into his face. "Are you ready?" Her voice was quiet, but intense enough to give him chills.

Falcon only nodded, not trusting himself to speak.

"Close your eyes," she instructed. He did, a moment later feeling her palms cool against his cheeks. They smelled strongly of the herbs she'd crushed between them. "Breathe deeply," she said. Her palms were soft but firm, cool but alive with some kind of energy Falcon couldn't have named. The feel of her flesh against his was reassuring, comforting.

Then the hands were gone. "Keep your eyes closed until I tell you to open them," Mary told him softly. He nodded, then heard a click, a quiet hiss. His nostrils filled with pungent smoke, probably from her burning the leaves and herbs.

"Breathe deeply."

He did so, drawing the warm smoke deep into his lungs. At first the membranes of his nose and throat burned and stung, but numbness quickly replaced the pain. The vapors seemed to fill his head; he could feel them billowing through his mind, mingling with his thoughts. Then Falcon felt as though he were pivoting slowly backward—*just like being too drunk*. He wanted to open his eyes, to stop the dizzying movement, but he kept them tightly shut.

"Breathe deeply," Mary repeated, her voice sounding so far away. "Breathe steadily."

He nodded. The sense of movement became more intense, yet less disorienting. He felt himself growing warmer, more comfortable and reassured, as if cocooned and sheltered from anything that could harm him. He felt his lips curve in a smile.

There was a sound in his ears, a quiet, musical humming. It was Mary, he realized. His fingertips and his lips began to tingle. Mary's humming took on a faint ringing tone. Falcon took another deep breath. . . .

And the universe opened up around him. He heard himself gasp.

It was as if he could sense the infinity of creation all around him, with himself at the very center. A tiny, infinitesimally small point. Alone, vulnerable . . . inconsequential.

But then the universe turned inside out; *he* turned inside out. The infinity was still there, but now it was inside him. The universe was an infinitesimal point, within the infinity that was Dennis Falk. He gasped again in wonder.

"Don't worry." Mary's voice came to him softly. "I'll be with you. There's nothing to fear."

"What's happening?" he asked.

"You're walking the path of the totems," she said quietly. Her voice sounded even more distant, twisted and shifted out of all human timbre. Her last words seemed to echo around him, *through* him. "The totems, the totems, the totems, the totems . . ."

In sudden alarm Falcon opened his eyes.

But it wasn't the grimy back room of the Buffalo Jump that he saw.

27

So this was Reservoir Park. The cab driver had known right off when Sly told him her destination, so there was no risk she was in the wrong place.

The cab driver. At first it had irked her that Falcon hadn't come back with the Callaway. But then she realized that she hadn't given him any reason to think she'd be needing the car so soon. Besides, the Callaway was definitely an attention-grabber, definitely not appropriate for this meet. The cab had dropped her off on Deming Drive, half a klick from the park, and she'd walked the rest of the way.

Reservoir Park was a rolling expanse of grass several hundred meters across. A promontory projected out into the reservoir, which, presumably, provided drinking water for Cheyenne. A gentle breeze was blowing off the water, chill and refreshing. Sly imagined that the place was probably a riot of colors in spring and summer, with flowers spilling out of the many soil beds that surrounded the grassy area. At this time of year, however, the flower beds were empty, leaving only plots of bare soil.

Near the far end of the park, just south of the promontory, was a circular building maybe twenty meters in diameter. That had to be the Roundhouse Moonhawk had mentioned. Sly walked slowly toward it, loosening her heavy revolver in its holster.

Drawing closer, she could see that the Roundhouse didn't have any walls as such, just pillars, probably ferrocrete, supporting a conical roof. For a moment she was puzzled, then realized it must have been designed as a shelter for picnickers in the event of a sudden rainstorm. She smiled wryly to herself. Maybe she'd been in the shadows too long. Sly had almost forgotten that normal people did things like go on picnics.

The Roundhouse was an excellent site for a meet, she had to admit. There were no other buildings, no bushes or trees nearby, nothing to conceal anyone who might wish to sneak up on her and her contact. The fact that she could see clearly into the Roundhouse once she got closer also greatly lessened the odds of a setup.

Sly checked her watch. Still more than ten minutes to go until the time of the meet. Cautiously, she did a full circuit of the Roundhouse, keeping about fifty meters out from the building, scouting the terrain for cover that someone might use to creep up on the meeting. Nothing. Nobody there and no way anyone could get within twenty meters without exposing himself. Satisfied, she crouched down near the bank of the reservoir and waited.

At exactly oh-one-thirty, a light came on inside the Roundhouse. Sly could see that it was from a camp-style battery lantern apparently resting on a table. In the yellow light, she also saw a small, slender figure standing in the center of the building. She waited a few minutes more, hoping to create some tension that would serve her interests in the negotiations. Only then did she slowly begin to move in.

The figure, presumably Hal, was turned north, away from the reservoir, in the direction of the main road leading here. Silent as a ghost, Sly approached from the opposite direction, from the reservoir side, able to observe her contact carefully as she did.

Hal appeared to be an elf, short for that metatype, but with the characteristic slender bone structure and slightly pointed ears. He wore blue jeans, a jean jacket, and motorcycle boots. His blond hair was short and subtly spiked on top, shoulder-length at the back. Slung over his shoulder on a padded strap was a metal case about the size of a briefcase. Sly smiled with approval. It looked like he'd brought her stuff.

She made it all the way to the edge of the Roundhouse's concrete floor before Hal heard the first sound of her approach. He spun around in surprise, but didn't reach for any concealed weapon. Sly stepped forward, holding her empty hands out from her body.

"I assume you're Hal," she said.

The elf gave her a grim, ironic smile. "And I *know* who you are, Sly," he said.

That voice, she'd heard it before. But where?

And then she remembered. On the Seattle docks, just before the sniper had opened fire. . . .

Setup!

Simultaneously with that horrible realization, the figure facing her shimmered like a mirage, changed. Grew taller and broader, its face twisting into more familiar lines. Even the clothing changed from casual denims to a semi-military uniform. She recognized the face grinning down at her. Knife-Edge, the leader of the Amerindian runners who'd tried to kill her at the Hyundai terminal.

Instinctively she threw herself aside, hand clawing for the big Warhawk. Too late, she knew, too slow. Knife-Edge was unarmed. But as the illusion magic ended and the runner was assuming his true shape, her peripheral vision caught other figures flickering into view around her. Illusions and invisibility . . .

She hit the ground, rolled, bringing her gun up. Trying to bring it into line on Knife-Edge.

She saw one of the other figures, a skeletally thin Amerindian with feathers in his hair and assorted fetishes

dangling from his belt, point his finger at her. She tried
to roll aside, as if the finger were the barrel of a gun.

The thin man's lips moved.

Oblivion followed, hitting Sly like a missile.

Consciousness returned as suddenly as it had fled. No
slow, drowsy transition, just a sharp demarcation sepa-
rating nothingness from full awareness.

Sly kept her eyes closed, forced her body to remain
perfectly still, not wanting anyone else to know she was
awake. It gave her time to run a quick inventory of her
physical sensations.

She was sitting upright in a padded, high-backed chair.
Her hands were secured to the arms of the chair by tight
bands around her wrists. Her ankles were tied together,
and broad bands encircled her waist and chest, binding
her body to the chair back. A padded headband was
around her forehead, positioned just above her datajack,
immobilizing her head. She didn't need to try to know
she couldn't move a muscle.

A sickening rush of fear shot through her. This was
exactly what they'd done to Agarwal. It took all the control she could muster not to buck and twist, fight against
the bindings. She concentrated on her breathing, keeping
it even, deep, and slow.

"Don't bother." The voice sounded close to her ear,
making her jump. "We know you're awake."

For a moment she considered bluffing it out, but it was
futile. Sly opened her eyes, looked around.

She was in a small, windowless room whose walls, floor,
and ceiling were of bare concrete. Her chair, in the center of
the room, was the only furniture. Three men stood around
her. Two she recognized at once: Knife-Edge, still wearing
his semi-military uniform, and the cadaverous, fetish-
festooned shaman who'd put her out at the Roundhouse. The
third figure was a small, weasely-looking woman who stood

well away from the others, watching with a kind of emotionless curiosity that made Sly very uncomfortable. Knife-Edge and the shaman both had pistols holstered on their belts; the woman was apparently unarmed.

Knife-Edge jandered up to Sly, crouched down in front of her until his eyes were on a level with hers. She tried to kick him, but her ankles were secured to the chair as well as to each other.

"I'm glad we can finally have a quiet discussion," the Amerindian said calmly. "This time without the risk of interruption."

"You should have been standing twenty centimeters to the left," Sly growled.

Knife-Edge touched his left side, where the sniper's bullet had punched through his body. He smiled. "That might have made a difference to me," he admitted, "but not to you. Even with my spine shot in half, someone else would have eventually been having this discussion with you, you know." His cold smile faded. "Now, I think you should tell me where the data is. I know you don't have it on you." He reached into his pocket, pulled out the passcard for the motel room.

"Hotels never put their names on their passcards anymore," he went on conversationally. "Normally I think that's a good idea. It reduces thefts. But at the moment it's very irritating. My guess is that the datachip we're looking for is in this hotel room."

Sly smiled grimly. "Lots of hotels in Cheyenne, aren't there, drekhead?"

"Which is why you're going to tell us which one it is," he said quietly. "You're also going to tell us where you've hidden the chip and how to get around any security provisions you've set up."

"Or you're going to work me over the same way you did Agarwal, right?" She tried to keep her voice steady, but didn't quite succeed.

Knife-Edge shook his head slowly. "That wasn't us," he told her. "That was barbaric and primitive. Dangerous, too. There's always the chance the subject will die before breaking. A weak heart, a brain aneurysm . . . so many things can go wrong. We've updated the procedure. The, um, persuasive benefits of torture without the physical risks." He chuckled, the sound sending a shudder through Sly's body. "Why damage the physical body at all when we can directly access to the mind?" He reached out and gently touched Sly's datajack with a fingertip.

Oh, Jesus fragging Christ . . . She flung herself against the straps that held her. Uselessly. They didn't give a centimeter, just bit deeper into her flesh as she struggled against them. She couldn't even tip over the chair she was strapped into.

Knife-Edge merely watched her dispassionately until she stopped, panting with exertion. He beckoned to the woman.

She approached, taking something from her pocket. A small black box not much bigger than her palm. Trailing from one end of it was a fiber-optic lead tipped with a brain plug. The woman took the plug, reached out to insert it into Sly's datajack.

"*No!*" Sly screamed. She tried to turn her head, to pull it away from the plug. But the headband, too, was tight enough to prevent any movement. She could do nothing as the woman slipped the plug firmly into the datajack. Sly felt the click as it socketed into place. Waves of sickening fear and despair washed over her.

"You can tell us what we want to know at any time," Knife-Edge said. "Then we'll turn off the box."

"And then you'll kill me," Sly spat.

Knife-Edge stood, shrugged. "Why should we?" he asked reasonably. "There's no percentage in it once we've got what we want."

"Liar!" she shouted.

Knife-Edge nodded to the weasel woman, headed for the single door. "Catch you later, Sly," he said tauntingly.

The woman pressed a button on the black box.

Images of defilement, degradation, and terror blossomed in Sly's mind. And overlaying everything was wrenching, burning agony.

Sly couldn't help herself. There was nothing to do but scream.

28

Falcon stood on a rolling plain covered with green grass and a profusion of wildflowers. The air smelled fresh and pure, untouched by man and his taint, as clean as it must have been when the world was new. A breeze stirred the grass, ruffled his hair, bringing him more distant scents of deep, old-growth forests.

How long have I been here? he wondered. A moment? My whole life? Forever, since the dawn of time? Deep within, he recognized that the true answer had something of all three.

The breeze brought him more than scents: the chuckle of a distant stream, a symphony of birdcalls . . . And, beyond them all, there was music. A low complex rhythm and melody. Strong and dignified, ringing with power. But joyful too, free and unchained. The music seemed to resonate within him, resounding with the fundamental frequencies of his bones, his nerves, setting up an echo in the very core of him. He could still hear it with his ears. But now he could also hear it with his heart. The music called to him, and he came.

He ran toward the distant source of it, ran faster than he'd ever run before, faster than any human could. Ran faster than the deer, swifter even than the eagle. There was no strain, no effort. His breathing was as slow and steady as if he were standing still, perfectly relaxed. But still he ran on, with every passing moment gaining more and more speed.

And running with him was someone else, effortlessly keeping pace. Mary Windsong.

And yet *not* Mary, not quite. There was something different about her appearance. Her hair looked more like the pelt of an animal, her nose and jaws more pronounced, almost resembling a snout. But the eyes were hers, as was the smile.

He bared his teeth in a wild, feral smile, and howled his joy to the infinite azure skies. "Why didn't you tell me it would be like this?" he cried to the girl.

Her laughter was like bright mountain melt water dancing over stones. "Would you have believed me?"

They ran on.

How long did they run, how far? The questions were meaningless here, Falcon knew. Here they experienced time, but were not *of* it. They were outside the world as he knew it. Maybe he should have been afraid, but with the wind in his hair and the music in his heart, fear was inconceivable.

Now he could see the forest rising ahead of him. Almost instantly they came to its edge, and were forced to slow down, to walk rather than run.

Sunlight lanced shifting golden beams through the leaves overhead as he and Mary Windsong walked along. He heard large animals moving on either side, invisible in the underbrush, flanking them as they moved. Again he probed his emotions for fear, found none. The animals aren't stalking us, he realized, they're escorting us.

The music still sounded, clearer and stronger now, its

source somewhere ahead. After some immeasurable time, they reached a clearing, a great grassy opening in the midst of the forest. Falcon stepped into the open, hesitated when he saw that Mary had stopped, still standing within the trees.

"I can guide you no further," she replied to his unspoken question, "but you have no further need of my guidance. See?" She pointed. He looked in the direction she indicated.

The clearing was no longer empty as it had been a moment before. A large animal stood in the midst of the open space. A wolf, gray-black and with hackles of silver, watched Falcon steadily.

No, not a wolf. This *was* Wolf.

Now, for the first time, he felt fear. His stomach twisted, his pulse pounded in his head. *I can't do this. . . .*

He looked back at Mary for help. She smiled reassuringly, nodded to him. *Go ahead.* He heard the words, her voice, inside his head.

The music was still there, around him, within him, still calling to him. How could he deny it? *This is what I've wanted all my life. . . . Isn't it?* He swallowed hard, stepped forward.

The first step was the hardest. As he drew nearer to Wolf, his fear lifted, to be replaced once more with anticipation—just as intense, but enabling rather than incapacitating. The creatures that had traveled alongside through the forest now stepped forth into the sunlight. Timber wolves, huge but still smaller than Wolf. They kept their distance, watching Falcon respectfully, pacing him like an honor guard.

And then Wolf was before him, its great gray eyes steady. The music faded from Falcon's ears, but continued to sound fully in his heart.

"Do you know me?" The words—clear and sharp as

crystal—rang within Falcon's mind. Wolf's mouth didn't move, but Falcon had no doubt whose mental "voice" he was hearing.

He swallowed again, forced words through a dry throat. "I know you." Only as he said it did he realize it was true. "I have always known you, just didn't know that I knew."

"As I have known you." Wolf moved closer; Falcon felt its breath warm on his face. "My song is within you, Man. It has always been there, though you could not hear it. Now you *can* hear it, and you can choose to follow it.

"But if you do so choose, it will be difficult, sometimes the most difficult thing you have ever done. It may demand from you more than you feel willing to give. But never will it demand more than you *can* give.

"Will you follow it, Man?"

Emotions warred within Falcon. Fear, exaltation, sadness, anticipation. He was overwhelmed by the enormity of what Wolf said—even more by what Wolf left unsaid. But the song still rang within his breast, and he could no more have answered differently than he could have stopped breathing. "I will follow it."

"Then you have taken your first steps on the path of the shaman," Wolf told him. "You will embellish my song, you will make it your own, as does each one who hears it with the heart. Now, I would teach you some other songs—lesser songs, perhaps, but still songs of power."

Falcon bowed his head. There was nothing he could say, nothing he wanted to say.

And that was when the first scream sounded in his head. A woman's scream, one of absolute agony, powerful enough almost to unseat his reason.

He spun, looked back at Mary. She still stood at the edge of the forest, watching him, the expression on her face confused now. The scream hadn't been hers; she hadn't even heard it.

It sounded again, louder, even more piercing. And this time he recognized whose voice it was.

Sly!

A third scream. He could *feel* her agony almost as if it were his own, feel her terror and her powerlessness. Could *feel* her calling for help. *Calling to him?*

He turned back to Wolf. The great creature seemed totally unmoved, as though not hearing the screams. "I would teach you songs," Wolf repeated.

"I can't." The words were out of his mouth even before Falcon could think.

Wolf raised its eyebrows in a human expression of surprise.

Falcon rushed on. "I have to leave this place. A woman is . . . a woman needs me."

Wolf growled quietly, the first actual sound Falcon had heard from the creature. Its eyebrows drew together in a scowl. "You would leave?" Wolf asked. "You would scorn my teachings? Who is this woman to you?"

Maybe I should stay. . . . But he couldn't, Falcon knew that.

He swallowed hard. "She is my friend," he said as forcefully as he could. "She is . . ." He paused; his eyes were drawn to the timber wolves flanking him.

"She is of my pack," he finished.

Wolf's scowl faded. After a moment it spoke, its mental "voice" tinged with amusement . . . and approval. "Yes, of your pack. You follow my song perhaps better than you know. You have *always* followed it." Falcon had the strong impression he'd passed some kind of test.

Wolf sat back on its haunches. "Go, Man," it said gently. "There will be time later for you to learn more. For now, go in peace."

And, without any warning, reality seemed to burst into a million fragments, flying apart around him.

Falcon was standing on a nighttime city street, Mary beside him. Looking around, he saw people passing by, but not many. All were going about their own business, but it struck Falcon as strange that none spared him or Mary even a single glance.

There was something strange about the street, something strange about the buildings. Everything looked too clear, too sharp. He could see into all the pools of shadows, even the deepest where no light fell. He turned to Mary.

"Where are we?" he asked.

"Outside The Buffalo Jump," she answered slowly, "but we're on the astral plane. Did *you* do that?"

Falcon shook his head slowly. He couldn't have done it; he didn't even know for sure what the astral plane was. "It was Wolf," he told her.

"Why?"

The terrible scream rang out again, shaking his mind to its foundations. *That's* why, he realized. "Did you hear that?" he asked Mary.

"Hear what?"

So this is just for me, whatever this is.

Though Falcon knew he'd heard Sly's scream with his mind, not with his ears, he thought he could sense the direction from which it came. He turned his head, scanning with senses he hadn't known he had. *It came from that direction.*

"Come on," he urged Mary. He started to run, the shaman—the *other shaman*—on his heels.

Running here was almost like running on the plane of the totems. He was moving much faster than his legs could possibly pump, and there seemed to be no effort involved, no strain. Though Falcon didn't know where the thought came from, the idea blossomed in his brain that his will was all that limited his speed here. He exercised that will, and his speed doubled, trebled.

At first he dodged around obstacles such as parked cars and buildings. But then, as an experiment, he ran directly at the wall of a building, passing right through it as though it wasn't there. He cried with exultation.

Another scream, much closer now, much louder—and much more terrible. Somehow he knew from where it came. A small building up ahead, the dead neon sign identifying it as a machine shop. The doors and windows were boarded up.

That didn't stop Falcon. With Mary close on his heels, he plunged into the building. Passing through the walls like a wraith, he found himself in a large, empty room. Dust and refuse were everywhere. No sign of life.

But—somehow—he could *feel* life below him. With nothing but an exercise of will, he passed through the floor.

Found himself in a bare concrete room. Two standing figures flanked a third, who sat in a high-backed chair. One was thin, almost skeletally so. Strange objects dangled from his clothing. Falcon saw those objects with some kind of double sight. He saw them as what they were—tiny amalgamations of wood, bone, and feathers— but also as what they *represented*—flickering, shifting concentrations of power.

He focused on the strange items for only a moment before his attention was drawn to the figure in the chair.

Writhing and twisting against the straps that bound her, face twisted into a rictus of agony, it was Sly. She screamed again, and this time Falcon could hear it both with his ears and with the strange internal sense that had led him straight to her. He realized only then that Mary

Windsong was still with him. The young woman stared, aghast, at Falcon's tortured friend.

The second figure standing there was a scrawny, soulless-looking woman. Reaching out to a black box connected to Sly's datajack, the woman flicked a switch.

29

0223 hours, November 16, 2053

God, let me die! Sly tried to scream the words, tried to beg for the release of death.

The agony thrummed and rang through every nerve fiber, burned through the marrow of each bone. Her head pounded with it, her stomach and bowels twisted with it. Sometimes it was formless. Other times it had a shape— trolls gang-raping her, tearing at her body; surgical instruments in the hands of a demented artist; fire consuming her from within; rats consuming her from without . . . Each time she thought she had reached the boundaries of pain, thought she understood its limits, the form changed—so fast she couldn't adapt.

All she could do was scream.

And then, the pain was gone. The terrible sensations stopped pouring into her mind, replaced with the very real sensations of her own body.

She was weak, weak as a baby or a woman who'd run a dozen marathons. Her muscles twitched and vibrated— an aftereffect of her convulsions, she guessed. Her clothes were drenched with sweat, her throat hoarse with screaming. She took a deep, shuddering breath.

"Falcon," she moaned.

But Falcon's not here, another part of herself answered wearily. Why did you call for him?

She opened her eyes, looked up into the face of the soulless technician.

"Do you want to talk?" the woman said.

Sly tried to spit in her face, but her mouth was too dry. "Go frag yourself," she croaked.

The woman shrugged, totally unmoved. She reached up to flip the switch on the black box.

No! Panic ripped through Sly's mind. *I can't take that again!* She teetered on the edge of the abyss, on the margin of madness.

Falcon? Again, impossibly, she felt the young ganger's presence, and it was that presence that brought her back from the brink.

As if it mattered. The woman's finger touched the switch. Sly braced herself, a useless gesture.

"*Huh?*" The scrawny shaman gave a guttural grunt, seemed to stare at something that Sly couldn't see. The technician jumped at the sound, her finger falling away from the switch.

And then, shockingly, fire blossomed in the small room, bursting forth from one of the fetishes festooning the shaman's belt. Like a fireball it bloomed, washing over the technician, igniting her hair and clothing, turning her into a flailing, shrieking human torch. Sly screamed as the flame also licked over her, but somehow the fire did her no harm. She felt no pain, saw no blisters bloom. Neither her clothes, her flesh, nor her hair ignited. Nevertheless, she clenched her eyes tight shut.

The firestorm was over in an instant. Cautiously, Sly opened her eyes once more.

The woman was dead, sullen flames licking over her body. The shaman, though, seemed almost untouched. His clothes were scorched—particularly around the fetish that had detonated—and his exposed skin looked red, but he was not significantly injured. (Spell defense? Sly wondered groggily. Was it that saved me too?) He snarled in anger, closed his eyes, and slumped against the wall. Sly realized he must have gone astral to cope with some magical threat.

He was in trance for only a few seconds. Then his eyes opened wide, his face twisted in an expression of disbelief and horror. He lurched to his feet—clumsily, like a zombie from some low-budget horror trid—and took a stumbling step toward Sly. The runner recoiled from the terrifying rage in the thin man's eyes. His mouth worked as though he were trying to speak, but only garbled moans and rumbles came out. A gobbet of saliva dribbled from the corner of his mouth.

This is part of the torture. The thought struck Sly suddenly. It isn't real, it's just another false scenario being fed into my brain. But regardless, she still struggled and strained against the straps binding her.

The shaman stopped beside her chair, reached out and released the velcro band around Sly's left wrist. She snatched her hand back as soon as it was free, clenched it into a fist, readied to drive it into the man's throat. . . .

With an immense effort, she forced herself to stop. He's setting me free. For whatever reason, he's letting me loose. She felt withdrawn, emotionally overwhelmed and totally confused.

Snarling wordlessly, the man freed her other hand, then bent down to release her ankles. While he did so, Sly undid the straps around her torso and the band around her head.

When he'd freed her feet, the shaman lurched back against the wall. His eyes rolled up in his head, and he slumped to the floor, whether dead or just unconscious, Sly couldn't tell.

For a moment, she just sat there in the chair. Then she reached up and carefully unjacked the torture device from her skull. The moment the plug popped out of her data-jack, she flung the black box against the concrete wall with a yell, flung it with every joule of energy left in her body. Laughed aloud as the plastic enclosure cracked, spraying broken circuit boards and fragments of integrated circuits across the floor.

She sat up, grabbed the chair arms and started to force herself to her feet.

But the world seemed to spin and tumble around her. With a groan, she sank back into the chair.

Sly felt like drek. Pure, unadulterated, pluperfect drek. Every muscle in her body ached; her joints felt loose; even her skin tingled and itched. Worst of all, though, was the feeling that her grasp on reality was shaky. Is this real? she asked herself. Did the shaman really free me? Or am I hallucinating?

Or—horrifying thought—was this only another part of the torture? What if she forced herself to her feet, left the echoing concrete room with its smell of burned meat, and ran outside into the night—only to have that feeling of freedom wrenched away? To open her eyes and find herself back in the chair, strapped in place, immobile. With the woman technician preparing the black box to feed another electronic fantasy—something even more soul-destroying—into her brain.

Sly couldn't stand that. If it turned out that's what was happening, she'd collapse right then. Surrender, give up the will to live.

And, yes, *break*. Tell them what they wanted to know. And didn't that very fact—the realization that this technique would succeed—make it even more likely that this was a simsense fantasy?

She closed her eyes. *This* is how I can beat it, she told herself. If I never believe I've got my freedom, having it snatched away won't frag me up. Who feels the loss of something they never had? She slowed her breathing, tried to relax her muscles.

She felt eyes on her—someone was watching her. *Is this it? Is this when the tech turns off the simsense torture box?* Despite her efforts at relaxation, Sly felt all her muscles tensing again. She opened her eyes.

Nobody was there. Well, nobody conscious, at least. The smoldering body of the tech still lay crumpled in the corner; the shaman still slumped against the wall, definitely unconscious or worse. Apart from them, the room was empty.

But frag it, she still felt the presence of somebody else there. *Knew* there was someone watching her. And, deep down, she also *knew* it wasn't someone watching her through a spy-eye. There was someone near her, she could sense it. Someone standing next to her chair, even though she couldn't see anyone.

A spectator—maybe Knife-Edge himself—under cover of an invisibility spell, like the back-up at the hosed Roundhouse meet? But no, she didn't think so. She could sense a person's proximity, but there was more to it than that. She knew this person. That's how it felt, at least— there was definitely a sensation of familiarity.

"Falcon?" The word slipped from her dry lips before she could suppress it.

It couldn't be. . . .

But—and now she was totally convinced—it *was*.

"Falcon? Are you there?"

How could this be part of the torture? They couldn't know that Falcon was working with her, that he'd come to Cheyenne with her. That he was her comrade, her chummer. Could they?

Panic suddenly washed over her in a wave. *Am I losing it? Is this what it's like to go mad?* She looked wildly around the room.

And yes, there was Falcon. Standing next to her, his

face twisted with fear, with horror. And with concern. She reached out to him, tried to grab his arm.

But her hand went right through his body. For the first time she could see that the young ganger's body was translucent, vaguely transparent. She could see through him, see the wall and the shaman's body behind him.

I am going mad! She closed her eyes again, tears leaking out from under her closed lids. *Ask me your questions, Knife-Edge. I'll answer them. Just don't let this continue.*

"Sly."

It was Falcon's voice . . . but not quite. There was something eerie about the sound, something . . . *ethereal* was the only word that fit. It was distant, too, as though he were speaking from a long way off, not from right next to her.

"Go away," she mumbled.

"Sly," Falcon said again, and this time she could hear the tension, the urgency in his voice. "Come on. You've got to get out of here, chummer."

She shook her head, closed her eyes. "You're not real," she whispered.

"Knife-Edge might be coming back." The panic in the ganger's voice contrasted with the peace she felt inside—the peace of fatalism, of surrender. "You've got to move."

"You're not real," she repeated.

"Frag it, go! You want to die?"

"Why not?"

"Sly, you *slitch*!" he yelled, the voice echoing strangely around the concrete room. "Die on your own fragging time! *Now move your fragging hoop!*"

"You're a ghost," she muttered.

"If I am, I'll haunt you till the end of fragging time. Now get your pudlicking hoop out of that chair and *move it*!"

She shrugged to herself. Why not? It wasn't going to do any good, of course. She'd get outside, and then the tech would turn off the simsense and she'd be back in the chair. But what the frag was the difference anyway? Listening to Falcon was just as bad—his voice reminding her that the only way she'd get any peace would be to tell Knife-Edge what he wanted to know. Reminding her that she'd be killing him too.

"Okay, okay. . . ." She forced herself to her feet again, clung to the chair while the world did its wild acrobatics around her. Clenched her jaw against the nausea that threatened to make her spew.

Took her first lurching step toward the door.

"That's it, move," Falcon told her.

"Go frag yourself, ghost," she growled.

Took another step. Stumbled over the outstretched leg of the felled shaman, almost pitched headlong to the floor. Reached out a hand to steady herself, felt the cold of the metal door against her palm.

Okay, I'm at the door. Now what?

Open it, idiot. She reached down for the handle, grabbed it. Twisted.

It didn't turn. *Of course not, it's locked.* Pounded her fist against the door in frustration at the futility of everything.

"Turn it the other way, frag you!"

"Okay, okay," she mumbled. Turned the knob the other way.

And the door swung open. A narrow stairway ahead, leading up.

Three or four meters, maybe, to reach the top. The way she was feeling, it could just as easily have been a hundred klicks.

But he won't leave me alone until I do it, will he? She started up the stairs, leaning against the concrete wall to keep herself upright.

It was almost too hard. Her muscles rebelled, her sense of balance swung like a compass needle next to an electromagnet. Her vision tunneled down to the size of a gun muzzle at arm's length. The sound of her breathing in her own ears took on the same distant echoing as Falcon's ghost-voice. *I'm not going to make it.*

But somehow she did. She almost fell when she raised her foot to stand on a step that wasn't there. Leaning against the wall, her legs quivering under her, she breathed deeply until her field of vision widened again. Not all the way: it was still like looking down a tunnel, with flickering, pixelating lights around the dark periphery.

She looked around her. A small anteroom, doors to the right and left, the staircase behind her. "Which way?" she whispered.

"To your right." The ghost-Falcon was still with her, seeming to stand right beside her. "It's not locked. Open it."

Only if you'll leave me be afterward. She grabbed the doorknob, turned. The door swung open.

A rush of chill air washed over her, partially clearing her head for an instant. *Outside. The streets of Cheyenne at night. Freedom?* She paused.

"What are you waiting for?" the ghost-Falcon demanded, nearly hopping from foot to foot with impatience. It was almost funny. "Well?"

How could she answer him? That she was waiting for the tech to cut the simsense. . . . Now, when she could *see* freedom a meter in front of her? Or when she'd taken the first couple of steps out of the building? Which would cause her the most torment?

"Move!" ghost-Falcon screamed.

She moved. What else could she do but play this out, follow the script to the last page? She stepped out into the night, filled her lungs with the cold night air.

Sly had come to an alley in what looked like a light-industrial neighborhood. Warehouses, disused machine shops, across the alley a boarded-up foundry identified as Cheyenne Chain and Wire.

Which way? And did it matter?

She turned to the right, took her first step away from the building that had been her prison.

The illusion didn't end; the tech didn't turn off the simsense.

Another step, then another. Increasing tempo, faster and faster, until she was into a shambling run. The air hissing in and out stung her dry throat, but the pain felt good. Who knows? she thought. Maybe they'll forget to turn the simsense off. Wasn't a convincing illusion of freedom as good as the real thing, as long as it didn't end? If you couldn't tell reality from illusion, why favor one over the other? Maybe her whole life had been simsense. . . . She ran on.

Her lungs hurt, her legs felt like they were on fire. The impact of each step pounded up her legs, through her spine, into her brainpan. A rushing filled her ears. The tunnel—with its flickering walls—drew tighter. The size of two fists at arm's length; one fist; a fingertip . . .

And then there was nothing but blackness and drifting stars ahead of her. A phantasmagoric starfield.

With something like relief, Sly fell headlong into it.

30

With a gasp, Falcon "fell" back into his body.

That was the only way he could describe it. One moment he was with Sly, running along beside her as she lurched down the back alley. The next he felt a kind of psychic wrench, then was back in his meat body, sprawled on the floor in the back room of The Buffalo Jump. He lay there for a moment, tingling all over. It felt like those times when you're half-asleep and you dream you're falling, but instead of hitting the ground you find yourself startlingly awake, staring at the ceiling, with strange sensations coursing up and down your nerves.

He turned his head. Mary was still in full lotus, swaying slightly. She still seemed to be . . . What, in a trance? Was that it? And then her eyes jolted open too. She stared at him. "What the frag just happened?" she asked quietly.

He forced himself to his feet—tested his sense of balance. The tingling was already fading. "I don't know," he said. "This is your thing, not mine. I've never done it before."

"But . . ." She paused. On her face was a strange expression, something close to awe. "But what you did . . ."

"What *did* I do?"

"You tracked your friend from the *astral*," the young woman said slowly. "You went to her. You slammed a spell into that shaman's fetish. . . ."

"No!" he yelped. "That was you."

She shook her head. "It was *you*. You cast a spell. Think back."

He tried to. He remembered seeing the room, seeing Sly strapped into the chair. The song of Wolf was still thrumming through his nerves, sinews, bones. He remembered the outrage, the horror, as he realized Sly was being tortured. And then . . .

And then Wolf's song had taken on a different tenor. No longer the quiet, steady power—like that of a slow-flowing river. It had changed, become angrier, fiercer—more like a storm-tossed sea. The song had filled him, overwhelmed him. He'd become one with the music, singing along with it.

And then the fireball had burst.

I cast a spell? Is that what a spell is?

"*I did it?*" he mumbled. Mary nodded. "What about . . . what about the shaman when he let Sly go?"

"That was me," Mary acknowledged. "A simple controlling manipulation. By that time I kind of understood what was going down.

"But then you manifested on the physical, didn't you?" she went on. "You made yourself visible to her, and you spoke to her. Didn't you?"

He nodded. "Shamans can do that, though, right?"

"Yes, but . . . drek, Falcon, they've got to *learn* to be able to do it. *Everything* you did tonight . . . It's like, it's no big fragging deal to ride a bike, but what you did— it's like some guy who's never ridden before swinging onto a combat bike and doing trick riding stunts!" She shook her head in amazement. "We've got to talk about this."

"Later." He jumped to his feet. "Sly went down. We've got to find her. Where the frag *was* that?"

Mary paused for a moment. "That place we saw—

Cheyenne Chain and Wire. I know it. It's south of town, near I-80. Industrial area."

"Take me there," he said flatly, heading for the door.

Mary hesitated for a moment, then, with a shrug, followed him out.

Falcon didn't know how Mary had sweet-talked the bartender—Cahill, she said his name was—into lending her his bike, and right then he didn't care. He sat on the back of the rumbling hog, his arms locked tight around the shaman's waist.

She was a good driver, not aggressive, not into high speeds or anything flashy, but stable and steady. Safe. Right now Falcon would probably have wanted to trade a little safety for some more speed. He knew enough, though, not to be a back-seat driver.

It took only a few minutes to reach the industrial area. The *feel* of the place—abandoned buildings, industrial trash, scavengers in the alleys—was right, even though he didn't recognize anything directly. Then Mary was cruising slowly past the front of Cheyenne Chain and Wire.

"She started off into the alley behind this building," Mary said.

"Which way did she go?" Falcon asked. "And how far?"

Mary shrugged. "I don't know. We'll just have to search." She turned the bike down the next street, cut into the alley behind the foundry.

A few minutes later—the minutes feeling like hours to Falcon—they found her. Face-down in a pile of refuse, a rat the size of a malnourished beagle sniffing at her. As Falcon ran up, the rat seemed to consider taking him on to protect what had to be enough food to last a month. But then the creature apparently decided discretion was the better part of valor, and made itself scarce.

Falcon crouched beside Sly, grabbed her wrist, felt for

a pulse. It was there—fast, but not strong. Mary squatted next to him, laid a hand on the fallen woman's shoulder. "How is she?" Falcon demanded.

"You could probably find out yourself," Mary said cryptically. But then she closed her eyes and slowed her breathing. After a moment she looked up. "Not good. Alive, but drek-kicked."

"Can you help her? Shamans can heal, can't they?"

"I can help her," Mary acknowledged. She glanced around. "But this ain't the best place." She hesitated. "We can carry three on the bike—just—but we can't go fast and we can't go far. Where do you want to take her?"

It was Falcon's turn to pause. The motel was too far and perhaps too dangerous, but what other choice did he have? If Sly still wanted to go through with this drek about cracking into Zurich-Orbital—assuming she didn't flatline, of course—she'd need her deck. Which was back at the motel. And the motel was much too far to take a wounded woman three-up on a bike.

"Can you wait here with her?" he asked. "I'll take the bike and go get the car."

Mary nodded.

"They might come looking for her."

The shaman smiled. "If they do, they'll find more than they bargained for. I'll summon a city spirit. It can conceal and protect us while you're gone."

"Good," Falcon said. "I'll be back quick as I can." As he swung aboard the bike and peeled out of there, he heard Mary begin to sing a strange, rhythmic song.

He was expecting some kind of trouble. Somebody trying to stop him from returning with the car, loading Sly into it, and cruising back to the motel. Hell, he was almost looking forward to it. He was cranked up, out on the pointy end, ready to kick some hoop. His machine pistol was locked and loaded on the seat next to him, and he found himself humming the song of Wolf through his clenched teeth.

But nobody tried to slot with them. In fact nobody paid them the slightest heed. Even when he carried the limp figure of Sly from the car into the motel room. Somebody was walking through the parking lot during the whole procedure, but the slag didn't even look their way. Falcon wondered if maybe Mary's city spirit was still looking out for them. He set Sly gently down on the bed, while Mary locked the door behind them.

Sly looked like drek—face pale and drawn, skin almost yellow. While carrying her, he'd felt tremors shooting through her muscles. And her flesh was cold. *Like Nightwalker when he died.* With an effort, Falcon forced that memory away.

He turned to Mary. "Fix her up," he said gruffly. Then, more tentatively, "Please?"

He tried to watch and learn as Mary sat cross-legged on the bed beside Sly, ran her small hands gently over his chummer's body, and began to sing.

But he couldn't. He couldn't sit still. He was filled with energy—energy to burn—and nothing to burn it on. So he paced and he fumed. He pictured Knife-Edge's face twisting in agony as he pumped bullet after bullet into the Amerindian runner's belly. Pictured him engulfed in flame, screaming as he burned like the woman in the torture room. Pictured him moaning in fear as his lifeblood ran into the gutter and he bled himself dry.

He couldn't bear to look at his chummer's pale face. She looked so young, so helpless, lying there. And that was perhaps the biggest crime of all that Knife-Edge had to atone for. He'd taken a confident, competent woman and turned her into this.

Why does it matter so much? he asked himself. I didn't know her from squat a week ago. She shouldn't mean anything to me.

But she did, of course. They were working together toward the same goal. They trusted each other, depended on each other. She is of my pack, he'd told Wolf. And that was the truth, simple and plain. He sat on the other bed, facing away from Mary and Sly. The Dog shaman's song filled his ears, and dire imaginings filled his mind.

Finally Mary's song faded away. He was scared to turn, to look. But he had to.

Sly still lay unmoving, but her color had returned to normal. Sitting next to her, Mary looked tired, her face sheened with sweat.

"Is she . . . ?" Falcon couldn't finish the question.

Mary just nodded.

Falcon came over and sat on the edge of the bed beside his chummers. He reached out, brushed a lock of hair back from Sly's face. "Sly," he said softly.

And her eyes opened. For a moment they darted about wildly, clouded with terror. Then they fixed on his face.

She smiled. A tired, worn smile, but a smile just the same. "It *was* you," she said weakly. "It was real."

He didn't trust himself to speak, just nodded. His eyes were watering, and he scuffed the back of his hand across them. It's all this blasting around when I should be sleeping, he told himself.

"How are you feeling?" Mary asked.

Sly smiled up at the young woman. "Good," she said. "Better than I have any right to expect." She paused. "You were there too, weren't you? I *felt* you." Mary nodded. Sly turned to Falcon. "How?"

It was Mary who answered. "Your chummer's walking the path of the shamans," she said quietly. "He sings the song of Wolf."

Falcon saw Sly's eyes widen, full of unspoken questions. Then she smiled. "Hidden depths, Falcon," she said. "Hidden depths." Cautiously, she pushed herself upright. ''Anything *else* happen that I should know about?''

31

0521 hours, November 16, 2053

At the suggestion of the young woman whose name Sly learned was Mary Windsong, they picked up and moved. Sly was pretty sure she hadn't said anything to her torturers about the motel—if she had, the three of them would already have been blown to drek—but it didn't make sense to take any chances they could avoid. Mary led the way, riding a hog much too big for her, her long braid trailing back in the wind. Falcon had driven the Callaway, Sly sitting in the passenger seat, her cyberdeck clutched protectively in her lap. They'd gone to some little tavern with the improbable name of The Buffalo Jump, then installed themselves in the tiny back room.

Sly was feeling better—almost back to normal, she had to admit. Sometimes she still felt tremors in her muscles, and sometimes when she shut her eyes—even if just for a moment—images from the simsense torture came back and she'd have to smother a scream. What would happen when she went to sleep? she wondered.

Both Falcon and Mary had been solicitous about her health. Maybe a little *too* solicitous, Sly thought at first, a tad grumpily. But then she realized that their concern wasn't misplaced. She *had* gone through a frag of a lot, and still felt like a wet bag of drek, despite help from the Dog shaman's magical attentions.

A strange dynamic seemed to exist between Falcon and the Cheyenne woman, Sly had noticed. At first she thought it was sexual attraction—the ganger was handsome in an unpolished kind of way, and the diminutive girl cute the way Sly had always wanted to be as a kid. But then she recognized that there was more to it, maybe much more. They had something important in common, something that underlaid their entire lives. Sly wondered if it was because Falcon was now "walking the path of the shaman"—whatever that meant.

"What do you need?" Mary asked her as soon as they reached the tavern.

Sly's first impulse had been to say something flippant like a liter of synthahol and thirty-six hours of sleep. But she put that thought aside at once. Knife-Edge was still after her. He'd gotten her once, and had no reason to stop trying. Holing up and waiting it out would be just plain dumb, she decided, particularly after Falcon told her what he'd learned about the Amerindian runner. *The Office of Military Intelligence—no drek.* That meant they were playing with the Sioux government, the military— maybe even the fragging Wildcats. No, holing up was not a good idea. This wasn't going to just blow over. She had to do something, *right now.*

And, no matter how much it terrified her, she knew what that something was. Zurich-Orbital again. Sly had to try, even if it killed her. But then, of course, there was the problem of cyberdeck utilities. If she was feeling really militant, she could go "naked" into the Matrix, depending on her skills to whip up the programs she needed on the fly. Five years ago she might have considered it. Now? No fragging way. Her conversation with Moonhawk—*the fragging double-crossing drek-eater*—had convinced her that she was too out of date for that. Phase loop recoursers—PLRs—wouldn't do squat against modern ice. What other unpleasant changes had she missed?

No, what she needed was all the edge she could get. And that meant up-to-the-minute varsity-league utilities.

Fortunately—and to her surprise—Mary had come to her aid when she'd mentioned the problem. The little shaman had some connections with the Cheyenne shadow community—including, it turned out, a couple of programmers and deckers. Mary took off with a list of the utilities and hardware Sly needed, returning less than an hour later with a collection of optical chips in a plastic chip carrier.

Frag, Sly thought as she loaded the last utility into the deck's onboard memory, why couldn't Falcon have met her a couple of hours sooner?

She set aside the last program chip, ran the deck through a quick self-diagnostic. The processor was having no problem running the utility code. The utilities themselves were almost implausibly sophisticated—at least, in comparison to what Sly had used five years ago. According to the deck's internal bench marks, most clocked in at a hair over rating seven. One read out at nine, and one peaked at an unheard-of *eleven*. (What's all this going to cost me? she wondered, then put the worry aside. Mary had given the stuff to her on credit, so if Sly got herself geeked, she wouldn't have to sweat it. And if she made it, any price would be cheap.) With the speed increases Smeland had wired into the circuitry, the combination of wiz utilities plus beefy processor turned the deck into a real ice pick.

Satisfied, Sly sat back.

Falcon had been pacing nervously. Now he came to perch beside her, concern written all over his face. "Are you up to this, Sly?" he asked quietly. "You don't want to wait? Like, give yourself some time to bounce back?"

She smiled at him, appreciating his apprehension on her behalf. She squeezed his arm reassuringly. "I'm up for it," she told him. "I'm ready." As ready as she would

ever be. But how ready was that? "What other choices
do we have?"

She watched him struggle with that, reviewing their
options—sadly limited—in his mind. Eventually his
shoulders slumped and he nodded. She knew how he was
feeling. Helpless, impotent. There was nothing he could
do to help Sly directly. She squeezed his arm again, trying to communicate a determination and confidence she
really didn't feel. *Maybe this is it.* She couldn't force the
thought from her mind. Sly used to think that the next
time she faced black ice, she'd get flatlined. And now
she was going up against the best. And maybe a military-
class decker too. Would Jurgensen be waiting for her
when she decked in? *Count on it,* she told herself.

Sly turned to Mary Windsong. "Can you watch me?"
she asked. "Monitor me magically, or something? If you
see something strange happening to my body . . ."

"If you start T-and-F-ing, you mean?" the young
woman asked.

"T-and-*what*-ing?" Falcon demanded.

"Twitching and foaming," Mary explained. "Like if
a decker hits some bad ice. Yeah, sure. You hit trouble,
I'll jack you out. I've covered for deckers before." She
turned to Falcon. "It's like watching a shaman's meat
body when he's gone astral. Yeah, null persp, Sly. I'll
move fast."

Sly nodded. There was no more anyone could do to
help. Maybe, if Mary was as quick as she thought she
was, and if she was watching closely enough, she could
jack Sly out before any black ice had time to fry her brain
or stop her heart. But how much faster did black ice react
these days? How long did it take killer ice to set up a
lethal biofeedback loop?

She looked down at the deck, the plug-tipped fiber-
optic lead coiled like a snake ready to strike. *No more
excuses,* she told herself, *no more procrastination. If I'm*

going, *go*. She picked up the brain plug, snugged it into her datajack. Felt the familiar tingling that told her the deck was on-line, ready to rock and roll.

She glanced up into Falcon's worried eyes. Gave him and Mary a reassuring smile. "Well," she said softly, "here goes nothing." She checked the deck's memory—utilities loaded, interfacing well with the MPCP and the persona programs. Ran another quick diagnostic, got a green board. No glitches, no anomalies. No more excuses.

"See you soon," she whispered, hitting the Go key with a sharp little tap.

She blew through the Cheyenne Matrix, danced across the datalines until she saw the LTG node high above the surreal city below her. Rocketed toward it, into it. Then the jump to the RTG, the universe folding around itself like an origami figure.

And, all too soon, she was hurtling toward the satellite link, the blue radio telescope construct on the dark plane. Instinctively, she looked around her for Theresa Smeland's armadillo icon. Laughed wryly at her reaction. I'm alone this time, she reminded herself. No back-up. Just me.

She saw the beads of ice sliding back and forth along the structural members of the satlink construct. Saw them pick up their tempo as she approached. Okay, she thought, let's see how wiz these utilities really are. . . .

Her samurai icon reached into a pouch on his belt, pulled out a tiny mask—like a harlequin's mask—and slapped it to her face. A tingle went through her virtual body as the masking utility activated. For an instant she thought it had worked. The beads slowed down again, back to their normal level of activity. But then, as she came within contact range of the satlink construct, the beads flashed again to high-speed, alert mode. Before she had time to try another utility, a dozen of the beads burst free from the construct, slamming into her icon. Nothingness engulfed her.

And then she was in the office once more, the perfectly rendered corner of the Matrix created by the UCAS military. No doubt some node running on hideously powerful military mainframes.

Jurgensen the decker was sitting at the desk. He looked up with an expression of surprise as her icon materialized in front of him.

"Waiting for me, Jurgensen?" she asked. And then she hit the army decker with everything she had. Triggered a frame—an autonomous program construct—and hurled it at him. In keeping with her own icon, it was a low-resolution Japanese ronin, armed with a *tetsubo* glowing the brilliant red of a CO_2 laser. As the frame leaped forward, swinging its studded mace, she triggered a "hog" virus—appearing in this node like a viciously barbed dart. She tossed it underhand at Jurgensen.

The army decker had responded quickly to the frame—*too quickly?*—holding a macroplast riot shield up before him, blocking the ronin's *tetsubo* blow. But that meant his attention wasn't focused on Sly herself for a critical instant. The virus dart flew true, slipped past the riot shield, bit deep into the icon's chest. Jurgensen howled in outrage as the virus code began to replicate in his cyberdeck, allocating the deck's operating memory to itself, preventing it from being used for anything else. Unless the decker didn't act fast to eliminate the virus, soon it would take over all unused memory, then start on the memory containing his own utilities, flushing them from the deck and eventually dumping him.

Of course, she knew, Jurgensen *would* act fast. She couldn't trust to something as simple as a hog utility to take him down. But, at least, for a couple of clock ticks he'd be occupied. Clock ticks she could use herself.

She fired up her first attack utility, and a heavy crossbow appeared in the samurai's hand. Aiming carefully, she triggered the bow, watched the bolt whistle past her autonomous frame, saw it slam into Jurgensen's chest. A frag of a good hit. For an instant, the decker's icon quivered, losing resolution. Keep on him, she told himself, don't give him a chance to use a medic program. And don't let him deal with the hog. The crossbow re-cocked itself, and she pumped another bolt into her opponent. Again his icon lost some of its resolution, but this time it didn't return to its previous, pristine state. Hurt you bad! she crowed inwardly.

Jurgensen snarled in anger. His riot shield vanished, a snub-nosed submachine gun taking its place in his hands. He triggered a burst into the frame that was still attacking him, blowing gaping holes through the ronin. The frame attacked again, slamming its *tetsubo* into the decker's head. But then, with a despairing, electronic screech, it pixelated and vanished. The SMG muzzle swung toward Sly.

She flung herself aside as bullets stitched the wall behind her. Simultaneously triggered one of the highest-rated utilities in her deck—a cutting-edge mirrors utility. As the code executed, her icon split in two—two identical samurai. The new icon—the mirror image—jinked right, while she flung herself low into the shelter of Jurgensen's own desk.

The army decker hesitated for a tick, trying to guess which was the real icon and which the image. Guessed wrong, and sprayed a long burst into the mirror construct. Giving Sly time to pop up and blast another crossbow bolt into him at point-blank range. Jurgensen howled, his icon pixelating like the frame ronin. Then he vanished—jacked out or dumped, Sly neither knew nor cared. She caught her breath, tried to slow her racing heart.

Just for an instant. And then what she'd been dreading—but, deep down, expecting—happened. Two nightmare figures, night-black and twisted out of true, loomed over her.

The golems. Golem-class black IC—according to Jurgensen, driven by a high-level expert system code. Smart—maybe as smart as a decker—fast and lethal. With brain-splitting roars, they lunged at her.

Sly backpedaled wildly. Her mirror image was still visible, but the golems were ignoring it, converging on her from two directions. She brought up her crossbow, pumped a bolt into the belly of the closest monster. No visible reaction.

What the frag do I do now? her mind gibbered wildly. Jack out, while I've got the chance? Give it up as a bad job? But that wasn't even an option, was it? If she ever wanted a normal life, she had to win now, once and for all.

She danced back another step as the nearest golem swung at her with a fist bigger than her head. So sophisticated was the ice code that she "felt" the wind of the fist's passage a centimeter from her face.

Another step back. Trigger a utility. Another step. Another utility.

The first—a modified "smoke" utility—filled the room with coruscating blue-white light, sheets and curtains of it, like heat lightning. Sly could still see the advancing golems clearly, but knew that the display was interfering with their perception of her. Not much help against something this sophisticated, but a whole lot better than nothing. The second utility surrounded her icon with another construct—a full suit of late-medieval plate mail.

And not an instant too soon. The golems were quicker than they looked. One had managed to close with her, slamming a massive fist into her chest. In the real world, the impact would have collapsed her rib cage, ruptured internal organs, possibly smashed her spine. But here, in the virtual reality of the Matrix, the blow crashed into her armor, making the metal ring like a gong. Still, the force was enough to stagger her, make her head ring like the armor. In the real world, she knew, her body had probably spasmed as the IC code had momentarily over-ridden control of her cyberdeck, dumping a damaging over-voltage through her datajack. Would Mary jack her out, or would she judge the damage minor and let Sly be?

The office didn't vanish from around her, so Mary had obviously decided to hang back. One of the golems was confused by the "smoke" display, swinging wildly at the sheets of light that surrounded it. Not so the second. It advanced on Sly, more slowly now, as though taking time to analyze her armor and find its weak spots. She tried to dodge to the left, but a sweeping arm blocked that move. She backed up again, felt the office wall behind her. No more retreat. No more options.

There was only one thing she could do. A big risk— but what part of this run wasn't a risk? She still had one utility left—a rating-eleven attack program. Maybe beefy enough to crash the golems, maybe not. But even pulling it out was a terrifying risk. It was experimental code, Mary had told her, nowhere near as "plug-and-play" as the other programs Sly had used up till now. Not only did it need almost all her deck's resources—so much so that she'd have to abort everything she was already run-ning to give the program what it needed—but she'd have to do some on-the-fly programming to tailor the code to its target and "lock it on." Which meant she wouldn't even have the option of maneuvering, of dodging the go-lems' blows; she'd just have to hang tough and take it.

And she wouldn't have the option of jacking out if things got nasty.

An all-or-nothing play. Did she have the guts to go through with it?

Do I have any choice?

Before she could think about it any further, paralyze herself with indecision, Sly aborted the other utilities she had running. The mirror image, the heat lightning, even the suit of plate mail—all vanished. With a growl of triumph, the two golems converged on her.

The construct of the attack program appeared in her hands. A bulbous, space-opera laser rifle. She swung the barrel up, pointed it at the nearest golem. It was cumbersome, clumsy, incredibly difficult to aim. (Sly *knew* that, in reality, her meat body was slumped on a couch in the back room of a cavern, her fingers flying across the keys of her cyberdeck. The clumsiness of the laser rifle represented the difficulty she was having in tailoring the code of a virus program, tweaking it so it'd crash the code of the intrusion countermeasures that were trying to coopt control of her deck. But, like any decker, she'd buried that reality deep. It was so much faster, much more efficient, to think symbolically. But also much more terrifying.)

She squeezed the rifle's trigger. With a loud *pah* of discharging capacitors, the weapon fired. A yellow-white bolt of energy burst from the muzzle, slammed into the torso of the nearest golem, punching a hole clean through it the size of Sly's fist. The thing staggered back, howling. She squeezed the trigger again.

Nothing. The weapon had a recycle time—representing the time it took to modify the code for another assault on the ice. The high-pitched whine of recharging filled her ears.

The golem was hurt—maybe seriously—but it wasn't going to back off. It lunged at her again while its comrade shambled to the side, trying to flank her.

The laser rifle beeped, and she triggered it again. The bolt took the attacking golem clean in its lack of face, tearing the head from its neck. The massive body collapsed to the ground, flickered, then vanished.

The second golem snarled, leaped at her. She couldn't move, couldn't do anything while the rifle recycled. A black fist slammed into the side of her head, smashing her to the ground. Her scream of pain seemed unimaginably distant in her own ears. The world blurred around her.

Through the crushing pain, she heard a beep. For an instant didn't realize its significance. Then, just as the golem swung another blow—a killing blow, this time— she squeezed the trigger.

The energy bolt plowed into the monster's belly, knocking it backward. It screamed its agony, flailing wildly at the hole torn in its torso.

But it didn't go down.

Crumpled on the floor, the rifle—useless until it recharged—in her hands, Sly watched death approach. Looming three meters above her, the golem snarled down at her. Enjoying itself. Slowly raised a foot high, ready to slam it down and crush her skull.

Too slowly. The rifle beeped. Sly clamped down on the trigger.

The energy bolt ripped upward into the construct at a steep angle. Blasted into its groin, tearing up through its torso, exiting from the back of its neck. It teetered there for a moment, then toppled toward her. Pixelated and vanished an instant before it struck her.

Sly just lay there, gasping. The laser rifle felt crushingly heavy in her hands—meaning that the programming effort of keeping the utility code running was becoming too much. She let it deactivate, saw the construct flicker and disintegrate.

I did it. . . . The metabolic poisons of fear and exhaustion were flowing through her body, making her muscles feel leaden, and giving her a sick headache. With an Olympian effort, she forced herself to her feet. Looked around her. The office was empty.

But maybe not for long. She had to get out of here *now*.

She took a moment to run a medic program, to restore at least some of the damage the ice had inflicted on her persona programs. She ran the construct—a complex science-fictional "scanner"—over her body, felt at least a portion of her energy returning. Some of the damage she'd suffered had been real, she knew, affecting her meat body directly—surges in blood pressure had probably burst capillaries, strained heart valves. But she also knew that those things would heal with time.

Which, of course, she didn't have now. She had to get out of this node—somehow—relocate back to the satlink. But how?

She started to initiate an analyze utility—hosed it the first time, had to try again. The utility's construct appeared as a pair of goggles, which she slipped over her icon's eyes. She started to scan the walls of the "office."

There it was, what she knew she had to find. A concealed "door," a rectangle of wall that shimmered when viewed through the goggles—a dataline leading out of this node. Another utility told her there was no security on the "door"—nothing to stop her from using it—but couldn't tell her what was on the other side. Apparently, there was some kind of discontinuity that blocked the utility's scan.

That was reassuring. She'd certainly experienced a discontinuity when she'd been shunted here. If she was lucky, this dataline would lead her back to the satlink. She took a deep breath, readied herself. And plunged through the doorway.

A moment of blackness, of vertigo and disorientation. And then the virtual reality reestablished itself around her.

Luck was with her. She was back at the satlink node. Actually *within* the construct this time. The blue structural elements formed a lattice around her. The beads of ice still shuttled up and down along the elements. Fear twisted her belly for an instant, but then she realized they weren't paying any attention whatsoever to her icon. Why should they? she reasoned. I'm inside now; they're looking for intruders coming from *outside*.

She looked around. The lattice-work parabolic dish of the satlink was above her, pointing up into the sky. When viewing the construct from without, she hadn't seen anything extending from the dish, anything that could have been the dataline to Zurich-Orbital. Now, from her new vantage point, she couldn't miss it. A faint, shimmering tube of sky-blue light, lancing into the heavens.

Z-O, here I come, she thought, then plunged into the dataline.

There was something . . . *not right* . . . about how Sly felt as she sped up the dataline. Some sense of . . . *disconnection*, though that didn't quite describe it either. At first she thought it was a mental artifact, some kind of aftereffect of her combat with Jurgensen, with the golems. But then she realized it had to be the time delay that T. S. had mentioned. Depending on the geometry of the link—the number of sidelinks necessary to communicate with the Zurich-Orbital habitat—the light-speed lag could be three-quarters of a second, an eternity at computer speeds. She tried to imagine what it would be like without the compensator chip that T. S. said was installed in the deck, then gave up; this disconnected feeling was disturbing enough.

She'd expected there to be something distinctive about the system access node leading into the Zurich-Orbital system—something that reflected its importance. But there was nothing out of the ordinary. It was just another SAN, following the Universal Matrix Specification standards, appearing as a simple door in a shining silver wall.

Sly stopped outside the SAN, ran a selection of analyze programs on it. As she expected, the door was a glacier—almost solid ice. Nothing lethal that the utilities could detect, but enough barrier and trace ice to overload a less powerful node.

Nothing that Mary Windsong's slick utilities—backed by the punch of Theresa Smeland's deck—couldn't sleaze their way past. The ice accepted Sly's forged passcodes, and the door swung open. She slipped silently into the heart of the Zurich-Orbital computer system.

Through an SPU—a sub-processor unit—and into a CPU. Probably one of many, she guessed. Most modern systems were "massively parallel"—the term currently in vogue—with multiple CPUs, sharing the processing overhead of the system. Cloaked, so that any ice or deckers in the CPU wouldn't spot her, she called up a system map.

Then, with stunning clarity she realized she'd reached her destination. She didn't have to go any further. There was a public bulletin board system—well, "public" with respect to people who had access to the Corporate Court's computer—to which all multinational corporations contributed. It comprised a single datastore connected to a dedicated SPU—which was, in turn, linked with the subordinate CPU where Sly was. All she had to do was upload Louis' stolen datafile from her cyberdeck to the CPU. Order the CPU to transfer it to the SPU, along with an instruction to post it in a read-only section of the datastore. Simple.

Too simple, part of her mind yammered. But no. It took just a couple of clock ticks to write the appropriate code, to feed it into the CPU's command stack. She watched an execution trace of the CPU's activity, saw her command get processed normally. Saw the creation of the data packets containing the paydata plus the appropriate instructions to the SPU. A few cycles later, she ran a listing of new postings on the BBS and saw the still-encrypted data appear, with file attributes of READ-ONLY and PROTECTED.

It would still be possible, but incredibly difficult, for someone to delete the file. The subordinate CPU where Sly was had the ability to post entries to the BBS datastore. But it didn't have the authority to delete a posting or even change its attributes or status. If somebody wanted to do that, they'd have to penetrate a lot deeper into the Zurich-Orbital system.

How difficult would that be? To find out, Sly ordered the subordinate CPU to display the security ratings of the nodes surrounding the central CPU cluster. Reading the lines of data, she had to suppress a shudder. Not a chance, she told herself. Any decker even *thinking* about penetrating the central CPU cluster might as well just shoot himself in the head. The result would be no less certain, and it'd probably hurt less.

I can't believe it. I'm out from under. . . .

It still didn't seem real. Maybe it wouldn't for a long time—maybe not until she'd returned to Seattle and saw everything was back to normal. But did she *want* to go back to Seattle?

She shook her head. Here in the middle of the Corporate Court's computer system wasn't the time or the place to worry about it. She reviewed things in her mind. Had she forgotten anything?

Satisfied that she had not, Sly jacked out.

32

It was like a bad case of déjà vu, Falcon thought. Sly
jacking in, doing . . . something. And then all hell
breaking loose around her, with him afraid to jack her
out before she was ready. Afraid not to jack her out,
because the woman-plus-cyberdeck combination—tied to
the wall, to the phone jack, and from there to the Matrix—limited their options so much. He didn't understand
what she was doing, not really. And the not understanding made it all worse.

There'd been no real warning. Everything had been
quiet, with Mary squatting on the floor next to Sly,
watching her carefully. At first Falcon had thought that's
all it was—just watching. But then he'd kind of . . .
opened up his perception—that was the best way he could
think of it. Opened himself up to additional data, data
that wasn't coming in through his normal senses. Kind
of the way he'd been opened to the alternate reality of
the plane of the totems. And then he'd understood that
Mary, too, was using senses other than the five normal
ones to monitor Sly and how her body was reacting.

Twice he'd seen Sly twitch. The first time like somebody had touched her unexpectedly. The second time like
somebody had goosed her hard—or like she was on some
kind of drug trip gone bad. He'd wanted to jack her out
right there, free her from whatever it was that was tor-
menting her. He'd turned to Mary, worried, questioning
her with his eyes.

But Mary shook her head. "She's hurting," the shaman said. "Hurting bad, maybe. But it's not critical yet." He'd wanted to yell at her, to say *any* hurting was critical after the abuse Sly had suffered from the black box in that small concrete room. But Mary just looked at him calmly. "This is important, right?" she said. And all he could do was nod.

And it was then the gunfire started. The booming of single-shot weapons, the harsh ripping of autofire. Muffled by the closed door, but obviously coming from the barroom of the tavern.

"What the frag is *that*?" Falcon demanded.

Mary hadn't answered at once, just rested her shoulder against the couch, closed her eyes, let her chin sink down onto her chest. He wanted to shake her, then realized that she'd gone astral—the same way he'd gone astral to find and rescue Sly. Falcon wanted to join her, but he didn't know how. Not by himself, not without the help of Wolf. He tried to summon up the song he'd heard in the forest on that distant plane. He was able to remember it, but no matter how hard he tried, he couldn't feel it vibrating through him like before, was unable to sing along with it.

Mary came back almost immediately, opening her eyes again, flowing to her feet. He knew at once from her expression that it was something bad.

"There's heavy drek going down in the barroom," she told him tersely. "Some new guys came in—strangers; none of the regulars knew them. They headed for the back room. Cahill"—that was the bartender, Falcon recalled—"tried to stop them. They shot him.

"There were five regulars out front—drinking their breakfast here like they usually do—and four strangers. There's a real pitched battle going on. Two strangers down, three regulars."

"What the frag do we do?" Falcon demanded. He

looked around the room. The only door led out into the
barroom—into the firefight. At first he'd liked the security that represented; nobody could come in from the
street or through some alley door without the bartender
spotting them and giving some kind of warning. Now he
realized the single door turned the back room into a trap.
No way out in an emergency. "Can't you do something?"

She hesitated, then nodded. "You watch Sly," she told
him.

"What are you going to do?"

"Summon a spirit," she said, her voice as calm as if
she was saying, "Get a drink." "I'll summon a hearth
spirit."

"How?"

She grimaced. "You want me to do it or *talk* about
doing it?"

"Go."

Falcon squatted down beside Sly, reached out and
rested a hand on her forehead. The runner's skin was
cool, but not cold. There didn't seem to be any tension
in her body—as if whatever it was that had made her
twitch was over. He didn't know whether to take that as
a good or a bad sign.

Mary walked to the center of the room, already humming a calm, unhurried song under her breath. She began
to move rhythmically in some kind of jerky dance, singing all the while. He watched her with his eyes, tried to
extend his new, unfamiliar senses as well.

To his meat eyes, nothing seemed to be happening.
But with those strange, arcane senses he'd never known
he had, it was obvious that something was going down.
He could feel a flow of energy, initially from Mary herself, but then shifting so that the flow came from outside—apparently from the structure of the building and
from the ground on which it was built. It formed a swirl-

ing vortex around her, totally undetectable by the normal
five senses, but obvious to his heightened perception.

Mary's song changed, took on words—words that
weren't English or Cityspeak, but that he could somehow
understand. "Guardian of hearth and home," she was
singing, "protector from the elements, protect us now.
Go forth now, great one, shelter your children." She
pointed to the door.

The vortex changed, drew itself together into something almost humanoid in shape. Still invisible, still unheard, but still easily assensed. And the shape walked
through the closed door into the barroom.

Mary stopped her song, let her shoulders drop. Wiped
a sheen of sweat off her forehead with the back of a small
hand. "That'll help for the moment," she said quietly,
"but there are more strangers coming. And they've got
their own shaman with them."

"So what the frag do we do?" Falcon had his machine
pistol out, was nervously flicking the safety off and back
on again.

"Bail out, that's the smart thing," the young woman
told him.

"But how? Out through *there*?" He pointed to the door
to the barroom.

Mary didn't answer him directly, just crossed to the
back of the room. Ran her hands over the wall. Falcon
couldn't see exactly what she was doing, but a section of
the seemingly solid wall swung open—a small concealed
door leading into darkness.

"Where does that go?"

"Into the storeroom," she answered, "then there's another door out into the back alley." She gestured to the
other door. "Let them chew each other up. We just bail."

He hesitated, looking at Sly. The decker seemed totally at peace, like she was asleep—or dead. He felt a
moment of panic until he saw her breast rising and falling

in a slow, relaxed rhythm. "No," he said at last. "I've got to let Sly have her shot. I owe her that."

"Even if it kills us?"

He didn't answer—*couldn't* answer.

"What if someone comes in the other way?" Mary pressed. "The door to the alley isn't hidden. They could try and flank us."

At last Falcon saw something he could do. He flicked the safety off his machine pistol one last time, made sure it was cocked. "You stay here," he instructed. "Watch Sly. Don't jack her out until she's done. You hear me?"

"What are you going to do?"

He shrugged. "Watch our backs. And anything else I can figure out." Before she had a chance to argue, Falcon had ducked through the small concealed door. "And close this after me," he added.

The storeroom was small and dark, cold and smelling of stale beer. Stacked against two walls were wooden cases—no doubt containing bottles of liquor—and metal kegs. There were two doors, opposite each other. One led to the barroom; the other, latched and barred, had to lead to the alley. The concealed door swung shut behind him, and he heard a lock click. He turned to see how well concealed it actually was, feeling reassured that not the slightest clue of its existence was visible.

He listened at the locked door, the one to the alley. Nothing. But did that mean anything except that the door was too thick for him to hear surreptitious movement outside? He hesitated, wishing for the ability to go astral like he'd done before. He tried to conjure up the sensations he'd felt on the plane of the totems and later, the oneness with the song of Wolf. It wouldn't come.

Well, waiting around wasn't going to help anyone. He snapped open the latches, raised the bar. Listened again— still nothing. Opened the door, and ducked back into the shelter of the wall. Again nothing—no grenade rolled and bounced into the storeroom, no high-velocity bullets stitched the darkness. Crouching low he stepped into the alley, pulled the door shut behind him.

As far as he could see and hear, the alley was empty. Nothing moved near him. Nobody pumped lead into his body.

Which way? Left or right? The Buffalo Jump was on the north side of the street, near the east end of the block. Which meant the nearest street was to the right. If he ducked around that end of the block, he was taking a real risk of running into the support that Mary had said was converging on the front of the tavern. He headed to the left, moving fast.

He could hear gunfire splitting the night. More than just the minor firefight that Mary had said was raging in the front of the tavern. This was more autofire, punctuated by the resonating booms that he'd come to associate with grenades. A real fragging urban war was going on somewhere. What the frag was happening? Was it like the ambush at the docks, where Modal had said multiple teams—all corp, the elf had guessed—were scrapping it out? It made an ugly kind of sense. Sly kept talking about the prelude to a corp war. Had it started, and already spread to Cheyenne? Frag, why not? Everything else is . . . what was Modal's word? *Fugazi!*

He ran on, crouched low, machine pistol held out before him, steadied by both hands.

Something was there! He *felt* the movement before he saw it. *Above* him, on one of the rooftops. He flung himself aside.

The crash of a powerful rifle shot, hideously loud. A round slammed into the wall next to him. Exploded violently. Fragments of ferrocrete lashed his bare face and hands. One splinter tore into the skin just above his right eye, temporarily blinding him with pain and blood. He brought his pistol up.

Falcon could see the sniper, a blacker silhouette against the black of the sky. The figure stood on top of a single-story building near the west end of the block. A faint blue glow, something electric. A sniper-scope—light amplification. The sniper was working the bolt on his rifle, jacking another round into the chamber. Bringing the rifle back into line.

Yelling with fear, Falcon clamped down on the trigger. The machine pistol chattered, bucking in his hands.

He saw the bullets striking sparks from the parapet in front of the sniper. Heard a double cough of agony, as multiple impacts drove the air from the gunner's lungs. The silhouette swayed, dropped. Something fell from the rooftop, to crash and bounce on the alley floor. The rifle!

He sprinted forward, scooped up the huge weapon. Flattened himself against the wall directly below the sniper's position. Maybe he's only wounded, Falcon thought. Maybe he's got a sidearm as well. . . . He looked up, wiping blood from his right eye.

It took a few seconds for his vision to adapt. Then he saw something hanging over the parapet. An arm. Something warm dripped onto his upturned face.

Blood. Not his own.

The sniper was down. If not dead, then incapacitated. *For the moment.*

Falcon looked at the rifle in his hands. A massive weapon, bolt action, with a magazine three times the thickness of the one—now empty—that fitted his machine pistol. The barrel was long and thick, with some kind of strange porting arrangement at the end. *A muzzle brake.* He stuck his finger into the muzzle, which was still hot from the passage of the bullet. The bore of the gun was wider than his finger. What did that make it? A fifty-caliber? What the frag kind of rifle was fifty-cal?

Then Falcon remembered something else Modal had said after the dockside ambush. Something about a Barret sniper rifle, wasn't that it? Nineteen-eighties vintage? If this was the same gun—and how many of those could there be on the streets?—didn't it mean it was the same corp team as the one that had hosed Knife-Edge's ambush? *The enemy of my enemy is my friend. . . .* He'd heard that somewhere. But could he believe in that now?

No! *Everybody* was an enemy.

He raised the rifle to his shoulder, tried the balance. It was a heavy, cumbersome thing, with an integral bipod mounted under the barrel. It had to weigh at least thirteen kilos—a massive weight to pack around, and useless for snap-shots. Thank the spirits. . . .

There was no digital display showing the number of rounds remaining, but a mechanical indicator on the side of the magazine told him the gun had four shots left. At first he thought the nightsight was dead, broken in the fall to the alley. But then he found the small toggle, easily within reach of his right thumb. He flicked it, and the scope lit up. Through it, the alley was bright as day, just a little grainy, like the view through a cheap portacam.

Falcon dropped the now-useless machine pistol. Hefted the Barret again.

He jogged to the end of the alley, stopped. Used the nightsight to scan the darkness. No figures lurking in the shadows, concealed by the darkness. He rounded the corner, headed down to the main street. Crouched low again and looked around the corner.

All the streetlights were dead—maybe shot out. The only light came from muzzle flares and the spray of tracers. A scene right out of some wartime nightmare. He used the nightsight again.

Even with electronically enhanced vision, Falcon couldn't make much sense of what was going down. It looked like a major pitched battle, with shooters hunkered down behind parked cars and firing from positions on rooftops or from windows. There were at least a half-dozen bodies sprawled in the street, dead or so badly chewed they weren't moving. Not shadowrunners, he didn't think. The bodies and the live combatants Falcon could see had a kind of regimented sameness to them, like they'd come out of an identical mold. Corporate street ops? Megacorp soldiers? It seemed likely. He guessed that at least three factions were involved, yet he couldn't be sure. Maybe somebody trained in small-unit tactics could understand what he was seeing, but Falcon was only a fragging gutterpunk ganger, for frag's sake.

The situation seemed static. Everybody had some kind of cover. Nobody was advancing, nobody retreating. Probably those who were dead had been the brave or the foolhardy ones, trying for some kind of territorial advantage. Or maybe they'd just gotten caught out in the open when the drek hit the fan. He settled the Barret against his shoulder, steadied it against the corner of the building as best he could. Found a small thumbwheel, turned it. Saw the scene jump into close-up as the variable scope changed its magnification. Saw a glowing set of cross hairs superimpose themselves over the image. He settled the cross hairs onto the back of a street op hunkered down behind a car on the same side of the street as the tavern. Remembered how this gun had blown a flaming hole right through the armored torso of the street samurai Benbo. Started to tighten down on the trigger, anticipating the sniper rifle's brutal recoil. . . .

Then loosened off on his finger. Who the hell do I geek? Falcon asked himself. Four shots remaining. There were at least five times that number of prospective targets. So what good would it do if he dropped four of them? After the first shot, at least some of the shooters would turn their own gunsights on him. One shot, maybe two if I'm lucky. Then I go down. . . .

He backed off a little, maximizing the cover provided by the corner of the building. What should he do?

Falcon couldn't stop the fight, didn't know if he wanted to. And he probably couldn't even affect the outcome in any meaningful way. *If I splatter four out of twenty gunners, so what?*

What was his purpose here anyway? To protect Sly and Mary long enough for the decker to finish what she had to do.

So that was his answer. He decreased the scope's magnification a little, increasing its field of view. Then he changed his point of aim to the front door of The Buffalo Jump. Settled his finger on the trigger. At the moment, everyone was pinned down. But if anybody broke cover, made a dash for that door, *then* he'd fire. *The first person to head for the tavern dies,* Falcon told himself. *And the second, and the third and fourth, if he could stay alive long enough.* Again, it might not make any difference in the grand scheme of things, in the final accounting. But it was *something*.

He waited.

The firefight raged on. Bullets slammed into parked cars, smashed masonry from buildings. A grenade launcher coughed; a car blossomed into a fireball, pouring black smoke into the lightening sky. Three figures that Falcon could see were hit, collapsing into the road.

Where were the fragging cops? he wondered angrily. *Don't they give a frag that there are armies blowing up the city?*

But these are megacorp armies, he reminded himself. *Couldn't some megacorp just as easily have bought itself the police department?* Frag, it happened in Seattle often enough—a large donation to the Lone Star Retired Officers Fund, or whatever fragging cover story suited the moment. The Barret was getting really heavy, the muscles in his forearms starting to quiver with the strain of holding it steady. He considered flipping down the bipod, then discarded the idea as cutting down his mobility too much. The gunfire rose to a crescendo.

And stopped.

Just like that.

One moment the air was filled with high-velocity ordnance, the paling of dawn lit, strobe-like, by muzzle flashes and the occasional explosion. The next moment, utter silence.

What the frag was going down?

Falcon could still see heavily armed and armored figures crouching down under cover, weapons at the ready. But nobody was firing, nobody was advancing or retreating. They just seemed to be waiting. *Waiting for what?*

For more than a minute, the street looked like a freeze-frame from some trideo. The only movement he could see was one mauled corp soldier, dragging herself agonizingly toward cover, leaving behind a smeared trail of blood. Another minute.

Then the movement began. Retreat, not advance. Through the nightsight he could see figures melting away into the darkness, leaving their sniper nests, leaving their over-watch positions. Slinking away into alleys, disappearing into buildings. A couple of figures—holding their empty hands away from their bodies—darted into the street to drag their dead and wounded out of the killing zone. Nobody cut them down.

What the flying frag was happening?

Within five minutes, the street was empty, the silence complete.

"It's over."

Falcon spun at the voice from behind him. Tried to swing the cumbersome Barret around.

A large hand grabbed the barrel, immobilizing the gun as totally as if it had been locked into a vice. Falcon looked up into the face of a heavily armored street op. Looked into the muzzle of an SMG pointing directly be-

tween his eyes. Every muscle in his body spasmed, as if muscular tension could stop the bullets from smashing his skull to fragments.

But the corp soldier didn't fire. He just looked calmly down at Falcon. "It's over," the man said again. Then he released the rifle barrel, turned and tore away in an inhumanly fast sprint.

Falcon watched him, letting the Barret's barrel sagging down to the ground. Realizing he'd been holding his breath, he let the air out of his lungs in a long hiss.

"It's over," he repeated. But what, exactly? And why?

Well, it was damn sure he wasn't going to figure that out squatting here.

He slung the Barret's strap over his shoulder and jogged back to the alley, to the rear door of the tavern. Went into the storeroom, rapped on the wall where he thought the concealed door was.

After a few moments he heard a click, and the door swung back. He stepped into the back room.

Mary was there. And so was Sly, who was longer jacked into her cyberdeck. She was sitting on the couch now, exhaustion written in every line of her body, a tired smile on her face.

He unslung the rifle, tossed it onto a chair. "What the frag is going on?" he asked of anybody who'd care to give him an answer.

33

Sly smiled at the young ganger—or should I think of him as a shaman now? she wondered. He looked almost as drained as she felt.

"It's over," she told him.

"*What's* over, for frag's sake?" he demanded. "What just happened? It's like . . ." He hesitated, searching for the right words. "It's like the fragging director yelled 'Cut!' and all the fragging actors went home."

She nodded. "I did it."

"Did what?"

"I uploaded the fiber-optic data to the Corporate Court bulletin board system," she explained. "It's on the system now, where every corp in the world can read it." She let herself relish the relief. "We're out from under."

"So why'd they stop shooting?" Falcon wanted to know.

"Don't you see?" she asked him. "Every corp's got the information. There's no percentage in coming after us, and there's no percentage in"—she chuckled— "wasting each other's assets. And you know that corps don't do anything if there isn't a percentage in it for them."

"So they stopped fighting. . . ."

"Because there was nothing to be gained by fighting anymore," she finished for him. "They called back their armies, all their assets." She shook her head. "I don't like the corps, but there's something to be said for the rational way they handle things.''

Falcon shook his head slowly. She could see him trying to understand. Then his frown softened, and he smiled. ''It's over?'' he asked, almost plaintively.

''It's over.''

They went back to the motel—the Plains Rest. Why not? As far as Sly could tell, nobody had figured that was their doss—And why should it matter now anyway? It was over! And what the hell, they needed somewhere to rest up. Somewhere to decide where they'd go from here.

Falcon had driven the Callaway, with Mary following along behind on her borrowed bike. Then again, maybe the bike was hers now. Its previous owner—the bartender—was dead. Falcon had insisted on taking along the massive sniper rifle—he hadn't told her how he'd come to acquire it, and she hadn't asked. They'd soon enough have plenty of time for stories. Sly had worried about the kid carrying such an obvious piece of ordnance openly to the motel room, but Mary had promised to handle it. Sly didn't know exactly how Mary had done it, but even though the ganger had brushed past a cleaning woman with the rifle slung over his shoulder, there'd been no outcry, not even the slightest hint of recognition that he carried a gun. *I should find out more about this magic drek*, Sly thought dryly. Now Falcon was lying on the bed, the weapon beside him as though he didn't want it too far out of reach. Once they were settled down—each with a glass of synthetic scotch from the bottle Mary had provided as her contribution to the celebration—Sly told them about her run through the Matrix. Was surprised to find herself shaking when she described the fight with the golem-class black ice. There were a lot of nightmares there, she realized, waiting to come and get her. She knew it would be a while before she'd be able to sleep without the memories returning to frighten her awake in a sweat-soaked bed.

When she'd finished, Falcon shook his head slowly. "So that's it?" he asked doubtfully. "No comebacks? No loose ends? Nobody coming to geek us?"

She smiled. "The corps are satisfied . . . if that's the right word," she explained. "The playing field's level again. Everyone's got the results of Yamatetsu's research. Nobody's got any kind of edge. There's nothing to go to war for."

"The corp war's over?" he pressed.

"It's over," Sly reassured him. "It's like I said, there's no percentage in it anymore. Everything's back to business as usual." She chuckled. "No doubt everyone's scrabbling to develop what they've got, to advance the technology. But they're all starting from the same point, so no one's got an advantage." She shrugged. "Probably the Concord of Zurich-Orbital's back in force—with some changes—and the Corporate Court's back on top of things."

"The Sioux government's cleaning house," Mary put in. "That's what I heard when I picked up the bottle. Closing down the OMI, and—"

Without warning, the door blew off its hinges. As Sly's ears rang with the overpressure from the explosion, she saw a figure standing in the doorway. A massive figure, bulky with armor, a large helmet covering its head. The transparent face-shield was down, but through the clear macroplast she could clearly see the face.

Knife-Edge.

Sly clawed for her revolver. Out the corner of her eye, she saw Mary fling herself into the dubious shelter of one of the beds. Falcon didn't dive for cover. He reached for the sniper rifle.

Knife-Edge raised his assault rifle, triggering a short, controlled burst. Falcon screamed as the bullets tore into him, the impact sending him rolling off the bed. Still clutching his rifle, he slumped to the floor face-down, motionless in a spreading pool of blood.

Sly brought up her pistol, squeezed off two rounds. Saw them slam harmlessly into Knife-Edge's heavy armor.

"Drek-eating *slitch!*" he yelled. "You fragged everything up!" He swung the assault rifle around.

She stared down the muzzle helplessly. *Nowhere to go!* Time seemed to click into slow motion, everything happening at a crawl. Instinctively, she tried to fling herself aside. Felt her muscles contract, felt her weight shift as she lunged to the right. *Too late, too slow.* Her own movements were as slow as everything else—as slow as everything but her racing thoughts. She saw the Amerindian runner's finger whiten as he tightened down on the trigger. She was right out in the open, no cover. No time to reach cover. I'm dead, she thought, expecting any instant to feel the bullets flaying her flesh from her bones. She heard herself start to yell, her voice pitched too low, like sound from a tape running slow. *"Noooo!"*

A big gun boomed.

In slow motion, she saw Knife-Edge's chest armor fracture under the impact, saw the fireball burst into life where the bullet struck him. Saw his chest cavity deform as the round tore through him. Saw it burst out the other side like a fist-sized glob of blood and tissue, with a dart of burning, molten metal at its core.

The runner's weapon came up, his death-spasm clenching down on the trigger. A long burst sprayed into the ceiling, tearing great holes in the acoustic tile. The impact of the bullet slammed him off balance, and he fell—slowly, ponderously, like a felled tree.

Sly's own lunge was carrying her off her chair, to the right. Nothing she could do to stop it. As she fell, still in slow motion, she saw Falcon. Somehow he'd managed to drag himself up onto his elbows, managed to bring the sniper rifle to bear. He was staring at the ruins of Knife-Edge, his mouth hanging open, eyes glazed with agony, face pale from wound shock and loss of blood. She saw him slump down again.

Sly hit the ground hard, too distracted to turn the fall into the roll she'd intended. As the impact drove the air from her lungs, time seemed to snap back to full-speed again.

Gasping, she forced herself to her feet. The room looked like a slaughterhouse. The air was filled with the sweet, sickening smell of blood—the reek of feces, of cordite, of hot metal.

Mary's head appeared from behind the bed. Looked at what was left of Knife-Edge, her face going pale.

"Do something for Falcon," Sly ordered breathlessly. Mary jumped to obey.

Sly looked around at the chaos. In the distance, she could hear the wail of an approaching siren.

"*Now* it's over," she whispered.

Epilogue

1430 hours, May 20, 2054

The mid-afternoon sun beat down from a cloudless sky, the small waves of the Caribbean Ocean shattering the golden light into sparkling shards. Without a breeze, it would have been brutally hot. But there was a breeze, blowing from the east—from the landward side—carrying with it the sweet-fresh smell of tropical flowers and verdant forest. The fourteen-meter powerboat—the *Out of the Shadows*—swung easily at anchor, a kilometer off the west coast of the island of Saint Lucia.

Sharon Young sat on the flybridge, sprawled bonelessly in the pilot's seat, a broad, floppy-brimmed hat sheltering her from the worst of the sun's onslaught. Her skin was tanned a deep mahogany. Little rivulets of sweat ran down her body, darkening the waistband of her sky-blue monokini. On the rail, within easy reach, was a large gin and tonic—real gin, still available and not prohibitively priced in the islands. On the deck beside her was a pair of binoculars—also within easy reach if she wanted to take a closer look at any of the other boats anchored in the bay, or examine the huge spear-like mountain that the chart identified as the Gros Piton.

She sighed. She'd been aboard the *Shadows* for almost two months now, cruising slowly—aimlessly, almost—through the island chains of the Caribbean League. Just taking it easy, unwinding slowly. Stopping wherever the mood took her, going ashore or simply lounging aboard. The Shadows had enough fresh-water capacity and storage space that Sly could provision the vessel for almost three weeks at sea without having to resupply. Which was just the way she liked it.

She ran a hand along the polished teak rail. *My boat.* She could still hardly believe it, even after two months.

After the debacle at the motel room, after the death of Knife-Edge, they'd gone to ground in the shadows of Cheyenne. Mary had stayed by Falcon's bedside the entire time—almost two weeks—that it had taken for magic and medicine to bring the young shaman-ganger back from the brink of death. During that time, Sly had spent a couple of hours a day wandering around the Cheyenne corner of the Matrix, just generally checking things out—watching the newsbases, monitoring megacorp activities in Sioux and elsewhere. Never trying to crack into anything that was protected, of course, and *definitely* never getting even close to anything that looked like it was related to either the Sioux military or the Corporate Court.

The corp war was over—all signs of conflict vanished as though they'd never existed. That had been obvious from the first moment Sly had started monitoring network activity, but it had taken her several days to completely believe it. There'd been hints of transfer payments between megacorps—no doubt restitution for "lost assets," personnel and equipment killed or mangled during the fighting. (She'd wondered what the dead soldiers would think about that. . . .) The Corporate Court had apparently been directing those transfer payments, and the Zurich Orbital Bank had been handling all the transactions. So didn't that mean that the Court was back in control of everything? Business as usual . . .

It had been harder to keep track of the maneuvering within the Sioux Nation's military and governmental apparatus, but in time she'd picked out a few "indirect indicators," which had given her some clue about what was going on without getting her close enough to trigger an alert. It had certainly looked as though Mary was right—the Sioux military had been doing some major housecleaning. The Office of Military Intelligence had undergone a massive purge—a "restructuring," according to the bureaucratese. Most of the big players in the OMI had been transferred elsewhere in the military complex, but some—including the head honcho, one Sheila Wolffriend—had simply vanished. Gone, never to be heard of again. End of story. Then the military had just closed ranks, and that was it. Business as usual there, too.

Toward the end of Falcon's convalescence, Sly had gathered up her courage and taken a look into the Seattle Matrix. *Status quo ante* there as well—no changes, everything running as if there'd never been a corp war on the horizon. She'd checked her own records, too, just to see if anyone had tied her in with the events in Sioux.

Somebody had, that had been immediately obvious. According to the files, Sharon Louise Young now had an account in the Zurich Gemeinschaft Bank. An account with a balance in the low seven digits. An off-planet account, free from any kind of tax and exempt from UCAS Internal Revenue Service scrutiny.

When Sly first saw this, she'd jacked out at once, sweating in panic. A trap? Somebody waits for me to make a withdrawal, and then everyone and his fragging dog jumps me. . . .

But then she'd gone back in and approached the information from a dozen different angles. There'd been no traps or traces around the account. Nothing other than the bank's own monolithic security. No deckers watching for access. Using various blinds and covers, shell companies and shills, she'd tried to withdraw some of the credit, transfer it to a blind account in a bank in Casper, Sioux Nation. No problem. The transfer had gone through faster than any bank transaction Sly had ever seen—no doubt the Casper bank had jumped frosty when they'd seen where the credit was coming from.

The next day the electronic mail message had arrived. Not at any of her shell companies or layers of protection. Delivered electronically directly to her cyberdeck. Addressed to Sharon Louise Young. From the Board of Directors of the Zurich-Orbital Bank. When she'd gotten over the shakes and the sweats—*how the frag did they track her down so easily*?—she read the message.

The account balance was a payment for services rendered, authorized by the Corporate Court itself. No specifications as to just *what* services, but Sly didn't have too much trouble venturing a guess. For stopping the corp war, of course. For letting everyone forget about geeking each other, for letting everyone get back to the profitable business of screwing the consumer.

The e-mail message had ended with a suggestion that there was "no need to contact the Court to thank them or to discuss this matter in any way." In other words, take the money, shut up, and get out of our hair for good. It had seemed like an excellent idea.

And so Sharon Young—Sly no more—was in retirement, long-awaited and well-deserved.

And, much as she hated to admit it, she was getting bored. She'd left Falcon and Mary behind in Cheyenne—with a fair chunk of credit each, of course—left her old life and the shadows far behind. But . . .

You could take the runner out of the shadows, but you couldn't take the shadows out of the runner—or something like that.

She sighed, finished her drink and went below.

The *Out of the Shadows* boasted a state-of-the-art computer system, complete with satellite link. It hadn't when Sharon first picked it up, of course; that had been the first of many modifications she'd commissioned for the graceful craft. She slumped down at the keyboard, idly logged on and requested a list of any electronic mail she'd received.

There was only one message. No originator ID.

Curiosity piqued, she ran a back-trace. No real problem. The sender had suppressed his or her ID, but hadn't buried it too deeply—as though he/she *wanted* Sharon to be able to run the trace if she wished.

As the information appeared on the flatscreen, Sharon sat back and smiled.

The transmission was from Cheyenne—from Falcon. She chuckled as she read the message.

A really hot run was shaping up, it seemed. Starting in Cheyenne, but maybe spreading back up into the UCAS and Seattle. Falcon had gotten a team together, but there was still one slot open—for a drek-hot decker. If the "lady of leisure" could fit it into her busy social schedule, would she consider it?

Sly shook her head slowly. I'm retired, she told herself.

But then another thought struck her. Retirement isn't doing nothing, she realized, it's doing only what you want to do. That was a new concept.

A broad smile spread over her face. May, she thought. I wonder what the weather's like in Cheyenne?